OPERATION: EYEWITNESS

OPERATION: EYEWITNESS

For Jim —

Here it is, enjoy!

Best Wishes —

Dave Wise

D. Rudd Wise

W. Rudd Wise

www.novelsbydrwise.com

To order additional copies of this book, contact:
Xlibris Corporation
1-888-7-XLIBRIS
www.Xlibris.com
Orders@Xlibris.com

www.novelsbydrwise.com

CONTENTS

CONTENTS

JESS HANES ADVENTURES

When Jess Hanes, a professional treasure hunter en route to the Middle East, visits the men's room at the Casablanca airport, he has no way of knowing that this simple act will thrust him into an international tangle of drug running, arms smuggling, and investigations by such agencies as Interpol and the CIA. Jess is the only witness to a murder inside the men's room, and the murder victim happens to be the brother of the king of Morocco.

ACKNOWLEDGMENTS

I appreciate everyone who had a part in editing and guiding me with this novel. Most of all, my patient wife, Rachel Marie, who pushed, prodded, read to me and loved me through to the final chapter.

A special thanks for their proofreading and editing goes to my sister Betsy Wise, Uncle Johnny & Aunt Rose Wise, cousins Cy Wise and Blaine Wise, sister-in-law Karen Sue Pierce, and to Wendell Norwood and Chuck Hernley.

Those who have helped with technical advise: Dave Eby of AeroFlow Systems, Craig MacNab of AM General Corporation; Terry Humphery of Ayres Corporation for his assistance with detailed aeronautical editing and proofreading of many special chapters in the use of Ayers aircraft; nephew Michael Pierce, Indianapolis corporate pilot, CFI, for his expertise.

For his critique, edit, rewrite, and promptness, another special thanks to Bill Greenleaf of Gilbert, Arizona.

CHAPTER ONE

Leaning back into the seat of a Royal Air Maroc 747 jet airliner headed for the United States, Jess E. Hanes felt the usual pressure forcing him deeper into the seat as the aircraft lifted from the runway. It banked over Casablanca, steadily climbing above the clouds, and he could feel the mental pressures fading away like the continent below.

The noise of his surroundings subsided until he could only feel a steady light vibration. The aircraft had reached its cruising altitude and began a level flight. Deep in thought, he was almost mesmerized watching the puffy clouds pass rapidly beneath them.

A flight attendant tapped Jess on the shoulder, bringing him out of his daze. Startled, he threw up his arm in defense. He could not see her clearly for his eyes were slow to adjust to the lesser light in the cabin.

"Mr. Hanes, sorry I startled you," she said quietly. "Would you like something hot or cold to drink?"

He returned a blank stare.

"Would you care for something to drink?" she asked again.

"Why, yes! Please . . . iced tea?" he asked, turning toward her in the seat.

"Iced tea with sugar, lemon?"

"Lemon. Thanks!" He replied while rubbing the right side of his neck. It had almost cramped while he had been staring so fixedly out the window.

His eyes finally adjusted to the interior light of the airliner, and he could see his flight attendant smiling while she continued taking the other passengers' orders. Then she returned to the upper deck galley serving area at the rear of his seating section.

Jess in his late fifties was in perfect health for his age, a retired military pilot with twelve years in the U.S. Navy and twelve in the U.S. Air Force while working as an undercover agent for the Secret Service.

Now, he was a world traveler, searching for hidden and lost treasures of the world. Jess was married for more than thirty years to the same beautiful lady, Marie Ann, whom he was returning to in Austin, Texas.

He spoke softly to himself while slowly shaking his head, "Lord, I need to get these tensions under control!"

Jess was not in danger any longer. He did not have to look over his shoulder, always reacting to every unusual noise or movement around him. He was tight as a fiddle string.

Seated all the way forward, the roar of the jet engines were behind him. The light vibrations finally began their relaxing effect. No one occupied the two seats next to him toward the aisle, so he was alone with his thoughts.

The Boeing 747 airliner was less than half full, and most of the passengers were seated in the economy middle and rear sections. Jess sat in the front row of the upper deck seats, with only four other people in the section. At the expense of the Moroccan government, he had selected his own seating. It was a good location.

The wall in front of Jess held a large rack full of magazines and current newspapers. He selected a *National Geographic* magazine, because they always had good photos and interesting articles. He was not really in the mood for reading, but just looking at the pictures kept him from thinking too much.

The attendant brought the iced tea he had ordered. She was an attractive, long wavy haired brunette in a light blue uniform, which fit her tall, shapely frame comfortably. She wore her uniform with pride and confidence. It was not tight like some of the others, who were obviously uncomfortable when bending over or kneeling next to a passenger.

Jess had also noticed that her face, with its natural beauty, was not covered with excessive makeup. Yes, she was a very attractive lady, perhaps in her late thirties. Madilene was on her nametag, which was attached over her jacket pocket.

"Thank you ma'am." Jess spoke like a true native Texan would to a lady.

"If you need me for anything, just push the button above you for service," she said. "I'll be in the back." She hesitated, then opened the overhead storage above him, moved a few items, and closed the door. She laid a pillow and blanket in the seat next to him. "You look like you could use these," she said with a smile, then returned to her duties.

Slowly stirring the ice cubes to get the tea colder, he took a long sip. Its taste was fresh, and its aroma was pleasing, just what he needed.

The pictures and articles in the *National Geographic* did not stop his brain from wandering off to other things. Taking a deep breath and laying the magazine on his lap, Jess returned to gazing out the window. He shook his head in amazement, just realizing the turmoil he had come through and survived.

Man alive! He almost said out loud. *I'm finally on the way! Here I am, going home to Texas after eight months of life threatening adventure and leaving behind nightmares of terror.*

Those were events he would not soon forget. How did he get himself into such a mess? He was just an innocent bystander who had been involved in international terrorist turmoil in Morocco.

Again, it was the age-old story of being at the right place at the wrong time or was it the wrong place at the right time for Jess?

#

It was August of the previous year when all his problems started during a layover in the Dar al-Baida International Airport, Casablanca. Jess, a professional treasure hunter, was in route to the Middle East. With a six-hour delay in Morocco, he welcomed the chance to be back in a country he had lived in thirty years prior.

Strange things can happen in international airport terminals where thousands of people are in transit. Not knowing one another, but thrown together in a split-second of passing, people glance at each other but do not really see. Occasionally, eyes momentarily meet, but otherwise no communication shared.

Jess moved through the terminal aisles, looking for his departure ramp before taking a sightseeing walk outside. He glanced at his ticket again for the gate number, and moved into the flow of people heading in that general direction.

The morning crowd pushed through the wide aisles. He noticed congestion ahead of him where three civilians and a big fat military man were quarreling. They were shoving and cursing each other. That attracted a small crowd in front of an empty ticket counter, causing the flow of people to shy around them.

One civilian was dressed like a banker, or politician, in a white summer suit. The other two, who wore similar light blue three-piece suits, had joined with the large military man in an intense argument with the gentleman in white.

Jess did not know why he had noticed the suits, but thought it unusual. He did not stop to watch, because common sense told him to keep moving. Not minding his own business had gotten him in trouble before.

As Jess pressed between people to pass around the small crowd, the large uniformed officer backed out into the aisle, almost knocking Jess down. He turned and glared at Jess for being in his way. The big man made gestures with his hands flapping in the air, shouting what Jess supposed were Arabic obscenities.

Because of his brute size, he had brushed Jess aside with little effort. He and the two blue-suited men hurried toward the main lobby, leaving the white-suited gentleman standing alone. Startled, Jess just stood there watching the three leave, realizing that the encounter could have been a bloody battle if they had come to blows.

The big military officer suddenly stopped and turned around, glaring back through the parted wake of people he had left behind him. His men were following so close they almost bumped into him. He yelled something and pointed toward Jess; or rather, at the white-suited man behind Jess. Jess quickly moved aside, turned around, and continued on his way.

The noise from the crowded lobbies eventually drowned out the confusion behind him. He followed the signs to the departure ramps and stayed with the flow of people ahead of him.

Seeing restaurants reminded Jess that he had not eaten for a while, and his stomach began to growl. While trying to make up his mind where to eat, he made mental notes on the different cultural clothing of the international travelers. He enjoyed watching and studying the people.

This is going to be an enjoyable layover, he thought to himself. *The flight for Dubai, United Arab Emirates, is six hours away. There is plenty of time to eat, browse and perhaps find a souvenir to send home.*

Suddenly, he had a call of nature, causing a frantic detour for the nearest restroom. That can be a threatening experience in a foreign country. But, when you gotta go, ya gotta—now!

Upon finding a restroom entrance marked with a silhouette of a man on the door, he rushed in. The heat from the Moroccan desert with the ocean's humidity made most of the terminal unbearable. But the temperature was cool inside the large, brightly lighted, high-ceiling restroom.

It was fairly clean for a foreign airport. There was a long row of washbasins on the left, and a row of twenty partitioned stalls across from them. He picked the last stall at the far end of the room. Standing inside the stall, he could not see over the top of the partition, and it reached down to within six inches of the floor.

Jess laid his satchel and attaché case against the wall, closed the door, dropped his pants and sat on the cold toilet seat. No sooner had he sat down, he heard shuffling of feet at the other end of the room. Low voices in Arabic bitterly argued. One loud husky voice was familiar to Jess, like that of the large military officer he had seen earlier.

The sound of three muffled gunshots startled him. Then, he

heard the sound of a body falling to the floor, which sent a sudden, icy chill down his spine. He sat motionless, barely breathing.

Be quiet, Jess! They may not know you're here, he thought to himself. *Maybe they won't notice this is the only closed stall door.*

He stood, pulled his pants up, zipped them closed and lightly bumped the stall door. It banged against its latch, and the sound was like a shotgun being fired. It echoed in the large room.

The men stopped talking and listened. Now Jess knew they would notice the only closed stall door. He held his breath, not wanting to make a sound, and did not even want to blink or think about them knowing he was there.

He started to step up onto the stool, and a coin dropped out of his pants pocket onto the tile floor, making enough noise to raise the dead.

One of the men ran toward the stall where Jess was, shouting in Arabic, "*BISMILLAH* . . . in Allah's name, you die!" and hurriedly tossed a bag toward Jess' stall. It scooted on the tile floor and swished under the stalls partition, bouncing off Jess' attaché case and coming to rest between his spread legs. It was a tan canvas bag, and he had little doubt of what it was: a satchel charge of explosives. He kicked the bag, shoving it out of the stall. It slid across under the lavatories.

He grabbed the top of the partitioned wall next to him. Lifting his legs toward the back wall, he pressed his shoes against it and hugged the partition as tightly as possible. He began to pray.

A deafening explosion shook the room, blowing the outside wall onto the grassy yard. At the same instant, the stall door blew in and slammed against Jess' back. The shrapnel had cut jagged holes in the door, which ripped into his skin, penetrating between the ribs, pinning him to the door and against the still standing partition wall. He could feel the sharp metal scraping his rib bones. Hanging helplessly, he was not able to extend his legs to the floor for support.

His head reeled from the concussion of the explosion. He could not catch his breath, speak or scream. The stenches of powder, dust, smoke and blood mingled, dripped down his shirt onto his pants, and then onto the floor. A thick cloud of dust settled over him as numbness and shock rapidly set in.

Jess began to lose his grip on top of the partition wall, and his weight pulled against the jagged metal, which was tearing further into his back. Not able to reach the floor with his feet, he hung helplessly by his back from the door—and passed out. The partition wall began to lean, and finally collapsed from his weight.

CHAPTER TWO

Work crews stepped aside when two Moroccan government officials slowly investigated the restroom with its missing outside wall and damaged inside stalls. Palm trees, flowerbeds and vehicle traffic could be seen through the large opening. A light breeze could be felt through the restroom from the missing wall.

Pointing and nodding to each other without a word, they finally began to examine the dead man who had been shot.

"Three bullets to the back of the head," said the tall official with the full black mustache. He was looking through the pockets of the dead man.

"Yeah! They faced him to the wall. Here are the three 9mm slugs in the wall with pieces of his forehead," said his stocky partner in Arabic. He rolled the white-suited dead man over on his back and looked through his other pockets. "How many government men killed this week? Four? Now we have the King's brother assassinated in a restroom." He shook his head in disbelief. "He was scheduled to leave for Saudi Arabia with the King tomorrow?"

"Yes, you are correct," said the taller man. "A total of four, and this one makes five!"

He moved back to the opening of the missing restroom wall. The porcelain toilet and fixtures from the stalls were sprayed in small pieces all over the room and embedded into the wall. The stall doors and walls had ugly holes torn through them. Water and dust covered the walls and ceiling from the explosion. Mounds of red dust had formed where Jess' blood had splashed on the floor. The dust and blood mixed with the toilet water from the broken water line had made streaked paths across the mosaic floor tile to the drain. No one had turned off the main water supply to the restroom.

"This was a tough spot to be in, in the last stall," one of the inspectors said. "They say he was still alive, hanging on the toilet door. It had to be unhinged from the stall to get him down. He was stuck to it!" He shook his head in puzzlement. "But why blow out this wall?"

"Inspector!" one of the policemen called to the tall official. "These are items found on the American who was taken to the hospital. His attaché case has a laptop computer, papers and maps in it. I have not looked through them." Closing the satchel and attaché case, he handed them to the inspector, "The airport terminal manager turned these over to me. He may have looked through them. I do not know if anything is missing."

"I will talk to the American Consulate when he arrives, and then we will visit the terminal manager," said the inspector. "Do we have any, 'willing', eyewitnesses to this mess?"

The others shook their heads and shrugged their shoulders as they continued with the inspection of the damage.

"I think we have seen enough," said his partner.

Chief inspector, Colonel Abdel Samain el Keime, stepped through the opening in the restroom wall and strolled across the grassy area toward his vehicle. The hole was large enough to drive a truck through. Samain turned to his partner walking with him and motioned for him to drive.

Inspector, Lieutenant Colonel Bushta Hammad Delai, smiled and made a snappy salute to his friend and partner, Chief Keime.

Their new American AMC vehicle, the famous high mobility, multi-purpose wheeled vehicle, better known as the "Hummer", was well equipped for the Moroccan climate and terrain. The light tan color of the vehicle did not reflect the sun's heat too well, for it was extremely hot. Both men avoided touching the roof as they got in. Once inside, Bushta started the engine, and Samain turned on the air conditioner.

Samain, the taller of the two, was the department's ace counter intelligence officer on international terrorism. The Moroccan government and Interpol were having serious difficulties in Northern

Africa with the traffic of illegal arms and narcotics, and now with the assassinations of high ranking officials by terrorists.

Bushta emptied the contents of the satchel on the small table between the seats and pushed his driver's seat back to have more room to lay the American's articles on his lap.

"We will wait just long enough to go through his belongings, and then visit the terminal manager," Samain said. "We can talk to the Embassy man later."

Even though he was in peak physical health, he was sweating more than usual. He turned two of the air conditioner's vents toward him. Frowning and wiping the sweat from his forehead, he began searching through the papers with Bushta.

"I will never become accustomed to this Casablanca high humidity," Samain said.

He reflected the ancestry of the Berber Atlas Mountain people with a strong square face, thick black hair and mustache, and jet black eyes. He had eyes that would pierce the guilty and console the innocent, and with a continuous smile, he could keep others off-balance, not knowing his mood or thoughts. He was a handsome man who was well dressed in his Italian sports clothes.

Born in Marrakech, Morocco, Samain as a youth was raised in France and obtained his high school education and college prep schooling there after World War II. While still a young man, Samain's father sent him to Harvard's International Law College in the United States. He then enlisted in the Moroccan Air Force for pilot training, where he flew their American F-5E and OV-10A Broncos.

After his discharge, his summer months were spent working with his cousin Bushta, his closest friend. Back in the early '60's, they worked for the U.S. Navy and Air Force Strategic Air Command on bases in Morocco, which are no longer open. His king Itssani V appointed Samain to his current government position, after Samain and Bushta had saved the King from a secret coup d'etat in 1983.

For his doctorate degree in 1994, Samain had done considerable research in the Atlas Mountains on the Berber tribe's dialects. Now in his mid-fifties, Samain was as sharp as ever, fighting his country's enemies, terrorists and drug smugglers.

Bushta Hammad Delai was raised in a very wealthy and prominent family in Morocco. The Delai family was known in the international political circles as the 'Lions of the Desert'. They were still held in high esteem by Arab tribesmen throughout the Mediterranean countries.

Bushta and Samain were each others most trusted and faithful friend. They worked hard in those hot summers long ago, providing for their young families. They did not depend on their families' wealth, but supported themselves while obtaining their higher educations. Bushta also graduated from Harvard with a Masters degree in International Law, and then became a military jet pilot for the Moroccan government.

Their training with the CIA and Moroccan Special Forces in Kuwait during the war against Iraq had marked them as tremendous fighters and thorough investigators. Investigations had taken them to all Middle East and European countries as Interpol agents, working against terrorist's activities.

This investigation was their first direct association with the U.S. Embassy related to an injured American, who may have been involved with an assassination.

They teased each other about the heat as they continued searching through the American's papers and satchel.

"You have never been able to take this heat," Bushta said in French, laughing.

This was considered a derogatory remark, speaking in French, because neither of them liked the French, nor their language. This attitude came from generations of French rule in Morocco. It had taken a long time for Morocco to get its independence from France, and speaking the language still left a sour taste for these two.

"Okay, Frenchie!" Samain teased back. "Your sweat smells of the garlic you ate last night." Pointing a finger at Bushta, he sneered, "Camels breath!"

"Enough, enough!" Bushta said. "Here, look at these things the American had. His attaché case survived the explosion in better shape than he did, and his laptop computer does not look damaged externally. We can test it when we get back to the office. The computer hard drive may be broken. If it works, we can find out more about him."

"Let me have his passport and visa. Whom did he work for?" Samain asked. Opening the passport, he frowned, "Jess E. Hanes?" His name sounded familiar to Samain. "He was born in Dallas, Texas, 1942. Texas! Remember the Texan we knew in Kenitra?"

Bushta was not listening closely to Samain's comments; he was carefully going through the contents of the attaché case. "Look at this! He was researching oil fields in the Middle East. Here is a map of the Persian Gulf with offshore wells marked. There are marks in the areas where Kuwait had their oil wells burning during the Desert War. And, here are a dozen or more photographs of those areas. He might be military or CIA?"

"I do not think so," Samain said, shaking his head. "It is possible he is a writer on a research trip. These pages of notes and small maps look like treasure hunter's journals or diaries. He may be an archaeologist. I think we know this Mr. Hanes," Samain said, handing the passport to Bushta.

"He does not look familiar from his photograph. But then, I could not recognize my own mother from most passport photos," Bushta said.

"His name does not help me. Do you know him?"

Samain nodded, "Yes, we both do, Bushta. Remember the days we worked for the U.S. Navy at Sidi Yahia and Kenitra?" They looked at each other and nodded affirmatively. "Think about it!"

"We do not know if Mr. Hanes will live long," Bushta said, becoming very excited with the new information they were uncovering. "So, we should go to the hospital first. Right?"

"Right!" replied Samain.

The Hummer came alive as Bushta stepped on the accelerator and sped from the parking lot toward the hospital downtown.

CHAPTER THREE

Jess woke up in bed in a recovery room, and remembered very little. When his eyes finally focused, all he could see were small, light green squares,—ceramic floor tiles. His face was pressed down into a wide opening of a special padded pillow at the end of a bed.

His vision blurred, and everything began to twirl around, so he closed his eyes. The motion stopped. He gulped and tried to take a deep breath. But, a sharp pain in his back cut short his inhaling.

Slowly opening his eyes again, he tried to move, but could not budge. He could not move his head to look around, and his feet were cold. He began to panic when he could not move his legs to put his feet under the covers to get warm. He tried to rise up on his elbows, but his arms were strapped down next to his body, and his ankles were firmly strapped.

A little confused, but quick to judge his situation, he knew he was not going to get up. Moving around caused pain in his back, to the point he felt like he could pass out.

Am I paralyzed? He thought.

Familiar smells brought him to full awareness. They were awful hospital odors: alcohol, ether and cleaning solutions. His head started to spin again, and he closed his eyes.

I'm either in a morgue or a hospital. My nose is itching, but I can't move my arms, only my fingers. Get a hold of yourself Jess; it can't be all this bad.

"My Lord, I'm paralyzed!" his voice echoed in the room. Talking to himself, he reasoned, "No, I'm not dead! I can see the floor. Cadavers are usually face up, so I'm not in a morgue. If I'm on a cold slab in the morgue, my nose wouldn't be itching. If I could only rub my nose before I sneeze."

He tried to take another deep breath to keep from sneezing. This caused great pain in his back, and he almost fainted.

"Oh! Don't try that again, dummy!" he said moaning. "That hurt!"

"Mr. Hanes, you are awake!" Said a soft, sweet, female voice from somewhere in the room, with either an English or Australian accent, very precise and distinct.

Frantically, he said, "Yes! And, I'm going to sneeze!" The more he held his breath, the tighter the back muscles became and greater the pain from his injuries.

Her long-fingered hand came in sight with a wash towel. It was cool and moist against his forehead as it draped down over his nose. She gently held the back of his head with the other hand. Leaning down next to his ear, "Go ahead and sneeze in the towel. I will hold the back of your head from raising too far."

The pressure of wanting to sneeze subsided, and he began to relax when it caught him off guard. He sneezed hard, not able to hold it back any longer. It felt like his back was being torn apart, and he moaned from the pain. She released the back of his head and removed the damp towel from his face. He broke out into a cold sweat.

"Are you going to sneeze again?"

"I'm not sure!" he replied. "Sometimes I do," hesitated, ". . .twice in a row. I'm cold."

"Yes, it is chilly. I will take care of that. I am your nurse, Miss Elliot. Let me help you relax." She tenderly wiped the sweat from his face and neck. "You could have ripped out the stitches with that sneeze."

"I could never hold back a sneeze like some people can. I have to let it all out."

He could feel her warmth moving along the side of the bed and her body pressing against his right arm, then her warm hand on his wrist. She took his pulse.

"We are feeding you intravenously, so we needed to strap your arms and legs," she said. "You have been unconscious for a long time. Three days to be exact."

He could hear her dress rub her hose as she moved around to his left side. Her warmth felt good.

"We could not let your body move while you were unconscious," she said with her pleasant foreign accent. "You could have pulled out the stitches from your back wounds. I must call the doctor immediately, now that you are awake. I will return shortly."

"No!" he howled. "Please put a blanket on my feet first. Please! I'm about to freeze to death in here. I feel like I'm stark naked."

"Take my word for it, you are well covered with a gown," she said. "I have already placed a sheet and blanket over your feet, Mr. Hanes. I will be right back."

Leaving the room, she closed the door softly behind her.

Jess was puzzled about being unconscious for so long. His dizziness came back while he tried to remember what had happened to him. What happened to his back that he could not move? Where was this hospital he was in? He closed his eyes again; trying to think clearly instead of looking at the tile squares of the floor.

He thought he heard movement in the room. He did not remember hearing the door open, and listened more intently, "Is someone else in here?"

"*La Bes, homdula*, Mr. Hanes." He spoke in broken English with a heavy Arabic accent, "I am Sergeant Alda, Casablanca Secret Police, Sergeant Aliba Hammad Alda. I stay with you from explosion at airport. You need something?"

"Yes, please! Touch my feet. Are they cold?"

Dreading the thought of having no feeling, he felt the warmth of the Sergeant's hands.

"Good, good! Just hold them for a few minutes, your hands are warm."

"Feet cold, Mr. Hanes," he said. "I hold feet for you, until doctor comes."

Why is this Sergeant in my room to protect me? From who? Anyway, this guy is handy to have around. Jess wondered if he was for hire and started to ask another question, but Aliba spoke first.

"You no move three days. Afraid you die! I carry you to hospital truck at airport. Door stuck on back."

"Thank you," Jess said. "What happened Sergeant, were you there when it happened? I don't remember much."

"When bomb exploded, I fall off bench. Uh! . . . ." He paused, then thinking aloud. "Bus stop. Wait for bus. Uh! . . . Dust and smoke covered grass lawn. I watch three men walk out hole in building. One big fat man in brown army uniform, try run to big black car like rich man owns." He hesitated and began massaging Jess' feet. "Smoke and dust come out hole, more. I hear moaning inside. I step in wall hole, no floor. I fell! In dust, I see dead man on floor. Shot in head, not know his face. Then you scream, bad pain!"

Bad pain, for sure! Jess thought to himself.

Aliba continued rubbing Jess' feet, "Dust and smoke bad, cough much. I not see you good. I try get door off, but not good! Wait, police come. Take you and door to hospital. We carry you to ambulance, door on back."

What in the world is this all about?

"Where am I?" Jess asked.

Aliba shrugged his shoulders, "Casablanca Royal Hospital."

"I remember . . . going to the restroom . . . at the Casablanca airport," Jess said slowly, trying to squeeze out more from his shaken brain. *I just went in to the restroom, and sat down on the toilet. Then gun shots and a green bag! Or was it tan? Explosives! That's right!*

Jess opened his eyes and closed them tightly again. *What happened next? I'm getting a headache from trying to remember.*

"I think I heard someone get shot, and . . . the next thing I remember . . . a satchel charge was under me between my legs. Right now, I don't remember anything after that." He was getting tired of trying to remember and was sleepy. "Why did they want to kill me? I didn't know who they were."

"Mr. Hanes, you see someone before going in men's room?" Aliba asked.

"Yes!" Pausing to consider the question. "I saw thousands of people in the lobby, but no one I spoke to. And, . . . I didn't linger or look directly at anyone. I didn't see anything or anyone who would want to kill me if I saw them." He paused again, "Let me think about it awhile. I'm sure not going anywhere. I'm thankful I'm not brain dead. Thank you, Jesus!"

Aliba smiled and gestured his approval, "You call on your God in restroom at airport. You thank Him now. Your God's Son, Jesus! Good you pray to Him. I pray to Mohammed, Allah's son, for you." He came closer to the head of the bed. "I get you magazine, doctor coming. I hear more, your Jesus."

"Yes, that would be great! Once I'm up on my feet, we can have a long talk."

Their conversation was interrupted when the nurse and doctor came in. Aliba immediately left the room.

"Good afternoon, Mr. Hanes," said the doctor. "You're a hard man to kill."

He shuffled to the side of Jess' bed, dragging the heel of one shoe. He had a bad leg from a World War II injury. Speaking thickly, like a German not accustom to speaking English, he said, "Let me look at wounds. I am Doctor Heitzik. Please excuse my English. It not good!"

"Sure Doc!" Jess replied.

Nurse Elliot pulled back the sheet and blanket, and the doctor lifted the nightgown. He felt lightly along the incisions with the tip of his fingers. The doctor's fingers were cold and Jess flinched. His touch caused a muscle spasm.

"Hey Doc! You'll freeze me to death before I die of these wounds. Please hurry and cover me up! I'm cold!" Jess' shivering became more violent. The goose bumps popped out all over his body.

"Blood circulation normal according to our tests and instruments. No permanent nerve damage. Good! No signs of infection except few spots of high temperature, some above normal. Hum, good! I will be quick. Checking reflexes!" He felt lightly along the bruised ribs, spine, and up to the base of the skull. His fingers hit nerve endings sending pulses of pain through Jess' back. He winced, but kept quiet.

The doctor checked around the wounds for redness and drainage. "Hum, good! Bruised neck muscles, will be better! Swelling down, good! We start therapy walking today. Easy stretch exercises next week when stitches and clamps are removed. Use another bag of antibiotics tonight," he said to the nurse. He continued his inspection of Jess' bruises. "Good, good! Much better! Hum, yes! Much better! Three days, you come long way!"

The doctor turned, "Good work, Nurse Elliot." He nodded his approval and shuffled out of the room, closing the door behind him.

That report sounds like I'm recovering pretty well. But, he didn't cover me up. I'll die of pneumonia first.

The sheet and blanket were pulled back over him, and warm hands began massaging his feet again.

"Bless you, Aliba, that helps!" Jess said sleepily.

"Mr. Hanes," Her sweet voice again, but stern this time. "Nurse Elliot. Aliba is out in the hall with the doctor and other government investigators. I will be the one to nurse you back to health. It is arranged for me to be here at all times to care for you."

In a softer tone, she continued, "I have ordered a heating blanket for you from our supply room. We usually do not have need for them."

"Thank you ma'am," Jess said. Closing his eyes, he could feel his muscles trying to relax. Nurse Elliot's warm hands massaging his feet put him to sleep.

CHAPTER FOUR

Samain and Bushta walked away from the doctor and approached the closed door to Jess Hanes' room. Aliba stepped between them and the door.

"Yes, may I help you?" he said firmly in Arabic.

"You know who we are," Bushta said. "It has not been that long since we worked together. We were here the first day when Mr. Hanes was brought in. We understand he is up and walking around. It has been over a week now." He flashed his credentials, and folded the wallet to put it back in his vest pocket.

"No!" Aliba said, reaching his hand out to receive the wallet. "I want to see!"

Reluctantly Bushta opened the wallet again and held it up to Aliba's eye level. Firmly gripping it, he permitted Aliba to hold only its corner.

"You know Mr. Hanes was not conscious when we were here before," Bushta said in Arabic. "We are returning his passport, computer and attaché case. It is urgent we question Mr. Hanes concerning the assassination at the airport."

With a stern set jaw, Samain did not offer his identification. Sergeant Aliba Alda acknowledged his superior by clicking his boot heels together and snapping to attention. He opened the door and walked in ahead of the two agents.

He immediately walked around Nurse Elliot, and to the head of the bed, next to Jess. Letting out a deep sigh, he turned around laying his warm hand on Jess' wrist.

"Excuse, Mr. Hanes," he said with a firm low voice. "Two government men about bomb at airport."

Nurse Elliot instantly became very angry, "Gentlemen! Next time, you will knock quietly, and wait for me to answer the door. He could have been completely uncovered." She turned and glared at Aliba. "Besides, he was asleep! Soundly asleep! He needs an enormous amount of rest." She faced the other two, "What do you want that could not wait?" She asked curtly.

"You not talk that way if you were Arab woman," Aliba stated harshly in Arabic.

"Really!" She replied in Arabic and continued her conversation to Jess in English with a low voice. Jess found out later she was fluent in six languages. With her back to the three men, she just smiled and continued attending to Jess' needs.

"Just one minute, please!" Samain interrupted the dispute. "All four of us must work together as a team to keep Mr. Hanes alive and safe. Stop this childish bickering. It is urgent we speak to Mr. Hanes privately, without these interruptions." Walking to the head of the bed, he continued, "And, immediately! With your permission, Mr. Hanes?" Samain added in good Queen's English.

"Yes, it's all right, if my attendants approve," Jess said, still not knowing who they were. When there were no objections, he said, "Sergeant Aliba, it's all right, thank you. Please come back in when they are gone. Stay close!"

"I will stay!" said Nurse Elliot emphatically as she continued rubbing the calves of Jess' legs. That was that!

Aliba headed for the door with an echoing sigh of disgust and muttered something in Arabic under his breath and reluctantly left the room.

Jess did not know these men, and did not want his bodyguard too far away. It surprised him that they let his nurse stay. Then he remembered one of the agents remark about the four of them keeping him alive and safe.

They were moving about his room with electronic detectors searching for listening devices, because a steady tone could be heard from one of their instruments. One of them searched under and around his bed. The sound was like a threshold tone of a metal locator, which was used by treasure hunters to find ferrous and non-ferrous metals. But the instruments they used were for detecting electronic frequencies, transmitted by small hidden transmitters.

"Sorry, Mr. Hanes, for the interruption," Samain paused, listening to his instrument. "We must check your room for electronic bugs. There must also be strict security with our conversations and activities from here on. Do you understand what I am relating to you, Mr. Hanes?"

"I'm not sure this is necessary," he answered.

"Your life is still in danger, especially if the assassins know you are alive here in the hospital," Bushta said. "We have made all arrangements for your safety and comfort while you are recovering from your injuries. While you are in Morocco, there will be one of us with you at all times. The American government is aware of your circumstances."

"What circumstances? Who was assassinated? What about my wife?"

"She is made aware of your conditions daily. She is prohibited from coming here at this time," Samain said. He leaned on the mattress at the head of the bed and spoke softly, "Our king demands protection for both of you."

Jess felt him move away, and then asked, "What does the king of Morocco have to do with my wife and me?"

"One member of his family was murdered in the restroom where you were injured," Samain said.

The room was quiet for a few long minutes. Too much information at one time was clouding and confusing Jess' mind.

From the window, Bushta could see over the other buildings toward the center of the city. "Beautiful view of Casablanca's gardens from up here, Mr. Hanes," he said. Motioning to Samain, he pointed out the window, "Okay! Our men are still in place on the roof and down on the street."

"Miss Elliot, how long does the doctor give for his recovery time?" Samain asked.

Shouting down through the pillow hole, Jess' voice echoed in the room. He had enough. "Hold on now! I'm flat on my stomach and can't see you face to face. You have me at a disadvantage. Who are you and why are you here? Why is my life in danger? I'm not in Morocco illegally! I was on a layover for a flight to Algiers and then on to Saudi Arabia. Evidently you know the rest!"

His nurse placed her warm hand on the back of his neck, leaned over and whispered in his ear, "It is all right! I know these two men quite well. Do not let them upset you."

"The two of us, Sergeant Alda and Nurse Elliot, are here for your twenty-four hour protection," Samain explained while moving around the room. "Mr. Hanes, we are government agents of Morocco and Interpol. We are like the U.S. Marshals in the United States. Our assignment is to protect our government officials from assassinations, and especially the King. Our job is to protect you at all times. I have authority to transfer you to secret locations when you have recovered well enough for travel." By the time he finished, he was standing in front of the closed door to the hall.

Bushta was still close to the window. Jess could sense his closeness. "The public and hospital staff will not see us together again for security reasons. Only Nurse Elliot and Sergeant Alda will be here night and day, until you leave the hospital."

"So you're stuck with being my baby sitters?"

"The two of us, your nurse and your bodyguard," Samain repeated.

Jess moved his arms, trying to relax the muscles, and felt the stitches pulling. It did not hurt like before, but felt odd, as if he had dried mud stuck to his back.

"Sorry, I can't turn over to shake your hands," he said. "They still insist on strapping me so I don't pull stitches apart. My back was all messed up when I was brought in here." Nurse Elliot unstrapped his arms and massaged them.

"At least that's what I've been told, and it feels like one big pin cushion."

"May I look at your back, Mr. Hanes?" Bushta asked.

"Sure! If my nurse agrees, I guess so. Just don't take too long, it's cold in this room."

"Yes. Quickly please!" She nodded her head in approval.

Bushta removed the bed sheet and blanket from off Jess' back, "Look at this!"

Samain came out of the bathroom where he was using his detection devices. He stood next to Bushta and whistled.

"How close do you think you were to the bomb blast, Mr. Hanes?" Samain asked.

Jess chuckled to himself, "I really don't know, because I can't remember much. But, I was close enough, as you can see! Maybe within ten feet, it was a large desert tan canvas bag . . . looked like a satchel charge left over from Desert Storm." He hesitated, and then continued. "But of course, they are all large, that close! It's only by the grace of God I'm still alive." He thought to himself, *How did I remember it was tan; maybe it was olive drab in color? It's been years since I've seen an explosive bag. I guess some things like that you don't ever forget, especially if you had to use them.*

The bed covers were placed over him again. Then, Nurse Elliot announced, "Mr. Hanes had a latrine door hanging on his back when they brought him in for surgery." She stepped around the two agents and continued her foot and leg therapy. "The explosion sent pieces of the metal through the door. It was a fragmentation bomb. The jagged holes in the door tore into his back, holding him against a wall."

Bushta smirked, "Why not take it off at the airport."

"When I saw him in the emergency room, they were prying his ribs apart to lift the door off," she said. "Aliba brought him in that way, door and all. The explosive device had to be a military issue, probably stolen from NATO installations in Europe and smuggled here."

Jess thought, *How come she knows so much about explosives and NATO stolen property?*

"Mr. Hanes, I would like to talk to you more in the morning," Samain said, pacing the floor. "I understand these clamps and stitches will come out tomorrow. The doctor told us you would be walking tonight without assistance. The fresher your memory is, the clearer the events at the airport will be. We need to catch those people quickly."

"Hold the phone!" Jess demanded. "All this conversation, and I still don't know who you two are. All of this has been confusing! What are your names? I want to see your ID? Please!"

After consulting with the nurse whether it was all right to talk longer with Jess, Samain brought his and Bushta's identifications to the bedside. Squatting down cross-legged, and sitting Indian style on the floor, Samain scooted under the front of the bed, leaned under until he could see Jess' face.

Looking up at him, Samain smiled, "Hello, old friend! It has been many years since we last were together. Do you remember Samain and Bushta at Sidi Yahia?" As he showed Jess their I.D.'s, tears came to his eyes from the emotions he was holding back.

"Well I'll be! Bushta! Samain! How in the world?"

"Old friend, we will take care of you," Bushta said standing next to the window at the head of Jess' bed. "We will explain more for you in detail, later. But when we went through your attaché case and computer, we began to realized who you were." He squatted next to the bed. "All your luggage has been taken care of, also. Try to stay calm and relax as best you can. We will be back early tomorrow morning." He motioned with his hand to Samain that they should be leaving.

Samain laid his hand over Jess' hand and patted it, "Nurse Elliot will take very good care of you. Jesus will heal you!"

Jess was almost speechless, and pleasantly warmed by the unexpected appearance of his two old friends. "Thank you, Samain! And, you too, Bushta!"

Bushta stood up and whispered in his ear, "Jess, we will be back as soon as possible. Everything is working out fine." Then they left.

Jess remembered that Samain had become a Christian some years ago. As a former Moslem, it must have been a shock to his family and friends when he changed his faith. *I wonder how the King had overlooked a Christian working for him, especially a converted Moslem?*

Jess' mind was working overtime, trying to piece everything together that had happened. How had Samain and Bushta become involved? Questions, Questions!

#

A week later, Nurse Elliot prepared Jess for their evening walk through the halls. Her starched uniform swished against her white-hosed legs as she brought a cane to him. He lifted each foot for her to position the slippers, because he still could not bend over to reach them. The warmth from her shoulder against his leg felt good. It was still cold in his room and any warmth absorbed quickly.

She stood up, looked him straight in the eyes and smiled. For the first time he realized she was his same height with her nurse shoes on.

Being so involved with his own recovery, only now was he really able to look at her. Miss Elliot's long, wavy dark brown hair hung across her shoulders. She had her hair in netting. Her nurse hat was pushed down into her hair, and looked like a white, lacy crown. Her hazel eyes glistened, and wrinkles showed a little at the corners with her big smile.

She looked as though she had spent time outdoors; her face was nicely tanned. She was about five feet ten inches tall with well-proportioned features. In her white uniform dress, white shoes and stockings, she looked to Jess like a bright angel with no visible wings. He supposed she was about forty-five, or so.

She noticed him staring.

"Please excuse me," blushing he apologized, trying not to say the wrong words. "My first real look at you is refreshing."

She smiled, "Thank you! With that observation, I will write on your chart that you are recovering splendidly."

She put her arm through his and guided him to the door. Her perfume was pleasant and feminine. Jess could feel her warmth pressing against him, holding him steady on his feet. She slowly moved an arms length away, standing in front of him, holding onto his shoulder. Stepping back with her hands on her hips, she looked at him.

"I do not think you need me or your cane any longer. You are ready for longer walks without support." Nodding her approval, she motioned him toward the door.

Aliba met them in the hall outside the room. "Okay, Mr. Hanes. We go. Nurse Elliot, I lead the way."

Jess noticed again, how protective they both were. Aliba was always moving ahead, checking hallways and entrances to rooms. Miss Elliot was constantly at his side, watching and observing him and their surroundings.

There were always four uniformed officers, two at each end of the hall, checking identification cards of people coming out of the elevator and the double staircase. Jess seemed to be safe for recuperating and well protected.

#

A week later, the three were walking together in the hall on the hospital floor three levels above Jess' room. These three unfinished inside floors were noisy with construction work, except during lunch and evenings.

On this evening stroll through the top floor, it was quiet, and their view of Casablanca was tremendous. All the construction workers had left for the day. The three of them were at least ten stories above the highest building in town.

Jess' ever-present companions were looking toward the Atlas Mountains, outlined by a bright orange moon behind them to the east. Its pale light made shadows of the city seem darker.

They moved to the west side to view the lights of the shipping harbor and the Moulay Youssef jetty through the hall windows.

Suddenly, to Jess' left a bright orange flash of light caught his attention in the shadow of a distant warehouse.

"What's that?" He asked, pointing?

Nurse Elliot and Aliba had seen it, too. The light disappeared, but a white smoke trail began to wind its way toward them with great speed.

"Look out, it's a missile!" Jess yelled.

The three fell to the floor in front of a leather couch, where Nurse Elliott and Aliba covered Jess with their bodies. There was a sharp explosion below, lifting them off the new floor throwing them against a cement pillar. The dust and debris settled around them, as they lay dazed.

The floor groaned and began to sag. Sounds of broken water lines and fire alarms began to pierce the evening stillness. Iron girders began grinding against each other in unnatural ways, running chills up Jess' spine. It was like raking fingernails across a chalkboard. The floor sagged again.

They were still in shock and for the moment did not know what to do. Finally, catching their wits, they scrambled up toward the level part of their floor next to a cement column. No sooner had they reached the safety of that portion of the floor, it began to collapse to the floor below. They had to grab the closest unmovable thing to hang onto in order to keep from falling with the floor. The hallway hand railing saved them from falling.

The floor they had stood on had completely collapsed to the floor below. Dust bellowed up to their level so thick they could hardly breathe.

Scooting their feet along the base board of the hall, they were able to move toward a stable section of the floor. Then, holding onto each other's hands for support and guidance through the dust in the air, they ran to the staircase. Coughing and spitting dust, the two men followed Nurse Elliot down to the floor level where Jess' room was located.

Aliba began choking from the dust, and another nurse put an oxygen mask over his nose and mouth. Nurse Elliot found two

more for her and Jess. They huddled together under a table at the
nurse station.

"Are you two all right?" Jess asked. "Your faces are covered
with white dust. All I can see are your eyes peeking out."

They took off their oxygen masks, and Nurse Elliot began to
laugh, trying to cover her fright. Tears made dirty streams down
her face as she tried to control her crying sobs. Jess was visibly
shaken, and Aliba's arms were wrapped around himself.

"I thought we would be crushed. It was like a giant hand
reached out and lifted us out of that hole. I was afraid of dying."
She continued to cry.

Aliba and Jess put their arms around her shoulders to comfort
her. She put the oxygen mask back on and took a deep breath.
Aliba spoke to her in Arabic, and she nodded.

He stood up, shook himself, and moved among the others in
the hallway, assisting them. Organized hospital crews hurried
through the halls, checking patients' rooms, and attending to those
who needed help. The after shocks of the hospital building settling
could still be felt.

Jess realized that other people probably needed Nurse Elliot's
attention more than he. "I'm fine," he told her. "Isn't there any
assistance you can give to the other patients?"

She removed her mask, but did not answer him. Instead, she
began using a portable transceiver radio, which she carried
constantly, talking in Arabic and French.

Aliba returned and listened to her for a moment. Then he said
something and she repeated it over the radio.

"We must leave before someone is killed," she said to Jess. "A
vehicle is waiting downstairs for us. Aliba knows the plan and he
will secure your belongings from your room. Come on!"

Nurse Elliot and Jess made their way down to a waiting vehicle
and sped away into the dark alleys of Casablanca. Their contingency
plan was in effect in order to keep Jess alive. Aliba would meet
them later at a different hospital, where Jess' own personal doctor
would be waiting.

An investigation of the missile fired at the hospital revealed that it had been the work of a terrorist group. They had fired the deadly missile that missed its mark, supposedly targeted for Jess.

How did they know where I was at that specific moment? He wondered.

CHAPTER FIVE

Weeks later, Jess was released from the other Casablanca hospital. He said goodbye to the nursing staff, but was disappointed that Nurse Elliot was not on duty when he left. Aliba escorted him down to the outpatient desk and into an adjoining office. Inside, the administrator placed a form on his desk for Jess to read and sign.

"Mr. Hanes, please sign on this line at the bottom," he said. "Our government will cover everything. Your bills have been paid."

"That's great, thank you! I'm happy to be getting out of here. I did have outstanding help in recovering from my injuries."

The administrator nodded and shook hands, bowed and returned to his other business. Leaving his office, they walked toward the hospital lobby. Aliba guided Jess away from that area to another office.

"Mr. Hanes, please, we do not leave hospital from front. We go this way." Motioning through the room to an outside glass hallway, he led Jess to the alley exit. "Safer this way," he said, as they hurried through a long hall. "Your three friends from the government are waiting for us in the back."

They continued through another hall until they entered a plush doctor's office, and then out to a storage room.

"Where is the back?" Jess asked. "Isn't this sort of a roundabout way to get there? What's the rush?"

"You in danger!" Aliba replied, breathing a little harder. They stopped at an outside door. "Wait here. I will look."

Aliba slowly opened the door enough to peek out. Passed Aliba's shoulder, Jess could see a light tan vehicle under the shade of a date palm tree. Aliba waved to the men in it, and they drove up to

the door as Aliba and Jess went out. The new tan U.S. military
Hummer vehicle looked great. Jess had wanted one ever since Desert
Storm.

The wide back door swung open and a familiar voice called
out, "In here, Mr. Jess E. Hanes."

He entered the full-size back seat, coming face to face with his
nurse who was seated in the middle of the back seat. "Miss Elliot,
what are you doing out here? What a pleasure! I thought you were
off duty this morning."

"Mr. Hanes, please move in further," said Samain from the
front passenger seat. "We must move with haste."

Aliba bumped against Jess as he pushed him inside just when
the Hummer leaped forward, causing Jess to fall against Miss Elliot's
soft body. He needed to step across her legs to the seat on the
other side.

"I'm sorry!"

He kept apologizing, while trying to keep his hands from
pushing against her in an ungentlemanly way. There were no
handles to grab onto. To keep his weight from pressing harder
against her, he put his hands on the back of the seat on each side of
her, and came nose to nose as the Hummer surged forward.

What an embarrassing situation! He knew then why he had
skipped garlic and onions with his omelet for breakfast!

Jess was a happily married man, but here he was with his arms
around a very attractive lady who he was pressing into the seat. He
could smell that nice perfume! She wore a tight, light blue business
pantsuit, not the usual nurse uniform, and it amplified her shapely
body.

He tried pushing back from her, but her weight held his hands
behind her, plus the acceleration of the vehicle did not help. She
smiled and slid her hands up between her and Jess, helping him to
move away from her. She scooted out from under him toward the
door, while he moved out of the way and sat between her and Aliba.

Why didn't she scoot over in the first place? Jess thought, just a
little aggravated.

"Jess, I had no idea!" she exclaimed, teasing him as she slowly gave him more space to sit. She rearranged herself next to the door as Jess grabbed the front of his seat between his legs and held on. The Hummer made its way through crowded Casablanca streets. He glanced at her, and she gave him a shy, pleasant smile.

"No harm done," she said. "But, it was nice while it lasted. You should buckle up though, we have a rough trip ahead." Then she settled back into her seat and buckled up also.

With a sheepish smile, feeling just a little embarrassed, Jess locked his seat belt as Aliba snickered, mumbling something under his breath.

"What did you say?" Jess demanded, looking out the corner of his eye at Aliba.

"Nothing important!" Laughing, Aliba slapped Jess on the knee. "We have fun trip? Ya?"

Once they were settled, Jess could see Samain and Bushta in the front seats. Neither looked back at him, but continued suspiciously scanning the cars and people on the streets. As quickly as possible, they sped through the narrow lanes and alleyways in the heart of old Casablanca, a city of over two million people.

Then they were absorbed into the center of a convoy of other Hummer vehicles that were waiting for them. The other vehicles parted, and theirs blended in with them, all the same color and type vehicle. Jess learned later this action was to help confuse anyone trying to follow them.

"We are insuring your safety out of the city," Bushta said. "Then our job will be to help convince you to join our efforts in finding the assassins and the ones who persist in killing you."

It did not sink in for Jess as to what Bushta had said; he was too engrossed with the turmoil around him. There were automatic weapons in racks on both back doors, and the cargo space was filled with supplies and suitcases. Nurse Elliot kept tight against Jess on the right, and Aliba on the left, while they watched out the window. It was as if they were using their bodies to shield him from danger.

OPERATION:
EYE WITNESS

A treasure hunter finds himself at the wrong place at the wrong time in Morocco

D. RUDD WISE

OPERATION: EYE WITNESS

A treasure hunter finds himself
at the wrong place at the
wrong time in Morocco

D. RUDD WISE

Jess E. Hanes, a middle-aged treasure hunter, finds himself at the wrong place at the wrong time at the Casablanca airport in Morocco. He is the lone witness of an assassination of a high government official, which plunges him into an international tangle of drug running, arms smuggling, romantic involvement, and investigations by such agencies as Interpol and the CIA.

Nice riding vehicle, for a truck, he was thinking. *Wonder if they're still so expensive for civilians?* Jess' mind became focused on the large number of people in the streets. The street vendors with their wagons and booths were all open for business. It was the famous Casablanca *Souk* or outdoor open marketplace; an open market similar to the big ones in New York City, Boston and Chicago, but more primitive.

Parts of the market would not have passed any health departments' inspection in the U.S. Products for consumption were open to the environment: flies, bugs, maggots, dirt, dust and handling by customers. For the pampered, modern, average American, the stench would be too much for shopping.

It was like moving back to the time of the Roman Empire, like the movies depict North African cities of the first century. Casablanca's inner walled city, the *Medina Souk* (old city market trading-place) bulged with vegetables, citrus, cloth in every color and pattern, meats of most every animal (except pork), every variety of seafood from snails to squid, and leather products of belts to camel and horse saddles.

If customers wanted milk, a fresh warm supply was right from a goat. But, no fresh clear water was available; however, only wines for the body's needs.

In the narrow streets, it was difficult to get through the throng of people. They were not willing to move for motorized vehicles. Progress was slow, and people refused to get out of the way, even when the bumper of the Hummer pushed them.

The men wearing their *jellabas,* a shapeless robed garment with long sleeves and hood, often homespun and striped, resisted being moved aside by slamming their fist on the hood and banging the door windows as the vehicles passed. The caftan (robed) women with their colored veils glared with resentment. Jess did not know what they were saying in Arabic, but the angry expressions on their faces spoke an international language that all understood.

Aliba stood up in the opening of the roof, shouting in Arabic, "Make way! Emergency! Make way! *Balek! Balek!"*

He and Miss Elliot had their hands on their weapons, ready for any confrontation. Samain and Bushta were busy driving and navigating. Jess was hanging onto overhead recessed ceiling handles with both hands. A shoulder harness would have been a welcomed item in the back seat.

They finally drove onto a dual lane highway, still in a convoy with other vehicles. The number of vehicles had grown, but now every so often one or two would turn off. The convoy finally lessened to three.

"Are we headed for the airport?" Jess asked.

"No!" Bushta replied from the driver's seat. "Hopefully we can convince you to stay with us for a while," he said. "I canceled your flight for the U.S., securing you a refund. Your wife has been contacted about this whole matter. We are requesting that you not leave Morocco at this time. We need your assistance in finding the assassins."

No one else made further comments about needing Jess' assistance. He looked perplexed, and became a little bit angry over the idea of not being able to continue on his business trip or even return home. It sounded like they wanted him as bait to catch the terrorists.

He did not want to start a commotion with all the tensions they were under at the moment, so he decided to save talk about this until they were stopped for the night.

They continued through the outer part of Casablanca, then turned north onto a gravel road in the country, then stopped. Samain was very quiet as he studied maps on his lap, and would occasionally glance out the window. He began using his radio, talking in Arabic. Aliba and Bushta also kept comments to each other in Arabic.

Miss Elliot glanced at Jess and said nothing. She did not have the beautiful smile he was accustomed to seeing; she was engrossed in her surveillance, and she had a stern look and a set jaw. Jess would find out later that these four made up a team that had worked together often, even though he was given a different impression at the hospital.

By the time they had traveled into the country for about half an hour, they all could feel the tensions ease. It was a beautiful, sunny afternoon, with a clear blue sky. Jess was surprised to see that their vehicle was producing no dust, which would have been seen a long way off. Evidently, the gravel was packed hard. He wondered what was happening; it was too quiet!

"Will all your conversation be confidential? I don't understand Arabic, and very little French. I'm enjoying the scenery, but I'd really be interested in what's going on."

"We are sorry, Mr. Hanes!" Bushta said. "We have been too busy with our routing and plans, not regarding you. You do not understand French or Arabic?"

"You have missed out completely," Miss Elliot said still holding onto her automatic rifle. She placed it in the pocket of the door at her side. "I will interpret for you as we go along. If you have any questions, let me know." Then she gave him that big smile of hers.

"We've been together for quite awhile. Can we drop the formal names? Call me Jess," he said loud enough for everyone to hear over the truck's noise.

Everyone nodded their heads in approval, replying in unison, "Yes!"

"Janet Jay Elliot," she said, as she extended her hand.

"May I call you Janet?"

"Yes, but you may also call me J.J. . . . . Jess!"

Aliba frowned at Jess. "No! It is not dignified to address my superiors by first name, Mr. Hanes."

"As long as we have been together, I would like to call you Ali, if you would call me Jess. We are friends now, not business associates. I would consider it a privilege and an honor for you to use my first name."

Aliba's eyes brightened as if Jess had given him a present. "Yes, a friend. I have come to like you as a brother. Closer than a friend." They shook hands. "Mr. Hanes! Ali, too short name. Please, Aliba!"

From the passengers' front seat, Samain said loudly, "Hey, back there, we have details to work out. It is a long trip to the Atlas Mountains. We must continue to be alert. Jess, the first stop is Rabat." He motioned with his hands. "Our king Moulay Ben Aladu Itssani, will talk to you in person. We are assigned to protect you until the problems are solved with the assassination at the airport."

"What does your king want with me?" Jess said thinking that was a most unusual request. He did not even know the king's full name until now, and certainly could not spell or pronounce it.

The prospects of catching the killers does sound intriguing, especially if I am able to meet the king in his palace, Jess thought. *It might be a good opportunity to get permission to research some old abandoned villages in the foothills of the mountains. That could prove very interesting for this ole Texan.*

"There is a plot to kill our king Aladu Itssani," Bushta explained. "You may have seen someone or something that the assassins think will hinder their progress in taking over our country with communism. His Highness has expressed ahead of time his thanks for your involvement in helping find the killers of his brother. We all want you to volunteer to help."

As Bushta slowed the vehicle to a brisk walking speed, Samain added, "We need your assistance in catching these assassins. Understand it may cost your life and ours, but that is the price we pay for such dedication."

After the vehicle stopped, Samain checked the maps with Bushta again, and turned in his seat looking straight at Jess, "It will also be harder for us to protect you at the same time. You must make the choice."

"We operate much like the FBI, CIA and Texas Rangers, as secret agents for the Moroccan government and Interpol," J.J. explained.

The vehicle started rolling again, and slowly gained speed as they exited the area of rolling hills.

"They killed the king's brother?" Jess said, trying to understand the situation. "So, that was the man who was shot in the restroom and the reason I was getting so much attention? Well! I'll be a monkey's uncle!"

Aliba and J.J. both looked at him, and then at each other shrugging their shoulders.

"That's another odd American expression. I really don't know where it originated from," Jess said looking at their puzzled expressions. He waved his hands, trying to dismiss his comment, "No, I'm not really saying that I'm a monkey's uncle! But, I don't know what help I'll be. Anyway, how does the Texas Rangers fit into this plot of things? What do you know about the Rangers?"

Bushta slowed to a crawling speed. Everyone continued looking for other vehicles and aircraft.

"We had an exchange program with all three branches a few years back," Samain said. "We have learned better ways of networking and of obtaining international assistance with satellites."

"I have two nephews in the Texas Rangers," Jess said. "Maybe you have met them? They're in the West Texas district."

"I doubt we did," Bushta said. "We spent most of our time down around the Brownsville area and up the coast line. We wanted to go to Langtry where Judge Roy Bean was to have controlled the law west of the Pecos River, but we could not fit it into our schedule."

"No, we did not meet anyone from that district," Samain said. "Did we J.J.?"

She just shook her head, no.

"But we liked Texas. Do you?" Samain asked.

"Remember?" Jess replied. "I'm a native Texan, and proud of it!"

"Have you ever met a Texan that was not?" Samain teased.

"Those we have met are 'true grit' Texans, the same as John Wayne," Bushta added. "You know, the Duke?"

"Not personally, but I sure like his western movies. He's my hero. You knew he died a few years ago?"

"Yes, we heard. But, back to business, gentlemen!" J.J.

interjected. "Our contacts in Oujda and Meknes have told us of another attempt to kill you, Jess. It is in the planning stage. Remember this, Jess," she said earnestly. "You are their key link to whoever did the shooting at the airport and who also tried to kill you."

"But you know I did not see or . . ."

"Yes, we know that," Samain said. "But, we do not think it matters to them now. You are considered a marked man, and there is a price on your head."

I wonder how much my head is worth on the foreign market? Jess thought. "If I'm not going home yet, this will put my wife in danger. I need to warn her. I've been gone too long as it is without contacting her." Patting his attaché case, he added, "I could use my notebook computer on the Internet, when we get to Rabat! I'm sure she thinks I'm dead, or being held hostage by some terrorist."

"We cannot take a chance, even with Internet," said Samain. "Please do not worry. That has all been taken care of. She knows what the situation is here daily, and she is in protective custody with the U.S. Marshal's agency. Also, the Texas Rangers in Austin, Texas, are escorting her."

"Why didn't you people tell me all of this before now?" Jess asked, getting upset.

"Twice our people stopped terrorists," Aliba said firmly. "Remember, they try kill you in hospital."

"Thanks to J.J. and Aliba, they did not get to you," Samain said.

J.J. tried to assure Jess, "We did not want to take a chance of losing security, and so we kept you out of that chain of information. We did not know how the drugs in the hospital would affect you."

"Once again, we cannot let you contact your wife, or anyone else in your family." Samain smiled, "It would be too risky for all of you. Hopefully, this will be over soon, and you can return home safely."

Samain and Aliba discussed the location of hideaways and the people they needed to contact. J.J. began spreading out aeronautical sectional maps for them to study in the back seat. She pointed out the different routes through the mountains they could travel once leaving Rabat. They were to keep moving until an undercover operation could be set up.

Jess had been in Rabat years ago, and the surroundings in the country outside of the city looked the same. Most of the back roads had fencerows of big-eared prickly-pear cactus plants and stacked rocks instead of barbed wire. They appeared to be the same species of cactus as those in Texas.

Jess thought, *The early settlers in Morocco must have brought the cactus over here from Texas. How else could a Texan look at it?*

His joking thoughts were covering his concerns for his wife and uncertainty about whether he should consent to go through with the developing plans.

There were Bedouin tents on the hillsides where men wearing turbans were riding horses at full gait, firing musket rifles into the air. They were celebrating the circumcision of a young man or someone was getting married. Also, many small huts and buildings were scattered in the countryside. Most of them were built with mud and straw bricks. They are called 'adobe' back in Texas.

Most of the road travelers were either walking or riding bicycles or carts; very few were in vehicles. Those not in vehicles would wave and smile as the Hummer passed.

Barefooted women with shear blue-veiled faces, wearing hooded *jellabas* with a straw basket on their heads, would turn and smile. Yes, their faces could be seen through some of the blue veils. Their differently tattooed chins displayed the Berber tribe to which they belonged. Some girls played with rope hoops along the roadside. Young boys would hit rocks with sticks made from tree roots, knocking them into holes or empty tin cans. They had their own special games.

A large sheep herd was crossing the road as the vehicle headed around a blind curve on a hill. Bushta slammed on the brakes, sliding the Hummer to a stop with gravel and dust spraying everywhere. The noise, gravel and dust scared the sheep. They began to run, bleating loudly.

Aliba stood up in the seat with half his body out through the roof of the Hummer. "I see long way! Safe to get out! Only shepherd and two sons."

Samain stayed inside and contacted someone on the radio, letting them know they were stopped and their location. The rest of them got out and stretched.

The shepherd, who was a good hundred yards away, yelled, "*Bonjour! Bonjour!*" He and his sons herded the sheep across the road and further down the hill, away from the road. Two black sheepdogs worked the left and right sides of the herd bringing them under control. The shepherds had trained the animals to respond with precision to their commands, by talking to the dogs in French, whistling, and using hand signals.

Bushta and Aliba continued to scan the horizon and the road ahead of them. J.J. walked along the edge of the herd and talked to one of the sons. He was smiling and waving his hand for his father to come to them.

The father bowed at the waist to her and shook her hand. Then in the Moslem way, kissed his own hand and placed it to his chest. It was unusual seeing this Moslem custom done with a woman. Men are usually given this greeting, and the women are mostly ignored in Arab tradition.

She came back to the vehicle with a big smile on her face, "He wanted us to take a lamb for not running over his sheep. I understand that has happened before, someone running over his sheep. I thanked him, but told him we had no room." She climbed back into the vehicle, leaving the door open.

Aliba, Bushta and Jess stood at the side of the road next to a deep ditch. Samain returned to the truck to monitor the radio. The sheep herd had all passed safely across the road, so the crew had slowly started back across the road to the vehicle.

Suddenly, Jess stopped and pointed back up the road in the direction from where they had come. He heard a familiar noise in the distance, one they all recognized at the same time. It was coming from the other side of the hill they had just come around. The sound was the beating of helicopter blades against the air.

There was no safe protection for them to get behind for cover. The vehicle was not a place to be, especially if someone began shooting from a helicopter. The fuel could explode.

They ran back across the road and jumped in the ditch. Samain yelled at J.J. to get out of the vehicle. They both got in the ditch on their side of the road and were exposed to the helicopter as it followed the road around the hill.

Jess had his head down and did not get a good look at it passing overhead. It kept right on going, scattering the herd of sheep as it veered away from the road and continued on down across the open fields into the lower valleys below. It looked as if the pilot had intentionally scared the sheep by splitting the herd with a low pass. The shepherds had another herding job ahead of them.

I don't think they saw us, Jess thought.

Samain was talking on his portable transceiver, and motioned for everyone to stay where they were. Either the pilot did not see them because of the shadow of the hill, or seeing the sheep scatter drew his attention.

But, will they be back? Jess wondered.

"Stay away from the truck, and keep watching the helicopter until it is out of sight," Samain shouted. "They may return. They seem to be following the road. Did anyone see markings on the helicopter?"

There were none.

Both Samain and Bushta had binoculars. They kept track of the helicopter and looked for others that could be following.

Down the hill from the road, the sheep were being rounded up, and the herders were still shaking their fists in the direction of the disappearing helicopter. The sheep were still bleating, and the sons were yelling at the dogs. It was too beautiful a day and countryside to be marred with violence.

J.J. and Samain stood up in the ditch, while the other three on the other side of the road strained to see the helicopter, and where it had vanished in the distant haze. Jess had set up in the ditch, and then lay back with his head in the dry grass. He looked up to see a red hawk soaring some distance above them, screeching its warning of distress. It was upset, too!

When the Hummer pulled back on the road a few minutes later, Samain began driving in order to give Bushta a break. Only the radio reception broke the quietness as they continued the ride to Rabat. There were no comments about the scare they had, but the tension was back. It could have been a setup, using the sheep to stop them.

They finally arrived at their destination just before sundown. Jess expected to arrive in front of a grand, spectacular, mosaic palace or government building adorned with Moroccan cultural antiques, but he was wrong.

East of Rabat, Samain parked the vehicle in thick brush that scraped the sides. They began unloading a small amount of equipment into one backpack. They were packing flashlights, a first-aid kit, bottled water, maps, a compass and a coil of climbing rope. Samain opened a bag and handed each of them a one-piece diver's dry suit and booties. Their first names were printed in white ink on the inside of each piece.

Jess thought it was sort of premature on Samain's part to have a dry suit for him. *How did Samain know I would be here?*

They slipped the suits over their clothes, and Jess was surprised they had enough room. It would be a safe bet that he would sweat-soak his clothes and hoped they would not be in the suits too long.

They were on the shore of the Oued Bou Regreg, a river flowing west from the Atlas Mountains down to the Atlantic Ocean through Rabat. At the river's edge, four Moroccan men were holding an eight-man pontoon rubber boat with an outboard motor. They had placed the backpacks in the middle, so Jess and the others squeezed between them and the rubberized sides of the boat. One of the four men waded out into the water, pulling the craft into the current, which swept toward Rabat. He stayed behind.

The sun was down, and the cool river breeze caused Jess to shiver. He pulled the divers rubber headpiece over his head and settled in his position with a paddle for rowing. No one had paid attention to his movements; they were concentrating on their location close to the shoreline.

The partly cloudy sky blocked the moonlight, and the darkness made it hard to see obstacles in the water. The craft slid easily over boulders and submersed wharf pilings as it drifted downstream. The two men in front had night-vision binoculars strapped around their heads. But, they did not seem concerned with the small bumps in the water.

After passing many freighters tied up to piers and small marinas, they quietly steered the rubber craft under a high pier, and waited.

It seemed like hours had passed when Jess looked at his watch. It was only eight-thirty; only one hour had passed.

The vehicle traffic across the river had almost ceased, and the only sounds were the wharf rats searching for food. Jess remembered the size of wharf rats in Morocco, which caused another chill to go up his spine. This also reminded him of his brother-in-law, who woke up one night in Vietnam with a large rat squatting on his chest, looking at him. Jess knew he would have nightmares too, after that!

The stench of this river is enough to gag a maggot, Jess thought, swallowing hard. The rotten odor under the wharf was getting to him. J.J. and Aliba had covered their noses with one hand.

After an hour of waiting, they moved into the current again and slipped by Rabat unnoticed. They paddled toward the center of the river into the swifter current.

An hour further downriver from Rabat, they paddled into a small cove that had a white, sandy beach, not far from the ocean. They could hear the waves, smell the salt ocean breeze, and feel spray against their faces.

Jess often missed the open beaches of isolated islands, because they were usually so clean. He remembered, *Back stateside, the beaches had become too crowded with sun worshipers, garbage and dead fish left from high tides.*

Three of the men who met them on the beach, stayed with the rubber boat and equipment. Jess and his three friends left their firearms in the boat, and started walking toward six men further up the beach that had automatic weapons and wore flak vests. They had been waiting for them. It looked like the beginning of a clandestine night raid, not Hollywood style, but the real thing. They gave vests to Jess and the others.

Jess could not see much ahead of them because it became darker closer to the cliffs. They followed the leaders, three in front and three following the crew. They used no flashlight, which led Jess to believe they had done this many times before.

Jess put his hands out in front of him as Samain and Bushta disappeared into the utter darkness. It was so black he could not see his hands in front of his face.

Someone grabbed Jess' left arm at the wrist, leading him in a downward direction. There were no stairs, just a gradual sloping down of the beach sand under their feet. Then rocks and boulders became obstacles, though he was still being led by someone's firm grip. Water splashed against the rocks and their rubber diving boots. They stumbled along, and could hear the echoes of their movements, as well as the waves hitting the walls inside the cave they had entered.

Ahead of them was a dim outline of the shore where they approached the ocean side opening of a cave. The glow of phosphorescence in the waves breaking on the beach produced an eerie green light in its foam. They began to climb up steps cut in the rock cliff.

The salty spray from the surf smelled unusually refreshing; it did not stink like some beach areas Jess had walked across. Even though the steps were slippery, he did not need to be led any longer. He could see fairly well now that the moon was out again.

Finally, entering a room illuminated with a red light, they

could see. A large, heavy door closed behind them, sealing out the ocean's noise. They removed the armored vests, diving suits and booties, and put on *babouches*, (slippers). Their clothes were not as wrinkled or sweaty as Jess had expected them to be. Wearing his blue jeans had been a good selection for the trip, but not for meeting the king of Morocco.

They climbed more stairs and entered a dimly lit storage room. Their companions hung their automatic rifles on a rack. Jess and the rest of the crew were escorted into another hall by two Moroccan guards dressed in Berber tribal clothes. They had automatic weapons slung over their shoulders. The crew looked like out-of-place tourists.

Removing their slippers in the hall, they were ushered into an oval room with carpeted floor and a burning fireplace. The warmth felt good to Jess after the cool dampness of the cave and tunnels.

A tall, well-built Moroccan guard prompted them to be seated around a large oval wooden table covered with a lacy white cloth. They were given a choice of brandy, wine or American coffee. Jess requested black coffee; Samain and J.J. ordered brandy, and the others wine. They were briskly served and left alone.

Samain and J.J. let out deep sighs as they tried to relax, sipping their brandy. The others sniffed their wine, smiled and took a sip.

The windowless room was very stately for its small size, and it seemed comfortable and cozy. Above them, a large crystal chandelier hung from the oval ceiling. The indirect lighting caused a mellow peacefulness throughout the whole room as the crystals reflected the light upon the walls.

Jess wondered if the king played the fine-looking ebony grand piano near the fireplace. Behind the piano, hanging from the wall, was a tapestry with a majestic mountain scene woven into it. Its purpose was to keep the heat of the open fireplace from escaping into the porous adobe walls.

They were alone only long enough to enjoy and finish the drinks. Voices in the hallway and the hurried shuffling of shoes drew their attention. Three men entered the room, and the crew rose to their feet. Jess knew that it would be expected of him to bow, which he did with the others, as their king entered the room.

Jess was pleasantly surprised to see King Aladu Itssani was dressed, as a king would be expected to dress. He was not in a European suit, but wore his tribal attire, having just left a Berber gathering of leaders to meet with the four. He was a man of great distinction with his short graying beard, tanned face, and unusual deep blue eyes. He was in his early sixties and looked to be in very good health.

He acknowledged their courtesy with a broad smile that seemed his nature and motioned for them to sit at the table again.

King Itssani bid them his greeting, "*La bes!*", in Arabic and nodded to them. It was his greeting of hello. He did not sit, but slowly moved around the table. Gaining eye contact across the table with each of them, he nodded and strolled behind those who were seated. Stopping next to a large ebony chair, he looked directly at Jess and smiled.

"Mr. Hanes," the king began. Jess started to stand, but Samain touched his arm for him to stay seated.

"I want you to understand at the beginning, I am not having you held against your will. You may leave Morocco when you wish," he said in clear distinct English.

He approached Jess and held out his hand to shake. Jess stood, bowed and shook the king's hand. The king held onto Jess' hand tightly with both of his as they looked straight into each other's eyes. "Welcome to our country. I regret the difficulty you have suffered, physically and emotionally. Please accept my apology."

"Thank you, Your Highness," Jess said. "I do accept your apology. My wounds are fully healed; I have been superbly taken care of. I am grateful to you and your people here." He hesitated, and then said, "May I speak freely, your Highness?"

The king nodded his approval.

"It was only recently I learned of your brother's death," Jess said. "I did not know he was the gentleman shot at the airport in Casablanca. Please accept my deepest sympathy, sadness and prayers for you and for your family. It was a most cowardly attack." Jess felt tears come to his eyes while the king continued to hold his hand. He was emotionally taken back by the king's openness toward him and his attitude for his family. He regained his composure.

"Yes, I will share your concern with my family," the king said.

He released his grip with Jess, and moved further around the table. Jess sat down with his emotions running high. The king turned toward Jess and smiled again.

"You must find the courage to help my people overcome terrorism in our land, without undue pressure from me. The only reason I requested you be brought here in this fashion was for your protection and the secrecy of our dealings."

He moved further around the table, "I have spoken to your president and his council for added support, should you accept. I have had you thoroughly investigated and arranged for your wife's protection in the United States." He glanced at those who had brought Jess, "This was at your friends' recommendation, and I understand you are an honest and just man.

"We cannot guarantee your complete safety until these people are caught and jailed. You have had a few close encounters in Casablanca, making you aware of the dangers you face." He was very serious and apologetic that Jess was involved. "The loss of my brother has been a burden for not only me, but for my whole family and our nation. He was held in high regards and esteemed by all, even admired by most of his enemies."

Pausing for a moment, he held tightly to the arm of his chair at the head of the table, "I understand you were present when the murder was committed, and that was also when the terrorists tried to kill you. Whether you can identify the one who pulled the trigger or not, please help me." Releasing his grip on the chair, he moved further around the table. "You will be used as bait to catch them . . . with your consent, of course. Will you assist with this undertaking?" he asked, standing across the table from Jess.

Jess looked at Bushta, J.J., then at Samain, Aliba, then stood.

"Your Highness, it will give me pleasure to join my friends

here in their efforts to catch these terrorists," Jess said, slowly bowing toward the king. "It will be an honor and a privilege to fulfill your request. I understand the danger that will come. Thank you."

"Done! You will be well compensated for the rest of your life. I will see you again." With a broad smile, he added, "Allah will be with you!"

He and his men hurried from the room and disappeared down the hall. The large scrolled door shut, and the room remained quiet for a few minutes.

When Samain rose from his chair, everyone else stood. He turned to Jess and grabbed his hand, "I have never known of our king to do this before. Usually, he delegates someone to take care of these matters. You are special to him, and he understands what you have been through and the dangers ahead." He released Jess' hand and motioned for the others to join him. "Any questions?" He paused. "No comments? If not, lead the way, Bushta. It will be dawn in five hours. We must be back on the road heading for the Atlas Mountains by then."

#

The undercover operation would be planned near Rabat and Kenitra, but Jess' training and physical conditioning was in need of attention first.

The four traveled to Ben Mellal and then south through Marrakech to the foothills of the Atlas Mountains. Their destination was one of the many remote fortress hideouts in the mountains, which the Moroccan government used for protecting diplomats.

Southeast of Marrakech, the road narrowed through the Tizi N' Tichka pass. The bumpy dirt roads to Taroudant, on the southeast side of the mountain range, covered them with dust. The map showed the Qued Sous River winding through the arid valleys to the ocean, not far to the west, at Aqadir. The east side of the mountains was rough and barren of vegetation, because rain seldom came over the peaks. Some water from snow at the higher elevations would make its way down the eastern slopes and collect in the rivers.

In many areas, the Qued Sous was used for irrigation of barley and wheat fields. The humidity was very low in that part of Morocco, because only a hundred miles further to the east was the mighty Sahara Desert.

Finally, they arrived at the small fortress, which was up near the snow line of the mountains. It was built into the crevices of a cliff high above the deep valleys.

CHAPTER SIX

At Ft. MacMahan, Algeria, an oasis in the northwest Sahara Desert, two men stood at an open window with no screen, on the second floor of a newly remodeled villa. They overlooked a courtyard of beautiful flowers and thick shrubs.

Mist from a water fountain sprayed over the greenery, giving an eerie false impression of a jungle setting. Even though the Atlas Mountains starved the Sahara desert of moisture, this oasis fort was furnished water from underground springs.

The sun had set long before this moment. The moon played its macabre shadows on the courtyard lawn, shrubs, fountain and buildings. The mosaic villa was beautiful by day, but changed to a ghostly, colorless appearance at night.

The pungent mist of the fountain, mixed with the exotic perfume of the flowers, filled the patio and could be sensed from the upper window. Only the locusts, crickets and harsh voices from the second-floor window interrupted the quietness of the night.

One man now stood at the window, and flipped the stub of a lighted cigarette out into the fountain. He turned and moved toward a tall, obese Arab military officer seated at a huge, dark mahogany desk. For a big man, he was a sharp dresser in his pressed tan uniform with silver aviator wings and a few impressive medals hanging over the upper left pocket.

Taking a flat gold case of cigarettes from his inside jacket pocket, the officer offered one. "Try this Turkish blend. I have them made by special friends in Tangiers. And, by the way, your cigarette butts belong in this ashtray, not my fountain." Smiling arrogantly, he added, "Or, would you rather try this Havana cigar direct from Cuba?"

Taking a cigarette, the other man nodded. "Colonel, you seem to have the best of everything in this God forsaken hole. But I'm not impressed! How much more time do I have to waste here? You know I'm behind schedule getting to Meknes? I thought Al Khartoum in the Sudan was miserable, but this!"

"I know this is not America, Mr. Hastings," Colonel Alvarez said. "But, you have only been here a short three days. Have not my companions been satisfying for you?" He pointed a finger toward a sheer drapery at one end of the room and motioned with it. Two women left their plush couch, slithered through the red drapes, and moved toward Hastings. The colonel laughed as Hastings pulled back from the women.

"Don't try to hustle me anymore," Larry D. Hastings said, waving his cigarette hand in the air. "I'm not interested in your whores. Your streetwalkers hold no interest for me. Besides, I can pick my own and not have to worry about diseases from the likes of these," he said defiantly, sputtering his words.

Hastings knew that the colonel was using him, but he had not found a way to escape from the colonel's domineering pressures . . . yet. Some day in the future, he knew there would be some way out of this line of business. He would have to keep his wits about him and try to keep this bully from intimidating him further.

"Hey, Mr. Hastings," said Alvarez, moving to the window. "I'll take your throwaways!" He turned around and opened his arms, and the women smiled. They bounced over to him, nestled in his arms, and then tried to make purring sounds. He patted them on their swinging backsides, and ushered them from the room. Upon leaving, they made rude slurring remarks and gestures toward Hastings.

"Hastings, you cannot upset them, because I am too nice to them," grunted the colonel.

Pulling at his beige sports jacket sleeve, Hastings continued, "Back to my questions, Colonel. I've paid you good American money to keep my business going in Morocco. This business front will fail if you're not careful. I don't mind running firearms, but drugs are not my piece of cake."

Many people, looking at Hastings, would think of a Florida car dealer. He was six feet tall, slender built, tanned, and wore a loud colored Hawaiian flowered shirt under his sports jacket. He had the shirt collar pulled out over the jacket collar with a wide gold chain necklace hung around his neck.

For a shrewd businessman, Hastings had permitted the colonel to intimidate him, and he was becoming frustrated. Hastings' dealings with this terrorist had snowballed downhill the last few months, and the snow was melting fast. He had not been able to cut relations with the colonel, nor eliminate the pressures. The innocent sales of months ago were only fronts for international drug dealings.

This uneducated Arab isn't going to get the best of me, Hastings thought to himself.

Hastings began pacing the floor. He was hot, wet with sweat, and had become impatient with the colonel. His jacket had turned dark blue under the armpits where sweat had soaked. He wiped his forehead and neck with a handkerchief.

"What's the holdup?" Hastings demanded. "I need to get back to my office in Meknes and make sure it's running correctly. You're wasting my time here, Colonel!"

Alvarez made no immediate reply to this.

Hastings put out his cigarette in the ashtray on the colonel's desk and moved back to the window. The pounding of a migraine headache had started like a bass drum. He took another cigarette from its pack inside his jacket pocket. His hands began to shake as he shielded the lighter flame. Puffing on the cigarette to keep it going, he blew out the smoke from his nostrils and mouth. His menthol cigarette tasted better in the dry desert air.

With the cigarette hanging from the corner of his mouth, Hastings began to cough. He yanked the damp handkerchief from his pants pocket again, took the cigarette from between his lips and wiped the corners of his mouth. Then he wiped his face and neck again. He fanned the handkerchief in the air to cool it and wiped his forehead. The wet cloth hit the hot end of the cigarette, knocking the red ash out the window. He flipped the cigarette out on the lawn in nervous frustration.

"You should not smoke," the colonel said, leaning back in his plush chair. "You have a bad cough, not that I really care! I do not want you spitting up blood and spewing it over my rugs." He watched Hastings closely, belching loudly with his mouth open. He had been eating garlic all evening, along with chewing and smoking his cigars. "I'll have to eliminate this infidel soon," he muttered under his breath.

Irritated, he left his desk and placed an arm around Hastings' wet neck. Six inches taller and over a hundred pounds heavier, the colonel dwarfed Hastings' six feet, 200 pounds. He pulled him close and moved closer to the window, pressing them both against its ledge.

Hastings was feeling worse, because he had not eaten a decent meal in over forty-eight hours. He was getting weak and shaky.

Under normal conditions, I know I could physically handle this smelly blob of an Arab, He told himself. *My martial arts abilities would do the job. But not now!*

"You know the king of Morocco is my top priority," Alvarez said, pushing Hastings against the side of the window opening. "He must be eliminated and replaced by his young brother, who supports terrorism with my supplies. Then the money I bring in through your business front will help me hire the people necessary to gain control."

Hastings coughed as the colonel blew his rotten garlic and cigar breath into Hastings' face. Then the colonel continued his intimidation.

"I do not like communists, except for the money I can make from them. When Morocco becomes a communist country, I will have one more avenue on my list to openly work." Arrogantly, he added, "With Libya, Algeria and Morocco for terrorist outposts, I can control this northwest part of Africa and southwest Europe.

And, I will have the control of weapons, which the terrorists require. When I receive the missiles they need, I will block the Gibraltar Strait shipping lanes." He pressed Hastings backward against the window ledge, laughed and pulled him away, releasing him.

Frightened by the physical pressure, and not being able to resist, Hastings started to speak to the colonel's back, but hesitated. He stepped back to the window opening in hopes of feeling a breeze. Putting his finger in the air to make a point again, he was abruptly interrupted when the colonel slapped the side of his pants with the palm of his big hand. Hastings jumped as if he had been jabbed with a straight pin.

"Yes?" the colonel said, smiling. "You were about to say something?" He picked up a Havana cigar and cut the ends off. He wallowed the large cigar between his moistened, oversized lips with a half smile. Leaning against the desktop, he took long draws from the cigar while lighting it, and then exhaled. This became a cloud of smoke around his head. Finally, he inhaled the cigar smoke deeply and blew it up to the twirling blades of the ceiling fan.

Smoke began to fill the room with a blue haze, vortexed by the motion of the blades. Alvarez enjoyed the power he had over Hastings, and continued irritating him with the cigar smoke.

Hastings became more impatient, "I don't want to know any of the sordid details of your business world. I want that money put into my Swiss account like you promised, and then I will go home to Florida. I need a rest."

"All in good time, Mr. Hastings. You are not finished in Morocco with our transactions," he said, moving back to the window.

Hastings stepped aside and sat on the arm of an overstuffed couch. He grew lightheaded from the tension, heat and smoke. His tanned face turned pale white.

"We may leave tomorrow morning before it gets too hot," the colonel said, placing his officer's hat on his baldhead. "I have a C-130 aircraft arriving tonight with cargo. Shall we go to dinner?"

At that announcement, Hastings had dry heaves and moved

to the window to spit. Then he headed for the stairs, keeping his handkerchief over his mouth to prevent vomiting.

Leaving the upstairs room, they went down into the courtyard. No air stirred in the patio, either.

Colonel Alvarez put his arm around Hastings shoulder again as they walked through the arched hallway, whispering in a low voice, "There is one more small problem I wish for you to take care of for me. I want you to annihilate someone! A witness is still alive who saw me kill the king's brother, the financial minister, at the Casablanca airport." Tugging on Hastings' shoulder with his large hand, the colonel pulled him tight against his side. "Well, this is an American I believe you know from your past. He is an old business acquaintance of yours from years ago, a professional treasure hunter now. A retired government man, was he not?"

Hastings frowned, and tried to compose himself, thinking of whom the colonel was suggesting. *I'm no murderer anyway*, he contemplated. *Damn it, I wish he would stop hugging me, and keep his mouth closed. That foul breath of his . . .*

The colonel's guessing game continued as he pressed the point, "Yes, Mr. Hastings, he knows you quite well. Did he not help put you in jail, when you were misusing illegal immigrants in Florida?"

Hastings' brow pulled down, "Are you talking about Jess Hanes? How did he get involved with you?"

Opening the car door, the colonel motioned Hastings in first. "Come now, you will upset yourself and will not enjoy your meal tonight," he said, crowding his large body into the back seat against his miserable passenger.

Cramped for space, Hastings began to sweat more profusely, while his large host panted from exertion after entering the vehicle.

No air-conditioning in this vehicle? Hastings thought. He reached for the switch to lower his window as the car moved forward. The wind felt good, even though it was hot.

"All right, so I'm not so clean," Hastings said. "Hanes knows nothing of my dealings with you here in Algeria. He doesn't know I have a business in Kenitra and Meknes. Why should I be responsible for doing away with him? I'm not an assassin. I'm no terrorist!"

"Oh, my dear friend, but you are! Just as much as I am. Now, let us talk about pleasant things, like the delicious food we are about to partake of. Jousting with you has given me an appetite that will be hard to satisfy."

Hastings suddenly reached his limit. He could not take anymore physical or mental abuse. "Let me out!" he yelled. "Let me out! I'm about to throw up!"

The car came to a screeching halt. Hastings and a smaller man from the front passenger's seat got out. They were left standing in the street as the limousine's back tires smoked from burning rubber. Hastings bent over the gutter with dry heaves, thinking his whole insides were tearing loose.

The colonel's loud laughing could be heard in the distance as the black limousine sped away through the narrow street.

Hastings hated that grinding laugh! He stood up in the fluttering moon shadows of a palm tree trying to catch his breath. Taking off his jacket and tossing it over his shoulder, he unbuttoned his shirt to obtain more air.

The little man with him snickered and began to laugh. He said something in Arabic, a dialect Hastings could not understand. Hastings waved him away. His stomach was beginning to settle down.

In the quiet of the night, an approaching large aircraft could be heard. The whine of its four turboprop engines drifted across the sand dunes toward the oasis. Hastings and his companion both looked toward the east, watching the aircraft's silhouette grow against the large yellow moon.

"I would be willing to sleep on that plane tonight and not go back to my room," Hastings said to the Arab, who could not understand him. "It couldn't be any more uncomfortable or hotter than now."

The short man had walked away from Hastings in the direction the limousine had departed. Hastings sighed and followed, and they slowly walked through the empty streets to the hotel.

CHAPTER SEVEN

Jess had forgotten how beautiful the Atlas Mountains were in September. This was the first opportunity to really look at them. It was a crisp, clear morning to do so.

The time had passed by fast while the crew worked him into physical and mental readiness for the undercover operation. Jess, Samain, Bushta, Aliba and J.J. became a close-knit team during that period of time. Aliba was still overly protective, and it seemed like he was always near-at-hand for Jess. Jess had hoped Aliba would back off some. Perhaps he should have said something about it, but that would certainly have hurt Aliba's feelings. He decided to think more about it before doing anything.

First, Jess intended to relax a little and take in the view from the balcony window outside the large conference room. Dark storm clouds were rolling down the high, snow-covered peaks toward the valley below. They looked threatening for some of the small villages. He could hear thunder rumbling through the mountains as lightning pounded the earth.

Altitudes separated snow and rain. To be so barren and hot thirty miles east from their location, and so green, wet and cool on the western side of the mountain range where they were located, left no doubt as to why there were big differences in tribal customs and cultures.

Jess remembered the Berber mountain people being known for their beautiful women and bright colored clothes. The mountain tribes, Ait Haddidou, Ait Morrhad and Ait Ali Ou Ikkou, were only a few of the 200 Berber tribes dwelling throughout the Atlas Mountains. Many were in the south-central part of the Mid-Atlas range, where he was located.

The stories had been told of the Berber men being fierce fighters on horseback, and how they despised communism. They had been the prominent tribal force keeping the Moroccan government from turning totally communistic.

Years ago, Jess had become personally aware that if a Berber became your friend, it was for a lifetime.

J.J.'s movement near the open fireplace interrupted his thoughts. She was across the room behind him. Without turning toward her, he commented, "I could live in an area like this."

Standing outside on the narrow concrete balcony, Jess' view was magnificent to the western horizon. Turning around, he could see how the crescent shape of the fortress was built into the narrow crevices and caves on the shear face of the high cliff. He wondered how long it had taken to erect this stronghold. After studying the structure for a few minutes, he turned around again to view the immense mountain ranges.

There were clear blue skies to the west, but to the east and higher up the mountain from the fortress, were black clouds of snow moving their direction. It made him want to go back inside with J.J. and stand in front of the warm fireplace.

"I was wondering who built this place and who owns it?" he said, walking back into the warmth of the conference room. "Maybe Samain has a map or blueprints, so I can snoop around in these halls and tunnels."

J.J. was lying on a large pillow near the fireplace. Patting the pillows, she got up and stretched. She had dozed off and was almost asleep when Jess went back into the room from the outside balcony.

She was full of answers for him about that old place and rambled for a while. "Samain told me that this area has belonged to the Berber tribes for centuries. Fires were started by lightning strikes, which burnt it down, and then it would be rebuilt. This was once their main hideaway from other tribes who tried to take their wives and fortunes." She walked over to the fireplace to get warm. "In World War II, they hid French and American underground agents up here."

"By the looks of things, it must still be used often," Jess said, stretching and yawning. "We've had everything we needed to stay here through these past months. Evidently, the government keeps it well stocked with supplies. I've not seen anyone here to bring in supplies, or to take care of the quarters. Someone must have come in everyday after we left."

"It does get cold up here, and fast," J.J. said rubbing her shoulders and arms. "Isolated and desolate places make me shiver. I really do not like the cold. And, being lonely." She stretched her arms out toward the flames to warm her and continued, "This fire feels fantastic!" Turning her back towards the fire, she put her hands behind her and closed her eyes. "I have wondered about that too. Who does keep this furnished? Every time I have been here, it has been fully supplied with wood, food, sheets and blankets, firearms and radio equipment. Whatever we have needed was here. Natural springs inside the fortress provide fresh water. I have never seen anyone bring supplies in, either."

The large room they were in was used for tribal meetings and was built hundreds of years ago. The dimensions were about sixty feet long by forty feet wide. It was hard to keep heated, so they had hung multicolored tapestries from the high cathedral rock ceiling down the rock walls to the floor to help hold the heat. The floors were hardwood with padded, hand-woven carpets that covered to within a foot of the baseboard. Tribal swords, shields, spears, bows and arrows, and ancient rifles hung from the wall. Roman weaponry, crossbows, lances and leather helmets hung above the fireplace.

A large wooden table in the center of the room had ten stools on each side with a stately chair at one end. A thick leather cover was wrapped around the stools to keep swords and other weapons from causing damage when someone sat on the stools. The backrests of the stools had Arabic lettering and tribal markings carved into the leather. The leather was dark and shinny in spots from the years of use.

The room itself was built into a crevice in the face of the cliff.

Its ceiling and inner three walls were bare rock. The large fireplace, without a mantel, was cut into the rock, except for the hanging tapestry. A brick chimney was built inside the fireplace to catch the smoke.

But Jess could not figure how the smoke got to the outside, other than through cracks in the rock. It really did not matter, since it worked. The warmth from the crackling firewood kept the room cozy and dry. Next to the fireplace was a huge woodbin, which must have held ten cords of wood.

J.J. had been lying in front of the hearth on a long crescent-shaped couch with over sized pillows. Two people could lie on one pillow and not be crowded.

I'll bet it was used for after-parley socializing, Jess thought.

He moved next to J.J. in front of the fireplace and warmed his backside. They stood there without moving or speaking for a long time, both in their own dream world.

The sunset caught their attention where rays came through numerous small windows above the balcony door. The glass panes caused the sunlight to be filtered into the dimly lit room. The refractions formed uneven heat patterns on the smooth floor and carpet, and upon the rock fireplace behind them.

It was certainly a serene and peaceful atmosphere for deep thoughts. No television, no blaring stereo, no traffic, no computers and no cell phones ringing; just the crackling firewood echoing in the stillness.

"This is a very romantic place," Jess said, not pushing for conversation, just commenting on the absence of the outside world.

Another hour of silence passed, and they continued to enjoy the warmth of the fire. When Jess noticed the hot coals growing dimmer and a chill began to creep into the room, he tossed three large logs in the fireplace and stirred the hot coals. Dusting off his hands, he returned to warming himself.

After staring at the flames licking around the dry logs and its bark turning red, he broke the silence. "You impressed me as a rare, compassionate, pretty nurse J.J." Not looking at her, he piled another armful of wood on the fire and had it roaring, which they really did not need. They moved further away from the crackling fire.

J.J. gave him no reply; only a forty-five degree side glance. Shifting her weight to one leg and cocking her hip out, she stretched as high as she could reach. The sun had set and the fire cast her shadow on the far wall making her twice her size. She pointed at the shadow and snickered, then turned to gaze into the flames.

"But now, through all this training with you and the crew, I understand you're an Interpol agent," Jess went on. "Spending these last few rough months up here with you and the guys, I could tell you had guerilla warfare training. What else are you?"

"Mostly lonely!" she said, softly. Shifting her weight to one side, she rested the other boot on the hearth. Taking a deep breath, she sighed.

Jess remained silent, watching her. He certainly had not expected a response like what was coming.

"I am always in the middle of upheaval and turmoil that never seems to cease. Always having to be on guard and being tense all the time, has taken its toll on me. I have to be on top with all the answers, all the time." She paused, collecting her thoughts as she moved away from the fireplace. "I am not bored, just tired! This is the first time I have really relaxed for years." The fire reflected on her long hair. Folding her arms and tossing her hair from side to side, she released another long sigh. She was a beautiful lady standing there in the gleaming firelight. "I am lonesome for my old friends. In this life style, I do not have many. So, I stopped getting close to anyone. They all manage to be killed, die or disappear."

She started to cry softly. Tears streamed down her cheeks, falling, soaking into her Alpine sweater. Trying to keep Jess from noticing, she turned away, sniffled, and wiped her eyes and cheeks with the heels of her hands.

"J.J., I'm sorry for being so nosey. I didn't mean to pry and upset you. I'm just trying to be a friend. You four have gone to extremes to keep me safe and I'd like to show my appreciation, but

I don't know how. I suppose this isn't the time or place for my idle talk." Jess cut his chattering and turned facing her. A moment of silence passed by as she pondered her thoughts.

"Yes! No! I knew that!" She sounded uncertain what to say.

"I knew the background of Samain and Bushta, but not you and Aliba. But, J.J. . . . " Jess hesitated. "Your experiences sounded so exciting when you would share them in the hospital. I thought you were just another nurse. It was no big thing, not knowing you had other interests," folding his arms across his chest he continued. "I figured this might be a good time to find out more about you. But evidently, I'm prying and talking too much again! If you're not in the mood to talk, I'll shut up and keep the fire roaring."

Moving close to her, he put his hand on her shoulder. She pulled away as if a bee had stung her. Jess returned to the hearth and faced the fire, not understanding the situation they were in.

What can I do to comfort her? He wondered. "Probably just keep your mouth shut, Jess!" he said under his breath.

It was quiet again. She just stood in the middle of the room with her arms folded, silent.

"Forgive me, I meant no harm," he said at last. "You have been by my side ever since the first day at the hospital. I haven't had the opportunity to really tell you how much I admired . . ."

"Jess, will you please shut up!" she cried, not holding back the sobs.

Her sudden outburst and crying startled him. He was speechless and felt helpless. *Now, what should I do? I better keep my thoughts to myself, unless she asks.*

"I became very fond of you with your Texas wisdom and philosophy," she said haltingly, after she had gotten her sobbing under control. "The times you would lay there on your stomach and tell about your love for God, your wife, Marie Ann, and your Texas, you . . ." She sniffled and wiped her nose. "You prompted me, unknowingly, to consider my relationship with God. I have been soul searching about where and what my life's priorities should be?"

J.J. would not look at Jess, but walked to the other end of the room toward the windows. She was searching within herself for something worth holding onto in her life. Her facial expression told him she did not seem bitter, but empty, longing for attention, affection and love from someone, somewhere.

"I have killed in this line of work," she went on, her voice steadier now. "You see, I am responsible for other people's death, trying to stop terrorists. I have even killed innocent people, as well as the terrorist. Sleeping with my enemy to get information is something I am not proud to admit, and I am not boasting, but at the same time, I am not apologizing either." She hesitated and took a deep breath. "Smoking and drinking are not vices for me, except wine at special times." With a sweep of her hands, she slapped her hips. "But, so what! God knows I am not perfect. Who is? I live in constant fear of death every day. It is to kill, or be killed! And I am tired of it all! Tired of it all!" She paced back and forth in front of the windows, then threw up her hands and cried some more.

Jess did not say anything; he was not the one with the answers. She had to work it out. It was one of those times when he wanted to put his arms around someone and hold them until the hurt was over, but he felt helpless this time. He was close to loosing control himself, because he wanted to comfort her and could not. He prayed inwardly.

Samain and Bushta had followed Aliba into the meeting room and stood quietly in the shadows, listening to J.J. Neither she nor Jess knew they were there, but the three in the shadows could feel the tense situation as it heighten.

"It hurt my ego to hear you relate your happiness and love, when I was so void of it. I am envious and jealous of what you have. Here I am, over forty and I am running out of time." She began pacing the floor in front of the windows again. "The only good I have really accomplished in years is nursing you back to health. Up to that time, I was pushing, pushing, pushing to stay involved in something. I cannot keep up this pace, mentally or physically, for much longer."

She slowly walked back toward the fireplace. Jess stood at the hearth with his back to her, listening to her every word and movement. She stopped in the middle of the room, still not knowing that others were there. J.J. put her hands on top of her head, and took a deep breath.

"Jess!" she blurted out, trying to hold back more tears, "I do not have anyone! I do not have anyone to take care of, no one to take care of me, and no one to love, or be loved by!" Now she was sobbing hard again. Holding her breath, she finally let go, "I permitted myself to fall in love with you. I love you, Jess Hanes!"

Jess turned around, stunned again, at what he was hearing. What had he done to cause such deep feelings? He was dumbfounded. She held up her hand to stop him from speaking or coming toward her.

"Let me finish. I must get this out or I will explode." She hesitantly walked over next to him in front of the fireplace, and put her hands on the edge of the mantle above it. The reflection of the fire danced on her face and glistened off her salty, drying tears. Trying to compose herself, she said, "I am not being very professional about this, but let me work on it. I am sorry for getting so upset."

Jess nodded, not knowing what to say. He thought, *Just be patient and listen. You might learn something, Jess.*

Looking into the fire, she took another deep breath and sighed, "I was a full-time registered nurse and taught at a small university hospital in Sydney, Australia. I was the Director of Nurses, which was a prestigious position." She walked away from the fireplace, and picked up one of the large pillows. Hugging it close, she sat on the couch. "I fell in love with my first and last love, a heart surgeon. We were married only two years. We had no children, because I wanted to wait awhile before starting a family. I was only twenty-six." Turning her back to the fireplace, wrinkles crossed her forehead as she squeezed her eyes tight. "Without warning, he died of a heart attack at the age of thirty-two. Job related stress killed him, they said. Joshua Elliot was dedicated, honest and a loyal young man, not only with his work, but also to me. Oh, how I loved him. That has been over twenty years ago."

Jess walked away from the fireplace to the balcony doors, and then slowly returned to the warmth of the fire. He watched J.J. trying to find the words to say.

She tossed the pillow on top with the others, blew her nose on a handkerchief, wiped her eyes, and continued, "I went back to school, and then to the U.S. to get my Masters in International Law Enforcement. I needed a career change! That was where I met your friends, Bushta and Samain. They introduced me later to this international business of fighting crime and terrorism. I met Aliba at the Crime Academy in Casablanca."

Jess thought she was finally slowing down when she turned to him, "I went to work for the Australian government as an Interpol agent. I had previous flying experience, so they sent me to twin-engine pilot training for the outback areas." Her eyes closed as she thought back to those times. "I spent many hours flying into those remote areas at low altitudes and landing in short openings. A majority of my flying hours were spent in a Vietnam aircraft, which was used by forward observers, the U.S. Marine OV10A Bronco. I enjoyed living on the edge of danger."

She began to pace back and forth in front of the fireplace again, "I crop dusted for a while doing investigations and did one parachute jump for fun. Hang-gliding and glider flying were great, too." She hesitated again, "I was always ready to jump in and do the impossible. Many times I did it, because I was a woman, and women were not suppose to do those dangerous things. I was not trying to prove that I was as good as a man at this game, but, I did like men's dangerous jobs." Pausing again, she smiled, "Here I am, still running around like a young woman, trying to do a man's job. I should have stayed strictly in the hospital field; I could have retired by now." She turned, and her red watery eyes met Jess', "I am tired, hungry and sleepy. Can we go eat?"

Jess smiled, "Yes, let's eat! I thought you would never ask."

The three men in the shadows made a quiet exit without either of the other two knowing they had been in the room.

"That's the best offer I've had all day. Let's go!" Jess opened his arms for her, and she stepped into them. He pulled her close as she nestled, lingering, not wanting to move. "Someday you will be as happy as I am. Your heart's heavy now, but I'll predict that your love will flourish again. The Lord has ways of straightening things out. Plus, He has all the answers, if we ask for them. I know that from personal experience."

She stopped crying and relaxed in his arms. Holding her shoulders, he gently pushed her away, then folded her hands in his and kissed them.

Looking into her pretty face, and locking eyes, he said as tenderly as he could, "I'm flattered, honored and touched by your openness."

Nothing was said for a few moments while they searched each other's expressions.

Jess broke the silence, "To the kitchen! I'm hungry, too!" Offering his arm, they walked toward the hall. "I smell food cooking!"

Passing through an arched doorway into a long wide rocked hall, they approached a row of large window openings on each side. As usual, Aliba was not far away. He had already checked the hallway and the outside, giving them an assuring nod. He was a shrewd bodyguard. Jess knew Aliba would put his life on the line for them.

Aliba acted hungry too, sniffing the air like a bloodhound. He smiled and led the way to the kitchen, "Food this way."

CHAPTER EIGHT

For the first time, after all the months in the mountains, Jess decided one morning to open the door to the outside balcony of his room. The April winds were not howling and the morning sun was warm, but the temperature was still below freezing making him catch his breath.

He stepped out of the bedroom onto the narrow balcony. The sun's golden rays came down in narrow beams above him from over the rugged eastern peaks. The sun was just high enough to throw shafts of light on the far valley to the west. He made the mistake of looking down at his feet.

It was as though he had stepped out into emptiness from an open door of an aircraft at 13,000 feet. The floor of the balcony was a crisscross mesh of rusty metal strips that left square openings at least three inches wide, perhaps to keep snow from accumulating.

Jess could see all the way to the valley below. The sheer, flat gray surface of the cliff was back under his room ten feet away. A portion of the room and balcony were hanging out in midair. The railing was a single piece of cork-oak wood less than waist high. It was farther than an arm's length for him to reach.

At that same instant of seeing the vast emptiness below and before him, another cold gust of wind hit him in the face taking his breath away. He panicked, jumping back against the door facing, and banged his head. His heart pounded so hard he could not catch his breath again.

Jess closed his eyes and drew in more of the cold air to help clear his mind. The spinning inside his head stopped. Blinking his eyes a few times, he regained his balance and slowly reached for the railing. Holding on tight, he looked straight ahead at the far mountains.

"Jess, get a hold of yourself," he whispered. The last time that happened to Jess was years ago, in a glass elevator in a big hotel in Austin, Texas. He had lost his equilibrium as the elevator rose toward the upper floors. He had to move away from the full glass walls of the elevator and grab the railing at the rear, near the door.

Again, it was the same old pilot's problem of vertigo. But in an aircraft, the yoke or stick and the seat belt secured him. Jess loved flying and had no fear of heights, but this was the second time he remembered losing his sense of security with heights, because he felt no control over the situations.

He regained his bearings and tightened his grip on the wooden railing with both hands. After inspecting every inch of the old railing before putting any weight against it, he forced himself to lean over it and look down. He took a deep breath and a long look at how the fortress was attached to the cliff. Forcing himself to relax, he took another deep breath of the cold, clean air.

The fortress looked like it had grown out of the cracks and crevices of the cliff, protruding some ten or more feet from its face. Jess straightened up, took another deep breath and finally began to relax. The vertigo problem was over, so he released his white-knuckled grip on the railing.

His thoughts were mixed, but calm. *I'll have to make a paper glider to sail and watch the air currents play with it. A hang-glider would perform great from up here.*

Taking another deep breath of cold air, he stepped back into the bedroom. The warmth of the fireplace felt great and relaxing. Suddenly, his stomach began a loud, long growl. Jess grabbed his leather jacket and headed for the kitchen for breakfast.

"Good morning Ali! Pardon!" he said. "*La Bes, hom dula,* Aliba! Did you have a restful night?"

He was in the hall hanging at arm's length from a beam above his room's entrance. "Yes, Mr. Jess. Good morning. *La Bes*! I had peaceful sleep in night. Cold air good for lungs and make me sleep." He released his grip and dropped to his feet. He beat on his chest, took a long stretch standing on his tiptoes, and reached for the ceiling. He was very muscular, like a circus trapeze catcher.

"That must have felt good," Jess observed.

"Yes! You try stretching, Mr. Jess. It helps relax you. Here! Jump up, grab beam over door," Aliba said and pointed. "Let weight stretch you." Then he patted Jess on the shoulder. "Back okay, now! Morning stretch feel good."

The beam was eight feet above the floor. He jumped and got a good grip the first try. Letting his muscles relax, he felt the weight pull his vertebra apart. All the conditioning they had put Jess through increased the strength of his arms. He certainly felt a difference. His back muscles stretched until he felt the scar tissues' resistance.

"Let me help you down. Do not drop weight on feet at once." He grabbed Jess around the waist from behind and lowered him to the floor effortlessly.

Aliba released his grip on Jess and moved his arms under Jess' armpits, clasping his hands together in front. Pulling upward, he stretched Jess. Then he jerked backwards. Jess could hear the vertebra popping. Slowly lowering him, putting weight back on Jess' feet, he patted him again on the shoulder.

"It help you," he said.

"Hey, that's alright," Jess replied. "I did feel some difference. But whether it was good for me, only time will tell." They headed for the kitchen.

"I have a question for you, Aliba. Who was the first to build this fortress?"

"Romans and Berbers. See Roman arches above big doorways and gate entrance?" He pointed to a center stone above the doorway. "Key! They call it keystone. Hold other stones in place." He jumped up and slapped the center stone above the doorway. "Keystone! I show you around tomorrow. We have a week of rest. Breakfast waiting now."

They carefully made their way down the narrow, winding tunnel, watchful of the wet rock floor, and entered the dining area off the large kitchen.

That was interesting, Jess thought. *I didn't know the Romans had gone this far south in Africa. I knew they built a city at Volubilis, northeast of Rabat, where the olive groves are located. I wish I had one of my metal detectors up here. It would be interesting to search this old fortress.*

Inside the kitchen cave, Aliba, J.J. and Jess were already on their second helping when Samain and Bushta came into the kitchen. They had been in radio contact with some of their other agents.

"This is a good breakfast, as usual," J.J. said.

Samain nodded, "Bushta prepared it this morning before you were awake."

"Early bird does not always get the worm!" she said. "An old Australian proverb!"

Aliba was about to ask what it meant when J.J. put a finger across his lips. Everyone laughed when he smiled in his questioning way and shrugged his shoulders.

"I'll tell you later," she said.

Pushing his coffee cup toward J.J. for more, Jess asked, "How come the U.S. isn't involved in this mess? I would have expected a visit from the Embassy or have the CIA come calling."

"They are involved, but in the background," Bushta said. "If we need assistance, it will be provided. We call the shots, and they support us where needed. The CIA is not always welcome in Arab countries."

Jess noticed that the others all had 9mm automatic pistols in their holsters and a bandoleer of rifle ammo hanging across the backs of their chairs. Each had an M16 rifle nearby, all except Jess.

He began to feel like he was missing something. *No weapon for me? Why not? I thought training was over and we had a week of relaxation.* Except for the training period, this was the first time weapons had been carried so boldly in the open since they arrived at this place.

After breakfast and before anyone suggested they get involved with a project, Jess said, "I sure do feel exposed and naked!" He put his hands in the air as everyone looked at him, surprised.

"What did you say?" asked J.J.

"He said he was naked?" laughed Aliba. He could not hold himself from laughing. He got up from the table and walked out into the hall.

"Why naked?" asked Samain laughing. "You look covered to me!"

"Your turn, Bushta," Jess said.

"With all those clothes," Bushta said, pulling on Jess' jacket sleeve, "you would think it was cold in here!"

"You wear what, YOU, need to keep warm, and I'll wear what, I, need to keep warm. You sound like my wife's folks in upper Indiana, kidding me about all the clothes I would wear when I got cold," Jess said.

"Hey, you guys!" said J.J. "He is right! He does not have a firearm! He has been handling all the automatics with excellent results in training. Why not now?"

"Yes, I carried a .45 auto back home. Under these circumstances, I figured you'd be issuing me weapons too . . . especially after proving I could handle them."

"J.J.'s new Colt Commander .45 would do the job, in addition to the 9mm Berettas already assigned to you," Samain said. "I will order her a replacement."

J.J. nodded, "I have it in my backpack. I will go get it."

After she left the kitchen, Bushta said, "We are waiting for special permission to back up our authorization for firearms for you. Legally, as a foreigner under Moroccan law, you are not to possess a firearm. I am sure King Itssani will give you the written permits, and you may take firearms home with you, if you want them."

"Certainly, that would be nice for my collection. I do remember the Moroccan law on firearms. Of course, I could use the bow and arrows or a crossbow, which are hanging in the other room."

Samain lifted his coffee cup in the air above his head. "Let us hope that we will not have to use any of these weapons." Placing the cup back on the table, he continued, "I hate killing. But to save other lives, there is no question that it is to be done. This does sound like, as you would say, Jess, a '*Catch 22*' situation; taking the lives of a few in exchange for saving hundreds of lives."

Aliba had left the room with J.J. and returned with a newly issued Thompson submachine gun. They handed it to Jess with a full bandoleer of ammunition. J.J. gave him her Colt automatic with two fully loaded extra magazines.

"This Thompson match her .45 auto pistol," Aliba said. "They same caliber." Smiling, he slapped Jess on the shoulder, "Not hurt back when you shoot."

"I have never used this weapon," Jess said, "but I've always wanted one. Is it as good as the older models?"

"We had the manufacturer change a few things for us," Samain answered. "Otherwise, it is the same weapon. It is fully automatic burst-firing with a selector switch for single or auto." He pointed to the selector switch. "You will have a burst of four rounds with one squeeze of the trigger. Also, you will find our ammo is for stopping two or four legged beast of prey." He said with a critical smile. "All our weapons are the best money can buy. You can shoot it now if you are finished with breakfast."

Bushta picked up Jess' flight bag, and said, "You will still have two 9mm pistols with extra magazines, plus that .308 automatic sniper rifle you used so proficiently."

"I don't know why I feel like I'm being setup as bait for this operation," Jess said kidding, knowing this was the plan he agreed to take part in.

"You are right on that point," Bushta said. "In addition, we are all as ready as a team can be. We will make a good team."

"Again! I know, you know and Interpol knows that I don't really have information about that shooting at the airport," Jess said. "If they know, why don't the bad guys know too?"

"Yes sir, you are partly correct," Bushta replied. "But, if they knew, why the attack at the hospital? All of this training is for our contingency plans for emergencies only. We do not operate like a gang of mobsters or terrorists."

Samain stood up and spread his arms to encompass everyone as a group, "The five of us are an elite team, and we will only kill in extreme circumstances. This may turn into one of those extremes, and I want us to be prepared."

They cheered and clapped their hands. Their mood was good, and Jess was grateful for the training.

Samain leaned over to the table and picked up a biscuit. He took a big bite, "This is good! Bushta's mother taught him how to cook. My mother taught me how to eat good cooking. We should keep him around for the kitchen duties, especially the meal preparations."

Everyone agreed, even Bushta. They were eager, because soon they would be on their way to the Casablanca and Rabat area. Yes, they would make a good team!

After finishing breakfast, they moved to a large table with all the maps and plans. After rehearsing them over and over again, they assured each other their backup plans were good.

"We should be able to plant Jess in the right spot to pull these terrorists into making a mistake," Samain said. "Jess, J.J. will give you refresher flight time in the agricultural spray planes we have. She will show you information on them later."

The information sent by radio had been updated every morning. The operation would take possibly three weeks to coordinate. But when the time came to capture the terrorists, only minutes would be needed. Fresh information was critical. Hopefully there would be no loss of life.

Samain stood back from the table and smiled broadly, with a twinkle in his eye. "Now that you are physically strong enough, we saved the best for last. Have you ever jumped from an aircraft with a parachute?"

"Nope!" Jess answered. "Never had the opportunity to jump from a perfectly good aircraft or a bad one."

"Tomorrow, we are scheduled to start with hang-gliders and then paraglider training for three days," Bushta said. "There may be times we will need to quietly drop in unannounced. Then, weather permitting, we will skydive. These high cliffs will give us maximum use of thermal."

Samain continued, "We will get out the gear and take you a step at a time through the procedures. No physical work, just hang and fly. Today, we will continue to rest and relax."

"The next six days will be enjoyable for you because you like to fly," Bushta said with a smile. "Then we head to Casablanca."

After exhausting themselves mentally until the late afternoon hours on plans, they took a break, got up and stretched their legs. Bushta brought over the ingredients for a serving of hot mint tea. He had tall clear glasses and a tray with a large ceramic teapot. He placed on the table a bowl filled with big chunks of sugar, and another bowl of fresh mint leaves with a pouch of special herbs and tealeaves. Then he put all the mint leaves in the pot and filled the rest of the pot with sugar chunks. He poured boiling water over the sugar, mint and tealeaves. Almost instantly, the sugar was liquefied. After stirring the mixture, he let the tea steep for five minutes, and then poured everyone a glassful through a strainer.

Samain motioned with a finger not to pick up the glasses; they were too hot. He handed them each a small towel to wrap around the glasses.

Bushta pointed to the coffee pot on the stove, "Coffee is ready after you are finished with the tea."

Then Samain asked, "Who can remember the last time this was served to him?" Looking at Jess, he nodded.

"Very vividly!" Jess said with a smile. "At Kenitra, in your home, Samain. It almost took the skin off my hand when I grabbed the hot glass. Yes, I do remember. That has been over thirty years ago."

"Many long years ago and good memories," Samain said, nodding. "We lost track of each other after you left Morocco. When we were in America, we could not find you. We did remember you were a Texan, but we had no address or telephone number."

J.J. moved over next to Samain, and put her arm under his. "Samain, Bushta and I became acquainted in Waco, at the Texas

Ranger Headquarters. We had special training with them and the Border Patrol on the Texas border, related to terrorists smuggling drugs and military arms. They are a good group to work with."

"While you were there, did any of you get out to west Texas for cattle drives or roundups?" Jess asked.

J.J. shook her head, "We were only with the Texas Rangers and the Texas Border Patrol. Why do you ask?"

"Bushta's biscuits remind me of home. My wife's recipe is from my father's sourdough biscuits. He was a chuck wagon cook on some cattle drives in west Texas. Have you ever tasted sourdough biscuits or bread?"

Samain and Bushta shook their heads, no.

"We had biscuits, but I do not remember sourdough," Samain said.

J.J. smiled, "I went on a roundup with cowboys in the outback of Australia. It is perhaps the same as in Texas. We had Australian cowboy style biscuits, steaks, gravy, barbecue and beans with all the 'trimmings'. The cook said he was from the state of Arizona."

"Well, you had a good taste of western hospitality then," Jess said. "Anyway, I love biscuits and gravy. Three meals a day would suit me," he took another swallow of coffee. The hot tea was too sweet for him. He had to wash the taste out of his mouth with a good cup of coffee, "Sorry, I sort of got off the subject." Reaching for another biscuit, he continued, "I promised to go along being bait, but don't leave me out on any of the details. I don't want to slip up by saying or doing something at the wrong time."

Aliba returned to the kitchen and sat next to Jess, and then poured himself some more mint tea. He was the only one of the group who could drink the tea boiling hot.

"Jess, you are our only hope in getting these people to expose themselves," Samain said. "We are confident you are ready, and you will have every detail we receive. Good results will come only as we work together as a single team. We are that team now," he said enthusiastically.

"The terrorists think you can identify the people who did the shooting at the airport," J.J. said. "It must be that someone very important in the Moroccan government was involved in the assassination at the airport."

Bushta nodded agreement, "They have always been one step ahead of us."

Aliba, with a distant look on his face, stood up and moved next to Samain at the stove. His expression had changed trying to remember something.

Samain stood in front of the old wood-burning cook stove warming his backside. J.J. had stretched her legs out, putting her boots next to the stove's side. Bushta and Jess stood at the other end of the stove warming their hands. Leaving their coffee cups on top of the wood-burning stove insured the cups would stay warm, too.

Everyone looked at Aliba, waiting for him to say something. A long period of silence in front of the warm stove was soothing the nerves. Aliba had remembered seeing three men at the airport who may have done the shooting in the restroom.

"Please!" Aliba said, holding up his hand to get attention. "Mr. Hanes, I remember! The terrorists say you saw someone. I did also! I told you in hospital, when you woke up." Turning to Bushta, he exclaimed, "I know the big man!"

They thought he was going to dance a jig before he calmed down enough to sit at the table. By then, all were ready for his information.

"What big man, Aliba?" Bushta pressed.

"I remember. He and two men. They run to big black car. Car like king has." Motioning with his hands, "Long black car," he said with a big smile. He was one happy man.

"That is called a limousine," J.J. said.

"Yes! Yes! Big fat man in army uniform! Sand, desert sand!" He hesitated again, thinking. "Arabs! The big man, I know. Somewhere . . . Kenitra, Rabat! Where?" Now he was getting himself flustered. "Maybe Agadir freighter seaport. I will remember!"

"Did you see him before the explosion?" asked Samain.

He shook his head emphatically. Sitting down, he leaned over, put his elbows on the table and laid his forehead in the palm of his hands, almost spilling the hot biscuits. "Where? Long car not parked in correct place with motor running. Car in bus parking place, not for diplomats. No! Bus parking. Bus parking place, and bus horn honking for car to move." He looked up, "Business man in blue coat, jump out of car shouting at bus driver. He opened coat, and bus moved away. People in bus point at him. Not unusual, until now. I know gun under jacket, light blue suit." Aliba's brow pulled down in concentration. "Let me think more."

Jess set his coffee cup down with a thud. Luckily, it was empty, or it would have been splashed all over the table. "I also remember a verbal fight and pushing in the airport terminal when I was trying to find a place to eat, just before I went to the men's restroom. One of the men, the loudest one, was a loud-mouthed big fat guy in a tan officer's uniform." Slapping his shirt over the pocket, he added, "He had silver wings over his chest pocket. You know, like most military pilots have. He did not impress me as the pilot type though."

"Big ugly Arab in uniform at airport," Aliba said. "They put cargo and fuel in tan, four engine cargo aircraft. Ugly Arab was telling men what to do loading it. Yelling at men!"

J.J., Bushta and Samain gave each other thumbs-ups. They all wore big smiles.

"Colonel Alvarez!" J.J. said. "Fantastic! Now we have a tie to both the assassinations and drugs."

"There is a group of businessmen here in Morocco who are fronts for firearms dealers from Libya and Western Sahara through Algeria," Samain added. "They have American drug money to push these arms into Somalia, Yemen, Iran and Pakistan. They keep small rebel groups well armed to support the Arab terrorist movements internationally. This Colonel Alvarez is our missing link."

"Our King Itssani is against those fanatics who were supplying the Middle East, and still do. He is against terrorists around the world who use Morocco as a trading point," Bushta said, pulling a large map over the other papers on the table. "Their missiles and firearms are being traded, not only for money, but also drugs." He pointed at different areas. "They are passing through Morocco, drugs going to the U.S. and the stolen arms going to the Middle East. Our country has become a transfer point for these shipments, and they are using some of our poor people. Our law enforcement is getting a bad reputation for not stopping that illegal traffic."

"Not only that," J.J. said, "American businessmen are fronts for some of the biggest movers of cocaine, hashish, heroin and opium. This Colonel Alvarez has been our missing piece of the puzzle. The Moroccan government has enough problems with opium poppy grown here illegally, without this other drug traffic. But now, we have a better idea of how to set our plans."

"Well, from the little knowledge I have about the middle-east," Jess said, "Iraq is still being supported by Russian factions. We should have cut the head off that snake while we were there during Desert Storm. They should have let my hero, General Schwarzkopf, do what he wanted to do in Iraq by getting into Baghdad." He tapped his finger hard on the table, "Mark my word, Saddam Hussien will be at it again, if not in Kuwait, he'll be striking somewhere in Saudi Arabia, Syria, Jordan or Israel."

Samain walked around the table. "The Islamic Fundamentalists were against Moroccan involvement in Iraq during Desert Storm. Our troops supported the U.S. ground forces, and I believe the information we have now relates to the I.F. supplying these terrorists again here in Morocco. Our conflict with Western Sahara has not helped to stop the migration of terrorists from the south."

Jess poured another cup of coffee. Putting his hand on Samain's shoulder, he continued to review the events in detail for them at the air terminal, and the information began falling into place. Aliba had jarred Jess' memory.

"Anyway, back to me," Jess said. "We know who this Arab is,

so how are you going to make me look good as bait to these people? Don't they know who I am, and what I look like?"

"Sure they do, Jess!" Bushta said emphatically, "They probably know more about you than you do. Perhaps, they also know we were close friends from years ago."

"This brings up one more subject I feel should be shared now," J.J. said. "One businessman here in Morocco involved with a terrorist group is someone you know personally, and he knows you. He will be your main objective."

Samain nodded, "Your right J.J. Do you remember Larry Hastings, Jess?"

"Hastings?" Jess exclaimed. "You've got to be kidding me! Old Larry Hastings from Florida, involved with terrorists? That's hard to believe." He could not help chuckling at the idea. Moving away from the stove, he sat at the table again, and began doodling on a note pad while nibbling on a warm biscuit.

"He taught me more about flying prop planes at low-level than the Air Force," Jess said. "We were in Vietnam, Cambodia and Laos when the U.S. wasn't suppose to have troops there. We flew everything from C-123's, A1's, L-28A Helio Couriers to OV10D Broncos." He took another swallow of cold coffee, "Whatever was available to fly the mission, we got in it and flew! Sometimes we had problems landing the first time, but we could always get it in the air.

"Larry was always into something wild. We were close once, but went our separate ways after the war was over. I knew of his work and operations in Florida." He sipped his coffee and scribbled on the sheet of paper. "Hastings had prison time back in the States for using his aircraft to smuggle in illegal immigrants. They didn't have their green immigration cards and he knew it. What's he doing in Morocco? Still selling aircraft, I'd bet?"

J.J. was shuffling through the maps and messages they had been looking at and finding what she had been looking for, and then pushed it over to Jess. "Yes! He is still in business, look at that. He bought a small aircraft factory in Florida, and builds small sports aircraft and crop dusters, then sells them internationally."

"Now these look like nice aircraft," Jess said appreciatively. "Bet he gets top dollar for them. This one looks like that Ayer's Thrush design."

"It is J.J.'s aircraft for a front in spraying fields," Samain said. "And yes, it is a Thrush turbo."

Jess looked at her and gave her thumbs up. She smiled and handed him other photos. "Hastings sells planes at an airport outside Kenitra. He is the front for that Colonel Alvarez for drugs and firearms through Morocco. That is who Aliba was talking about," J.J. said.

"I'm beginning to see how you will fit me into this mess," Jess said.

Samain nodded, "It is beginning to come together. Hastings also has chemicals for crop spraying and a flying crew to do the job. In his hangars, he has a good maintenance crew to keep the aircraft flying. They do major overhauls and restorations. Remember Kenitra?"

"Yes, back when it was Port Lyautey," Jess said. "I have some good and bad memories of those days. That's another story in itself."

"Would you like to do more aircraft flying?" Bushta asked.

"Sure! If it's some flight time in one of these crop dusters, I'm ready anytime. With those powerful radial engines under the cowling, it would be fun. I've never flown turbo spray planes either," Jess said, handing J.J. a sales brochure.

"The turboprop engines are relatively quiet, powerful and easier on fuel consumption," she said. "I am sure you would not have trouble flying the aircraft we have available."

Aliba began scowling and put his hand on top of Jess' hand, "You fly, I stay on ground. Enough flying in Army. Man has no wings, why get off ground to have fun!"

They all laughed.

"Okay, friend of mine! No flying for you unless it's absolutely necessary," Jess said, making a promise he was not authorized to make. "What else can you remember about the men at the airport?"

"We know him. He main problem now," Aliba said. He left the room and headed for the main exit.

"Jess, now you have an idea how we will bait the hook for these terrorists," Bushta said. "You are the pilot, and J.J. will be your flying boss. She, too, is a master pilot," he reminded Jess.

They all continued sharing the maps, messages and information about their plans for infiltrating Hastings' flying business.

The rest of the day was uneventful, so they talked mostly about personal things. Aliba, J.J. and Jess wandered around through the fortress, being snoopy. After supper, Jess excused himself and went to his room.

The others lingered near the kitchen stove and discussed their projects. "Now, any comments or suggestions about Jess' progress? In your opinion, is he ready?" Samain asked.

Aliba nodded his approval.

J.J. nodded too. "I have to make sure he can handle our aircraft safely and accurately. With all of his flying ability, there should not be a problem. Other than that, he is ready. For what he has survived, he is in great shape physically. I believe he has surprised us all with his sharp abilities."

Bushta folded his hands and leaned his elbows on the table, "I agree, he is ready. He was slow acclimating to our standards of operation, but that was worked out. I am surprised at his fast physical recovery and ability to handle all the aspects we have confronted him with. His endurance is fantastic, even though he is not fast on his feet." He said, with a broad smile, "But again, he could spend all day climbing these cliffs and ridges, and not breathe hard. It would be a benefit to have him as an Interpol agent."

Samain rubbed his cold hands together and stood, "Fine, if nothing else, that will be all for tonight except for Aliba breaking out the hang-glider bags. We will start the first part of his training early in the morning. Zero five hundred hours for breakfast, Aliba.

Tomorrow we fly the thermal at twelve hundred hours from the slope near the west gate."

#

That night in bed, Jess kept milling around in his mind the facts as he knew them and searched for what else he could remember about the Casablanca airport. He would doze off and wake thinking about it. *Aliba remembers a light blue suit on that man who made the bus move. Then the men at the ticket counter wearing light blue suits. And now we have the main supplier, Colonel Alvarez. What else is important to remember? And how did Hastings talk the Moroccans into letting him set up a business in Kenitra?*

Suddenly a fist banged on Jess' bedroom door. Startled, he sat straight up in bed. Grabbing the gun under his pillow, he replied, "Yes!"

"Mr. Hanes, breakfast, twenty minutes. Big day ahead," Aliba yelled through the door.

Jess looked at his watch, he had been awake most of the night.

#

Well-clothed for the cold altitude and wind, the team grouped together on the slope above the edge of a shear cliff. A distant valley to the west could be seen between high, snow covered ridges and plunging canyons. The wind blew steadily up the face of the cliff, lifting clouds with it, which surrounded the busy team.

The wet mist covered everything that was exposed, and froze on the cold metal frames of the hang-gliders. The black fabric of the gliders resisted the moisture, which slid off to the ground. The team was out of the strong wind blowing up from the cliff's edge and did not have to anchor the gliders.

After additional instruction for Jess, Bushta strapped himself to the sling under his glider. Samain, J.J. and Jess listened to Bushta's final in-flight course they would fly. They were to follow him down to the distant valley, an hour's flying time. If anyone had problems along the way and had to land, they would mark their spot with a smoke flare so the others could find them and land close to assist. They had radios to communicate with each other in flight and with Aliba who was to meet them below. He had left three hours prior to their departure.

Bushta grasped the crossbar of the glider and lifted the black wedge-shaped wings above him. The sling was one piece of nylon canvas formed to his front torso with straps and a harness around to his back, almost like a girdle with velcro straps through metal double buckles. The buckles were attached together in the back to a nylon rope by a snap safety hook, and then it was connected to a metal ring on the underside of the wing.

When gliding, his body would hang suspended under the wings mid-section and by shifting his body weight to the left or right; he could cause the glider to turn. If he pulled his weight forward of the crossbar, the glider would dive. Pushing his weight further aft or behind the bar, the nose of the glider would raise.

"Jess, do not forget when you reach the edge of the cliff, there will be an upward force of wind. It will lift you abruptly," Bushta said almost out of breath as his excitement increased. "Keep the nose of the glider down and veer to the right away from the fortress. The wind will smash you against the face of the cliff if you let it take you to the left."

Jess could hear him clearly on his headset. "I understand!"

Bushta ran toward the cliff's edge and leaped out into space. The upward draft of the wind caught him and slung him abruptly high above the other four on the slope. He shifted his weight forward bringing the nose of the wing down and descended between the rugged mountain peaks towards the lower canyons. J.J. followed Bushta, then Jess and Samain.

The harsh updraft lessened when Jess hurtled out into the vastness below, and was momentarily hung in space straight out from where he had leaped. When he pushed his weight to the right and foreword, the right wing dipped and the nose dropped down. He slowly began to descend on the glide path the other two had taken. The view was breathtaking. This, plus the excitement of gliding in the open at the high altitude in thin air, caused Jess to gasp for breath. He became slightly lightheaded, but it quickly disappeared.

This is fantastic! Jess thought. *This has to be better than jumping out of an aircraft in a parachute, even though I've never done that.*

"This is great!" he shouted. "I don't have words to express what I'm feeling. J.J., I'm to your right and above you."

Suddenly, a red tailed hawk swooped passed Jess, screaming as it returned to its nest in the crevice of a cliff.

"Just a warning, Jess," Samain said from above. "It will not leave the nest again until we are out of sight."

"No problem for now," Jess said. "It certainly caught me off guard."

J.J. was suddenly caught in an updraft and rose some 100 feet almost instantly. Then a down draft sent her further below her original altitude. "Watch out for that spot you two!" She warned, getting back under control.

Jess dipped his left wing and nose down to go around where J.J. had passed through. He glided further down the canyon towards the distant valley.

They drifted lazily with the wind currents, enjoying their soaring wings, playing games circling each other. Almost two hours had passed quickly when their landing area came into view. Aliba was waiting, holding up a pole with a long red streamer at the top. It hung limp for the lack of wind.

They all landed without mishap. Aliba had warm stew and coffee ready for them inside a walled tent he had erected. They ate heartily and rehearsed their trip, packed and headed back up into the mountains.

They spent the next four days gliding and sailing the currents to different landing areas. It was a thrilling experience for Jess.

CHAPTER NINE

Back on his return flight home, the steady light vibration of the huge 747 Moroccan airliner continued calming Jess' tensions. It was hard for him to believe he had been in Morocco over eight months.

He smiled, thinking about his narrow escape from death and the unlikely teaming with two old friends, Samain and Bushta. Remembering his two new friends, J.J. and Aliba, caused Jess to laugh outwardly to himself.

Jess' smile caused his flight attendant, coming from the first-class galley, to return the smile. She had been observing him for a while and was staring at him. His smile widened when he noticed her and pointed his finger at her.

Coming to his side, she asked, "Must be good memories? I've been watching you the last hour or so. You had a serious frown most of the time, looking out your window. And now, you have a big smile and laughing."

Jess nodded, "Yes, very good memories, renewing old friendships and acquiring new ones in Morocco."

"We will be serving a lunch shortly. Would you care for something more to drink now? We have little more than four hours to John F. Kennedy International Airport, if the weather holds."

He lifted an inquisitive eyebrow, "Expecting bad weather?"

"No, not really," she said. "Just showers."

"Good. I'll have American coffee, please. Black, no sugar."

"Will South American coffee be all right, it's freshly brewed?"

"Certainly! As long as you don't run out and we have to return to Morocco for more," Jess said jokingly, being reminded of a coffee commercial on TV. *Anyway, a fresh cup of coffee would hit the spot,* he thought.

The freshness of its brewing could be smelled throughout the cabin.

Jess returned to watching the bright soft clouds beneath them and continued to relax. *It's too bad man can't make a pillow as soft as those clouds look. Silly thought to have.*

"Mr. Hanes, here you are. Fresh, hot and black."

He released a tray in the armrest next to his seat, and raised it into place across his lap. He knew the fresh coffee would perk him up.

"Thanks!"

She smiled and returned to her duties preparing lunch. The other flight attendants swaggered down the aisles of the 747 as they served passengers. Jess' attendant was the senior attendant by the way she directed the others. After lunch was served and everyone had finished eating, and seemed content, she returned and sat next to him.

"Excuse me, Mr. Hanes. May I sit with you? Do you mind having me for conversation?"

"Why, yes! And no, ma'am! I would be pleased!" he said turning in his seat and leaning his left shoulder against the backrest. He watched her face change from a tensed look to a relaxed smile as she talked. *She must have needed a break from her routine.*

"This is a nice location you have picked to be seated," she said with a hint of a Texas accent. "It's pleasantly quiet compared to the other sections. Tell me about your friends you spoke of earlier and especially about the big smile you had awhile ago."

"Well, where should I start?" Jess said, staring passed her with a faraway look in his eye. He thought this was a little unusual for him to be so willing to converse with a total stranger, especially a woman and after his past ordeal in Morocco.

Oh well! I'll never see her again after this flight. This might prove interesting. Besides, she wasn't quite a total stranger. He knew her name was Madilene Ash from her nametag.

"Let's see now. About eight or nine months ago, I was on a business trip heading for the Middle East, with a stop in

Casablanca. A most unusual thing happened to me in the airport terminal men's restroom."

He began telling her his story about the assassination. An hour and a half later, the lights came on in the cabin galley for the attendants to serve drinks and snacks.

Madilene unfastened her seat belt and stood up, straightened her skirt and fluffed up her long brunette hair.

Smiling, she said, "I'll be right back. I have a few things to check. Need anything? I really don't want to miss any details of your intriguing story."

He shook his head, no, and thanked her. For a total stranger, she seemed very interested in Jess' story. *I'm a better storyteller than a storywriter.*

It had been a lop-sided conversation, though; Jess had been doing all the talking. They had not talked about her at all.

She was a pretty lady, not a stunning beauty, but pretty, attractive, and very attentive, somewhat overly so. *Now that's exactly why I've been so open with her. So, I'd better be careful what I say.* He had to admit that talking to Madilene had helped him rehearse the details. *I don't want to forget anything, especially when I tell Marie Ann about it.*

Madilene returned, smiled and sank into the seat beside him with a sigh, "I'll be glad when this turn-around is over. It's been a long flight." She leaned back into the seat, crossed her long, shapely legs, folded her arms, closed her eyes, paused and said, "Where did you leave off? I remember! You were setting up a sting operation in Kenitra."

Jess look out the window. *She had a good memory. She must be taking mental notes in order to remember that. I'll continue the story and give her a short history background of that area of Morocco.*

Jess resumed his story where the team had left for Kenitra, north of Rabat, on the Oued Sebou River. He described the geography of the area where the mouth of the river emptied into the Atlantic Ocean on the west coast of Morocco. Up the river was

Port Lyautey, (Kenitra), a city of international commerce, with a population of about 150,000 people.

In World War II, the French and Germans fortified Kenitra. They were protecting a large airfield, which the Allied Forces needed for operating out of North Africa. Allied Navies bombarded the beaches at Mehedia, near the Kasba fortress at the mouth of the river.

In short, the Allied Forces overran and captured the defenders. The French accepted talks with the Allied Commanders and turned the area over to them. France was convinced that Hitler did not have the answers for French Morocco. Morocco and France fought against the German forces until the war ended.

The Sebou River was only deep enough for small freighters and ocean liners, and small vessels such as an American destroyer. At the docks, the river was not really wide enough to handle a larger vessel, especially when it needed to be turned around for going downstream.

"Why Kenitra?" she asked. "I thought most of the fighting was around Casablanca and in the eastern part of the Sahara Desert in Morocco and Algeria? Isn't that only a limited farming area, and one of the largest cork producing areas of the world? There are no big industrial factories at Kenitra, . . . are there?"

"You're right," Jess answered. "At that time, it had to do with fighting Rommel in North Africa. Kenitra had the largest and the longest asphalt runway in that part of North Africa. The Allied Forces needed that base to operate from." He held up one finger to interrupt her next question, "But for the undercover operation I was with, it was the best area for our base; mainly, because Hastings' business was located there. You seem knowledgeable of that part of Morocco."

"In this job, I'm required to know about the different countries we service. I don't know a lot of history on Morocco, but my hobby is artifacts and geology." Madilene turned in her seat for a better position to face Jess. "Knowing four languages fluently has become most helpful . . . not only in my job, but also in my hobbies."

"How about that!" Jess said, stretching his arms above his head. "I'm a retired government employee and retired from the military. I've flown and instructed flying in most popular single and multi-engine prop aircraft, and I've spent some time working with law enforcement in my home state of Texas. I'm now considered a professional treasure hunter, which started years ago as a hobby searching for Civil War relics."

You're shooting off your mouth, he told himself. *She's not interested in your life's history. Just continue with your story.* But, the expression on Madilene's face told him she was taking it all in.

Mr. Hanes, you are a very interesting storyteller. How many books have you authored? Madilene thought to herself.

"Anyway, back to the story," Jess said. "We're going to be in JFK shortly and I won't be finished."

She laughed, "That's all right, we have plenty of time."

There will be plenty of time? She doesn't know me when I really get started! Jess thought.

He leaned back against the side of the seat next to him, with his left shoulder pressed into the seat so he could face her better. He was getting a sore neck sitting the other way.

She leaned back against the edge of the seat next to her, facing Jess and curled her legs underneath her in the seat.

Not a very ladylike position with a short skirt, Jess thought. *It will be up around her belly button if she squirms around much.* She surprised him with her relaxed attitude, especially while on duty. The other attendants did not seem to mind what she was doing.

"Before my flight was disrupted in Casablanca, I was headed for Dubai, United Arab Emirates," Jess said. "My research was on Roman vessels sunk in the Straits of Hormuz, off the coast of Oman, in the early first century."

After giving her his short, unsolicited verbal resume, he took a deep breath, "Maybe someday I'll get back over there. I was hoping to get the problem solved fast in Morocco, but it got more involved as days passed. I'm thankful it's over! Right now, all I need is rest at home and some T.L.C."

"Tender loving care. Yes, I can tell you're easily excited about things you like to do. I didn't know a Texan could talk so fast and so long without taking a breath," laughing she stretched her long legs out in front of her to the bulkhead wall.

"Well, you're nice to sit here and take it. You're a real trooper, and don't tell me, 'It's my job!'"

"That's right, it is part of my job to be of service to our passengers. You happen to be my special one on this flight."

What did she mean by that? Yeah, I know, I'm just another pretty face! I'm not that good-looking, so it must be my story. Samain must have put her up to this. It really doesn't matter, I'm enjoying the company, and she helps the time pass faster.

"I'm sorry!" she said. "I hate to sidetrack you from your story again, but I'm needed up front. It won't be too long until we land. I'll check on your JFK to Austin connections prior to our arrival." Rising, she started to leave, but turned. "I would like to hear the rest of your story." Then she headed for her workstation.

"I'll be happy to tell you the rest, if you have a layover in JFK?" he called to her. *Hold up Jess. You're getting a bit too friendly now. Maybe she didn't hear me.*

She came back and sat on the edge of the seat. A serious look on her face turned into a pleasant smile, "I would be pleased to have dinner with you at the airport." She extended her hand, "Thank you for the invitation."

What are you doing Jess? Oh well, what's done is done!

"Then I suppose we should introduce ourselves," he said. "I'm Jess Hanes." It just rolled out of his mouth like it was the most natural thing for him to say.

She grabbed his raised hand and pointed to her nametag. "Madilene Ash. My friends of course, call me Madi. Please wait for me at the ticket booth where we load and off-load passengers. See you later, Jess."

Leaving him for her duties, Madi became immersed in attending to others in the forward cabin.

Jess pondered what had taken place and what was coming.

The layover would prove very interesting. She was older than the rest of the attendants, and did not seem to have a flighty attitude. He felt comfortable and at ease with her.

Something about her reminds me of my sweet wife back home in Austin. Her smile and attentiveness captivate me, like there is no one else around, just the two of us. She puts me at ease almost immediately. Homesick, Mr. Hanes? Yes! Homesick!

CHAPTER TEN

Jess finally found an empty phone booth in the JFK terminal. As crowed as the lobby was, he was happy to be back stateside. Fumbling for a quarter, he located one in a handful of foreign coins. It had been a long time since he was allowed to talk to his loving wife.

"Hey, Marie Ann! Love! I'm at JFK airport," he said.

"How was the trip, Mr. Treasure Hunter?" she asked. "Sure missed getting your long letters. Did you find your sunken ship? I thought you might have been stuck on one, haven't heard from you for so long."

Jess' voice cracked trying to control his emotions, "I was stuck, but not on a ship. I'll have to tell you more when I get home. There's so much to catch up on."

"Your aircraft mechanic, Jason, has been trying to get a hold of you for a long time. I told him you were out finding our fortune. He just wanted to talk to you about the annual inspection coming up on your aircraft." Her excitement was evident, and she began to sniffle.

"I'm doing fine, Love. How about you?" He had ignored her comment about his mechanic.

"I'm all right, now that you're on the way home. By the way," she added, trying to laugh through the tears, "your junk mail is stacked sky-high."

"Love, don't cry. Everything is fine, and I'll be home shortly. I know it's easy for me to say."

"Yes, it is easy for you to say, but . . ." she hesitated. "Jess, I had different people from the government stopping by asking for you. I got sort of suspicious and contacted our nephews with the

Texas Rangers. Charles checked it out, and these people were assigned to protect me from Arab terrorists." Now she was slowly calming down. "He said they had been observing all of my activities for my safety. I also had a couple of visits from a lady who was a federal marshal. Then I did get scared, not having you here and not knowing how you were."

"I'm sorry, Love. Are you going to be all right?"

"Yes, I'm trying to be patient waiting for you to get home."

"It does sound like they have kept you aware of what has been happening. Did the federal marshal tell you where I was, and why they were protecting you?"

"No! That scared me. I thought you were a victim of terrorists in the Middle East. She said you were safe and in good hands. Also, they didn't have any idea when you would be home, or when you would be able to contact me." She paused, and Jess could hear more sniffles. "I'm so glad you're coming home. When do you get into Austin?"

"Later this afternoon, Sweetheart, at Berkstrom International," Jess said. "Contact Charles or Jack, and find out if they can take you to the airport. I'm sure one of them would be more than happy to be assigned as your bodyguard. I'm glad you're all right! I sure miss you, Love."

"Miss you, too," she said holding back the tears again.

"I don't want to give you a lot of information on the phone. It's still not safe."

She began to cry, "I'm fine now that you're coming home. It's been almost a year! Too long to be apart, especially not hearing from you."

"Yes, Love, eight months was too long! I'm sorry, and I'll try to make up for it when I do get there. I'll be home as fast as these planes will get me there. I'll be pushing all the way home."

"Be very careful of strangers, especially foreigners," she said.

"Okay! Keep close to our nephews," Jess warned.

"I'll call them again, as soon as you hang up. I'm waiting for that big smile."

"Good! God bless you, Angel. See you soon."

"Bye for now," she said. "I love you!"

"Love you, too," he answered, and started to hang up the phone. "Wait! You still there?"

"Yes!" she said.

"Forgot to tell you something. I've got a hot date for dinner here at the airport. Her name is Madilene Ash, one of the airline attendants from the flight over."

"Sure you do! I bet she's about my age, brunette, but taller, good looking," she teased.

"You know her?" He asked, teasing back.

"Perhaps!"

"Let me think . . . yeah, she's a brunette, about that age, taller than me, attractive and she is . . ."

"Hold on young man!" she interrupted. "Who is this lady you're talking about?"

"She reminds me of you when she starts talking," he said. "She kept me company coming back."

"I'll bet she did! I have a good idea what went on. YOU talked all the way. Better go eat and get your strength back. You'll need it when you get home. My 'honey-do' list is volumes long now."

"Okay, Love, see ya!"

"Bye!" she said again.

Jess hung up the phone, picked up his bag and headed for the restaurant. His thoughts were on his wife. *What a Sweetheart I have. People can't believe we trust each other the way we do. But, during thirty-one years of marriage, we have learned how to trust. You can bet that I'll receive the third degree when I get home, especially when she hears I was almost killed. Those months in Morocco without hearing from me had to be hard on her.*

At least when I was in the Navy, she got letters about every day while I was gone. Over thirty years of marriage, and she still puts up with my absences. Separation is rough on both of us. I'll have to take her along on my next trip. She usually enjoys our traveling together.

#

In a quiet booth in the business lounge/restaurant of the airport, Madi and Jess relaxed after finishing an unusually good meal. Madi was pleasant, had a great smile and was easy for Jess to talk to.

The waitress came over to the table. "Anything more? Desserts, coffee or drinks?"

They both shook their heads.

"No, thanks," Jess said. "May we stay here until my flight time?"

"Yes, sir." She left the check and returned to serving other tables.

"I'm not surprised you don't drink," Madi said. "You don't seem the type to me."

"I haven't had a drink since the Lord straightened out my life back in 1961," he said. "I was in Morocco, in the Navy."

"Yes, I understand what you are saying. But, what about continuing your story? You were talking about Kenitra and setting up that sting operation."

"Fine. Perhaps I can tell you some time about what happened in 1961," Jess offered.

Madi looked him straight in the eyes, "I'm sure that story is just as interesting as this one. But finish this one for me first. With all these experiences, you should write a book."

"That's what my wife tells me," he said. "I would spend another lifetime trying to learn how to write. Then I would have to get another computer for that, and I'd never get anything else done."

Madi nodded, "Computers have a way of holding a captive audience. They can be very intimidating, too."

"They certainly can be! But another computer would keep me home longer, except for trips on research. No . . . then I would be right back to square one. Foreign trips again."

She laughed and moved closer to Jess on the leather booth seat. The late afternoon crowd had arrived, and the noise of the restaurant picked up.

Jess continued his story with Madi, where he was to encounter the main 'weak link' of the terrorists' activity—Hastings.

"With the information filtered to us, we felt he was under pressure to move cargo, and he wanted out. In exchange for his information concerning the assassination, a safe haven anywhere in the world would be offered." He glanced at his watch out of habit, not really seeing the time. "We had to get into his business, deeper than the prior Interpol agency had been, and stop the main supplier."

Jess opened an unused napkin on the table, took a pencil from his shirt pocket, and began drawing on it.

"Kenitra, Port Lyautey, was a very busy inland seaport on the northwest coast of Morocco," he said. "The river, Oued Sebou, flows through the city from the Atlas Mountains in the east." He turn the paper napkin and marked it, "Where the river empties into the ocean, high on its southern shore cliffs, a large, abandoned Portuguese fortress, the Kasba, continues its overview watch to the west. Further south along the ocean shoreline, beautiful rough cliffs face the Atlantic Ocean where high waves and wind erode the rocks and beaches. Above the cliffs to the east, the land becomes rolling hills and valleys with deep blue lakes."

All the time Jess was talking and drawing, Madi sipped coffee the waitress warmed up for them.

"You know the westerners from the U.S., the French and other Europeans have helped modernize Morocco," he said. "Because of that modernization, many small airports, away from the cities had become busy hubs, especially, during the planting and harvesting seasons." Jess took another swallow of his coffee.

"Some of these smaller airports . . . ," Jess circled areas on the paper napkin with his pencil, ". . . have commuter aircraft and agricultural spray planes. At various times, these aircraft require maintenance and are sent to larger airports for servicing."

Doodling on the napkin, Jess resumed his story, "One small airport in particular, well equipped, south of Kenitra, handled most of the servicing required for smaller aircraft. This was the focal point of our operation with Larry Hastings."

"The plot was to move into the Kenitra farming area for aerial spraying of crops. The plan was to use me as a setup for getting involved in crop dusting. I had grown a nice salt and pepper beard and mustache, which helped hide a familiar face," Jess said and hesitated trying to gather his thoughts. "Hastings had not seen me for years, and I had lost almost forty pounds in the hospital, although some of my weight had been gained back in muscle while training in the Atlas Mountains. Hopefully, I wouldn't be recognized by Hastings or any other terrorists in that area."

Jess paused talking to Madi, suddenly realizing it must be close to flight time. Glancing at his watch again, and then at Madi, he began searching for his ticket.

With a puzzled look on his face, "What was my flight number?" So far, the search through his pockets had not turned up the ticket. "Which pocket did I put it in?"

Madi reached for her purse and pulled out an envelope, "This Delta flight goes direct to Austin and doesn't stop in Dallas or Chicago. Guess what? I'm on your flight." She waved a ticket folder. "Don't worry about the other ticket. I have your new one! You can get a portion of the other one refunded when you get to Austin."

Jess found his original ticket in his hip pocket and gave her a suspicious look.

"Your original ticket has a longer layover here," she said. "Then add your flight to Chicago from here and a lengthy layover there. Then your final flight would be from there to Austin. I don't know why they didn't route you direct to Austin from here; it's shorter in time and less money." Madi stretched her legs under the table with her arms above her, and then gathered herself back. She leaned against the back of the booth. "Anyway, I took the liberty and changed it for you. Hope you didn't plan spending time in Chicago?"

"No, not really. But . . . I'm surprised you did it without asking me first."

"While I was changing, I checked the departures and knew if I didn't do it for you then, you wouldn't have a seat on the direct flight. I hope I'm not in trouble!"

He shrugged, "No problem! I'll be home sooner with the direct flight. Thanks!"

To his surprise, she was very excited about being on the same flight. She hurriedly continued talking, as if she was being pressed for time. Grabbing his arm, she tugged and motioned for him to follow her out of the restaurant into the busy rush of passengers.

"If you would like, I can get us on board early so we can get to our seats without waiting," she said, another trace of Texas accent coming through. "Knowing the hired hands around here help."

"What takes you to Austin?" Jess asked over the noise of the crowd, following her through another crowded lobby hallway.

"It's my second home. I have an apartment there and spend most of my spare time at home in the hill country around Llano. I own a couple of small ranches near there."

"Well, I'll be. You're not originally from Texas . . . or have you lost your accent?"

"I'm a native Texan, too, born in Kerrville, raised in Odessa. Taking all those language courses through the years has caused my accent to disappear. But, I can add it if you like."

"Sure! Why not! We're almost home."

"I'm not on flight status now, so we'll take a shortcut to the plane," Madi advised. "I'm anxious to hear the rest of your story."

He followed her to a side door next to a ticket booth and down two flights of stairs, through a baggage handling area onto a loading ramp.

Jess, is she for real? This could be a come-on to set you up for the terrorists.

"You know your way around here pretty good," he observed.

"I know this place like the back of my hand. We can use some short cuts to our aircraft."

Moving up another stairway, down long hallways, they came

to activity in a large baggage loading area. Two security men approached them as Madi held out her identification.

Jess was uneasy about the two men. *They don't look foreign. I guess they're okay. But I better stay on guard, just in case I'm being sidetracked.*

"Hi Madi!" one of them called to her over the noise. They nodded and pointed toward the nearest aircraft.

As they walked under the front of an airliner and around the huge nose wheels, Jess realized he was looking up at a Boeing 747. *Boy, the pilots sure sit high above the ground in these jumbo jets.*

"We'll have to go up these stairs to the passenger loading platform and then through the forward door entry of the aircraft," she said, leading the way.

It was becoming difficult for Jess to keep up with her; she was definitely in good physical condition. He could feel sweat running down his back from climbing behind Madi. He wasn't out of breath until they topped the stairs. At the top, she looked back down behind them and waved at the two security men, and then entered the loading platform compartment. In the hallway of the raised platform, they paused to catch their breath.

A moment later, they entered the front doorway of the immense aircraft and felt the cool, air-conditioned breeze rushing passed them into the platform hallway.

Another attendant smiled, "Hello, ya'all. May I see your tickets, please?" She definitely had that familiar Texas accent. She and her companions wore fancy blue western outfits, along with swanky blue boots to match. A white Stetson hat hung down between their shoulders on their back, held in place with a braided leather stampede drawstring around the front of their necks.

Madi showed her ID and Jess showed his new ticket. They exchanged a few pleasantries, and then Madi motioned with her finger to follow her up the stairs to the second level. "I made arrangements for your ticket seating to be changed. Here we are," Madi said, "best seats on the plane."

She had picked the same seats Jess had on the previous flight.

The three seats on the right side of the cabin next to the windows were vacant. That row was a great choice for flying. No one would be walking on their feet trying to get to their seats.

Jess was curious, *How did those security people know we were okay? What about firearms? We just got off an international flight, ate out of the security area, and came directly to the aircraft with no customs to go through. Looks like a big hole in their security.*

After they were settled in their seats, Madi introduced Jess to more of her attendant friends. She motioned for one of them to come to her.

"Coffee, Jess?" Teasing him, she added, "They shouldn't run out!" After the attendant had gone, she tapped him on the knee with her finger. "Now we can relax and enjoy the flight."

"I have a question."

She smiled, "Yes!"

"How did the security men know we're not armed with a weapon?"

It dawned on him that Madi had slipped them passed security. *It was very swift efficient work, how did she manage to do it? I was a witness to it happening.*

"I've never changed aircraft like this without being searched by the customs people. We didn't go through detectors, and those security men did not stop us. Looks like a breech of their security system where a terrorist could take advantage. We could have weapons."

With a sly smile, she locked eyes with Jess, "I might as well tell you now. I knew you would be questioning me about getting us here. We do have a weapon . . . at least I do."

He stared at her, "What have I missed here? You're not carrying a . . ." He almost choked, and looked around to see if anyone had over heard their conversation. "Are you serious?"

She opened her purse just far enough for Jess to see a Mauser 9mm automatic pistol. He grabbed her hand on the flap of the purse and slapped it closed. Looking her straight in the eyes, he started to speak.

Madi interrupted, holding up her finger to her lips. "Not so loud. We don't advertise these things." She laid two impressive identifications on his lap: a U.S. Marshal's badge with ID, and her airline ID. Then smiling proudly, "I wear two hats. I'm a government Marshal, when I'm not in flying status. I've been assigned as your escort from Morocco," she said with a smile of pride.

"You knew all about me before I got on the plane in Casablanca?"

"Not about all your experiences in Morocco. But you did a good job of filling me in," Madi said. "I was to keep my eye on you in case of any trouble that might be following you. We're concerned about possible terrorist problems! I didn't know any of the story as to your need for escort, other than there were attempts on your life in Morocco. My job is to protect you all the way home. That was orders direct from the White House."

"You're great!" Jess burst out. "You sure know your business," nodding and crossing his arms. *She could just as easily have been a terrorist setting me up. Jess, count your blessing! It's aggravating that I'm so easily charmed by another pretty face.* "You really worked me right to where you wanted me. Boy, I'm a sucker for beautiful women."

"Thank you," she teased. "Don't be so hard on yourself. You're not the first one I have deceived in order to protect someone. It's my job to be the best, and I'm still learning."

"You really set the hook and reeled me in! My Angel told me about ladies like you, and I didn't listen." Jess starred out the window.

"Angel must be your wife, Marie Ann, in Austin?" she said.

Almost snapping his neck, he turned and glared at Madi. His eyes wide open giving her a surprised expression.

Madi smiled, "Jess, I've spent some time with Marie Ann. In fact, we've been out to dinner a few times in Austin. I found out she likes barbecue, too."

"You both knew about this and neither of you told me? You were the one she mentioned on the phone. All the time I thought she was home alone with no help." He shook his head.

"You have quite the two nephews, I've dated them both!" She said matter-of-factly. "Yes, very much the Texas gentlemen like their Uncle Jess." Madi pushed her purse and bag under the seat. "Your sister, Liz, south of Austin? Now there's a lady who definitely loves her Appaloosa horses. How long has she been doing that, twenty or thirty years? That's a beautiful ranch she has at San Marcos. She's retired Civil Service also, right?"

"Do you need anything, Madi?" one of the attendants stopped to ask.

She shook her head, "No, thanks."

Jess sat dumbfounded and irritated, not looking at Madi. "Okay, where do we go from here?"

Madi stood up, stretched and whispered, "Remember this, you are not unique to the world of terrorism, espionage and gangsters. Many people have been lied to and taken advantage of, injured physically and or mentally, and even killed! You and your lovely wife are lucky, but you're not out of the woods yet. That's why I'm chained around your neck until you get home. Now, please let me finish my job getting you there!" Softly, she added with a worried expression, "Please?" She stepped into the aisle, "Would you excuse me a minute? I need to go wash my face and put on makeup."

"Sure, you've earned the trip!" he said sarcastically. *She sure knew how to put me in my place. She's a master at her job.*

One of the attendants talked with Madi after she started back from the ladies room. Then she smiled and returned to her seat next to Jess.

"Madi, I apologize for getting so angry with you. I know you were only doing your job." Jess put out his hand.

"Accepted, Jess." She shook his hand. "That was a normal reaction for most people when they find out that they have been deceived. No hard feelings, I hope, because we probably will be seeing a lot of each other in the future."

"Okay, that's settled. Now, what else is behind that badge? You're the second mysterious woman I've met since I left home."

"Maybe I can share that later, but for now, we had better relax and take a nap. Coffee is not really what we need. With all the excitement you have been having, the jet lag is catching up with you. Let me find some pillows. We have almost an hour before boarding time."

She opened the overhead compartment and handed Jess two small pillows. Then she leaned over and helped place them behind his head. He seriously believed she did not realize how she exposed herself with her low cut blouse. He caught himself staring and shifted his eyes up to hers. "Sorry! Didn't mean to stare. I apologize."

Embarrassed, she clasped the blouse closed, "I'm the one to apologize. I knew I should have pinned that closed in the ladies' room a while ago. This fits too damn tight anyway." She sat down next to him and used a western-style brooch to close the gap in her blouse. "I apologize for flaunting myself in front of you. I'm never careless in my appearance like this. Jess, please forgive me?"

"Certainly, Madi, no harm done."

Madi's face was red from embarrassment. *Be a gentleman, Jess,* he thought to himself, *and don't make any more comments. She's upset, and we are both tired. She was right; the fatigue from the long day of flight from Morocco was getting to both of us.*

He was mentally exhausted and had no trouble putting his head on the pillows and keeping his eyes shut. The light vibration of the aircraft was soothing, and the soft pillows were just what he needed. Relaxed? But, not completely! Not until he was home.

CHAPTER ELEVEN

Jess felt a gentle nudge on his shoulder, and heard voices in the background. He opened his eyes to see nothing but soft pillows. Closing his eyes again, he felt another nudge.

"Jess, how about some fresh brewed coffee?" Madi said.

Jess thought, *That was a short hour.*

Squatted down against his knee, Madi offered him a cup of steaming hot coffee. He blinked and sat up in the seat. Their section of seats had been roped off for privacy. She had also changed blouses and braided her long hair into a single pigtail while he slept. She was wearing blue jeans and western boots.

"Are you awake enough for coffee?" she asked.

"Sure! Let me stand up for a few minutes, how long till flight time?"

Madi stepped back as he stood. After a good lengthy stretch, he accepted the coffee. It was freshly brewed. He felt ready for another twenty-four full, adventurous hours.

She smiled and sat down. "About ten minutes and everyone will be on board. Are you feeling some better?"

"Yes, thank you. Any suspicious characters come on board?"

"So far, just you and me," she said laughing. "Just us kids!"

"How about a game of cribbage?"

"Cribbage? There's a game I haven't played for years. I don't think they have cribbage on board."

"I have a portable with a lot of miles on it," Jess said, then sipped his coffee. "Or . . .would you rather hear the rest of my tall tale?"

"Your story is more interesting. Let me order a thermos of coffee." She signaled to one of the attendants.

"Sure, but first, which way to the little boy's room?" he asked, setting the coffee cup on a seat table. She pointed toward the front. He excused himself and headed that way.

Jess returned to his seat and Madi poured more coffee. He glanced out the window and saw the baggage crew loading the final wagonload of luggage into the aircraft's freight compartments below. For a moment, he was not paying any attention to Madi, who was patiently waiting.

He turned to her, "Sorry! Guess I'd better finish my story. Where'd I leave off?" He asked this purposely; wanting to see how closely, Madi had been listening before.

"J.J. and the undercover operation were set up!" She grinned. "See! You tried to get me on that one, didn't you?"

"Yes, I tried!" he said, laughing.

Resuming his story, he told Madi how J.J. became his agricultural agent for spraying farms. The undercover team had arranged for all the government forms and permits required to be made for them. From Spain, they purchased two older but well-maintained crop duster aircraft to use as trade-ins, and had them flown by other pilots to a small airfield near Kenitra.

Jess had spent three weeks flying the turboprop engine crop dusters to get back in the groove. Additional hours were spent in the big radial engine aircraft, because they did not know which type of aircraft was to be used.

He loved the sound of that power and the way the heavy aircrafts responded. To Jess it was like driving a big V8 engine in an American automobile up Pikes Peak compared to the little engine in a VW car.

J.J. had given Jess long hours of refreshing training in another aircraft used by the U.S. Marines in Vietnam, the North American OV10 Bronco. That was an aircraft model he would like to own someday, if he could afford it.

The plan began to unfold one early morning after sunrise, as Jess flew to Kenitra from the small airfield where they hangar their planes.

Meanwhile, J.J. was making trade arrangements for one of Hastings' new Cloud Duster aircraft at one of his business locations near Kenitra. Jess and J.J. were to meet there. There was nothing wrong with the aircraft Jess was flying, but trading it was part of the setup. This was to be their part of doing business with Hastings.

Hastings' main office was located in Meknes, some distance east of Kenitra. That was where most of the money exchanges were made. Their business cover was aircraft sales, aviation fuels, agricultural chemicals for crop spraying and leather hides from Bedouins. His sales and service was at the airport southwest of Kenitra, called Tourisme.

CHAPTER TWELVE

Heading west toward the coast of Morocco from Meknes, Jess flew over familiar lakes he had fished years before. They were a deeper blue from the air, and had greener vegetation around them than what he had remembered. He passed over tall electrical lines and the railroad, which were parallel with the coast. Flying between Rabat and Tourisme airports, he climbed from 1,200 to 3,000 feet above ground level, (AGL).

Jess felt the cool wind resistance increase the closer he flew to the shoreline. The head winds ate up the fuel fast. The updrafts from hitting the cliffs pushed his altitude 200 feet higher in a matter of a split second. Taken by surprise, and taking his breath away, he regained level flight and brought the aircraft back down to 3,000 feet.

The updrafts at that altitude had not been that bad the prior weeks. He grabbed the stick with both hands and pressed his knees against the inside skin of the aircraft. He did not have to fight the rudder pedals, but his knees were getting sore pressing against the wall. The abrupt change in altitude put his heart in overdrive, pushing the adrenaline. Jess was glad he did not get dizzy pulling low G's, as he had months earlier.

He finally got control of the craft, and his heart rate leveled out, also. Out past the cliffs and over the pounding surf, he dropped below the height of the cliffs. Pushing the right rudder with a little aileron to the right, making a slow turn north, Jess came parallel with the white beaches. He dropped to within thirty feet above the water. The strong crosswinds subsided away from the shoreline.

At the mouth of the Oued Sebou River, Jess made a forty-five degree bank, heading up over the river. Its boundaries were high cliffs off his right wing toward the south. And, to his left, were low beaches toward the north. With the slow easterly banking of the wings and pulling the nose up a little, he rose to a hundred feet; the same altitude of the old Portuguese fortress, the *Kasba* or *Citadel*. He flew passed the ruins of the old fortress, and its graves of American, French and German soldiers in its cemetery. It made an impressive view from that height. It would have made a great photo for his picture album, but no camera. That seemed to always happen, no camera when he needed it. He would have to make arrangements to visit there again.

Further up the river, he could see dredges, loaded barges and other heavy river equipment lining the south shore piers. Rows of large fuel storage tanks rimmed the north shoreline. As he flew over the workers on the docks and in the farm fields, they looked up and pointed. Most of them had never seen a yellow, two-winged aircraft before, especially flying that low.

Other higher buildings and high-voltage tension lines loomed up ahead. Pushing the throttle forward for more power and pulling back on the stick, he climbed to 2,000 feet with little effort.

From the higher altitude, he could see the Tourisme airport about five miles south of town. It had more hangars and a longer active runway than where their aircraft had been stored. He could see other aircraft to his left, in the distance, making their approaches to the larger commercial airport at Kenitra. He stayed out of their traffic area.

Jess made a routine downwind entry into the flight pattern about 1,800 feet, and noticed a C-130 cargo aircraft turning off the runway onto a taxiway. No one else was in the pattern for landing. He pulled the carburetor heat knob out and reduced the engine rpm for slow flight. He set the flaps for twenty degrees, lowered the nose to obtain his approach angle of descent. After finishing the base approach and entering the final, he lowered the flaps again to thirty degrees.

The light tan military C-130 aircraft at the other end of the runway had taxied and turned around in a large parking area. He wondered what they were doing there. *Perhaps the Moroccans had purchased the cargo plane from the U.S. He did not see any markings on it.*

There was no need using the radio, because the small tower had given him clearance to land with a steady green light. Wobbling the wings and turning on the landing lights in reply, he lowered the remainder of the flaps and adjusted for the wind from the left and set the aircraft down for a nice three point landing.

He taxied passed the large C-130 aircraft, and waved at the pilots still in the cockpit. They waved back. He continued taxing to the smaller aircraft parking area. Parking next to a line of new two-seated Moroccan white Ayres Thrush, agricultural aircraft, made his yellow aircraft look well used. A very organized display of single and bi-winged aircraft lined the tarmac, so he shut down right next to one. His dirty yellow machine stood out like a sore thumb.

After putting wooden chocks in front and back of the tires to keep the aircraft from rolling, Jess pulled his flight bag out from behind the seat and stuffed his headset in its side pouch.

He stood in the seat, which was a good spot to survey the airfield for his next move. Setting the bag in the seat, he continued to mess around inside it with his hands while checking out the field complex. Finally, he closed the bag and dropped it to the tarmac.

All of these actions were purposeful. Jess wanted to attract attention that would not be missed.

The Cloud Duster hangar and sales business office were along the west flight line tarmac. Picking up the bag, he headed in that direction. His greasy, dusty flight bag was borrowed from another pilot.

Jess swaggered down the tarmac toward the sales hangar, letting the bag bump against the leg of his flight suit. He remembered how the A10 Warthog pilots would swagger while walking with maps in the pockets of their lower flight suit pants legs. The white scarf around his neck fluttered over his shoulder in the breeze, and his goggles were pushed up over the cloth helmet on his forehead. He was putting-on-the-dog for anyone that would be watching.

"Hot pilot, right!" he snickered under his breathe.

Between Jess and the office, out from one hangar, another row of three new models of Cloud Duster aircraft were tied down. One was almost a copy of the T-6 Texan fuselage with the big radial engine, a popular tail dragger. It had one long canopy with two separate slide openings. This tail dragger really caught his eye. It was a crop duster painted canary yellow with light purple stripping along the length of the fuselage. A tail dragger is an aircraft with a landing wheel under each wing and one smaller wheel under the tail. The leading edge of the big engine cowling, the wing struts, the landing gear housing and the wheel skirts were painted metallic purple; and even the leading edge of both wings with the de-icier boots were purple. Jess did not think the boots should have been painted, but they were.

To Jess, it appeared to be a strong structural design with many new modifications. Remembering, *the only common problem flying the tail draggers was the landing of it. Sometimes they really could get 'squirrelly' in cross winds during landings and takeoffs.* Crosswinds cause a weather vane effect due to the large rudder, creating what is called a 'ground-loop', and the high engine torque on takeoffs could cause the same problem. He was willing to bet it would be great maneuvering in the air.

Stooping over and walking under the cowling, he dropped his bag next to a small pool of oil on the tarmac thinking, *that dribble doesn't look bad.* Touching the surface skin of the Cloud Duster aircraft was like nothing else, smoother than silk. Jess reached up and wiped his fingers around inside the exhaust pipe of the 1200 horsepower Wright R1820 radial engine. Lightly ringing the inside, he wanted to sample for oil deposits; and there were none. It was evident there were low flying hours on the engine, because of very little oil leakage on the tarmac.

Now, what was in the cockpit?

After pulling a portable platform stand over to the aircraft,

Jess locked its wheels. The stand was used to reach hard-to-get areas for repair and cleaning. From the top of the platform, he had a good view down inside the front seat cockpit. The canopy was open, so he leaned in. He held onto the side of the cockpit with one hand while shielding his eyes from the sun with the other to see the controls.

No wonder there were so many antennas! Jess thought. *Look at all the radios and navigational equipment! Clearly, this aircraft was built for other than just crop dusting, probably transoceanic flights, too. A global positioning system, GPS, with a moving map display, is installed right in the center of the instrument panel.*

"There's a lot of money tied up in this one aircraft," he whispered. "The instrument panel is full of gauges, dials and meters. There's a color weather scope for IFR flying, and even an INS mounted under the instrument panel between the pilot's knees. I wouldn't want the bill for this aircraft," Jess said, getting off the platform and moving it away from the aircraft.

He grabbed one end of a blade on the three-bladed propeller and pulled it through six revolutions. No oil leaks, yet! Great!

Climbing up on the wing root next to the fuselage, he stepped up into the front cockpit seat. *For short-legged people, that could be threatening,* he thought. Then he stretched and stepped around the canopy that separates the two cockpits, and got into the back seat. Most back seat instrument panels did not have much mounted on them, just essentials for basic flying. But this panel was crowded with instruments. It was a duplicate to the front panel, and everything looked in place, nothing lying loose.

Moving back to the front seat, Jess reached back over the center section of the canopy and pulled the back seat slide-canopy closed. He sat in the seat and made himself at home getting familiarized with the layout of controls and instruments.

In a pouch on the left side of the seat frame, Jess found the aircraft's registration, airworthiness certificate, navigational maps, and an empty candy wrapper with melted chocolate still clinging

to it. That made him hungry for a candy bar. He put the wrapper
back where he had found it.

Wanting to make sure he wasn't about to start a faulty aircraft,
Jess thoroughly read the logbook and mechanical forms, then
reviewed the aircraft checklist for starting procedures.

"HEY YOU!" yelled a deep voice from a loudspeaker at the
hangar office. "GET OUT OF THAT AIRCRAFT!" A big guy at
the hangar was waving at Jess.

Ignoring him, Jess buckled the seat belt and shoulder harnesses,
hunkered down to get comfortable and quickly readjusted the
harnesses. It was a nice seat, felt like the comforts of home. He
looked over his shoulder and saw the big guy running toward him
for all he was worth.

Jess locked the canopy, turned the main power switch on,
turned on the fuel pump, and then the ignition switch. The engine
turned over through three revolutions and produced a belch of
black and white smoke. Then stopped. He turned the ignition
switch again and with one more revolution of the propellers, the
engine fired and a ball of flame erupted out of the exhaust.

Jess scanned the gauges as the engine came up to the correct
rpm. The oil pressure indicated in the green, amps good, vacuum
correct, and temperature low, manifold pressure in the ballpark.
The engine backfired, and a ball of fire erupted out of the exhaust,
and then it ran smoothly. He continued the checklist, increased
the rpm for the magnetos check. Leaving it run at the high rpm,
the engine ran smooth as silk, and then he reduced it to idle.

Making sure the brakes were set, Jess increased to maximum
rpm and added a little pitch to the prop for a good tail lift off
when he pushed the stick slowly forward.

The roar of the engine reminded him of a well-tuned expensive
'hog' motorcycle. *There is no comparable sound like that of a radial
engine, great power!* He smiled enjoying the roar.

Jess did not know where the big guy from the hangar was,
because he had not looked. He increased the propeller blade pitch

on the engine; the backwash of the propellers' wind knocked the guy off his feet.

The wheels were chocked, brakes locked, which kept the plane from moving forward. Knowing this, Jess checked some of the aircraft's responses. He had not planned or intended to knock the guy down, but it added nicely to the big show he wanted to make.

"Play it to the hilt, Jess!" he said with confidence.

In the rearview mirrors mounted on the canopy, Jess saw the guy lying in the grass with his hands over his head. Jess backed down the throttle to idle, pulled back on the stick to lower the tail to the ground. With the ignition and master switches turned off, he waited for the prop to stop churning.

Opening the canopy, Jess unbuckled the harnesses, stood up and leisurely got out onto the wing. He stepped off the wing backwards to a step protruding from the fuselage, and then stepped to the ground. As he turned around, a big shadow enveloped him and a huge fist caught him squarely in the nose. The big guy could not have missed!

Jess bellowed loudly and reeled around blindly, "My nose!" He fell against the fuselage and bounced flat on his back on the tarmac. The goggles felt like they had been permanently planted into his forehead. Pushing up on one elbow, he cupped his nose with the other hand. It was bleeding so badly, he could not stop it with the palm of his hand and fingers. "You broke my nose!" he howled.

The big guy bent down handing Jess a handkerchief, and then lifted Jess up by the nape of the neck with one hand. Jess knew he would be hung if his feet came off the ground.

Laughing, the big guy said, "This isn't your plane! Sorry about your nose, but I had to stop you from leaving. My boss wants to talk to you."

Jess' eyes were watering so much he could not open them. Blood had drained down his throat, and he began choking. He coughed up a chunk of blood and spit it in the grass. The big guy released his grip on Jess' neck, dropping him to his feet. Jess' knees almost buckled beneath him. He could feel his face swelling and becoming numb to the touch. His nose, which felt like it was spread all across his face, continued to bleed.

With his hands guarding his face from another blow, Jess backed away from the big man. He could not see to protect himself and banged his right hip into the edge of the flaps on the wing.

Rubbing his hip, he muttered, "Those darn sharp edges hurt. Hold on a minute! I can't see a thing," he said, getting sick to his stomach. "I couldn't leave now, even if I wanted to. Dang it all! You sure caught me off guard!"

"Hey! I didn't hit you that hard. You just walked into my fist," the big guy said with a little chuckle.

Jess stood there with one hand over his nose, eyes watering like mad, and the other hand shielding his face from the sun.

The big guy reached for Jess' wrist, "Hold onto my belt. I'll lead the way."

"Yes, sir! Lead the way." Jess grabbed for the back of the guy's belt. As they walked, the jarring of Jess' boots on the tarmac caused his head to hurt. Moaning, he grit his teeth and demanded, "Slow down!" He yanked on the belt, but it was like a toy poodle pulling on a rope around a Brahma bull's neck. It did not slow the man at all.

"Is that your flight bag under the nose of the yellow duster?" the man asked.

"Yes!"

"I'll get it after you talk to the boss," he said sternly.

"Man, I'm getting too old for this rough stuff," Jess said, trying to control the bleeding. He was getting a fierce headache, and his stomach was beginning to churn. He was also getting mad.

"You did not have to hit him!" came an angry voice that Jess recognized. "He is my pilot! Now, he can not fly today!" J.J. ran over to Jess and grabbed his arm. "Let me look at you. My God, SAM, you are a mess!" Jess' beard was soaked with blood and started to stink from the heat. "Your nose is broken. Here, SAM! Sit down on this bench in the shade," she said sternly, guiding him over to it inside the hangar door entrance. Jess slowly and carefully sat down.

"No kidding, Dick Tracy! I could have told you that!" Jess said as J.J. lifted his bloody, bearded chin. "Anybody got a couple of aspirin? My head is split open! And, I need some water to wash my mouth out!"

"Yes, I have some aspirin in my purse," she said, "but I should not give them to you while you are still bleeding. They may thin your blood too much." Putting her hand behind his head, "Lean your head back on the top of the bench so I can put my wind-breaker under it for a cushion. Be right back."

"Yes ma'am, whatever you say," Jess said trying to calm down.

"Sorry I hit you so hard," said the big guy. "Do you have a contract to crop dust around here?"

"I did! My boss was buying a plane here for me to fly for her." Jess held his hands over his eyes. "Damn, it hurts! I need some air!"

"Hey, Charlie! Bring that floor fan over here!" yelled the big guy.

Jess felt the cool breeze from it, and a moment later, he heard J.J. running back to him.

"Here we go," she said, stepping in front of him, blocking the wind. "I have a washcloth, water, and some ice in a towel. Let me clean you off. Lean over a little and put your chin in my hand." She began wiping off the blood from around his nose and off his eyelids. Bending closer to Jess' ear, she whispered, "Why am I always elected to clean the blood off of you?" The fan noise covered their conversation.

"Because you're so great at it."

"This may hurt," she said again, removing the goggles and cloth helmet. She pushed his chin up to look at the inside of his nose. "A Band-Aid will take care of that cut, but your nose bone is shattered. That is were all the blood came from, way up inside your nose. It will take awhile to heal."

J.J. discussed with Jess and the maintenance chief who hit him, as to what needed to be done on the older aircraft Jess had flown in. A couple of their maintenance crew began pulling it to the hangar for an inspection.

"He sure bleeds easy," the big guy said.

"No! You just hit me at the right spot," Jess said with his hand over J.J.'s, on his nose. "Okay, I'll be all right for now. Thanks J.J." He held her hand away from his nose.

"It can not be all that bad, SAM. A little cut like that with a broken nose. I can not feel a thing!" she teased in her Australian accent, placing a tin cup in his hand. "Here is a cup of water."

"Sam?" The big guy began to laugh, "So that's your name, hotshot? Small name for a small man." He walked away.

"J.J., where did he go?" Jess asked, trying to stand.

"He went in the office. Now will you please calm down? You are not in condition to tangle with anybody," she said sharply. "For someone who has a low threshold of pain, you are sure anxious for a fight."

"Okay! Okay! Just bluffing!" Jess said. "Anyone else around?"

"No!"

"That was quick thinking with the name," he whispered to J.J. "We slipped up on that one. Where did you get the name?"

"You ask too many questions, SAM!" she said, pressing his head back onto the top of the bench. "Keep your face looking up. It will help stop the bleeding. Do not open your eyes. Let them rest while you can. Try to keep from swallowing blood that drains down your throat. Spit it out in this towel that is over your shoulder." She patted it.

"You are a sweet talker! You could talk me into almost anything. What next?"

"First things first. Let me finish taking care of you, and we will come up with something of a contingency plan. The paperwork is completed on the aircraft swap."

J.J. tenderly washed Jess' face, forehead and beard again. He was thinking, *She's quite a lady! She always has to patch me up,* "That feels almost as good as rubbing my feet at the hospital," he said. "And . . ."

She interrupted him with a jab in the ribs with her fist. "Shush!"

Jess tried to open his sticky eyelids; they were crusted with blood. J.J. gently washed them until he could open them completely.

"You sure look good!" Jess said.

She smiled and nodded, ignoring him. "On the surface, I do not see any problems. The swelling is down enough for me to see your eyes. They are, of course, blood shot and you are going to have two black patches around them." Smiling broadly, she added, "An old-fashioned shiner!" She stood up, leaned over to Jess, and whispered, "Now listen to me. We have the hook baited, and the little fish are about to bite. Then the bigger fish are next. Your act was really good. Thanks!" Walking away from him, she shouted for others to hear, "I'll try to make different arrangements."

J.J. walked further into the hangar, and he heard a screen door open and bang shut. Jess was thinking he would never live this down, once J.J. told Bushta, Samain and Aliba.

He dozed off in the cool of the hangar, and was awakened by J.J.'s voice.

"Larry Hastings, this is my pilot, Sam Jones."

"Sam, don't get up!" Hastings said as Jess removed the iced towel and slowly sat up straight.

Jess extended a hand to shake, wondering if Hastings would recognize him. It had been many years ago since they had seen each other.

"Looks like you ran into a brick wall," Hastings said.

"You're right! He was ten feet tall and about four hundred pounds of wall," Jess replied.

"That was my chief mechanic, Eric Johnston." Hastings spoke with a deep Southern accent. "He's a good mechanic and pilot, and can fix anything that flies! Eric's been with me for about six months."

"What about this?" Jess asked, pointing to his nose. "Can he fix what he breaks?"

"I'll take care of that," J.J. said. "We should be going now. Can you stand up without being dizzy?"

"Let's find out," Jess said, standing up slowly. "Just a throbbing

head pain when I stand. Hold on just a minute! It will go away!"
He reached for the bench to steady him. Bright sunlight reflected
off the hangar floor through the opened doors. "Sunglasses would
help," he complained.

She offered her arm, and Hastings stepped toward Jess to offer
his support.

"Thanks, but I have him," J.J. said putting her arm around
Jess' waist and pulling his arm over her shoulder.

Shielding his eyes from the bright sunlight, Jess said, "I can
stand by myself," as he easily pushed away from J.J.'s support.

"I just need sunglasses from my flight bag. But, I don't know
what the big guy, Eric, did with it."

"Please let me give you some support," J.J. offered holding
onto his hand.

"Thanks, I'll be all right."

"You're an American, too?" Hastings asked.

"Yes, Texan! To be politically correct, I'm a Texas-American."
Jess thought, *Might as well get that out of the way. Anyway, nothing
like a proud Texan. I couldn't hide my accent.*

"I'll get your bag for you, Sam," Hastings said. "Where would
it be?"

Jess pointed to the plane, "It's under the nose of the first yellow
aircraft."

Hastings went to the flight line with Eric following halfway.

"Maybe he will look through your bag and see your fake log
books," J.J. said. "Yeah! He is looking in your bag. Great!"

They watched the two return, when J.J. squeezed Jess' arm.

Hastings held the sunglasses and bag out to Jess, "Sorry about
the problem with your nose, but you asked for it. The way you
jumped into my aircraft, we had to stop you some way."

"I know that now! I just couldn't keep my hands off that yellow
paint job," Jess said, nodding. "I guess we'd better go, before I get
into more trouble."

J.J. tightened her arm around his waist and gave him another
tug. Over her shoulder, she said, "Mr. Hastings, would you have

my new plane flown over for me? Sam is not flying for the rest of this week."

"Sure, no problem. About zero eight hundred, tomorrow morning?"

"We will be waiting," she said.

When they were out of earshot, Hastings said, "Now, that looks more like 'lovers' to me, not pilot and boss!" He snorted while he tried to laugh. "She's a good looker, plus, I can't see what she likes about him."

Eric replied, "Naw, she doesn't impress me to be that type of woman. She just cares about her pilot not being able to fly."

Hastings just said something under his breath and walked toward his office. Eric joined his crew checking out the aircraft that Jess had brought in for trade.

J.J. and Jess started out of the hangar door toward the parking lot, when it occurred to Jess. "What plane did you trade for?"

J.J. didn't answer right away. They had reached her car, and she opened the passenger's door. "Now, we have to rearrange a few plans on the way back. I'll drive!"

The tan C-130 aircraft parked at the end of the airport in the 'holding area' next to the active runway began taxing toward the hangars on a parallel taxiway. Two of its four turboprop engines were running, and the back loading ramp began to lower. It had been there since Jess landed earlier.

It was only after they reached a smooth road, that Jess took a deep breath and rested his head on the back of the seat. He needed a good shower or a long soaking in a tub. The stench of blood in his beard was overwhelming, but the wind from the open window helped a little.

"Which plane did we buy, you asked?" J.J. started laughing. "It was the nice yellow one you tried to steal!"

"Really? Great choice," he said, "But! I wasn't trying to steal it. I was just trying to attract attention, like a hot-jock pilot would. Had I known Eric would be breaking my nose . . . if I had known what he would do, I would have . . . well, I would have!"

CHAPTER THIRTEEN

"They should arrive in less than an hour from Kenitra," Samain said to Bushta. "Jess and J.J. have become good actors in this operation."

The two men were waiting at a small private airfield north of the city of Meknes, a short distance from the olive groves at the ruins near Volubilis. Both men were restless. Sitting on the hood of the Hummer, they squinted when looking into the west for any sign of an aircraft.

Samain lit two cigarettes and handed one to Bushta. Bushta placed it in the corner of his mouth and took a deep draw. He then went around behind the vehicle and relieved himself.

From the rear of the vehicle Bushta spoke loud enough for Samain to hear, "Jess will fly above J.J. on the road. You know he can slow down to her speed without any problems. Slower if needed. They may not be traveling the main road, where she usually travels faster than 200 kilometers per hour."

It was quiet at the airfield. The only personnel were those in the maintenance shops and two sentries keeping curious people away from the parked aircraft. The wind sock hung limp from its pole.

The airfield looked like a museum with old aircraft in front of the older hangars: World War II, Korea, Vietnam and Desert Storm vintages. All had been refurbished, given fresh annual inspections, and were in good flying condition. They were the property of the Royal Moroccan Air Force.

The two men continued to sit watching in the silence of their own thoughts. Almost like clockwork, they both took out a cigarette pack and offered each other a smoke. Refusing a cigarette from one another, they took one out of their own pack and lit it. The boredom of waiting was getting to them and their patience was growing shorter. Not knowing what had caused the delay of J.J. and Jess' arrival was worrying them. The two-way radios were even quiet.

"How did they get out of Aliba's eyesight?" Samain asked.

"I am not sure they did," Bushta said. "His cousins own helicopters in Rabat." He paused, cocking his head to hear better. "Listen! That is the beating rumble of helicopter blades."

Samain pointed passed the west end of the runway, "Look! Out there in the distance to the southwest."

A dark blue helicopter approached the small airstrip just over a grove of olive trees. It settled down in front of a Quonset hut next to the hangars. Before the engines were turned off, Aliba was out and running toward the two men at the Hummer.

"Mr. Hanes and the nurse coming!" he said, panting. "I wanted to shoot big blonde at hangar. He hit him in nose."

"Who did what? Where?" Bushta asked, looking questionably at Samain with a shrug of his shoulders.

Looking back at Aliba, Samain asked anxiously, "Is Jess all right?"

"Let me find breath to speak," Aliba said leaning against the front of the Hummer. After a few minutes, he said, "I no like to fly. Helicopter no good, no wings!" He pointed toward the helicopter. His two cousins walked toward them with their automatic weapons slung across their shoulders. "I was too far away to help. Mr. Hanes, his beard full of blood from nosebleed. He look terrible bad through my binoculars," Aliba said, all excited. "His nurse took him to the hangar. He sat on bench. Then put cloth on nose and wash his face and beard. She most affectionate with him."

"Aliba, her name is J.J.!" Samain corrected. "Please call her J.J., not NURSE! Now tell us what happened." Samain pressed for a straight answer.

Pointing at the other end of a grass runway, Aliba said, "Ask them! I report what I see. Her car at entrance of airport. She drive fast to get here."

The car turned onto a parallel taxiway and sped toward them.

"The big cargo plane loaded before I come," Aliba continued to give details to Samain as everyone gathered around the car.

J.J. related the story, with Aliba's help, and they all began laughing. Jess was not going to move off the comfortable car seat to take on any more abuse. He was too tired, upset and downright embarrassed!

Bushta leaned through the driver's open door, shaking his head, "We did not teach you how to duck."

Jess tried to smile, "I will next time."

CHAPTER FOURTEEN

"What was all the excitement in the hangar?" Colonel Alvarez asked Hastings as they walked toward the rear opening of the cargo ramp inside the C-130 aircraft.

"Just a little misunderstanding," Hastings said.

He was going to say more, but when they stepped onto the tarmac, the screaming engines of a commuter jet passing by on a low flyby cut him off. He and Alvarez turned and walked back up the aircraft's ramp, holding their hands over their ears. They continued through the cargo bay toward the flight deck area. The noise of the cargo crew taking netting and binder straps off of the cargo pallets echoed inside the bay. They were getting ready to swap cargo.

Hastings and the colonel climbed up a short ladder to the flight deck and sat in seats not occupied by the flight crewmembers. The area had more open space than most large aircraft, but it still was cramped with radio transmitters, navigational equipment, and seats for the pilot, copilot and navigator.

A small bunk bed hung from the overhead at the back of the flight cabin with a crewmember snoring away. The pilot and copilot were in their seats with headsets on and scanning their sectional navigational maps.

Hastings squirmed around in a bulkhead fold-down seat, and hesitantly spoke to Alvarez, "Ah . . . a young woman bought one of my new yellow aircraft. No sooner had she bought it, a crop duster landed and the pilot went over to her new aircraft and got in. He started it, and we thought he was trying to steal it," motioning with his hands. "Good thing it was chocked. Then Eric ran out to stop him, and the back wash of the prop knocked him down."

Hastings was in tears laughing so hard. But, Colonel Alvarez was bored with Hastings' story and really was not paying any attention.

"Eric got up and was waiting for the pilot when he got out of the aircraft," Hastings said. "Once the pilot got on the ground and turned around, Eric had zeroed in on his nose with his fist. Blood flew all over, and the pilot was covered with it, beard and all." Still laughing, Hastings slapped his thigh. "In short, he was my customer's pilot. Now I'll have to fly the plane over to them tomorrow. He couldn't see to fly today with his eyes swollen shut."

All the time Hastings was talking, the overweight colonel walked back and forth on the flight deck. His neat tan uniform was wet with perspiration, and the medals on his chest clinked against each other. His silver winged medal had been recently polished.

Hastings left the navigator's seat to stir the air around him. It was getting stifling hot with no air flowing through the flight deck area, and no air conditioning.

He began following the colonel, taking short steps not knowing when the colonel would turn around. In the limited space of the flight deck, the colonel took up most of the empty walking space.

Abruptly, Colonel Alvarez turned and stuck out the palm of his hand and slapped Hastings in the chest, stopping him. His large mouth and huge ugly slobbery lips held a chewed stinking cigar. His big bulging black eyes emphasized his demands.

The colonel wore a white Arab turban headdress, which brushed against an overhead cable trace, tilting it to the back of his head. Aggravated, he grabbed the turban before it slid completely off. His large black bushy eyebrows pulled back as his eyes glared at Hastings, as if it had been Hastings' fault. He bared his yellow teeth, and breathed his foul tobacco breath into Hastings' face, almost nose to nose. Even though his cigar was not lit, he had been chewing it.

"Stand still! You make me nervous with all that talking. I cannot think with all your jabbering. Sit!" He pointed to the fold-up seat. "Sit, you miserable little man, or I will throw you out of here."

He turned again and tried to lean between the pilots' seats to look out the windscreen. He was becoming exasperated and impatient having to wait for the other aircraft to deliver illegal firearms. His cargo of illegal drugs needed to be off loaded and exchanged quickly and promptly.

Colonel Alvarez moved behind the copilot seat and peered out the right window. Leaning against the backside of the seat and over the right control panel, his eyes narrowed as he looked for an aircraft in the distance.

"This is another cargo delivery overdue," the colonel said. "He has those Cloud Duster parts crates with my shipment of missiles and firearms in them. Half is to be in Oujda tonight and the rest for Libya." He shook the radio operator's shoulder. "Confirm the drop in the Azores. Make sure my people are there now. Tell them to wait until this shipment arrives, or until they hear from me. They are not to leave until then. This shipment will be late leaving here. We wait one half hour, no longer!" Turning to leave the flight deck area, he barked an order to the pilot, "Keep a sharp eye for that C-123. Start the other two engines when you see it."

Hastings followed the colonel down into the cargo bay and back to the ramp. They slowly walked down to the tarmac and out into the grass. The colonel threw his cigar away, and they both lit a cigarette. Moving away from the plane, they looked to the west for the other cargo aircraft.

"Hastings!" Pointing his finger at him, "You make sure your mechanic, Eric, stays busy during the transfer of this cargo," the colonel said. "I do not trust him. He is too curious for his own good. He impresses me as a troublemaker. I have been watching him and his helper."

Hastings motioned for a group of workers in one of the hangars to meet him halfway. Two of them started forklifts and drove out of the hangar toward the C-130. The others pulled a trailer loaded with cargo netting.

He spoke to Eric and pointed to the hangar, "And, when that

is finished, you can go home for the evening. See you before takeoff tomorrow morning, zero eight hundred."

The colonel was chewing a fresh cigar when Hastings went back to him standing in the grass between the taxiways. He walked back toward the C-130 with Hastings in pursuit.

"Colonel, Eric is okay," he said, dismissing Alvarez's concerns. "He's my best mechanic."

In the distance, a trail of black exhaust smoke could be seen trailing a high-winged, twin engine, cargo plane making a long landing approach. The colonel moved back up the ramp inside the C-130 and on up to the flight deck area. He pointed to the hand mike of the radio.

"Is the radio on?" he asked in Arabic.

The pilot nodded affirmative.

Alvarez keyed the mike button, and spoke in Arabic, "Point one and two, see any police? Turn your lights on if you see them."

Two negative replies came back.

He pointed to the radio for the co-pilot to switch frequencies. "Abdelli, can you hear me?" he called.

"Yes, Colonel!" the reply came. "Wheels down, ready for landing. I have clearance to land. I will taxi and park with tail to tail."

"Thirty minutes for transfer!" the colonel said. "Do not turn off your engines! No more time to waste. There is room to park wingtip to wingtip."

After a moment a disgusted reply, "Yes, Colonel!"

"The police are not aware of my shipment, so get in and out fast," he said.

"Yes sir," was the reply again, with a sharp tone of voice.

#

When Eric Johnston heard the C-130's other two engines start, he stopped his work. Walking over to the hangar's opened overhead doors, he saw a C-123 had taxied into position, and transfer of cargo had started almost immediately.

Hastings briskly headed back toward the hangar, and Eric put his camera away and hurried back to the engine he was repairing. One of his best mechanics, Charlie Overly, brought some parts over to him as Hastings entered the hangar. It was too dark for Hastings to see very well, because his eyes were still accustomed to the bright sunlight.

"Boss, you want me to finish this engine inspection?"

Charlie asked Eric, speaking loud enough for Hastings to hear. "It's complete on the aircraft fuselage, and I've put its inspection covers back on."

Charlie was a small, wiry man of about forty. His long brown ponytail hair did not fit the culture. He looked like a typical cowpuncher, always wearing a greasy western hat, even while working. He was a rugged looking individual from Oklahoma with a long nose and tattoos on both forearms. Aside from that, he had a pleasing smile and an unusual horse-knickers laugh. Charlie's laugh would make most people laugh along with him. He was a very likeable guy.

Eric had a sick frown on his face when he turned to answer, "Sure, Charlie. That will work out fine." He walked away after handing a couple of open-end wrenches to Charlie. Picking up a shop rag, he wiped his greasy hands on it, and tossed it to Charlie. "The American pilot I hit has me worried," he said as Hastings walked up to them, joining the conversation. "I can't concentrate. I've got a bad headache."

"Don't worry about Sam," Hastings said. "He's just another flashy hot pilot. He didn't swagger out of here after you punched him." Thinking of the scene again made him laugh, "Anyway, I thought you were going home."

"It wasn't really that funny, not to him," Eric said, rubbing the back of his neck. "Yes, I'm leaving now. I've got a splitting headache. I shouldn't have hit him. I could've grabbed him and carried him to the hangar."

"Head really hurts?" Hastings asked.

"Yes! I'll be at my apartment, if you need me," Eric said. "Charlie will finish up this engine. He needs the overtime."

"Yeah!" Charlie replied. "All the overtime I can get will be great on payday! I'll call you later."

"I'll see you in the morning," Eric said.

"There's some aspirin in the office," Hastings said. "Take that vacation if you want. You guys can swap when you get back."

Eric nodded, "I'll get some aspirin and head out." He walked over and whispered, "Charlie, do call me later! And, keep an eye on what's going on out there. They may be onto us. I do think we are missing our chance by not securing both of those aircraft and searching their cargo. But, damn it, I can't get the authorization."

"You're probably right," Charlie said, not looking up from his work. "But, we can't do anything until you get the okay from the Moroccan Mokkadem, or that government agent, Samain Keime. If it was my decision, I'd shoot the nose gear tires right where they sit. They ain't gonna fly then!"

Charlie was a young mechanic who loved his work. He was single, and a sharp individual. He got his first job in one of Hastings' Florida repair shops after leaving the U.S. Air Force. He and Eric got their Air Frame and Propulsion licenses from the same school in Oklahoma, and went on to get their aircraft inspector certifications.

Neither Charlie, nor Eric, was aware of Jess' cover. They both were CIA agents, working with Bushta and Samain on surveillance at the airport; plus, they knew J.J.

Hastings was their number one man to observe. It was also the third time the C-130 had off-loaded Hastings' cargo onto another aircraft at this location. The Arab colonel was also being tracked.

Eric got in his car, making a mental note to have Charlie get the police dogs to search the new yellow aircraft that night for drugs and explosives. He pulled a portable radio from under the seat. Releasing the lever on the side of his seat, he tilted it back.

Then he leaned his head against the edge of the passenger's seat and closed his eyes.

He could not let himself relax too much for now, so he held the transceiver up to his mouth and pressed the transmit button, "Hotel Two, Hotel One," he called.

"Okay, Hotel One," was the immediate reply.

"Transfer is being made. Is chase plane in the air?"

"Yes! The NATO flying radar AWAC plane is in the north and is waiting over Gibraltar," was the reply.

"I'll let you know when he's off the ground," Eric said.

"Okay, Hotel One."

Eric changed frequency on the radio and called again: "I.P., Big Daddy calling."

"Hello, Big-D," came a female voice.

"Transfer made, pass the word. NATO's AWAC aircraft is on station now. I'll have your plane sniffed tonight with dogs."

"Great! Big-D," she said. "I will expect you tomorrow afternoon. You know our plans are changed because of my pilot. Can you be here at thirteen hundred instead of zero eight hundred? I know you are not feeling good!"

"Affirmative!" Eric said, "Sorry about your pilot! I didn't know he worked with you. Is he an agent?"

"He will be okay. Negative on an agent," J.J. replied, "See ya!"

"Out!" Eric replied.

After Eric had left the hangar, three men forced Hastings and Charlie into the C-130 at gunpoint. Someone also had overheard part of Charlie and Eric's conversation. Also, Eric was not aware that one of the colonel's men had been watching him use the transceiver.

Eric drove toward Kenitra, taking a roundabout way. He passed the huge prison on the south bank of the Sebou River. Driving on the narrow streets into town, he came to the wider busy main street and made a right turn. He slowed and turned into a driveway from the main street between two parked cars, crossed the sidewalk, and then drove through a narrow entrance between two businesses.

An overhead door raised, and he parked his late model white Citron sedan in an enclosed courtyard. The door closed behind him shutting out the street noise.

When the door was fully closed, lights of the patio flooded the shaded area. Two Doberman dogs ran out to his side of the car, and sat down patiently waiting for him. A woman in a blue *jellaba* robe and veil came to the edge of the second floor balcony. She nodded to him as he got out of the car.

Eric was welcomed inside the second floor villa by the tall, beautiful woman, who had removed her robe. She wore a beige European business suit, which caused the blue veil to look out of place. She opened her arms to him. Even though he was a big man, she too, was tall, well proportioned. Her arms almost encircled him. They held each other for a long moment, not saying a word.

She stepped away from him and removed her transparent veil, smiling. "Home again to me! You look overly tired for coming home early," she said.

"Lovely lady, I have a headache! Probably from aircraft fuel fumes," he said to his wife.

She put her arm through his while walking further into their large high ceiling apartment. She sat on an oversized couch with a row of massive, thick pillows and motioned for him to come to her. Moving the pillows, he stretched out on the couch, put his head in her lap, and sighed deeply. She opened his shirt and massaged his chest muscles, then rubbed his forehead and temples.

"Eric, I know you like working on those small aircraft, but how much longer do you have to work for Hastings?" she asked, caressing his forehead. "We should be close to catching him with a shipment without you spending more time at the shop. It is no longer safe for you and Charlie. Our undercover activities still frighten me. More so, now as we get closer to those terrorists."

He sighed, but did not reply.

She changed the subject, "Sweetheart, do you wish to eat early or have a glass of chilled wine first? I will prepare a good meal while you rest?"

"Gina, wine would be fine," he said wearily. "My beautiful wife, forgive me. I didn't ask how you're feeling?"

"Very well, thank you," she said. "I slept late this morning, but was awaken with radio messages for you from Holland. NATO will keep track with their AWAC aircraft over Gibraltar. They are temporarily over the Rota, Spain, area. I heard you talking to J.J. a while ago. You sounded upset."

"Yes! I hit J.J.'s pilot and broke his nose. It has me upset, because I didn't have to hit him. I didn't know who he was, but he got in one of the aircraft and started it. I thought he was stealing it, but he was out of it when I hit him." Relaxing a little, he added, "I will have to leave this line of work, if I don't get my reactions under control." He drew another calming breath. "Why should I let hitting a guy bother me? I've fought five men at one time and busted their heads together, usually over nothing. And it never upset me! I'm getting overly stressed, permitting these small aggravations to get to me."

Eric sat up and crossed his legs. Gina held his left hand with both of hers, rolling his thick gold wedding ring around his finger with her fingers. She was worried about him, and how intense he became on these special assignments. He was only in his late forties, and he had hoped his new job in aircraft maintenance would help relieve some of his stress. He really loved working on aircraft, but the spy business was getting to him.

"J.J. must have scraped the bottom of the barrel to come up with him," he went on. "We have two separate shipments to track out of Kenitra, and he had to cause delays by his actions today. Why did she hire him anyway? He's not in law enforcement?" He shook his head brushing his hair back out of his face. "One part of the shipment was to go to Oujda, and I'm not sure where the balance of it goes; probably in the Western Sahara. I think J.J. will be covering Oujda, and we will take the other one. Hastings wants me to be at the hangar before zero eight hundred, which means earlier than that. We need to have the dogs check J.J.'s aircraft. I'll have to leave for Meknes tomorrow and be there by twelve hundred." He gave her a big smile, "Can we be packed by then?"

"I can go with you again?" clapping her hands with joy. "Yes, I have everything ready, except loading the radios." She jumped up and began dancing around him on the pillows. "But first! I will prepare a big meal for now. You rest and I will waken you when I am ready."

Gina gracefully moved across the carpet to a recessed bar cabinet. Wine glasses bumped together with their high-pitched rings. Jubilantly, she poured one of the glasses almost full of Eric's favorite wine.

When she returned to him, he was sound asleep. She smiled down at him, sipped the wine and set the glass on a small Moroccan hand-carved table next to where he was sleeping. She let him rest and hurried into the kitchen.

Eric was an American with Swedish parents and Gina was from Sweden. They had meet and married at a ski resort north of Aviano, Italy, in the Italian Alps. After working as NATO agents in Bosnia, they spent three years in the Swedish army paratrooper division as demolition experts.

Their current Interpol assignment in Morocco was to keep track of Hastings and the arms' shipments in and out of his business areas. As yet, they had not been able to catch him with drugs or firearms in his hangars, aircraft or warehouses.

The antiterrorist group they were working with knew Colonel Alvarez was transporting across northern Africa, but they could not locate his contacts in Morocco. Their problem was finding the shipments' pickup and delivery points; then stop them.

J.J. had told Eric and Charlie to prepare for leaving the area for a week. Hastings had given them the time off not knowing they were following him. It seemed that the time was right to catch him with an illegal international shipment. They had been hesitant, because they wanted the suppliers captured at the same time.

CHAPTER FIFTEEN

Everyone settled down from the major events of the day in a small cafe in Meknes. They had assembled in the rear of the kitchen, discussing Jess' broken nose and the possible contingency plans.

Aliba, Bushta, J.J. and Jess huddled near a cook stove in the back. When the temperature dropped below sixty degrees Fahrenheit, everyone knew where Jess would be—near the warmest fire.

Aliba's cousins owned the establishment, permitting occasional secret meetings like this one. It was damp and cold that evening, because a cold front blew in from the eastern slopes of the Atlas Mountains. The only heat was from a fireplace in the front dining room and the large cook stove in the kitchen. Jess could not understand why they insisted on meeting there.

Samain clapped his hands for everyone's attention so that he could start his briefing. Finally, everyone quieted down.

"We will have a quick review of tomorrow's schedule," Samain said. "Since Jess has volunteered his 'acting' services with his big nose; we are attracting good attention from Hastings as to our spraying activities. In fact, he may want to spend time with you, Jess."

He turned on the Cappuccino maker behind him; it went through its paces. While it was brewing, Samain continued, "Jess, when Hastings arrives tomorrow morning, portray a desire to get better acquainted with him. You should have some ideas as to how he thinks and what he likes. Whatever detailed information on these terrorists you can draw from him, no matter how insignificant, we will use it. He should know where they have moved their transfer points and how long they will be there. We know you two knew each other quite well, so do the best you can to prevent him from recognizing you. The beard and broken nose certainly helps."

Everyone laughed and agreed.

"Okay?" Samain asked, "Any questions, Jess?"

Jess shook his head, no.

"Jess' code name is Samuel A. Jones, referred to as Sam. He is our major key to this whole operation." Looking at Jess again, Samain added, "We suspect the terrorists know you are around, but they do not know what you look like. As yet!"

Jess thought he had been prepared for this, but now they were right down to the deadline, and he was getting sweaty palms. Most of them had turned to look at him. He tried reading their expressions.

Smiling, he raised his hand and waved confidently to them. "I'll do my best to keep a level head, duck and concentrate on what I'm doing. No more macho man! I will tell Hastings I'm looking for adventure and more money."

No one grinned or laughed this time.

Jess began to realize how much he had become involved in this anti-terrorist activity, and how much they were depending on him. He had agreed to lie, cover-up, or whatever, in order to counteract the terrorists efforts.

With a clear mind, how could he do it? He had tried to keep from lying about anything, until this act he staged.

Yes, he thought, *what about the false front I played and got my nose broken? I certainly had prior knowledge of what I was doing then. It was plain as the broken nose on your face, Jess; a double standard could lead to confusion and danger.*

It was a heck of a time to start thinking about honesty. The die had already been cast.

In the first place, if I tell the truth, I would never have to tell another lie to cover up the first lie. But this may be a time that a false front could save lives. What a dilemma. Jesus, what do I do now? Don't let me be deceived or deceive others.

J.J. stood up and stretched, "Well, gentlemen! I'll give Jess our flying orders in front of Hastings for spraying on Friday, east of Tahala. Hopefully it will be warm with no wind. For now, the weather reports are good for the next two weeks. It will be in the seventies to lower eighties during the day, with low humidity, but close to freezing temperatures at night." She walked to the wall maps; "Jess' eyes will be good by then. Between tomorrow and Friday, three days, Jess and I will fly the new yellow Duster and the Bronco. Hastings will have the Duster here by thirteen hundred this afternoon."

"It is after midnight," Samain said. "Meeting is over."

She nodded and turned to the maps, "We can scout around the areas south of Jerada and refuel at Oujda. There may be drop points for the terrorists near there. That is all I have," she said, and moved back to the warm stove. Jess was not the only one there that was cold.

"Eric and Gina will be here at thirteen hundred," Bushta said. "We should have another meeting here with everyone tomorrow, at the same time."

Jess was surprised with this statement from Bushta. *Who were they? Isn't Eric the one I just met? The one who broke my nose?*

He made a sour looking face. Bushta nodded at him, took him aside and explained that Eric and Gina were both with the CIA and Interpol. Jess was shocked.

"For now, we will go back to the hangar and get some sleep," Samain ordered. "J.J. has bunkroom number one. So, gentlemen, stay away from her sleeping quarters!" Snickers arose from the men.

J.J., Samain and Jess left in the Hummer. They gave him more details on Eric and Gina. Bushta, Aliba and his four cousins left in another vehicle.

Once in the hangar bunkroom, Jess climbed into bed with his clothes on.

Jess did not remember anything until almost sunrise, when he heard someone sneeze. Then, he forced himself out of bed.

The six-o'clock sunrise came too early on that next day, a crisp bright morning. Their late night meeting cut into his beauty sleep. He slowly got up, showered, dressed and headed for breakfast.

Passing the hangars, he saw the security crews were already on the ramp preflighting aircraft. The old converted silver warbirds reflected the sunlight like spit'n polish museum relics.

Six two-seated Thrush spray planes with PT65 turbo engines were in a row and tied down. Jess walked between two of them, heading for the kitchen. They were painted white except for the wing tips and rudder, which were Moroccan red, with a gray stripping down the side of the fuselage. Two Ayres 600 Thrush radial engine aircraft were in the hangar for annual inspections. Jess' love affair with aircraft continued to grow.

Almost to the kitchen, Jess stopped and looked back at the Thrush turbos with the big 1230 horsepower engines. Something was unusual about those turbo aircraft! Then it dawned on him that their propellers had five blades, instead of the usual three or four. He planned to ask Samain about them.

In the little kitchen next to the office, Jess could smell American coffee brewing. He pointed to a cup on the drain board next to Bushta and made his normal morning grunting sound. Bushta nodded for him to help himself.

"As you well know, I'm not much on conversation this early in the morning," Jess said. "I'm better after my first cup of coffee. I can be a regular broken-nose bear this time of morning."

Bushta chuckled under his breath, "Yes! Broken nose!"

They had French bakery dainties that morning, but Jess wondered where the eggs, bacon, biscuits and gravy were? He figured it would be too much to ask for home cooking. The typical continental breakfast would not last long; Jess was hungry. He picked the two largest croissants on the plate from under the plastic lid.

With a mouth full of pastry, he asked, "What's the need for a five-blade prop on the Thrush sprayers? Does it give that much more power?"

Bushta swallowed a mouth full of coffee, and then replied, "Yes, it gives greater power and speed for the amount of horsepower that is available. It helps at slower speeds, plus it is very quiet. We can be on top of illegal opium, poppy and marijuana fields before their security knows we are there. We can spray half a field before they see or hear us."

"Well, I'll be! That's great!"

Just as he sat next to Bushta, to talk more about the five-blade propeller, Eric and his wife, Gina, arrived hours early. Eric was red-faced when they came through the door.

"Folks, we have a serious problem," he said. "Will someone call everyone in here. This is an emergency! I'll explain once everyone is here."

Bushta handed them cups of coffee, and they sat together on a wooden bench, across the table from Jess and Bushta. Eric had the same look on his face as he'd had when he hit Jess. Their eyes locked and he returned Jess' nod.

In five minutes, everyone crowded together in the small kitchen: pilots, flight line crew, government agents and security.

"Eric, what is this all about?" Samain asked in French, while J.J. translated for Jess. "Sounds serious!" Samain said.

Eric stood with the coffee cup in his hand, rubbing his index finger around its lip. Looking at each person straight in the eyes, slowly and deliberately, he moved between the tables, making his way back to Gina. He looked at Jess again and pointed at him.

In French, he asked, "Is Sam cleared to hear what I have to say?"

Samain and Bushta affirmed Jess was cleared for anything he had to discuss. "With top-secret U.S Pentagon clearance," Bushta added.

J.J. translated for Jess. That was sure news to Jess; he looked at Samain and shrugged. He returned Jess' shrug with an affirmative nod.

Regaining his composure, in English Eric continued, "We just found out this morning . . . that Larry Hastings and Charlie Overly were forced on the C-130 at gun point last evening at the airfield. They are being held hostage." Loud talking and chattering started among the crew. Eric took another sip of coffee, and then rubbed the cup rim with his right thumb. He raised his hand for silence,

"My oldest living friend is in their hands. Our info from the AWAC aircraft, off the coast of Libya, gave the C-130's present location at Ft. MacMahan in Algeria."

There were numerous loud negative remarks, all in foreign languages Jess could not understand. But he understood the emotional response.

Samain spread a map on the kitchen-cutting table to get the crease out, and then nailed it to the wall. Eric pointed out the route the C-130 had taken from Kenitra.

"They left the airfield, flew south to Mali, and then back northeast to Libya. It landed near the border of Chad. It must have refueled. Then it took off and landed back in Algeria. This C-130 is the same one we have kept track of these past months. We suspect Colonel Alvarez has both of the men and will use them as hostages for ransom or swap for political prisoners. We should have jumped those two aircraft while they were on the ground together yesterday."

Eric handed the information from the AWACS to Samain and stepped back. The silence was overwhelming; they were stunned with the latest twist of events.

Jess thought his stunt at the airfield must have stirred up a hornets' nest and caused two men to be taken hostage. He cleared his throat and stood up, "Sorry you guys! I certainly didn't expect my little act at the airport to cause this situation. And I thought you were one of the bad guys," pointing at Eric. Jess walked over and stood toe to toe with Eric, looking up.

Looking down at Jess and poking his big finger into Jess' chest, Eric said, "Yeah! . . . And, I didn't know who you were, either. In fact, I'm still not sure!" Smiling and gritting his teeth, Eric continued to press the point. "Your playing around with that aircraft impressed me as another hot pilot showing off. You definitely got my attention. I seriously don't think any of the colonel's crew knew any different. You sure had me fooled." The tension melted as he grinned suddenly and took a step back. Leaning toward Jess, Eric swung his big arm around his neck and pulled him close.

Everyone gasped as to what Eric might do.

Jess was too slow to use any marshal-arts protection and thought his neck was going to break. "Sorry about the nose!" Eric said.

"It's a good thing you're on our side and you apologized to me!" Jess replied. "I was about to clobber you on the chin! I'm not tall enough to hit you in the nose." He winced, as Eric squeezed again, "Not so hard, my nose and head are still touchy!" He released Jess. "By the way, I'm really Jess Hanes, alias Sam!"

Eric looked down at Jess and smiled, "I figured as much. But let me say, I'm the one who dropped the ball. I think they found us out through my lack of communications security at the airport. I'm the one that needs to apologize about them being taken."

Samain came over and grabbed them both by their shirtsleeves, separating them. He pulled them to a couch like a couple of young boys and pointed for them to sit. They did!

By that time, everyone was talking, and their voices were getting too loud for the small room. Samain shook his head, held up his hand for everyone's attention, and pointed at the two he had escorted.

"You two can talk about that matter later. I do not care who is at fault! The priority now is to get both of those men back safely! This will be a tough job for us. All other arrangements and plans are canceled. Hopefully, we will get Colonel Alvarez in the process of getting Charlie and Hastings back.

He moved over to the three computer monitors and entered information into each of them. He ripped off the printer paper and straightened up. Reading the replies in French, he slapped the side of his head muttering something under his breath. J.J. had moved over next to Jess, interpreting for him.

"We may have spies among us. Someone must have leaked information about our operation. Jess, your sporting scene yesterday did not cause this hostage problem. In fact, I still do not believe they know who you are by sight."

Everyone looked at each other with frowns. This was a blow, which caused suspicions to be planted. Who had given information to the terrorists?

Eric spoke first with a smile on his face. "I disagree with the spy bit, and I'm not positive I know what happened. But, I remember one of the colonel's crew watching me in the car while I was using the transceiver. But why they panicked and grabbed them both, I don't know. I've used a radio in the open many times, and Hastings has used one also." He continued to ring the lip of his coffee cup with his finger, "Again, the colonel doesn't have the capability to lock-on to our time-shared frequencies. I don't think they know any thing more than I represented a threat to them."

J.J. walked around offering coffee and tea to everyone, while Samain was contemplating the situation.

"You may be correct, but we still must be careful with our actions and reactions around those we do not know," Samain said, leaning against the wall map. "Charlie is smart. He will contact our people in Ft. MacMahan when he has a chance, if that is where they are. We do not know for certain the fort is their correct location."

"You are right, he is sharp," Bushta said. "Another point to be made: they were transferring pallets. Right?" he asked looking at Samain. "Could there be something on the pallets which caused them to panic, when Eric was seen using the radio?"

Samain shrugged, "We can speculate all day long. So, what facts do we have? Gina, please write these on the chalkboard."

Bushta and Samain stood in front of the large tactical aeronautical wall map of Northwest Africa. Everyone pulled up chairs to observe and listen to the exchange of ideas. They not only needed to bring the terrorists under control, but now, they had Charlie and Hastings to find.

This changed attitudes toward Hastings. Now he was seen as a hostage rather than a terrorist. He and Charlie may have posed a threat to the terrorists, and now they were in danger of losing their lives.

CHAPTER SIXTEEN

Somewhere west of Ft. MacMahan in Algeria, Larry Hastings began to shiver as the temperature dropped. He and Charlie Overly were tied to stakes; spread-eagle on the dirt floor of a small thatched roof hut. They lay on their backs, side by side, with their heads at each other's feet.

The desert had turned cold after the sunset, and both men could feel the change in temperature. They were in need of water and food, which were in crocks on a shelf near the corner of the missing door. At that time, neither of them knew about the life sustaining provisions.

The guard was to give them water and bread, but had not done so. He was outside puffing on a cigarette. They could smell the smoke from a Turkish tobacco that smelled like burning horsehair.

"Sure would be nice to have some water," Hastings called out.

"Hey, partner," Charlie whispered. "Save your breath. If you can't speak Arabic or French, he won't understand you. He'll ignore us anyway."

"I can try. *Parlez vous Francais?*" he yelled. "*Comprende Espanol?* You speak English? . . . French?"

There was no movement or reaction from outside. They could hear other people talking in Arabic in the distance, but neither could understand the dialect.

The thin camelhair ropes cut into their wrists and ankles. Those tender areas began to burn and sting. Even though they had been on the hard ground a short four hours, it was beginning to make their muscles tighten up. Small insects and vermin crawled across their uncovered skin and under their sleeves and pants legs.

Squirming and blowing at the menaces only caused them to bite and sting the more.

"We better figure out a way to escape this hell hole, or these pests will eat us alive," Hastings complained.

"I'm sorry for not complying with the colonel's demands, but I wasn't about to give him any information on anything," Charlie said. "His threat to torture my sister and her children in Florida will never happen. I don't even have a family of my own. I'm surprised he didn't shoot us."

Another hour of silence went by, other than Hastings' moaning, as the insects crawled over his skin. He turned toward Charlie, and with agonizing effort said, "Charlie, I'm the one who got you into this mess. You have nothing to apologize to me for. I wouldn't tell him either, and I DO have a family to worry about."

They heard voices coming closer. An Arab soldier stepped into the hut and spoke to them in English. "What is it you wish to say?" He asked threateningly.

"Water! Please can we have some water?" Hastings urged.

"Certainly! You sit up, I give you water." He laughed and walked out. The men outside began to laugh and went away.

The two hostages continued in their miserable state, tossing and turning the remainder of the night. They did not speak to each other until daybreak.

Lifting their heads, they could see the outline of a distant high wall and palm trees. They were inside an old fortress or a walled oasis somewhere in the desert. The comfort of the sunshine on their cold bodies warmed them from the desert cold night and brought them to life again.

"We need a plan," Charlie said. "Did they search you when we were forced on the aircraft?"

"No! They sure didn't," Hastings answered.

"Me neither!" Charlie replied, "Do you have a knife?"

"Yes. It's just a small pocket knife, but I always keep it sharp."

"I have one of those all-purpose tools in my fatigue pants pocket," Charlie said. "It doesn't look like you can get to yours, either. Can you reach my pants pocket, the one on the outside, along my leg?"

"I can reach the top of the pocket. Let me shake your pants leg. Maybe it will come out the top, if you could bend your leg up a little."

Charlie could only bend his leg a few inches above the ground. He bounced his leg as Hastings shook the pants leg. The tool scooted nicely out of the pocket onto the ground. He carefully pushed the tool toward Hastings' hand by the use of his hip and then his thigh. The knife moved easily across the hard sand floor.

Hastings strained at his bindings. The thin rope cut veins in his wrists as he twisted and strained. The rope absorbed his blood from the deep cuts. Hastings' blood caused the rope to begin slipping on his wrist as he struggled to reach the tool, without him realizing it.

Suddenly, his right wrist and hand slipped through the rope bonds. Reaching across his body, he grabbed the tool.

"I've got it!" he exclaimed, almost a shout.

"Keep it down! They'll hear us," Charlie said, as they heard two voices outside.

Hastings lay back down, placing his arm out in the position it was in. He slid the tool inside his shirtsleeve, where the blood had now soaked the cuff. It almost fell out because of its own weight lying in the warm, moist blood, which continued to flow freely from Hastings' cut wrist.

The two guards could not see well in the hut after being in the bright sunshine. The inside of the hut was dark. They walked in, looked around, and started back out. Then one of them knelt next to Hastings and began searching through his suit coat pockets. Finding nothing, he opened the coat and checked the inner pockets.

He found what he was looking for, American cigarettes. He patted Hastings' left pocket and pulled out a cigarette lighter. Grinning, he flipped the lighter open and grunted his approval. Standing up, he placed a cigarette between his lips and lit it. Taking a deep drag, he held the inhaled smoke in his lungs for a few seconds, and then slowly let the smoke out of his lungs through his nose. Stepping between Hastings' legs, the guard kicked him in the crotch with his heavy army boot.

The guard laughed at Hastings' scream of pain. Stepping back next to Charlie's head, he kicked him in the ear with a backward swing of his boot. Charlie did not move, but Hastings continued to moan from his groin pain and swore an oath at the guard. Laughing, both guards went back outside.

"Charlie, I think he ruptured me," Hastings moaned. "I'll never be the same." He drew a ragged breath, and turned his attention back to their problems. "How do I use this tool?"

No reply. Hastings grimaced as he rose up on his free arm to look at Charlie. Blood had oozed from Charlie's ear opening. He was unconscious.

Hastings began to shake from loss of blood from his cut wrist and became dizzy. He lay back and stretched his arm out on the ground next to the wooden stake. He gripped the stainless steel tool tightly. It was slimy with blood, and slipped from his grasp as he passed out.

The dirt floor soaked up Hastings' blood under the tool and his wrist. Insects were attracted to the blood and the wounds of both men.

A few hours passed when Hastings regained consciousness and slowly sat up. Under his breath, he swore at the insects and wiped his bloody wrist on his pants. That caused the clotted wound to bleed again.

Looking at Charlie's ear, Hastings could see it had stopped bleeding, but he still lay motionless. Hastings grabbed the tool again and put it in his other hand that was still bound by the stake. With his free hand, he opened the multi-tool and unfolded the knife in the handle. After cutting his own rope bonds, he started on Charlie's, while listening for the guards. He could hear no one.

Only after convincing himself no one was close by, he searched the inside of the small hut, contemplating how to escape. How in the world would they get out alive?

He left Charlie where he lay and moved against the wall of the hut. There was only one window with a view to the west, and it was without a screen. He knew it was west, because the sunlight flooded through the door earlier, behind him. Now the sun cast a shadow of the roof outside the door entrance and the sunlight was coming through the window onto the floor. There was enough light he could see farm tools in the corner. He was thinking, *Those could be used as weapons.*

Hastings slowly peeked out the window. He could neither hear nor see anyone. They were not in a fort, but in a small, walled village. The walls looked to be twelve feet high, even though they were not higher than most of the huts and buildings inside. The village was located on a hill, and Hastings could see mountains far to the west. A large unguarded, well-traveled, entrance was in that direction. He could not see to the east because of other buildings.

West toward the Atlas Mountains would be the way to go, if I get us out of here. Their exit out of the village was no further than a stones' throw. *Once outside the wall, which way should we go?* Hastings' thinking was not too clear.

"Don't change your mind now," he whispered to himself. "West! Toward the mountains would be best. That's back to Morocco. Hope I'm strong enough to carry Charlie."

Slowly and quietly, he examined the things in the corner. He could not move too fast, because of the pain in his groin.

"I'll take that ax handle, broken hoe handle, water jugs and a crock of food," he muttered. "Phew! Sure doesn't smell good. Probably spoiled. We'll be dehydrated completely if I don't carry enough water. I'd better take more water than food."

He sneaked a peek outside the door to make sure the soldiers were out of sight. Hastings closed the knife in the small hand tool and put it in his pants pocket. Checking Charlie's left neck for a pulse, he found it to be strong and steady.

He lay down in his spot next to Charlie and spread himself again. He was thinking that he better rest before night set in. What could he do for Charlie?

"I guess nothing right now. We both need water."

His thoughts became jumbled and confused due to the loss of blood and the afternoon heat. Hastings could not stay awake and dozed off mumbling to himself.

"Tonight . . . must do something tonight. Water . . . must get water! We're in the desert . . ."

Hours later, the cold night wind woke Hastings with his muscles aching and twitching. The crawling bugs had disappeared when the cold set in. Charlie was shaking uncontrollably and moaning. There were no lights; no fires and no one talking near the hut.

Hastings leaned over and checked Charlie's forehead for high temperature, but it was cold to the back of his hand. Slowly rising to his feet and moving to the doorless entrance, he stepped outside. Except for the moon, there were no visible lights anywhere and no guards.

"They have left us in an abandoned village," he whispered. "I can't imagine not leaving guards, unless they left us here to die."

He slowly crept around the outside of the hut, looking for any sign of movement. He went back inside to secure the food, water and tool handles, and then to help Charlie. He found two ragged sheets of canvas to use for protection from the sun's heat and cold nights.

After he gathered the items to survive the desert journey, he cut Charlie's bonds and sat him up. Covering him with the canvas, Hastings woke him enough to slowly give him water to drink.

Taking a few swallows, Charlie opened his eyes and nodded for more.

"We've got to get out of here, Charlie," Hastings said urgently. "Can you stand up?"

It took some earnest convincing, but Hastings finally got Charlie to stand, and helped him to walk around inside the hut. He gave Charlie the broken hoe handle to lean on, then picked up the remainder of their supplies.

They slowly headed west, leaving the abandoned village behind.

CHAPTER SEVENTEEN

Three days after the terrorists kidnapped Charlie and Hastings, the rescue teams were ready to fly to a Moroccan village east of the Atlas Mountains. The rendezvous was on the border of Morocco and Algeria, a few miles east of Rissani, Morocco.

The operations at Meknes had been contracted for spraying fields along the Oued Rheris and Ziz rivers as a cover for their activities. If they had found poppy or marijuana fields, they would have sprayed the fields with special chemicals.

Now the five white Thrush turbo aircraft and a desert tan camouflaged OV-10 Bronco aircraft were readied for a rescue operation. A late meeting was holding the team up. They were waiting for approval from the Algerians on the rescue flight to cross over into their country.

Everyone waited in the briefing room. Some tensely drank final cups of coffee before their takeoff, while others anxiously paced the floor. Coffee sometimes caused problems flying, creating the need for frequent pit stops, but they consumed it anyway.

They were prepared for the action to come. The last minute information had been briefed and the refueling at Marrakech had been completed.

Samain was intently looking at a monitor of a computer crypto decoder, reading the message that was coming in from the satellite. He raised his hand with one finger pointing to the ceiling and looked back at everyone, insuring he had their attention.

Turning around he said, "Okay! Here is the new plan. There is still no approval to enter Algeria, but we will leave now, anyway. We will have two separate flights of aircraft, one south to Marrakech, and the other to Fez. Approval will come while we are airborne."

With his pointer placed on the eastern part of the map at the border of Morocco and Algeria, he said, "J.J. will be in charge of the northern flight of aircraft. She and Jess will fly the Bronco, as planned, to Rissani. Thrush numbers one and two, will go with them to Fez to refuel. These three aircraft will take the northern route to Rissani. Pilots in numbers one and two are familiar with the Berber dialect of those northern and eastern tribes, should J.J. and Jess need assistance.

"The rest of us will fly south to Marrakech to refuel and meet our groups in Rissani. We should receive approval for flying into Algeria before arriving at the border area. Safety and security are the reasoning behind two separate flight groups." He pointed to the wall clock, "Set your watches on my mark, fifteen after the hour." For a short pause, everyone watched the second hand of the clock move toward the twelve o'clock mark.

"Mark! Any comments or questions?" There were none. "Okay! Allah be with you. For you Christians, may Jesus protect you. Load up!"

The rescue team cheered and headed to their aircraft. It looked like a flight of aircraft readied for a war zone. It would prove to be almost that, before their return to Kenitra.

The morning twilight had brought clear blue skies to the east over the mountains. At 3,000 feet AGL, Jess' group headed due east for their first fuel stop in Fez, Morocco.

Jess had not been in Fez since the early '60's. J.J. told him about the changes in Fez as they flew, and that he would not recognize the new city. The old walled inner city, the Medina, would be the same, just as it had been for over a thousand years, since 790 AD.

In the flying formation of three aircraft, they changed position and speed with the two white Thrush turbo aircraft. The OV10 flew behind and to the right of the Thursh aircraft, since their cruising speed was slower than the Bronco's.

All three aircraft's GPS indications matched, as did the INS. These systems gave longitude and latitude, speed and time of arrival to the next ground reference, called waypoints. The systems were working accurately, because they matched the visual ground references marked on the flight maps as each plane flew over.

The maps gave locations of high voltage tower lines, locations of railroads, highways and back roads, caravan trails, location and height of foothills and mountains, transmitter towers, and locations of buildings, oasis, ruins, etc. Sighting these ground references enhanced safety and made for accurate flights.

Jess reverted back to some basic map pilotage navigation. He had marked his map with straight lines between each waypoint, and Z's on each line every ten miles of the route. Then at each Z, a mark was made showing the distance from their base and the time lapse, and the distance to their destination.

Comparing that information with the GPS and INS, confirmed their positions. As he found ground locations and identified them as they flew over, Jess would put a check mark over it with a grease pencil. Those marks could be wiped off later. All this extra work helped Jess become familiar with the lay of the country.

The pilot in the lead aircraft was navigating right on course.

In good flying weather, Jess did not like to rely strictly on the electronic avionics systems in any aircraft, especially if he could see the ground and identify landmarks. Over the desert would be different, where there were no landmarks. Then he would rely on instruments. But instruments have been known to stop working or give erroneous information. Like all computers and instruments, if wrong data is entered, you get wrong results.

J.J. communicated with the NATO radar aircraft E-3A AWAC. The AWAC radar crew tracked the transponder signals from Jess' flight of aircraft, which showed up on their radar screens. They monitored the flights progress until its arrival at Rissani. After refueling in Fez, they would continue tracking the flight.

The Bronco aircraft Jess and J.J. were flying was to be used for search and rescue. It was one of twelve purchased from ex-US Marine Corps OV-10A's. It had been refurbished in 1981 to a 'D' model, and was equipped with Radar Homing and Warning System,

(RHAW), for detecting launched missiles and radar. The Bronco's, Forward-Looking Infrared, (FLI), for night reconnaissance and the chaff/flare systems to confuse radar detection and heat-seeking missiles had been removed to give room for cargo.

Three or four heavily loaded paratroopers or passengers could use the rear cargo compartment. In short, they had a rugged little aircraft that would get them in and out of almost any area, with its special equipment and Short Take-Off and Landing, (STOL), capabilities.

The Bronco had the same Garrett turboprop engine manufacture as the two Thrush aircraft they were flying with. It had two powerful modified 1,040 hp engines, for a maximum cruise speed of 288 mph. The white Thrush had a single PT6A, 850 horsepower engine with speeds over 180 mph.

Sitting in the higher observers seat of the Bronco, Jess had a superb all-around view from behind J.J. who was in the pilot's lowered front seat.

The aircraft could be flown from the rear seat in case the pilot was disabled. It had new style tandem ejection seats, which could be ejected in an emergency egress. If necessary, they could be ejected up through the canopy.

Jess did not go along just for the ride, but was going to talk J.J. into swapping seats for take off in Fez and fly the Bronco from the front seat. He had many hours flying it in Vietnam as a U.S. Air Force pilot with the U.S. Marines, and it had only required a short period to become familiar with aircraft again. They had taken care of that during his previous training.

J.J.'s landing in Fez was a very smooth touchdown. Following the other two aircraft, they all taxied into an exceptionally large hangar. The hangar doors were shut after the propellers stopped turning. Jess thought they were only refueling in Fez.

When the ground crew were out of hearing distance, Jess cornered J.J. under the wheel well of the Bronco. "No refueling? What's happening?"

"We are still waiting for approval to fly into Algeria," she said, leading the way. "So we will eat while they fuel. There is a snack bar on the second floor. I will tell you more once we are ready to leave."

Jess noted that J.J. was certainly in shape, because she was not even breathing hard after her fast pace up the stairs.

The hangar was large enough to store four jumbo 747-jet liners. Looking down from the railing of the top stair's platform, the hangar size made the three aircraft look small. They were the only aircraft in it.

Sunlight flooded the inside of the snack bar through windows across the east and south side. It was more like a restaurant than a snack bar, with a beautiful panoramic view of the city and the Atlas Mountains.

In a booth next to a window, J.J. shared plans, which were given to her over the radio. Jess did not know if the other crew knew English or not, but they continued to eat without saying a word. They probably already knew what was happening. It did not take long for her to finish; she was hungry, too.

Jess was satisfied with the two French bread sandwiches and Coke. It was not anything fancy, but it did fill the void.

He wondered if Charlie and Hastings would survive this ordeal. He prayed silently for God's protection.

The waitress told them the aircrafts were fueled and moved out of the hangar. *Refueling in a hangar?* Jess had never heard of such a thing. *That wouldn't happen back in the states or in the military. Don't recall ever seeing an aircraft fueled in a hangar. Of course, it might be done somewhere and safely. Just because I haven't heard of it doesn't mean it's not done.*

Once outside, Jess saw that his concerns were unfounded. The Bronco was chocked outside the hangar in the shade with the canopies opened, along side the Thrush aircraft.

Why did we taxi into the hangar? Jess questioned himself. *I bet we took on some kind of classified cargo. An external auxiliary fuel tank has been mounted underneath on the centerline of the fuselage. That would give us a ferry range of 1,382 miles, give or take a few.*

Protruding from both lower sides of the Broncos fuselage, were sponsons angled downward. These housed two 7.62mm machine guns with 500 rounds of ammunition stored in their weapons bay. Under the sponsons, were attachments for hanging four Zuni rocket launchers or rocket pods, depending on their future missions requirements. Other pylons under the wings could carry AIM-9D Sidewinder missiles.

This type aircraft flew many sorties for support of U.S. ground troops in Vietnam, especially flown by the Marine forward observers.

J.J. was smiling broadly while she and Jess preflighted the Bronco, like she had a secret. They walked around behind the cargo bay, where she slapped it a couple of times, then winked at Jess.

What's that for . . . a loving-swat on the aircraft's rear-end? Jess thought to himself. Then he heard a voice talking to J.J. in Arabic from inside the cargo bay. She nodded to Jess and slapped it again. They had cargo that talked! The suspense heightened!

J.J. pointed to the front seat for Jess, and he obliged her. They buckled up, removed the safing pins from their ejection seats, stuffing them in Velcro pouches mounted on the kick panel next to their right leg.

Jess checked the startup list and began turning on required switches and operating levers, then motioned for the other pilots to start their engines. He, too, started the left engine, then the right one, while J.J. turned on other equipment. All instruments were in their required green ranges.

Jess and J.J. set their individual altimeters with the correct barometric pressure received from the control tower. Then they readjusted the heading indicators with the magnetic compass, and continued their checklist.

While completing their checklist, J.J. explained about the three jumpers in the cargo bay. Then she received authorization for entering Algeria.

Jess motioned for the chocks to be pulled away from the wheels by the ground crew and pointed to the other two aircraft. He taxied across in front of them, and they followed him toward the runway's holding mark. The Fez airport tower controllers had not granted permission for takeoff.

They would takeoff in a three-aircraft formation to head south toward Boulemane in the mountains. *In a few hours we will be on the east side of the Atlas Mountains, unless,* he thought to himself, *we detour and not go directly to Rissiani.*

Because of Arabic spoken by the controllers, J.J. interrupted instruction for Jess on their procedures for leaving the control airspace at Fez, "We have takeoff clearance. Proceed out on the runway. Take us vertical to 5,000 and circle for the others to catch up."

"Roger!"

Jess taxied the Bronco out onto the active runway with its nose wheel on the white line. Stopping and setting the brakes, he was ready. The two white Thrush aircraft followed behind, off both wings, waiting for Jess to power up and head down the runway.

After making a slow scan left to right across equipment and the instrument panel, Jess lowered the flaps ten degrees. He advanced the two throttles on the quadrant forward for a full power takeoff. Propellers set, the nose of the Bronco pitched down from the force of the engines against the wheel brakes.

"Ready back there?"

"Ready!"

Jess released the brakes and felt the little aircraft jump forward as the two engine's propellers friction burnt the air, bit into it, pulling the aircraft to liftoff speed. Even with its relatively light load, the Bronco hit the rotate speed for liftoff in less than twenty seconds. But Jess kept it on the runway until the aircraft strained to lift.

He eased the stick back and the Bronco lifted into the air, smoothly responding to his command. He switched the flaps' lever to its closed position and trimmed the aircraft for low-level flight, to gain speed. The speed rapidly increased, and he then pulled the stick back into his lap and trimmed for maximum angle of climb.

In a tight, sharp, circling climb, he passed through one, two, three, and four thousand feet without any noticeable strain of the Bronco. He began to flatten and widen his climbing spiral up to 5,000. Leveling off and trim, he made his circles wider and dropped the left wing to vertical, holding his altitude, watching the two white aircraft climb to 5,000 feet. Once the two were heading to the east, Jess came in behind them slowing his speed to match theirs.

"Jess, go ahead and take the lead," J.J. said. "You know the route."

"Roger that!" He pushed the throttles forward again and passed over the other two aircraft, and settled down in front of them to match their cruising speed of 160 knots.

Then he relaxed his grip on the stick, checked his heading, altitude, flight control trim, and settled in for the few hours of flight.

CHAPTER EIGHTEEN

Jess had five more hours of daylight and plenty of fuel to fly the two hours to the Algerian border from Fez, Morocco. The flight had been uneventful and the Bronco was handling perfectly. He was getting bored following the planned course and wanted to fly the Bronco through some loops, rolls, vertical climbs and military maneuvers to take care of his fidgeting. He was about to rub holes in the seat of his flight suit.

J.J. interrupted his thoughts about every fifteen minutes with idle chatter, which was all right. She was either getting drowsy or making sure Jess did not dose off.

"Question for you, Captain."

"Yes?" she answered with a chuckle.

"I'm getting bored, so tell me more about our cargo?"

"I thought you would never ask. We will drop them off close to Igli, Algeria. Then we will head back to Rissani. They will be our forward observers on the ground. Our two Americans are with Colonel Alvarez somewhere west of Ft. MacMahan. We will have the other five spray planes spraying poppy fields at Rissani, for distraction, while you and I wait there for further instructions."

"Okay, then what?"

"It will actually be a low-level parachute drop, near Igli," she added.

They had passed over mountains at 10,000 feet in clear skies when J.J. instructed Jess to descend to a lower altitude through the canyons. He really wanted to slam the throttle forward, loop back over, roll around the other two aircraft, and speed on ahead. But, he had to restrain himself from jumping the gun. Plus, his passengers would not like the G-forces.

They now would fly strictly VFR, using visual ground reference points and not relying strictly on instruments, as they slipped through the lower mountain passes following the road from Boulemane to Itzer. They then continued on to Midelf and Rich. Jess continued to check off each ground marker on his map. That broke the monotony.

The western terrain changed abruptly from tall, green pines to scrub cedar and underbrush further east, to barren ground, sand and heat toward the Sahara Desert. The western white water streams disappeared, and the creeks, ravines and gorges became absent of moisture higher into the mountains. Over the divide on the east side, the terrain was lacking greenery and running streams. Very few gravel roads headed out of the mountains. Jess saw only a small number of people on foot and some riding camels. Many of the caravan trails vanished due to the blowing desert winds behind them.

The course flown by the small formation of aircraft avoided big cities and crossed very few small abandoned villages and ruins.

After flying eastward out of the mountain passes, they turned toward Ksat es Souk. They were on schedule.

Maintaining an altitude of 300 feet above the arid land below kept them off most portable radars that could be searching the border. Jess flew through violent turbulent up-drafts created by the rising ground heat, and at times, the flight was like a roller-coaster ride. It was a struggle for the two other aircraft to stay in formation with him. They had to slow their speed due to the turbulents.

"Jess, we better start drinking extra water to keep from getting dehydrated," J.J. said. "It has been awhile sitting in this direct sun, and you have been working steadily. Do you want me to take over?"

"Nope! I'm doing fine, thank you. These up-drafts are keeping me alert. I'll get some water."

They had six plastic quart water bottles in a Velcro bag strapped to each seat. Water always tasted good.

After another hour of flying, the junction of the rivers, Oued Rheris and Ziz, came into view. The other two white turbo aircraft banked to the left while Jess continued straight ahead on course. The other pilots were to land at a small airstrip east of Rissani, where they were to meet Bushta and Samain with the other three aircraft.

Jess and J.J. were about two miles south of the airstrip, and it looked to be a longer grass strip than his map indicated. He could see two small hangars. Samain and his flight had not arrived from Marrakech. The map markings ended at Rissani.

J.J. began receiving details to continue their flight into Algeria. Jess changed to the course J.J. had given him and flew on across the border. He did not mark the new course on the map in case it should fall into the wrong hands.

There were no ground reference points in the desert, and the Sahara was a big place. So, Jess checked their position on the GPS and INS, which matched J.J.'s. They had to fly totally by instrument now. The fuel quantity was double checked by Jess, and it was okay. They headed toward Igli. Somewhere across the other side of the Oued Saoura, they would lighten their load of paratroopers.

Descending to 200 feet off the desert floor, their flight became a rough ride again. The heat from the great Sahara rose from the desert with a rush, and it was a tough job staying at the correct altitude in those updrafts at a higher speeds. Jess decreased the speed from 463 knots, (approximately 288 mph), to 200 knots, (125mph). The slower speed helped control the Bronco in the bumpy wind.

J.J. gave Jess a new heading change after talking to the air traffic control (ATC) in Bechar, Algeria. They crossed the river by going twenty miles south around Igli Oasis, and then east between Mazzer Oasis and Beni Abbes Oasis.

"Thirty minutes until drop time," J.J. said.

The leader of the men in the back responded, "Roger!"

Jess thought, *Well! Someone can speak English.* He continued scanning his instruments and the horizon. He scanned as far behind them to the left as he could, then around to the far right. It was an endless desert and nothing in sight.

Whoever answered in the rear did not talk at all through the whole flight, until now. He told Jess and J.J., in English, about their plans of leaving a special laser marker in the sand for the pickup return. It would be in approximately the same spot where they were to be dropped. The Bronco laser detection system would spot it.

Jess could not believe two Egyptians and one Israeli would work together on a project like this. They had grown up together in Jerusalem and trained together in their separate armed forces. All three were college graduates and had been together many years. They talked about their promises to keep peace between themselves and not let old family traditions bind them in hatred against each other's race. They were counter-terrorist specialists from Interpol.

J.J. spoke to them in Arabic, Yiddish, French and then English for Jess, all in less than ten minutes. Jess was learned a lot from that lady of many talents.

Thirty minutes vanished fast and it was now time to drop their cargo. The thirty-second countdown started when J.J. had turned on the cargo door red light, indicating it was unlocked. Jess maintained 200 feet and reduced speed to 160 knots. He slowly increased altitude to 500 feet.

J.J. signaled and yelled, "JUMP!"

They were gone in a matter of seconds. She activated the door switch, and the door closed and locked.

Jess added speed and circled wide, descending to 100 feet. They watched the three touch down on the desert floor between sand dunes. Each one unharnessed their parachutes and waved that all was okay. Then they began burying the parachutes.

J.J. said something on the radio, and the crew on the ground answered and waved again.

"Jess, keep this altitude so I can get a satellite fix on our position," she said. "Go back over them and I'll set the coordinates in my GPS and INS."

"On my mark!" Jess said as he banked sharp and passed over them again, "Mark."

"Thirty degrees, five minutes, five seconds north latitude," she said. "Zero degrees, meridian."

"Got it written on my arm," Jess said. "I'll insert that info into my instruments, too."

"Great flying! We have matching coordinates with them on the ground," she said. "I will change frequency and tell AWAC."

After she finished her transmission, Jess told her to hang on. He pushed the throttles all the way forward for maximum speed. Pulling back hard on the stick, they went vertical and over the top to an inverted dive. Flipping over to an upright position, he pulled out of the dive and regained a level flight at 1,000 feet.

Jess heard a grunt from J.J. overcoming the G-forces they had pulled.

The blood drained out of his head and went straight to his feet. While puffing hard to force air into his lungs and blood to his brain, a little vertigo and gray vision momentarily blurred his sight, and his head began to spin.

They only pulled 5-G's on that change. Jess thought he might get really dizzy on that maneuver, but his head cleared fast and he did not break into a sweat.

"J.J., you recovered from that change?"

"Yes, no problem at all! I am glad you got that out of your system."

"Hold on, here we go again!"

Making a steep turn on the right wing tip, Jess brought the Bronco around and leveled off, heading west for Rissani. All they had to do was to wait for the three men to get the hostages and contact them. Then they would fly back in for a pick up.

The sun was down behind the Atlas Mountains, casting beams of light above the Bronco to the east. Flying direct to Rissani, it did not take long to arrive at the unusually long grass airstrip.

Using their landing lights, Jess slipped the Bronco down between the airstrip lighting and taxied to their parking spot next to five white Thrush turbos.

That wasn't grass we landed on, just a green paved runway. Jess thought to himself, *Fooled me again!*

There was a camouflaged C-130 cargo plane parked off by itself at the other end of the strip with Moroccan markings on it. Uniformed men off-loaded an odd looking aircraft, but Jess could not tell what it was from where they stood.

Jess and J.J. walked toward a jeep that was approaching with Samain, Bushta, Aliba, Eric and Gina, who had flown in earlier. The two sat on the wheel wells, dangling their legs over the side, without a word from anyone. They were a tired group of pilots.

The driver turned toward a deserted area, away from the flight line. There were no hangars, just low, rolling hills. The ground suddenly sloped down in front of them in the dark, and the driver flipped off the headlights. They had entered an underground concrete tunnel lined with red lights.

The driver parked the vehicle, and they all walked to an elevator. No guards anywhere, which Jess thought was unusual.

Maybe they have hidden T.V. cameras? On the elevator, Jess felt it move up. *I was faked out again. Instead of moving down, we're moving up. Now wait a minute! There are no big buildings above ground. What's happening? We must have gone down the tunnel farther than I had thought. The darkness messed up my perception.*

Through the door, they stepped out onto an inside perimeter balcony with offices and a security post. From there, a huge underground hangar sprawled out before them. It was filled with modern Moroccan military jet aircraft purchased from other countries. The McDonnell Douglas version of the Harrier, F-16 Falcon, F-18 Hornet, Mirage F1 and three other NATO aircraft set ready for use.

Jess had never been in an underground hangar with this many aircraft. He made a fast count of twenty.

There were three elevators for moving aircraft up to ground

level. The elevators were built on the same design as those on an aircraft carrier. Jess wondered how many hangars they had like this?

It looked similar to the hidden bunkers that the Saudi Air Force had in the desert, but larger. *Desert Storm uncovered many secret places in the desert,* Jess thought.

All Jess remembered up topside was the simulated grass landing strip, concrete taxiway, parking ramp and two small hangars.

At the guard desk outside the elevator, they were given security badges with their photos. Looking at his, Jess began wondering again, how much they did know about him. More than he really liked. Where did they get the recent photo of him and all the clearances marked for passage? This was becoming a little bit disturbing to Jess, as well as invigorating.

A fully armed officer in his battle dress uniform, (BDU), usually a camouflaged colored uniform to fit the geographic location, led the group to a briefing room with overhead TV monitor screens.

One monitor displayed the area where they had dropped the three paratroopers. Their position of progress was updated every few minutes, which was a combination of satellite information with airborne AWAC inputs.

The crew was lead to private quarters and fed. It was nice to relax. They were told that Samain and the others would join them shortly.

I guess we just wait for the jumpers to call, Jess thought to himself. There was very little conversation as they all tried to relax.

CHAPTER NINETEEN

Larry Hastings and Charlie Overly wandered west across the Sahara Desert in Algeria toward the distant Atlas Mountains in Morocco.

The tarp Hastings had brought proved to be a lifesaver. During the day, they used it for protection from the scorching sun. Using two hoe handles, which Hastings had taken from the hut, they would stick them in the sand and drape the tarp over them for shade. At times, a strong wind would blow their makeshift shade away, and they would spend precious energy and time retrieving it.

At night, with virtually no moisture in the air, the heat dissipated quickly and was replaced by biting cold; that was when they did most of their traveling. They put on all the clothing they could wear, most of which Hastings had stolen from a Bedouin camp, and wrapped pieces of the tarp around themselves. Since they had no compass, they used the North Star and Evening star for directions. They drank from the water pots Hastings had replenished, but he found no food to pilfer.

Charlie was becoming more coherent and was able to hold a better conversation with Hastings. They decided not to trust the merchant caravans crossing the desert. With the need for food and medical attention, they might have to steal again, which was not a good thing to do in the desert.

Hands could be cut off, Hastings thought to himself, *or we could be shot for stealing. At least we have water for now, which will keep us going for a while longer. Then again, we could be used as slaves. Or worse yet, shot!*

Their wounds had started to heal, but blistered lips and foot sores were becoming a big problem. Hastings could hardly walk without the hoe handle to support himself. Charlie was trying to be of help, but he was too weak to carry Hastings' weight. He was still suffering from headaches, dizziness, and occasional disorientation from the boot kick to his head.

On the third night, they spotted lights in the distance to the west in the direction they were headed. Hastings did not know if the lights were ten miles away, or just over the next ten sand dunes. *Maybe there,* he figured, *we can find a radio to use or transportation to get out of this miserable sand box.*

They sat on the west slope of a warm sand dune to rest. The moon was almost down to the western horizon. Sand poured inside the heels of Charlie's boots where the soles had separated. He took them off and poured the sand out while his mind wondered. He pressed his tired feet deep into the warm sand. It felt soothing to his aching feet.

He thought to himself that he should continue letting Hastings believe he was just an aircraft mechanic. Nodding and muttering under his breathe, *No sense in breaking security here in the middle of the desert, or anywhere else.*

"Hey, Mr. Hastings!" he said, slurring his words, "I wonder if the satellites can detect us down here at night. I think they can if they know our latitude and longitude. Those things are so great, they can read a book over your shoulder."

"I suppose you're right. How can they do that at night without infra-red detection?" Hastings replied in disgust. "Yeah, I know! They have those too, and they're probably listening to us babble-on now."

"I've heard of the infra-red systems," Charlie said, putting his boots back on. "But, I'm not up on those outer space things. Only what I see on the TV or read in the newspapers. They could detect our body heat sitting against this cooled-off sand. Wish I had my thermal underwear."

"You know what you can do with all that wishing?" Hastings asked.

"You know how to pray, Mr. Hastings? It sure does come in handy in tight spots. At least it did for me in Vietnam and Saudi,"

Charlie said. "Yes sir, it sure did! Can't beat talking to the Lord when you're in trouble."

"If I had to pray every time I got in trouble, it would be wasted," Hastings said. "Anyway, why wait until I'm in trouble? God has better things to do than listen to me."

"Well, I didn't mean just when I was in trouble or made a big mistake. I mean praying, anytime, anywhere and for any circumstances, in difficulties or out, for rough decisions or easy ones. You know, just talk to the Lord, like we do with close friends or family," Charlie said, and rested back against the slope of the sand dune.

Hastings sat up on his knees, leaning against the hoe handle. Staring into the bright starry night, he sighed and started to speak. Then he sat back on the heels of his boot. "If I didn't know better, I'd think you were preaching at me."

"Don't mean to preach. Just sharing my thoughts on God's answering my prayers."

"Have you prayed about our situation, yet?"

Charlie stood up and stretched, "Yes Sir! Ever since they took us into that C-130 back at the hangers."

"Really?"

"Yes, Sir! I don't lie!"

They sat in the quietness of the desert night pondering their own thoughts. Hastings yawned and lay back on the sand. A few minutes later, Charlie stood up and stretched.

"Are you ready to hike a little further before sunup? My head's feeling better now."

Hastings moaned and shrugged his shoulders. "I guess so!"

They helped each other move toward the distant lights and talked about things back home in the good old USA.

They had not gone far when they both stopped abruptly, and looked at each other in the darkness. The moon had disappeared behind the horizon of sand dunes.

"Hear that?" Charlie asked, squeezing Hastings' arm.

"Yea . . . what was it?"

Listening more intently, they both strained in the stillness to hear. Charlie turned around, speaking softly, "We have company behind us!"

"I don't see anything," Hastings said, moving closer to Charlie. "Do you?"

"Not yet, but I can smell them! Jackals!"

"Is that what I've been smelling? I thought it was me."

"They must have been stalking us for sometime getting their courage up to get closer," Charlie said. "If we had a spotlight or flashlight, we could see their eyes shining."

"Will they attack?"

"Not unless they are real hungry, or want to have something to play with," Charlie replied bringing his hoe handle across his body. "If they charge, use your hoe handle to knock them off."

The two men stood back to back, waiting for the jackals to attack. They had never had to fight off a dog before, much less a pack of wild ones.

Hastings heard Charlie talking to Jesus about the pack of jackals and he replied with a fast, "Amen!"

Suddenly there was a snap, an arc, like a high current of electricity, then three in a row. A jackal yelped, and then another as the snapping continued. Then it was quiet again. All they could see were small flashes of light, like a static arc, in the direction of the yelps, as the pack of dogs ran south.

"God just snapped his fingers at those dogs, and they took off with their tails between their legs," Charlie said sticking his pole in the sand and clapping his hands.

"You really believe that!"

"Sure as I'm standing here!" Charlie whispered, still intently listening. "That was His answer to our prayers for help."

They could still hear the jackals' yelping in the distance when an arc would hit its target. It was almost too dark to see anything, except the stars and the distant lights to the west. Neither man moved; they held their ground, still back to back.

"Where did that last snapping noise come from?" Charlie whispered.

"Came from back of me, in your direction," Hastings answered.

"The jackals went off to my right," Charlie said.

"I can't see anything, it's too dark. Now what do we do?"

Charlie turned around holding onto Hastings' arm, and pointed toward the lights. "That's the way to continue, don't you think?"

"You're the boy scout, not me."

"For not being a scout, you sure have natural survival instincts," Charlie replied.

That little incident woke them up, which had renewed their strength to continue westward.

But both of them were thinking about what had happened. What was the noise they heard? Was it actually God's intervention? Charlie thought so, and Hastings was willing to accept it that way.

"Thank you, Father!" Charlie prayed. "In Jesus name, for answering our prayers!"

Hastings added another, "Amen!" Then he said, "Do you really believe God made the snapping noise that scared them off?"

"Yes, I do! I've experience answered prayer before, in many different ways. God promised to keep His angels hovering around us."

"You believe there's angels, too?" Hastings asked as they climbed a sand dune.

"Sure do, because the Bible says He has stationed them around His children individually. There were many times, after the fact, I knew the hand of God took care of a situation, because it was out of my hands to do anything about the circumstances. I just prayed, and God worked it out."

"I didn't know you were so religious. I've never heard you say anything about God at work."

"Well, like my Grandmother use to say, 'Live your life before men, as if you were the only one that Jesus could be seen through.' In other words, live your life like you know Jesus would have you to do, and others will see Him in you."

Hastings paused, out of breath, waiting for Charlie to catch up. "I thought church people were suppose to stand on street corners preaching and handing out pamphlets?"

"Some do, some don't! It all depends on where the Lord has you in your life. Like right now," Charlie paused to catch his breath from struggling in the sand. "I'm sharing God's love with you. I could quote scripture to you, if you would like for me to, but I don't force it. If I can talk about God's love and what He permitted Jesus to do for us, I do it as the opportunity presents itself. But, again, I don't force my views on people."

"We don't have anything better to do, and it's too dark to read, even if we had something to read," Hastings said. "So, go ahead! See how long you can remember scripture. I've never heard anyone but preachers quote the Bible."

Charlie began his scripture quoting, starting with St. John 3:16, "Sure, let's try one you probably have heard before, 'For God so loved the world, that He gave His only begotten Son, that whosoever believeth in Him should not perish, but have everlasting life.'"

"Yeah, I remember hearing that! For a mechanic, you'd make a good preacher! What does that 'begotten' mean anyway?"

Charlie defined it as being 'born' and continued explaining Jesus was born of a virgin, Mary; conceived by the Spirit of God, and not of man. He asked, "You ever had anyone introduce you to Jesus Christ?"

"No, but I'm not really interested now. Keep doing your scriptures though," Hastings said. Other questions came and went as the two men trudged over the dunes.

Finally, needing to rest, they sat down on a high sand dune. Walking in sand all night had been hard work for their legs, more so because of their weakened physical condition. They had consumed large amounts of water, even though the temperature had been low that night.

The morning was a beautiful twilight before the sun rose. The cloudless sky was clear and free of pollution. The stars gradually faded away as the two men stopped again and rested against a cool sand dune.

The distant lights they had seen earlier were gone. There wasn't even a sign of life: no town, no movement, no tents, no camels or mules. Who made the lights and where did they go?

In the far distance, the Atlas Mountains could still be seen. They looked to be further away that morning than they did the evening before. The two men were seemingly moving in the right direction. Or, was it a mirage? Had they been walking in circles, or, on a straight westerly course to the mountains? The desert brought many unanswered questions.

Hastings helped Charlie make their shelters ready for the hot sun on the east side of a sand dune and drank a small mouthful of water. They only had a few water containers left.

CHAPTER TWENTY

The three paratroopers, Interpol anti-terrorists, code name of Star One, had been searching for Larry Hastings and Charlie Overly. Starting in Ft. MacMahon, it did not take them long to find the trail of the two hostages.

They talked to a merchant caravan chief and bought information for ten pieces of gold. He told them a large aircraft had landed outside the fort, but it had left. Two Americans where taken by camel to a village about ten miles west of there.

This information was radioed to Samain by satellite. Star One activated their personal locators for the satellite tracking and compared that information with their portable GPS units. When the transmission was received at Rissani, their location was marked and a search pattern was charted. They were to move north of their location to find a trail from the fort to a small Bedouin village where the hostages where taken.

A caravan left a few hours before the Star One was ready to leave. After catching up with them, they purchased three camels and obtained additional information for tracking the two hostages.

That night, the third night, after Hastings and Overly headed west, Star One came across a two-man trail leaving the Bedouin village. No one had been found in the village where Hastings and Charlie had been prisoners, but the trail led the search team to the hut where the two had been tied. The blood-soaked sand and ropes were still next to the stakes. After contacting Samain, they continued to follow the trail westward out of the village.

The next morning they found the spot where the two men had been circled by animals, perhaps wild dogs or jackals, but no sign of an attack.

A windswept trail continued leading Star One toward the mountains. They came across two broken clay jugs in the footprints of the men. The trail had become fresher, which meant the two men should not be too far ahead. Riding the camels, Star One should find them before dark, especially if the two had stopped to rest during the daylight hours.

CHAPTER TWENTY-ONE

At the Force One base in Rissani, Jess had poured more iced tea into his tall glass and returned to the communications room. He had found salty peanuts in bags in the lounge, and consumed one already. No wonder he was thirsty, he was fidgety and could not sit down for very long. Jess was trying to figure out how he could locate Charlie and Hastings faster, because waiting for Star One to find them was getting to him.

"Samain, will all of you come over here a minute?" he said at last. "I've got a suggestion!"

After they had all gathered around, Jess leaned over a large desk with an aeronautical chart of Algeria and Morocco. Jess pointed to their location at Rissani. Putting a clear sheet overlay on the map, he drew a line from Igli to Ft. MacMahon. Then he circled Star One's last position and where they were to be picked up by helicopter.

"Okay, now! The last position of Star One is here, approximately ten miles west of the fort. Our two men are making a straight run toward the mountains, more to the northwest, than due west. At least this is the direction they took from the village." He turned the map around so its top edge would face north. It was easier for explaining that way for some people. "If we take four Thrush and the OV10, we can search low between Igli and El Golea on this line, then turn where these two lines intersect and head toward the mountains."

Everyone seemed to understand what Jess was after and nodded their approval.

"Samain, I don't mean to jump ahead of your plans. I'm just making a few suggestions. I'm tired of just sitting here doing nothing."

Samain motioned for Jess to continue.

"If J.J. or I flew the OV10," Jess said, "there would be room for all five of them, one in the back seat, and four in the cargo compartment. Five aircraft would fly approximately a thousand feet apart, covering over a mile sweep with the OV10 Bronco in the middle as command aircraft. The Thrush can match up with the OV10 for slow flight, which I don't think will be a problem. If it turns out to cause difficulty, we can solve it on the way. At that slow speed, we shouldn't miss any trails or people."

Again, everyone was holding his or her comments until Jess finished.

"We should be able to pick up Star One and haul them to the other two when they are found. It depends on the fuel consumption for loitering time of the Thrush. They may have to return before we can pick them up." Jess took a deep breath, coughed and continued, "Top off fuel in the Bronco and not take the external fuel tank. We can replace that weight with an additional M60 machine gun pod, if we decide it is needed." He looked around, "That's it. I'm open for any comments, good or bad."

He stepped back from the map to give them a little time to take it in, and then he pointed to each one of them individually for a comment. All he received were smiles and thumbs up, until it was J.J.'s turn.

"I think it will fly, but I would rather you fly the OV10 and let me fly your left wing in a Thrush," she said. "You have more military time in it than I do."

Bushta and Samain agreed it could work, but they wanted to check on a helicopter first. If one was available, they suggested it should be used instead of the spray planes, with the OV10. The Bronco would be used for flying cover for the recovery team and survivors.

Samain gave his approval after a Huey UH-1N military helicopter had been assigned to them. Bushta and Aliba would stay behind for backup and assistance with the Moroccan officials. J.J. would fly with Jess in the OV10.

"We leave in one hour," Samain said as he looked at the communication center's wall clock. "The aircraft are ready, and so are we. Set watches on my mark, on the zero eight hundred hour." He paused. "Mark, zero eight hundred."

Everyone gathered their gear and equipment, and got on the aircraft elevator with the Huey helicopter to go topside.

CHAPTER TWENTY-TWO

The OV10 Bronco and the UH-1N Huey helicopter headed out on the rescue flight. Both aircraft were armed to the brim, because they did not know what could be confronting them over the desert in Algeria.

Jess changed his mind about additional firepower and left the external fuel tank installed, topped off with fuel.

Once in Algeria, they were only an hour east of Igli when they got a fix on the Star One crew. They had found the hostages and were secured, but the two were in need of immediate medical attention. It was a good decision to take the helicopter with medics on board.

The helicopter settled down on a hard spot between two giant sand dunes as the five men, two hostages with the three rescuers were helped inside. Frightened by the noise of the helicopter, their camels loped off across the dunes.

Jess and J.J. were twenty-five hundred feet above them, making a wide banking circle. Just as he leveled off for heading back, a light tan C-130 aircraft made a high speed, low pass over the helicopter. Their attention had been on the loading of the hostages, and did not see the aircraft's profile against the desert floor.

The vortex and backwash of the big cargo aircraft caused a momentary loss of control in the helicopter. Like a yoyo on a string, it bounced up and down above the ground. The pilots sat it back down on the hard desert floor to regain control.

"Get him, Jess!" yelled J.J.

"Wait, Jess!" Samain yelled. "Can you I.D. its markings?"

The big aircraft passed from right to left under the Bronco. Jess pulled the nose up, dropped the left wing vertical, and inverted his Bronco in a dive toward the big aircraft. The C-130 climbed from its low pass and turned to make another run at the Huey.

The sun was in Jess' eyes as he brought the plane's nose and gun sight down at the oncoming tan giant, leading its approach. He armed the M60 guns in case there would be a need to stop the big plane. Evidently, they had not seen the Bronco above them as they headed for the helicopter again.

"J.J., can you see any I.D.?" Jess asked. "I have my hands full keeping my sights on him. I'm pulling up and back over to dive on him when he passes the Huey."

"No markings of any kind," she shouted as Jess circled around and continued the dive toward the C-130.

"It looks like Colonel Alvarez's aircraft that took Hastings and Charlie hostage," Jess said. "I'm sure it's the same as the one I saw at Kenitra. Samain, permission to fire?"

"All he has done is pass low, keeping us on the ground. Fire your guns into the cargo area. That will let him know you are onto him."

The C-130 passed over the Huey, climbed and swung back toward the helicopter just as Jess pulled the trigger with a burst of 7.6mm from the M60 under the fuselage. His shots were on target, punching holes in the top, from behind the wings to the tail. He pulled up hard and came back over and dove toward the big plane again. This time, he came in behind and high trying to catch up, but the C-130's 370 mph plus was too much.

Jess made a tight circle over the helicopter and leveled off toward the big aircraft, waiting for them to come around again, to meet head on. They still had not seen the Bronco, but certainly would once it was in their line-of-sight to the helicopter.

"J.J. are you still back there?"

"Yes! Yes! Are you going head on?"

"If that's what it takes to get him out of here! Samain, should I fire into the cockpit area head on?"

"If he is suicidal, you will have to get out of his way or he will ram you, or perhaps dive on us. Has he made his turn back?"

"He's turning, but has not come around toward us yet," Jess said.

The big cargo plane was out about four or five miles from the helicopter and continued a slow bank at 3,000 feet. They were not sure who had jumped them, and it did not look like they would buzz the helicopter again. Jess banked back to the helicopter, slowing down so he could keep an eye on the aggressor as he continued his wide circle.

"Get out of here, Samain!" Jess yelled. "He's standing off right now! We will follow you, keeping an eye on him." He continued, "J.J., there are binoculars back there in the bag on your right. Let me know when it's hard for you to twist around in your seat to keep track of him, and I'll swing around until you can see. He may follow us back to Morocco."

She found them and got a visual on the large plane. "Looks like he is catching up, but staying way out to our left. I do not see any more aircraft or ground support."

"We have him spotted now too, J.J.," Samain said calmly. "We have our mini-guns mounted, so let him pass again. We will both give him something to think about. I have requested an escort for him."

"How did he find us anyway?" Jess asked.

"He has friends with eyes and ears. In case we get jumped again, stay in this configuration. You continue to observe up there, and we will stay low," Samain said. "I think he is being tracked now by satellite. He will be tracked all the way to where they force him down. We will cross into Morocco north of Rissani, in the foothills of the High Atlas Mountains, near Rich. ETA is one hour. We will refuel there."

Suddenly, two F5 Tiger II jets came from behind Jess and up along his left wing. They had Moroccan markings on them, but they were not yet over Morocco. The pilots waved, giving thumbs up signal, and headed toward the C-130. It had turned north toward the Mediterranean Sea as the F5's escorted him north.

"What a welcome sight," Jess said relaxing his grip on the stick handle. He trimmed the Bronco again for level flight and put his arms over his head, and then behind his back, stretching.

"We called our air force on the second pass of the cargo plane," Samain informed them. "Algerian authorities approved immediately."

"Great, Samain!" J.J. said. "I am happy we did not have to engage that big aircraft again. I think Jess would have played out his head-on-run."

Jess laughed and continued to scan the western horizon for any further aircraft. J.J. kept the binoculars pressed against her eyes, also watching.

The cool winds flowing off the mountains hit the hot desert air creating a rough up-flowing turbulence. Jess descended to 2,000 feet above the helicopter, 4,000 feet above the ground. The blue mountains ahead of them had cast shadows toward the edge of the desert. Deep gorges cut through the barren eastern plains and fingered out toward the Sahara Desert.

Over an hour had passed, and the tension that had gripped them both dissipated as they headed west.

"J.J., you sleeping back there?"

"Yes, just closed my eyes long enough to doze off, almost broke my neck nodding."

Her adrenaline was high from the excitement. She stretched, yawned, and put the binoculars up to her eyes again. Suddenly, two white horizontal trails of smoke caught her attention, coming out of the mountain's shadows, on their right side.

She had her mouth open to scream a warning to Jess when one missile hit them.

Jess did not see the missiles; he only felt the terrific concussion of the explosion that was deafening. The force of the impact caused his helmet to bang against the right side of the canopy. His shoulder harness was not tight enough.

The Bronco began a violent downward spiral, as the right engine and wing folded up over against the center fuselage. The propeller blades chopped into the empty cargo bay, behind J.J.. The binoculars where knocked out of her hands and bounced against the instrument panel on the left. She grabbed her seat handles to keep her hands from being flung around.

In those fractions of a second from the initial missile hit, Jess screamed, "EJECT! EJECT!"

Wind whipped through the broken canopy as Jess pulled the ejection 'D'-ring for both seats, hoping J.J. was ready. With another deafening explosion, they crashed through the top of the canopy in their ejection seats, being protected by headrest canopy breakers and the helmets they wore. Their heads were forced down between their shoulders as they were shot out of the Bronco.

J.J. had been ejected up first in an opposite direction from Jess, in a split second delay of each other. The sudden G-force caused Jess to temporarily blackout for a few seconds. They didn't have time to pull the helmet face-shield down before ejecting from the aircraft to protect their eyes and faces from the wind.

After a few seconds from being ejected from the aircraft, he regained his senses and slapped the harness release that freed him from the Bronco's seat, and pushed safely away from it. Jess saw J.J.'s parachute out of the corner of his watering eyes when her chute popped open. Only a few seconds of time had lapsed from the initial missile hit until they were floating down in their parachutes.

The sudden jerk of the chute opening caused Jess to lose control of his bladder. *What a revolting development!* He thought. "I don't have a change of clothes, either! Well, dog-gone it!" he said, feeling the warmth of his urine between his legs run into his boots. *What a mess this will be.*

They were not much over 3,000 feet above the ground when they ejected. The Bronco exploded in a deep ravine, spewing aviation fuel over a large area. The external tank blew, shaking the whole area. The 7.62 ammunition cooked off in the heat, firing in all directions.

J.J. had drifted east of the plane about half a mile. Jess had lost sight of her near a deep ravine when an updraft caught him and swept him into the face of a canyon wall. He impacted with it and veered away, then a sudden down draft dropped him brutally to the ground. The impact knocked him out. Later, he thought his knees had come up through his rib cage.

J.J. had been semiconscious descending in her parachute. Near the ground, it caught an upward gust of wind, raising her off the ground and slamming her back against a boulder. Her feet were only a foot off the ground as the parachute lost its lift and folded over the boulder.

She unlatched the chute harness and fell to the ground, trying to catch her breath. She leaned back against the boulder and pulled off her helmet, then threw it to the ground. Crossing her arms in front of her, she grabbed her sides under her armpits and let out a loud cry, trying to breathe out. She collapsed sideways.

On the escorted C130 aircraft, Colonel Alvarez was so mad his red face broke out in a sweat. The cigar in his mouth was soggy from his chewing it. He was swearing at someone on the radio about being shot at and harassed by Moroccan jets in Algerian air space. He was upset with the two Moroccan aircraft escorting him toward the Mediterranean and shook his fist at them.

He had given orders for his terrorist brothers to watch for the helicopter and two-engine aircraft entering Morocco from the east. Whoever could shoot them down would be rewarded with one million francs in gold.

CHAPTER TWENTY-THREE

The second missile had caught Samain's helicopter in the tail rotor and exploded. The shrapnel from the missile ripped through the fuselage, penetrating the fuel tanks. Fuel spray covered the craft and ignited. Burning, the Huey spun out of control and just before it hit the ground Samain jumped out through the open door. It exploded upon impact, throwing other bodies from it. Dust and black smoke billowed up, hung in the air and then settled, covering the crash area. At the low altitude of 2,000 feet with the helicopter spinning, no one had a chance to jump out with a parachute.

Samain hit the ground flat; face down, from his ten-foot jump from the helicopter. Dazed, he lifted his head, slowly shaking it. He jumped to his feet to run away from the crash, but the helicopter's secondary explosion blew him airborne some fifty feet further up the side of a small rise. He lay unconscious on the edge of a rocky caravan trail with the back of his clothing smoldering from hot oil spray. He was bleeding from the mouth and ears.

Still dazed, he slowly opened his eyes, then closed them and groaned. When he pushed up on his left elbow, bruised ribs made him catch his breath and cough, which only caused more pain.

Finally setting up, he opened his eyes again and blinked, trying to clear his vision. Two columns of smoke, which could be visible for miles, rose from the two downed aircraft. An additional explosion sprayed helicopter parts and pieces in all directions. The concussion knocked Samain onto his back again.

In the shadow of the mountains, Samain finally struggled to his feet feeling the chill of the mountain wind. He checked his body for broken bones and cuts. His clothing had been ripped and burned. It seemed everything was in place, but his sides ached with pain from what felt like broken ribs.

"Help me! Somebody! Help me! Please!" A voice shouted.

On the other side of the burning helicopter from Samain, someone was shouting for help. He could not see anyone for the smoke, but that was where the voice was coming from. Unsteady, he made his way down from the caravan trail toward dried, smoldering brush and around boulders on the other side of the burning debris.

The wind twirled the heavy black smoke low to the ground and sent it back up in a vertical pillar. The smoke encompassed Samain as he held his breath. He bent over, covered his face with his forearm and began to cough, and then fell to his knees.

"Over here in this cactus!" the frightened voice shouted. "Anybody! I can't move without getting jabbed with cactus needles. No wonder they call this God-forsaken stuff, prickly pear!"

Samain's coughing caused him to close his eyes. The pain inside his chest was terrible. He squinted, and through the smoke, he could see someone waving their hands from the center of a big cactus plant.

Slowly getting to his feet, he stumbled toward the trapped waving hands.

"Please help me! I can't get out of this mess, and I'm about to bleed to death!"

Samain recognized the voice as that of Hastings. "You picked a nice pin cushion to lie in. Nice choice!" Samain said and tried to laugh, but restrained himself. It was a suitable place for such a person, he thought to himself. He had no compassion for a man like Hastings.

Samain eased in between the cactus-needled ears, and let the long sharp spikes pierce his clothing, but not penetrate his skin. He tried to lean over, but his damaged ribs caused him to stiffen. Gritting his teeth, he moaned. He grabbed his rib cage with his arms and finally straightened up, taking a slow, deep breath.

Hastings could see Samain was in pain, because trails of blood still flowed from his mouth and ears, and his face showed it.

Samain slowly bent over again and lifted Hastings by his belt, as Hastings put his arms around Samain's neck. Stepping backwards out of the cactus, he turned, loosing his grip on the belt. They both fell to the hard, dusty ground.

Samain was close to loosing consciousness, when Hastings grabbed his shoulder lightly. "Can I help you? What can I do to stop your bleeding? You don't look too good!"

"Thank you!" Samain said. "I needed to hear that report, Doctor! You do not look too good yourself. You have blood all over you!" Samain said.

"I don't think it's all mine! Is it?" Hastings said, looking at himself.

"Yes, you are bleeding from the ears and mouth," Samain said as he crumbled to the ground.

"You're bleeding, too," Hastings said. "Let me pull you by your shirt over to the shade of that boulder. You will need water before I do. But where do I find it in this God-forsaken place?" It was becoming hard for Hastings to move, because the cactus needle poison was making his body swell.

Samain had passed out and could not answer. Hastings got a firm grip on the shoulders of Samain's shirt and dragged him to the shade of a small boulder. He removed his own undershirt and wiped Samain's face and ears with it. Hundreds of small needles clung to his shirt and he had to be very careful not to transfer them to Samain.

The bleeding was not coming from inside Samain's ears. Both had been sliced by pieces of flying metal from the helicopter.

Hastings opened Samain's mouth to make sure he had no foreign material inside, and wiped it with his fingers. A few teeth being knocked out caused the bleeding.

Hastings found his pocketknife and cut a couple of clean strips from his shirt. Then he placed them in Samain's mouth on the bleeding gums and closed the lower jaw against them, so the cloth would help slow the bleeding and keep it from draining down the throat, "Now there! That's the way a dentist would do it," he commented to himself.

Hastings checked under Samain's shirt for other cuts and his legs for damage. There were only small injuries that had stopped bleeding. Samain had huge bruises all over his body.

"How do I get us out of here?" Hastings whispered. It was becoming more difficult for him to move, and he could barely talk from the lack of air. The needle poisoning was causing his muscles to swell, cutting off his breathing.

Hastings took the remainder of his jacket, rolled it with his swollen hands, and made a pillow for Samain's head. He could not think of anything else to do except find water.

"Where do you find water in this God-forsaken barren land?" he said to himself. He had no desert survival training, only jungle training in Vietnam. "But how do you get water out of dry land? I've heard about chewing the heart of cactus, but which ones?"

The sleeve of Hastings' shirt had become increasingly tight from the swelling of his body. He was becoming sick to his stomach and lightheaded.

"I better find some water and help before I pass out too," he muttered, shielding his eyes from the rays of the sun setting behind the mountains.

With difficulty, Hastings managed to climb up on top of a large boulder to survey the area for others who could be alive and to find water. Then he saw the black smoke of the Bronco aircraft in the distance. "Sam and his boss, J.J. . . . did they crash too?" *They were all trying to rescue Charlie and me. Then Colonel Alvarez's C-130 buzzed us, and now this happened. Where is Charlie? Why did God let this happen to Charlie?*

In turning around on top of the boulder, Hastings lost his balance and fell headlong into gravel at the base of the rock. He lay motionless.

CHAPTER TWENTY-FOUR

Colonel Alvarez was met by Algerian authorities at the International Airport, Sidi bel Abbes, Algeria, and was escorted to a military lockup near the terminal building. Most of his men were killed by gunfire when they resisted arrest on the aircraft. A shipment of drugs on his aircraft was removed and burned by the Algerian military next to the airport runway.

That was the report Bushta and Aliba received while waiting for the rescue team to arrive at Rissani, Morocco. When that good news was shared in the control room, everyone clapped and shouted praises to Allah for another drug and arms dealer taken out of operation.

An alarm sounded in the control room from a speaker next to a transmitter/receiver radio. Two officers began monitoring the signal and directed the overhead view of east Morocco to be displayed. An international distress signal had been received by an orbiting satellite and retransmitted to alert stations in the North African and Southern European countries. It was an emergency locator transmission from either a crashed aircraft or a downed pilot, or both.

A sickening quietness came over the control room as the coordinates were fixed. Bushta and Aliba stood behind the controller's desk watching the large overhead monitor pinpoint the signal. It marked the location north of Rich in the foothills of the Atlas Mountains. That was the return route of the rescue flight.

Bushta grabbed the transmitter's hand mike he had been using to talk with Samain and Jess earlier, "Force One, Force One, do you hear me?"

No reply.

"Force One, can you hear me? If you cannot talk, key your radio."

Silence. He adjusted the squelch in order to hear any weak transmission. Still no reply.

"This is Main Force, calling Force One."

Silence.

The control room was a busy beehive of people doing their jobs sending out the report of a crashed aircraft. They suspected both the OV10 Bronco and the Huey helicopter were down; two separate signals were being received from the same location. Bushta summoned the rest of their rescue team and moved to a private room.

Trying to keep his emotions under control, Bushta put his hands on his hips and finally spoke. "It will take the military precious time getting airborne, but we can put the Thrush spray planes in the air now. They are checked out and ready to roll! Who wants to ride along and help out? This will be very dangerous."

All hands were raised, which meant all aircraft could be manned.

"Allah is with us! We go!" Aliba yelled.

"Hold it one minute!" Bushta said. "We have one hour until it is completely dark. We will fly low and straight to Rich. Once there, we will fly to the east and continue to the downed aircraft. We should be there in an hour. If lucky, we will find a place to land and look for survivors."

On the taxiway, Bushta gave thumbs up to the other pilots and their passengers in the Thrush spray planes; then started his engine. They taxied behind him out to the runway and took turns leaving. Flying in a tight vee formation, the five aircraft headed north. Time was running out, for the sun was sinking fast behind the Atlas Mountains.

CHAPTER TWENTY-FIVE

For thousands of years, the wind had collected dirt and dust from the barren hills and mountains, carrying them down through the canyons, depositing a portion of its collection against the walls at each twisting bend.

But the evening was deafeningly quiet, except for an occasional explosion from one of the downed aircraft, echoing in the distance. An aerial view would show Jess and J.J. lying motionless and separated by deep ravines.

Jess slowly sat up. He had trouble unbuckling his parachute harness because he was covered with slippery red hydraulic fluid from the Bronco.

The harness stirred a cloud of dust as it dropped behind him to the ground. Fortunately, the chute did not drag him while he was temporarily unconscious. It had collapsed behind him. There were large outgrowths of cactus around him; he would have hated digging cactus needles out of his hide.

Where's J.J.? Jess thought.

He tried to stand, and felt a sensitive spot on his hip as he rolled over to get up. He must have bruised it hitting the ground.

Sounding like an old man with all the groaning, he stood and scanned his location. *Where did he see her last?* He decided he would be able to get a better look from a hill close by. First, though, he hid his gear.

No need carrying all the extra weight around in this rugged country, Jess thought as he removed his flight helmet, tossing it under a growth of prickly pear cactus. The cracked helmet was covered with red hydraulic fluid. Sand stuck to it as it rolled into an animal den under the cactus. Jess wadded the parachute into a small roll and stuffed it into its nylon chute harness bag, which was soaked with the sticky fluid. After packing it all in the den, he covered the entrance with rocks and dead branches from underbrush.

"Hope there's no critters down in there," he said to himself. "You better remember this location, you may need that gear later."

Making a mental note of the location, Jess started up the hill. He stopped and took a couple of swallows from one of his plastic water bottles he had in his flight suit, and then washed his mouth out. The water was hot.

Kicking up dust as his heavy boots scrubbed the dry ground, he began looking for his survival kit that hit the ground before he did. It had been dangling on a cord under him when he came down. Jess continued up the loose, rocky hill toward large boulders, he could see the seat kit in an outcropping of rocks. He felt relieved finding it.

Jess' side was sore from hitting the ground so hard, but overall, he felt pretty good while climbing the rocky hill. He leaned over and reached down between the large jagged rocks, lifting out the kit. Then he straightened up.

"Aye! Don't raise up so fast!" His loud voice echoed in the hills. Quietly, he muttered to himself, "I better not do that again!" It had caused pain in his head. "Must've gotten a concussion from that missile blowing up."

Rubbing his neck, he strapped the kit on his back and inventoried the rest of his survival gear. The Colt .45 automatic pistol was still in its shoulder holster. The three, ten-round ammunition magazines had stayed in their snug pouch. All four small bottles of water survived in the pockets of his flight suit. The emergency radio transponder was still secure in the vest pocket, along with a military style compass.

"So, let's get this show on the road," he told himself. "Come on, Jess! Get your act together! Turn the radio on and call J.J."

Jess pulled the small radio out of its pocket, turned it on, hoping the batteries were still good. Then he keyed it, listening for a click. It worked and he nodded satisfaction to himself. He extended the antenna and transmitted.

"J.J., can you hear me? J.J., where are you?"

He reset the squelch so he could hear the maximum distance the radio could receive. He could only hear the noisy background.

"Come on, J.J.! Do you have a copy? This is Jess!"

Silence. *Nothing! I'd better get up on higher ground.*

Another explosion from the crashed OV10 Bronco shook the whole area and echoed through the canyons. Black smoke continued to swirl around the remains, climbing to thousands of feet straight up.

That would be a good marker for someone, plus it could be seen for miles. Whoever shot us down may start looking for survivors. I better keep a low profile getting up to the top. The whole rescue is turning into a bloody mess, and I'm getting deeper into it.

He prayed quietly to himself, "What do I do now, Lord?"

After a long climb to the top of the hill, Jess had a better view and a better chance of contacting J.J. He thought he was in better shape, but he was puffing from the steep climb. He could see more smoke half a mile down the mountain from the Bronco to the north.

"I bet the helicopter was hit, too. When I find J.J., we'll have to go over there," Jess said to himself.

He transmitted again. "J.J.! This is Jess. Do you hear me?"

A soft whisper came back to him, "Yes, Jess. Get your damn head down! Get under cover! I can see you, and they will, too! There are five Arab terrorists with firearms running toward you. They just passed me! That is why I could not reply sooner. Turn around, and you will see them. The smoke is blowing between you and them. Get down!"

Dropping flat, Jess crawled behind a couple of large cactus plants growing from under a boulder. The earpiece for the radio was hard to get out of its pouch, and he dropped it in the sand. Fumbling for it, Jess finally held on and stuck it in his ear, sticky sand and all. Then he plugged the other end into the jack of the radio.

Jess' flight suit soaked with the red hydraulic fluid was now soaked with sweat on the inside. His hands were gritty with sand and slimy from mixing with the fluid.

While looking for the Arabs, he stuck his hands in the sand next to his leg, hoping to wipe the fluid off. He was thinking, *They must be down in the valley to the east. If I could see them, I would have some idea where she was located.*

He fumbled around in the flight suit leg pocket for small night binoculars. The mountain shadows were getting too dark for Jess to see well.

"What's that noise? They're right on me!" he whispered, pushing further under the cactus. The needles scrapped against the survival kit strapped to his back, making an awful noise. He thought for sure they would hear it.

The five Arabs ran right passed him and kept right on going. The noise they were making running through the rocks and gravel would wake up the dead, and had nicely masked his noise. They were not silent in their pursuit of hostages.

Jess crawled from under the cactus and around to the other side of the boulder for better protection. They were up on top, looking around. Then they headed down the hillside toward where the Bronco had crashed.

Crawling further around the boulder on a narrow ledge, Jess pushed gravel loose down the side of the hill into a ravine behind him. The Arabs were making so much noise, talking, dodging rocks and cactus; they did not hear the falling gravel.

"They are out of sight, so better move, Jess!" he whispered to himself.

He slowly moved further around the boulder and leaned against the rocky face of the bluff. His binoculars were messy from the red fluid, but the lenses were clean when he removed their cover.

"J.J. where are you? Can you still see me?"

"Yes, but find another spot to hide. I can hear more people coming in a truck."

Jess hurried down the hill toward her. Their Arab visitors on foot could not see him, but the noise of the truck echoing in the canyon was getting closer. He ran as fast as he could, dodging rocks, boulders and small brush. A group of cactus and small trees ahead of him would make good cover.

Again, the survival kit made a shield from the cactus needles as he pushed under them. A sharp pain went through his left ankle, and at the same time, cactus needles pressed through his sleeve into his arm, above the elbow. Yanking his arm away from the needles, Jess pulled his knee up far enough to look at the ankle. It was so swollen, the bootlaces and eyelets were pressing into the skin of his foot and ankle. He had twisted it coming down in the parachute, and the cactus needles had penetrated through the high top of his boot. The needles did not break off in the boot or in his ankle.

Boy, that aches! He thought, rubbing his ankle. "The desert heat is drying me out. Better take a couple of aspirin and a swallow of water!" Jess whispered to himself. He had always found talking to himself was helpful in sorting out things under pressure.

Finding the aspirin in the survival kit, he took a mouthful of water, swished it around in his mouth and slowly swallowed it. The aspirin had dissolved in the water, making them easier to swallow.

"If these Arabs hear me talking to myself, they well shot me on the spot!"

After taking another swallow, Jess took a deep breath. *Anyway, Jess, that's the least of your troubles right now. How can you get to J.J. and find a way around those Arabs? We need to get to the helicopter before they do!*

He set up on his knees to sneak a peek through the cactus. "Listen to all that noise! There it is, an old WWII half-track truck coming down the creek bed. Sure is noisy! Not quite like they are depicted in the movies, when they quietly sneak up on the enemy."

The Arabs had to go around hills to get to the Bronco that would take thirty minutes or so. That meant they did not know where J.J. and Jess were hiding.

"Where are you, J.J.? They can't see us now?"

She stood up about twenty feet away, which startled Jess. He almost drew his gun from its shoulder holster.

Hobbling over to her, and throwing their arms around each other, they held tight. Then, held each other at arm's length. Her face was badly bruised and cut, and her lips and gums were bleeding. Her hands and flight suit were also covered with that blasted red hydraulic fluid.

"Thank the Lord you're safe!" Jess said. "Are you all right?"

J.J. wobbled unsteadily, then lost her balance and fell against Jess. "As you would say 'Let's don't count our chickens before they hatch. We ain't out of this yet!'" she said, trying to steady herself. "I am still dizzy from the explosion. I have previously thrown up a couple of times. Maybe I have a concussion."

"Come on, we need safer cover until it's completely dark. Let me help you," Jess said, putting his arm around her waist.

She moaned, "Not too tight, I have bruised or broken ribs."

He eased up on his hold and let her clutch onto him with her own strength. Even in the dark, Jess could see that her face was white and twisted in pain.

"Jess, where will we find safe hiding?"

"We'll find something!" he said. "I've been wondering the same thing about Samain, Charlie and Hastings in the helicopter. Evidently, they were hit with a missile, too?"

Jess and J.J. stayed in a ravine, hoping to find a place to hide. The two had only covered half a mile, when they needed to sit down to rest.

"There were two missiles coming, . . .one at us and the other at them," she said, gasping from pain. "But I did not have time to warn anyone before they hit. It was like everything was in slow motion and nothing would come out of my mouth until it was too late. I am sorry!" She was almost in shock and beginning to cry.

To keep her from getting more depressed, Jess tried teasing her, "J.J., you talk too much! Save your energy. You'll need it. Anyway, no one could have avoided being hit." As he spoke, he was constantly watching for the enemy, and at the same time hoping to see someone familiar.

They began moving again, still looking for a hiding place. J.J. was beginning to get heavy as she became weaker. If Jess had to carry her, he would need to find some place without delay.

"Neither of us had the Radar Homing and Warning systems turned on for early missile detection," he said. "Who knew they were around, anyway? We sure didn't! I bet they were hand held missiles, don't you?"

There was no response from J.J.; she had passed out.

"This may be against doctors orders for someone who might have broken ribs," Jess said. "But, here goes anyway. If you can hear me, J.J., I'm going to pick you up as gently as I can. The only way we can keep going is if I carry you."

Jess turned her facing him, put his head under her right arm pit, leaned down, put his right arm between her legs, and slowly lifted her onto his back and shoulder. Grabbing her right wrist with his right hand, Jess had her in the old fireman carry. No problem with her weight now, but he had to be careful not to bounce her weight on those bad ribs. His twisted ankle complained, but he could still carry the load.

Further down the ravine, he could see a hole in the wall about the size a man could crawl through. It was a natural opening to a cave, not man-made. Jess rested J.J.'s back against the wall near the entrance and sat beside her. Something at the opening moved, and a desert rat with her little ones scurried back inside, disappearing into the darkness of the small cave.

"They must have a nest back in there," Jess whispered to himself.

He peered inside the cave using his mini-flashlight and could not see anything, then turned it off. He crawled in backwards, pulling J.J. with him. He hoped the jostling would not cause her additional internal injuries. She still did not respond to his questions, but she was breathing deeply and sounded like she was asleep. He looked at her more closely, but could not see her face very well in the dim light coming from the outside of the cave.

He again turned on his flashlight and shined it on the wall next to her head, then slowly moved the light beam across her face. She had a large black bruise above her right eye. Her nose and upper lip were cut, but both had stopped bleeding. He felt her forehead and found that she was burning up with fever.

Jess soaked his red bandana handkerchief with water from a plastic water bottle. Putting the wet cloth on her forehead, he let the water drip down over her eyebrows, and wiped the dust off her face. After folding it again, he pressed it across her forehead.

"J.J., are you thirsty?"

"Please!" came her faint reply.

"Just take a small mouthful and wash the inside of your mouth. Then spit it out and take a couple of swallows."

He held the water bottle to her lips, and she took a small amount. He washed her mouth with the wet cloth. Pouring more water on the cloth, he fanned it in the air to cool it, and then placed it on her forehead.

"I'm going outside, so try not to move. I'll be right back."

Outside the small cave, Jess took a compass, a hand held global positioning unit (GPS), and a map from his flight suit leg pocket. He figured their location was exactly thirty-two degrees, twenty-one minutes, five seconds north latitude; and three degrees, four minutes, fifteen seconds west longitude. The map showed ruins, mines and forts not too far away.

Putting it all back in the pocket, he extended the antenna on his radio again. They had been on the ground over two hours without any sign of rescue, and it was extremely dark.

"This is Force One, calling anyone! MAY DAY! MAY DAY! MAY DAY! We have two downed aircraft! MAY DAY! MAY DAY! MAY DAY!"

He waited through a long silence of static, and then tried again with no reply. Looking at the radio, *maybe the battery is low. Nope!*

The little red light isn't lit to indicate low batteries. He repeated the call and waited. No reply.

He was about to turn off the radio to save the batteries, "Force One, Force One, I hear your may day. This is Echo Triple One. U.S. Air Force AWACS. Do you copy?"

Jess choked back his emotions, and finally answered with a shaking fist in the air for joy, showing his relief. "Yes, Sir, Echo! I read you loud and clear. I'm turning my transceiver 'ident' on. NOW!" Then Jess released the button.

"Copy your identification and location. Save your batteries. We have help on the way!"

"Roger! WARNING! WARNING!" Jess said. "We were shot down with missiles. I do not know what kind they were. Our RHAW system was not installed. WARNING! There are missiles in this area. Copy? We are Americans and Moroccans. Groups of men are chasing us. I will transmit again, when it is safe! Copy my last?"

"Copy your last on missiles in area, and you're in danger. The two Moroccan jets that covered you on prior activity, will be at your location shortly. Force One aircraft are heading your way now. We will advise them of the missile threat! Copy?"

"Echo, I copy. Force One down and out."

Crawling back in the cave, "Thank you Lord Jesus," he whispered, and gently shook J.J.'s shoulder. She did not respond. He set her up, leaning her against the wall.

"Come on, Nurse Elliot! We have to get out of here. Those Arabs may have monitored my distress call. . . J.J.!"

He gently shook her again. Her eyes opened, but she could not seem to focus. Her hand came up around the back of his neck, and she tried to speak.

"J.J., I will have to pull you outside and pick you up again. Do you understand me?"

Her mouth moved slowly, "Yes, I understand . . ."

It is hard dragging someone when you're on your knees, Jess thought. He gripped the survival kit straps around her shoulders and pulled. *Great! She slides easier than I thought across the sand.*

He had backed partially out of the entrance when an explosion erupted above the cave. Rocks, dirt and dust covered them. He didn't like going back into the cave, because the entrance could collapse. But, there was not a safe place out in the open, either.

Jess pulled J.J. back inside the cave.

"Get her back here as far as you can Jess!" he said, shouting at himself and pulling on her flight suit shoulders.

He rose up too far and banged his head on the ceiling of the cave. It forced him to his knees. He bumped it right in the soft spot.

"Damn it!" Jess said. "Sorry, Lord, but that hurt like blazes!" He rubbed his head, wondering why rubbing always seems to sooth the hurt. "Jesus, we're still in need! What do I do now?" He asked out loud while rubbing his head. "J.J. talk to me. Where do you hurt?"

No reply.

Kneeling next to her, he lifted her head onto his lap and patted her face. Her cheeks were cold. It was so dark he could barely see her.

The cave opening was partially shut from the explosion. Jess could not see outside, nor hear anyone above them. He was not going to dig out to take a look, not right then. If that truck was close, he knew he would feel its rumble on the ground. All they had for protection were two handguns, and that was like peashooters compared to what the Arabs must have. The best protection was concealment.

They were cramped against a sand pile at the back wall of the cave. Turning on his mini-light again, Jess leaned on his elbow to feel J.J.'s forehead.

The sand floor gave way under his elbow, and he was up to his armpit in a hole. Pushing out of it, he pulled J.J. away and leaned against the wall. The sand continued to sift down, with chunks of the sandstone floor scooting through and disappearing into the hole until it was large enough for two people to drop through.

It must be deep, he thought.

A nice cool breeze flowed past them from the hole toward the partially closed cave entrance.

Another explosion above them collapsed the entrance completely, which stopped the cool airflow. Dust from the cave boiled over them. Jess grabbed the damp red bandana from J.J.'s forehead and covered her eyes, nose, and mouth.

He pulled his undershirt collar up over his nose and mouth, taking short breaths. Fumbling for the mini-light, he finally found it and turned it on.

When he shined the light on J.J., he saw that dust had collected on the damp bandana, cutting off her air supply. When he lifted it from her, she breathed easier. He shook off the dirt and placed it over her face again.

Jess pulled her over on her back toward the hole in the cave floor, crawling spread eagle to equalize his weight. He flashed the mini-light down into the hole and could see a lower level of the cave.

"Great! It's bigger than this one we're in. J.J., I should be able to reach the bottom by stretching out."

Jess turned her over on her stomach and took the bandana from her face. He grasped her wrists and used her for an anchor, lowering himself until he had firm footing. When he pulled her down on top of him and fell backward with her, her weight knocked the breath out of them both when they hit the bottom. Jess rolled her off, onto her side.

"Sorry, J.J., I know that hurt. Are you all right?"

The fall caused her to start coughing and gagging on the damp bandana. Shining the light on her face, he yanked the cloth away. She caught her breath, and her large blue eyes opened wide. They were overflowing with tears.

"It's okay! It's all right, J.J.," Jess said, pulling her close.

"Where are we?" She squinted, "I can not see with the light in my eyes!"

Jess turned it off, "Sorry about that!"

Moaning with pain, she slowly put both of her arms around his neck. Scooting closer to her, he held her tenderly, not wanting to injure her further. Jess held her that way until she began to relax, and her breathing became smoother.

"We need to let our eyes get accustomed to the dark," he told her. "That cave floor above us fell through under my elbow. Plus, they blew up the entrance. We're in another cave below the other one. The air isn't stale down here, so there's got to be another opening somewhere. Once our eyes get adjusted, we might be able to see light."

J.J. relaxed her grip on Jess' neck, slumping next to him in his arms. They both took a few deep breaths of fresh air. It was nice and cool. He turned over on his side, pulling his arm from beneath her, straining to see moonlight, none anywhere.

"Sorry about my strong body odor," he apologized. "I had an accident when the parachute opened. This stink of aviation fuel and hydraulic fluid doesn't help either!"

"We both stink badly," she replied. "Just imagine what it would be like to sit in a nice tub of hot, soapy water and soak."

"That would be fantastic! But I don't see anything like that in this hotel."

Turning on the flashlight again, Jess searched the cave floor for something to burn. Dried desert plant roots were hanging from the ceiling. He crunched some of them into a ball and used waxed twine from the survival kit to wrap it. He knew it should burn for a few minutes.

"What are you going to do now, Jess?" she asked.

"Well, I saw this done in a movie once. It might really work. We should be able to tell where the air is coming from with the flame of these burning roots. You feel like moving?"

"No! But, we must find a way out. I do not like dark closed-in places. Plus, it is cold and damp in here."

When Jess lit the roots, they discovered a light breeze was

coming from their left. He handed the flashlight to J.J. to turn on, because the roots were not making much light to see by.

Holding on to each other, they stumbled through the small cave. The burning roots only lasted about fifteen minutes. The two wonderers continued in the same general direction where the wind was coming from and growing stronger.

Then J.J. began gasping as if she couldn't take a deep breath. She fell against Jess, dropping the flashlight. She had fainted, so he gently laid her down on the cool cave floor. "J.J., where do you hurt?"

No answer. Her breathing was shallow and quick.

Jess felt around until he found the flashlight and banged it against the floor. Nothing! He opened the cap on the end, moved the batteries around and put the cap back on. There was still no light from the flashlight.

Bulb must be damaged, he thought.

Taking the cap off again, he felt for the spring and removed it. Carefully snapping the extra bulb from its holder, he put the small bulb in between his lips. Then he took the lens and bad bulb out of the other end. After he replaced the bulb and put the old one between his lips, he reassembled the flashlight. It worked! Jess spit out the old bulb and heard it bounce.

"We have light again, J.J., can you hear me?"

Her pulse was weak, and her forehead was overly hot to his touch. He had to get her out of there.

Putting the flashlight in his pocket, he held up both of J.J.'s arms. Lifting her to her feet, he leaned down and pulled her over his shoulders once again. With his free hand, he flashed the light in the direction they needed to go.

Further through the cave, bats hung from the ceiling. It reminded him of the Carlsbad Caverns near his home in West Texas. The ugly bats would come out of those caverns so thick, it looked like a black cloud. They gave him the shudders like wharf rats did.

They reached two openings to the outside, one on each side of the base of a large boulder. They looked good, but low and narrow.

Jess propped J.J. against the wall and checked her pulse at the side of her neck. It had slowed, and her temperature seemed lower. But, she still would not respond to him.

"I hope you don't get chilled in here," Jess said, rubbing his hands together. "I'm going to dig this sand out of the way, so we can squeeze through here. Okay, Nurse Elliot?"

Jess moved the sand easily with his hands, but he was cautious. He did not want to create a cave-in, or cause the boulder to slide into the cave, blocking the small exit.

After about ten minutes, he stopped for a long break. He had worked up a good sweat. With J.J.'s water container, he dampened the bandana again and wiped her face.

Her lips moved. "That feels good, Jess," she murmured.

He smiled, relieved to hear her voice, "Welcome back to the land of the living. How do you feel now?"

"Better! Can I have some more water?"

"Sure, why not? You need refreshment," he said, feeling for her hand to put the water bottle in. "What about some aspirin with that water? It should help those painful ribs. I'll take more for my ankle."

"We both had internal bleeding. I suggest we wait before taking aspirin. It will thin our blood too much for now," shaking her head in the dark. "I will be still."

"Okay, Nurse!"

She smiled and closed her eyes.

"I'm going to pull us up through that hole over there, after we rest for awhile. After that, I'll go find out what's happening. Okay?"

"Whatever you wish, sir," she replied, still sounding dazed.

Jess and J.J. came out of the cave next to the large boulder, where he had just enough room to pull her through. She moaned from her rib injuries. He cradled her in his arms and leaned against the boulder. The sun had disappeared behind the mountains, and it seemed to be getting colder. The sand had absorbed heat from the sun and it warmed their legs. The moon would soon be up.

Jess was thinking about making contact on the radio. *There should be 'friendlies' around somewhere*, he thought, but he had not heard or seen anyone. He pushed the radio's earpiece in his ear again, so his reception would not be heard. Getting shot at again would not be welcomed.

Jess was thinking, *The bad guys who were shooting at us must have given up.* He could not see or hear them, so he took a chance.

"Maybe Samain can hear me, if he hasn't been captured by the bad guys." He operated the radio, "This is Force One. Anyone copy this transmission?"

Nothing, just noise on the airways.

He tried once more, "Force One calling, Echo, U.S. AWACS. Do you copy?"

Silence.

"Echo, this is Force One. You copy?"

No reply. Frustrated, he turned it off.

J.J. began to cough again. The cold mountain breeze was chilling her. Jess remembered that their survival kits had a solar blanket in them; that would keep her warm in the night. He rummaged through her kit and found it!

"Thank you, Lord," he whispered.

"J.J." he said, "I'll wrap you in this blanket, and then I'll get you more food and water. Feel like eating something?" he asked as he sealed the blanket around her. Then he turned on the mini light to check her.

J.J. attempted a smile and nodded her approval. She rested upright against the side of the cave opening and closed her eyes. The color in her face began to come back and she breathed easier. She did not have the burning forehead temperature like she'd had earlier.

After they finished eating their ration of food and water, Jess checked to see if she was comfortable. J.J. wanted to lie down, not horizontal, but against a slight rise in the warm sand. He elevated her head with the survival kit, and she gave him a smile that was worth a million bucks.

He whispered in her ear, "We'll get out of here, I promise!" He leaned close to her to help shield the mini-flashlight with its red lens and spread a map over her lap. "Can you see this?"

She nodded yes, and her eyes followed the light beam.

"The map shows mining five miles away at Ksar Morhel, straight as the crow flies. Then ten miles south are two forts. Wonder if they are still used by the Moroccans?" He shifted the map. "These ruins are only three miles away, but probably not inhabited, which is in the direction of the crashed helicopter and Samain. It crashed on the side of this hill." He pointed to the map. "Beni Bassia is ten miles, but it's over here on the other side of Ksar Morhel."

Jess turned off the light. He was not sure if he should leave J.J. and go look for Samain? If he left, hopefully, he could find his way back to her. Jess was trying to sort out what would be the best move to make.

Letting her rest for an hour or so, would be better.

He decided to go down toward their crashed aircraft.

If the bad guys didn't leave any men behind to guard the wrecks, I'll be able to find Samain, Jess thought. *I've got a gut feeling he's okay. Then I can come back for J.J. . . . Hopefully, these Arabs think we are all dead.*

"J.J. are you feeling better?"

"Yes, much better," she whispered. "But, my ribs are sore and aching. My stomach is not bloated, so perhaps I should take those aspirin."

"How many three or four?"

"No! Too many will thin my blood too much, just two, please. I will be okay."

Jess gave her the aspirins and checked her blanket to make sure she was secure, then felt her forehead again. He took one of his water bottles and placed it inside the blanket in her hand. He lightly patted the Berretta 9mm in its holster under her arm, and she smiled.

"Try to drink as much as you can, without upsetting your stomach," he smiled. "Listen to me telling a nurse what to do! Anyway, let me put this earpiece in your ear and the boom-mike about here." He moved the mike close to her lips, "Softly talk to me on the mike."

"Testing!" she said.

Jess nodded her transmission was good, "Good! Me too?" he replied, into his mike?

J.J. nodded, and Jess gave her thumbs up and patted her on the shoulder. *She'll make it all right,* he thought.

"You would make a good trail boss in the outback," she told him. "And, yes, I will relax as best I can. What are you going to do, Jess?"

"Don't talk anymore, just listen," he said. "Uncomfortable?"

She shook her head no.

"Well, Missy, it's like this," he whispered in her ear. "I'm going to mount my white charger and go for help!" He kissed her on her forehead.

"An Irishman?" She whispered, grinning at him.

"No! I know I don't have a booming bass voice, but maybe a little close?"

"No way, mister! Stop avoiding my question. What are you up to?"

"I'll find Samain or anyone else that may have survived the helicopter crash. I'm going over to the Bronco first to see if anyone is snooping around. Samain may have gone over there by now. Hopefully, the bad guys don't have him."

"You need my automatic?"

"No, you may need it. When I come back and get close, I'll call. You'll know me by Tex, and then if a second transmission is necessary, I'll talk Irish."

She tried to laugh, "Will I recognize your voice?"

"Probably not, little lady, but I'll try! If you hear someone other than me, get back inside the cave. The moonlight will help us when it comes up. Anyway, we could be the only survivors. I won't leave you stranded, that's my promise! I'll be back for you!"

She nodded, "Okay . . ."

Jess crawled away from her to the top of the hill.

CHAPTER TWENTY-SIX

Bushta and his flight of Ayres Thrush aircraft landed on an airstrip northeast of the town, Ksar es Souk, south of Rich. They were warned of the missiles used to shoot down the Bronco and the Huey helicopter.

After refueling, they waited for further instructions from the King of Morocco and NATO. The king may drop paratroopers into the area of the missile firing. They had heard the last Mayday transmission from Jess, but had not received his exact position.

Bushta, Aliba, Eric and his wife Gina monitored the radio, listening for Force One. They all had gathered at Bushta's aircraft and waited as the full moon came up. The sky was clear, and everyone had commented on how bright it should be great for night reconnaissance.

The four had made their recommendations to the king about using two spray planes and the converted sprayer, Ayres Vigilante, in the area of the downed aircraft.

The Vigilante had a surveillance and weapon systems, which were state of the art. It could operate from short, unimproved fields and was capable of seven-hour missions at speeds ranging from 60 to 220 mph. It had four pylons under each wing and could carry 1,200 pounds of ordnance on the inboard pylons, and 350 pounds on the outer three.

Stored on the pylons for this mission were two 50-caliber gun pods, two 2.75 rocket pods and two AIM 9 Sidewinder missiles. Hopefully, they would not be in missile danger, but they had installed a small electronic countermeasures pod to interrupt radar, just in case.

They waited for an exact location of the survivors from the

AWACS aircraft. For some reason, the two Moroccan Air Force jets had not located the survivors. They had returned to their base to refuel, because no air refueling was available.

Bushta wanted to rescue his friends and not wait for strangers to do it. He did not want others to think he was incompetent to make the rescue.

Finally, at twenty hundred hours, 8:00 p.m., they received approval to make the flight to Bouanane. It was 70 miles east, then north to the two old Legionnaire forts, and on further to Ksar Morhel. If nothing was seen, they were to return to Ksar es Souk. The search could take three or four hours.

Bushta and Aliba were in the blue Vigilante aircraft, Eric and Gina in a white Thrush, leaving the remainder of the crew on standby with their three aircraft at Ksar es Souk. Once in the air, they were to stay in touch with NATO AWACS observers to the north.

Flying at 500 feet above ground level, they followed the hills and mountain terrain toward Bouanane. Bushta communicated with his Moroccan Berber tribe's spotters on the ground on special radio frequencies. Aliba monitored Eric and Gina's conversations with the AWAC's tracking team. If the tracking team heard anything, Aliba could let Bushta know over the intercom system in the aircraft. They all wore night vision goggles to help the search.

There were only a few people traveling the caravan trails and highways after dark. The two aircraft banked toward the north from Bouanane and headed for the two forts.

The French Foreign Legion had abandoned the forts years ago, and then the Moroccan government had secured them for outposts. But, Berber tribes actually controlled the area, politically and economically. These remote locations kept the authorities informed of unauthorized crossings along the Algerian/Moroccan border. Trails and gravel roads led up through the mountain passes to the north toward the mining districts.

It was a smooth flight for the two Thrush turbo aircraft. The mountain turbulence had died down, so there was no buffeting of the aircraft by disruptive winds. Flying slower, (140 mph), with a full fuel load, crew of two, and ordnance on the one, neither aircraft had problems carrying its cargo. With the Pratt & Whitney PT6A engine, at 1,376 shaft horsepower and a five-blade propeller, the two aircraft could range better than 500 miles without refueling.

Both Eric and Bushta had more than 1,500 hours each of flying time in this type of aircraft and handled them like they were part of it.

They detoured from their scheduled flight plan and began flying up and down valleys, darting down to almost ground level over creek beds, checking every questionable object. There seemed to be nothing out of place or unusual on the ground below. The two pilots continued talking to each other about things to investigate and valleys to search.

"We should fly north of Ksar Morhel and circle low over the ruins and come back south," Bushta suggested. "That will give us a good view of the mining camps on the east ridges."

Eric had just taken a bite of a sandwich, "Sure! That's fine with us." He smacked his lips close to the boom-mike.

"I couldn't wait any longer, I'm hungry."

"That is a good idea. If you are hungry, eat now," Bushta said, as he and Aliba opened their zip-lock bags.

It was a good thing Gina had prepared for the trip. She knew there would be three hungry guys on her hands before they returned.

Soon after they finished eating, they made their first pass over Ksar Morhel toward the ruins.

"Not much excitement in that little place," Gina said.

"Right, even the streets are rolled up," Eric replied with a chuckle.

"What is rolled up? I did not see!" Aliba asked as he strained to see what Eric had seen.

"Aliba, that is an American expression," replied Gina. "It means, no one is out on the streets, and the lights are turned off."

"Okay, thank you," he said, shaking his head.

The American AWACS aircraft gave them Jess' co-ordinates, which caused a shout from Aliba in Arabic, "Allah, be praised!"

"I'll bank right and you go left in the valley at the ruins," Bushta said. "Go two miles and come back. Meet us over the ruins where Jess' co-ordinates are."

"See ya!"

The two pilots broke away from each other, one headed east and the other west down through the valley. They made their two-mile runs and headed back to the ruins. At the slow speed they were flying, they would spot anything moving.

"Bushta! Turn around! Smoke!" Aliba said with urgency. "I see smoke in valley. Black smoke!"

"Eric, did you hear that?" Bushta shouted.

"Yes, we're on the way!"

Bushta pushed the throttle to its limit and pulled the stick back into his stomach. He could hear Aliba's sharp shriek from the gravity force as they reached the top of their short loop and dove for the ground vertically. He snap-rolled and pulled the nose up level at 30 feet above the ground. He then spotted a narrow column of black smoke, which he had missed on their first pass.

Aliba was having problems keeping his light meal down. Gasping for air, he told Bushta he was about to vomit.

"Use the oxygen mask, but do not vomit in it. Breathe in oxygen deeply, slowly. That will help!"

Aliba reached for the mask as he removed the night goggles. Gulping oxygen, he tried to relieve the pressure in his stomach. Dropping the mask, he grabbed the empty zip-lock bag his sandwich had been in, and filled it. Zipping it closed, he stuffed it under his seat. He took a couple swallows of water and sat back in his seat. *That was close,* he thought to himself as he put the night goggles back on.

The black smoke was coming from the smoldering crash of the helicopter. Bushta had made two circles when Eric arrived.

"We will land in the valley on that gravel road, just below the helicopter. We have not seen anyone!" Bushta said.

Eric followed Bushta down into the valley and continued to circle. Bushta landed, then taxied to a good spot for take off. Eric and Gina saw the OV10 Bronco further up the hill from the crashed helicopter.

"The other aircraft is up the hill from the helicopter, Eric," Bushta said. "We are on Jess' co-ordinates."

"Yes, we see it! Okay, let's take a look," Eric said as they banked sharply and flew low along the lower ridge of the hill. "I don't see anyone up here. We're coming back down to land."

He circled and landed in the valley, parking next to Bushta's aircraft.

They all converged on the downed helicopter. The first person they found was Hastings, whose swollen body caused Gina to gasp. He was unconscious and not breathing normally. The cactus needles had poisoned his body, causing swelling and infection. Bird and animal waste, and other bacteria on the needles passed into Hastings' bloodstream, because they had pierced his body for a long period of time.

Eric and Gina began tending his wounds and tried to get him to drink water with aspirin. Hastings could still swallow and breathe, even though his face was not recognizable and his joints had vanished under the bloating.

Bushta found Samain, and Aliba continued up the hill to locate Jess and J.J.

Samain looked terrible, with bruises, cuts, oil and dirt all over him. His speech was not very coherent. He had inhaled so much smoke his throat was sore. It was difficult for him to swallow water or speak. He wanted to stand, but he was too weak.

With a piece of aluminum surface skin from the Huey helicopter, Bushta made a lean-to for protection from the cold evening, but held off building a fire. They didn't know where the people were who shot down the aircraft.

Eric approached Bushta, "I haven't seen anyone else. Sure is quiet and desolate out here tonight."

"I think there is a pack of jackals close," Bushta said. "I can smell them."

"So that's what I smell? Smells like rotten eggs!" Eric said.

"I don't think they will attack as long as we are moving around Samain and Hastings," Bushta said. "They usually wait until an animal is crippled or dead, before they get close. Cowards! As children, we would yell and throw rocks to chase them away."

Eric nodded, "The other people must have burned in the crash." *We should identify the bodies: two in the Bronco, five or six in the Huey,* he thought to himself. "I'll keep looking around and then go help Aliba at the other aircraft. Where is my good friend, Charlie?"

"It is a nice full moon," Gina said. "We should not have to use flares or flashlights."

Aliba searched close to the OV10 Bronco, but did not find anyone. No one was in the wreckage and the seats were missing. He put the night-vision unit back on and searched the area. A reflection from the moon on metal caught his attention. It was half a mile from him and seemed to be coming closer. He could see the form of a man, so he crouched down.

With his radio he called the others, "Someone come from the east on foot. I do not know who."

"Stay where you are, Aliba, until we identify who it is!" Bushta said. "It could be someone connected with shooting down these aircraft. Where exactly?"

"Coming from valley! East."

The silence of the barren foothills was deafening.

Then a familiar voice came from the radio. "Bushta, if you guys would shut your mouth long enough I'd tell you who I am. Where are you?"

"Mr. Jess!" Aliba yelled as he stood up and waved his hands.

Three rifle shots rang out, echoing between the hills. Aliba fell to the ground, not moving. Everyone dropped to the ground at the sharp rifle cracks.

"Stay down," Jess said. "There was a truckload of Arabs trying to find J.J. and me. They are still out here somewhere!"

Jess could not see anyone or determine where the rifle sound came from, mainly because of the echoes in the valley. He had not seen a muzzle flash either. He unholstered his Colt automatic pistol. The shots did not seem far away, but he could not see much for lying on his stomach.

"Are you on the ground, Bushta?" Jess asked.

"Yes, literally!" he answered.

"I didn't hear your aircraft. How long have you been in the area?"

Eric interrupted, "Aliba, are you all right?"

A long wait, no answer. Jess popped his head above a mound of sand and down again, he still could not see anyone. The Arabs had to be monitoring the radio again.

"Aliba, this is Jess. Where are you?" More silence. "Where was he, Eric?"

Eric whispered, "North side of the Bronco! He stood up and waved to you. Then they shot him. Haven't seen or heard him since."

Jess unzipped the flight suit leg pocket and pulled out the binoculars. "I was almost to the helicopter when I heard the shots," Jess said over the radio. Thinking to himself, *Dang it, Aliba! Why did you stand up? Maybe I can find you.* He turned over and peered through the dead underbrush. *Where is our crew? Whoever shot us down knows we are near the crashes. We didn't hear the jets that were supposed to come back and give us air cover.* He continued scanning the area with his night lens binoculars. *But, I haven't heard any aircraft or trucks. Maybe they came by camel! We couldn't have heard anything in the cave anyway. J.J.! I better tell her.*

"Hey there, J.J.! Keep your head down. Someone has shot Aliba. The others of our crew are around here somewhere. Are you feeling better?"

"Yes, very comfortable, under the circumstances," J.J. replied. "I heard everyone on the radio, and then shooting. I hid."

"Great! Just stay there until we get organized. I'll be there as soon as possible." Then he asked, "Bushta, do you know where I am?"

The radio was quite again.

Whispering to himself, "Shut up Jess! You know they can hear you, and they probably know exactly where you are."

Peeking over a clump of grass with the binoculars, Jess found the two Thursh aircraft parked on the road below. But one looked different for some reason, besides being painted a dark color. He couldn't see anything along the hill toward the crashed helicopter. No movement was visible.

"What about the Bronco crash area up the hill from me?" Jess whispered. He slowly turned over on his back, trying not to kick rocks or make noise. When he stretched out his arm to turn over to look up the hill, his hand touched something warm, moist and soft.

He jerked back! His heart pounded in his ears. Looking closer at what he touched, Jess saw a body with ripped clothes. It stank of blood and burnt flesh. He turned it over.

"Good Lord! Charlie?" Jess whispered. The only other time he had seen Charlie was in the hangar after Eric had broken Jess' nose. Even so, he recognized Charlie.

Charlie's eyes seemed open and he smiled, but could not speak. Jess put his finger to his lips for Charlie to be quiet, but he could not see. Charlie's eyes were just empty black sockets.

Pulling himself closer, Jess whispered in a charred hole where Charlie's ear used to be. It had been burnt off. "Be still, Charlie! We are still in danger."

He replied with a weak, "Okay! Who are you?"

"I'm Jess Hanes, the pilot that Eric punched in the nose."

Charlie tried to reply, but nothing came out. His clothes were almost burnt off his body, and he was covered with dirt and dust from crawling. His hair was missing on his face and head; just black, burned flesh remained.

With the binoculars back in the leg pocket, Jess took out a water container and gently poured it over Charlie's face. It hurt him, but he smiled again and nodded his approval. The water washed most of the sand from his forehead, and a little flowed down off what was left of his charred cheek. If Jess had touched Charlie's lips with the water container, they would have stuck to it.

Charlie raised his hairless head, and Jess put his arm under it, pouring another small amount of water in his opened mouth. The burnt skin from his neck rolled off onto Jess' sleeve. He gagged, almost vomiting.

"I'll give you a little water at a time, or do you want to hold the bottle?" Jess asked.

Charlie reached for the bottle and held onto it like it was gold. Jess scooted around, and then lay on his side and leaned against an outcropping of rock. Hopefully, they could not be seen as he pulled Charlie's back against himself, keeping him on his side. Charlie took a mouth full of water and slowly let it trickle down his throat. Jess could feel Charlie's tight muscles begin to relax.

After a few minutes, Charlie indicated he wanted to lean against the rocks. Jess helped him slide over to it, and took his pistol out of its holster again.

He leaned over with his ear next to Charlie's, so Charlie could hear the radio conversation from the earplug. The smell of his burnt flesh really got to Jess and he gagged again. Taking a deep breath, he used the radio, "I found Charlie. He's not good, Bushta. Do you know our location?"

No reply. Maybe the bad guys were too close to him.

"I know where you are, SAM. Remember, that's what your name use to be? This is Eric. We are on the same side 'Good Buddy'."

"No more bloody nose?" Jess said.

"No more bloody nose, I promise! How's Charlie?"

"Burnt bad, really bad," Jess whispered into the radio mike. "I don't know if anything is broken, but he's drinking water right now. Where's Samain and Bushta?"

"Bushta went to help Aliba," Eric said. "He got shot while waving at you. We have Samain and Hastings in a safe place. Haven't found anyone else alive. Heard your transmission to J.J."

"Roger," Jess said.

Suddenly, out of nowhere, there were paratroopers falling out of the sky all around them. Jess did not know they were there until they hit the ground next to them.

One, an officer by the rank on his shoulder, yelled orders in French and then Arabic. He and two other soldiers set up their own bodies as shields in front of Charlie and Jess, with their backs to them. They were wearing flak vests and fatigues. Jess could hear automatic rifle fire up the hill from them, but it was too dark even with the moonlight to see well.

Who were they shooting at up there, Jess wondered. *I thought Moroccan jumpers would be in desert BDU's, not old style brown fatigues. These guys don't look sharp enough for the Moroccan elite corp.*

Two old Sikorsky HRS-3 helicopters hovered near the Thursh aircraft. The helicopter above Jess and Charlie had high intensity floodlights. Wherever they would shine the lights, shots could be seen blasting up the dirt. The hill was swarming with uniformed men. It was a wonder that their own people were not shot.

"Bushta, tell the officer in charge I need assistance getting to J.J.," Jess said on his radio.

The three soldiers in front of them stood up. The officer turned and knelt next to Jess. He spoke in broken English. "Mr. Hanes, we will assist you. The king has sent us. I am Brigadier General Hamad Rashid."

A general drops out of the night to rescue us? I didn't know troops were on the way? Something just doesn't seem quite right. How did this guy know my name?

"This way, General, thank you!" Jess said, "Charlie, you're going to be all right now."

Two men helped Charlie onto a stretcher, which was taken from one of the helicopters, and carried him down the hill. The general and Jess, with half dozen other paratroopers, headed out to find J.J.

Jess became uneasy about the general and his men. There was no organization about their search, and men were running around half crazy, firing at anything. They were even falling over each other. It was like each one tried to find someone before another soldier could.

"Hey, gal! We're comin' to getcha'," Jess said in his best Texas drawl on the radio. "The Moroccan paratroopers have arrived. Stay hid!"

"I'm a'waitin'!" she replied.

One of the two helicopters followed above them. Jess stopped and checked his compass, thinking. *The creek bed is over there, and thirty degrees to the right should be the two large boulders.* "Over this way, General. Let me confront her first, so she doesn't get scared."

"That will be fine. Lead the way!" the general said, motioning with his gloved hand.

Following Jess was the general's radioman. He had an automatic weapon slung over his shoulder, which was pressing against the radio. He was unbalanced with the weight he was carrying. The general followed in behind them.

Bushta began whispering something on the radio, "No! Wrong! . . . Terrorists' troops, not Moroccan! Not Moroccan!" Then there was jumbled noise and no further transmission.

Jess was still using the earpiece and strained to hear another transmission. *What are they saying, . . . terrorists? These troops are the bad guys! Lord, how do we get out of this one?*

"J.J., did you hear the last transmission?" Jess whispered. "If so, stay put, don't show yourself!"

The general yelled over the helicopters noise, "Mr. Hanes, did you speak to me?"

Jess shook his head no, and then started veering up the hill, away from J.J.'s hideaway. The general's radioman stopped abruptly and pressed his headset tighter to his ears with both hands. The general tried to push passed him, slipped on rocks and fell headlong into cactus.

Before the soldier realized what he was doing, he grabbed the general's leg and started pulling him from the cactus, and fell headlong into the cactus himself. Both were screaming at each other in Arabic, which was being transmitted over the radio.

There were a dozen soldiers crowded around the general, shouting, pushing and ignoring Jess. He ran into the darkness of a ridge and then toward the crash of the Bronco, being careful of his movements in the moonlight. The spotlight of the hovering helicopter was on the general's activity around him.

At the OV10 aircraft, Jess jumped into the wreckage and hid in the black oil under one engine. He covered his face, neck and hands with the sticky stuff, even though it began to burn his skin. He wiped off the oil, as much as he could, from his face and neck onto his sleeves. That stopped most of the burning sensation.

The remains of the cockpit were upside down, so Jess crawled under and up inside. Surprisingly, for the condition the aircraft was in, it was not in bad shape on the inside. He pulled himself into the empty space where the back seat was before they ejected. There was just enough room for him to squeeze his back and butt into the collapsed cargo compartment. Lifting his feet, he could rest them on the underside of the damaged instrument panel. His ankle began to throb again.

Hopefully, the soldiers won't come looking for souvenirs tonight, Jess thought as he hunched down and closed his eyes. *Rest would be nice!*

But, Jess could not afford to sleep.

I need to think about what to do when the sun comes up, or even before then. What about the others, especially the wounded ones? Those of us left alive, how can we get together? We can't use the radios. I need to get back to J.J. as soon as possible. Hope they give Charlie good first-aid!

It was not long before the noise of the helicopter's blades began to fade in the distance.

"Where are they going?" Jess' mind raced with questions, *Hope they are taking the wounded out? Did they find Aliba? Was he all right?*

The general was still shouting at his men, but his voice was getting distant.

They must be going down to the Thrush aircraft I saw earlier, Jess thought to himself. *I bet they don't know how to fly them. That would be too much to expect. If they leave them alone, that will be our escape. We could squeeze three people into one aircraft.*

"Jess, you'd better wait a few hours before you stick your head out of this wreck," he whispered to himself. "Get as comfortable as possible, but don't you dare go to sleep. Okay, self! What do I do to stay awake? Pray! Yes, pray. That's not a waste of time. Lord, give us special care, please."

He began to repeat what he could remember of the 91 Psalm, silently: 'H*e that dwelleth in the secret place of the Most High, shall abide under the Shadow . . . of the Almighty. I will say of the Lord, . . . He is our Refuge and Fortress: our God; in Him will we trust. Surely . . . he shall deliver us from the snare of the fowler, and from the noisome pestilence.' . . . In Jesus' name, Amen.*

Jess nodded off to sleep.

CHAPTER TWENTY-SEVEN

Cold air blew up Jess' ripped pant legs giving him a chill. He was curled up in a knot, trying to stay warm in the cramped space in the wreckage.

He tried to jerk to an upright position, but the survival kit on his back had wedged behind a vertical panel. He snapped back, banging his head on a metal bulkhead frame. He felt panic about to take over.

"Come on, Jess!" he said gritting his teeth and rubbing his head. "Get a grip on the situation! Now . . . take a couple of deep breaths of cold air, clear your head before you move again."

Shifting his weight, he was able to straighten up. Quietly, slowly, he lowered his feet to the ground, knelt, and then sprawled flat in the debris on the ground.

Thinking to himself that he should not make so much noise, he whispered, "Just stay still for a few minutes."

He was finally wide awake, and made sure no one was around before standing up next to the fuselage. *Take it easy on that ankle. It could become a problem,* Jess thought to himself, *if you're not careful. Good thing I was wearing high top boots to give my ankle support. Funny, it doesn't throb.*

He turned and peeked over part of the wreckage, thinking, *The hill seems to be vacant of soldiers. Maybe they set up camp near the aircraft. I'll have to get myself a pair of these night binoculars when I get home. Using them is like someone had turned on the lights down in the valley. It's strange, though, no one is around the aircraft, no campfires, and no sentries. They must have dug holes to crawl in for the night.*

Jess hoped J.J. was still safe and comfortable. There was no movement around the boulders where he had left her.

He sat under the shadow of the wing, out of the moonlight. The aircraft wreckage behind him was black from being burned, and it would not cast a silhouette of him. His flight suit reminded him that it was soaked with black oil. The wind made the sticky stuff cold, and it was causing him to chill. A gust of frigid night wind hit Jess in the face, causing him to gasp. He needed something to wrap himself in. Otherwise, the wind could give him a cough and a runny nose.

He remembered that the ground was still warm from the day's sun. "Warmer than the air, at least," he whispered. Jess lay on the ground and crawled around a large clump of desert *esparto* grass to look across the ravine where J.J. was supposed to be. The warm ground felt soothing to his cold body.

There was no movement of anyone in that area. He still wanted to use the radio to find out who was alive, but did not dare to. The valley toward the aircraft was quiet and absent of soldiers. Charlie was not where Jess last saw him in the stretcher.

"Hope they have him in a burn center by now," he whispered to himself. "Where is everyone? What time is it, Jess?" He glanced at his watch. "Zero six fifteen, not much time left before the sun comes up, and it's a clear morning. Wonder if there's dew in the desert on a morning like this? Guess I'll find out shortly."

Jess kept scanning the hills and ravines for any sign of movement.

The soldiers could not have gone far on foot. What happened to Eric, Gina, Samain, Bushta, Aliba and Hastings? Jess was still full of questions. *Did the three guys that went into the desert to rescue Hastings and Charlie, get away? Who was killed in the helicopter, if anyone?*

"Time will tell Jess," he whispered. "Just take things as they happen. Be prepared for whatever comes. The Lord will provide the answers."

Jess decided to make his way over to where he left J.J. It needed to be done before daylight.

CHAPTER TWENTY-EIGHT

The cave was cool, but not cold like the breeze outside. The light from the moon had moved across the floor at the cave entrance to the east wall.

It had been four hours since J.J. had seen or heard soldiers at the small entrances of the cave. She had watched their boots kick sand as they ran passed, but they had not found the opening between the two boulders. The radio had been silent after Jess' last transmission for her to hide.

J.J. stood, stretched and winced at her rib pains and bruises. She stepped out of her survival blanket holding her ribs with her arms. She put the water bottle away after washing down a chocolate bar from the ration of food in her survival kit.

With the radio earpiece still pushed into her ear, she checked the squelch. Kneeling, she looked up and out of the opening of the cave. She could not see much, because she was looking at a hill of sand.

Almost holding her breath as she strained to listen with her empty ear, she slowly crawled out through the opening to the top of the sand mound. Each reach with her arms made her ribs hurt. Peering around the boulders on each side, she did not see anyone. The deserted hill and its rugged valley were quiet. The stars were bright that clear morning, even though it was almost sunrise.

Still cold from the night, J.J. sat in the sand out of the wind. The sand was not as warm as it was earlier. She had leaned against the boulder at the entrances, hoping it still had warmth from yesterday's sun. It also was cold.

"I should cover up in that blanket again before I get chilled," she whispered to herself, not really wanting to move.

J.J. felt stronger, but knew she needed to be very careful and stay where she was at the cave. She also was wondering where the Force One crew had gone.

"Hey, baby sister, want to go for a walk?" came a sudden, whispering voice above and behind her.

J.J. dove headlong through the cave opening, sliding on her stomach on the sand. Barely noticing her pain, she turned over and sat up straight, with her automatic pistol pointed at the hole. Then she realized it was Jess who had softly called out to her. On her knees, she crawled up to the opening again and peered outside, being careful not to stick her head out.

"Jess, is that you?" she whispered.

Suddenly, he appeared face to face with her, scaring her so much she fell backwards, down to the cave floor. He was right behind her sliding on his stomach. They bumped together and rolled with their arms around each other.

"J.J. it's me, Jess!" he whispered in her ear.

They were arm in arm, holding tightly to each other, with pain and all. She began to weep and buried her face in the curve of his neck. She abruptly pushed to arms length, laughing and sputtering. The side of her face was black where something had rubbed off of Jess.

"You hurt my ribs falling on me that way!" She complained. "What in the world do you have on you? You are slimy, and you stink of burnt oil!"

"It's the crowd I run with," he said teasingly. "We never take baths! Anyway, the moonlight won't reflect off your face now. It's oil from the Bronco. I used it all over my exposed skin, little lady. Want some more?"

"Engine oil can be poisonous and hazardous to your health!" she replied, matter-of-factly. "It absorbs through your skin! Besides it burns my skin!" Pausing and holding her breath, "Enough of that!" She threw her arms around his neck. "Just hold me, Jess! Easily! You scared me!" She nestled her forehead into the curve of his neck again, and relaxed against him. "I did not know what was happening, and I imagined everyone was taken prisoner. Where did those troops come from?"

"They probably came from Algeria, sent by Colonel Alvarez," Jess said. "It's clear that he has good contacts in this part of the country. I'll bet he's the one who called for the missiles."

Her tight hold around his neck relaxed, as she looked straight into his eyes, nose to nose, "Jess, thanks for coming back for me. I was afraid I would have to survive this alone. I love you, Jess." She kissed him tenderly, oil and all. Pulling back, she moved to his side and lay tightly against him with her arms around his smelly flight suit.

Jess put his arm around her and held her. They rested until their hearts stopped beating so hard and fast.

"Are you cold?" J.J. asked.

"Not really, but it is chilly in here," he said. "Once calmed down, I get cold. Let me get our blankets." Jess moved away and got the blankets. "We need to get to the other aircraft," he said. "There's two Thrush aircraft in the valley, which Eric and Bushta flew in. I didn't see anyone near them, and I'm surprised the soldiers didn't burn or take them. I reckon they could send pilots back to fly them out."

They lay close together for a short time, and then Jess slowly moved away and set up.

"They may not consider them military aircraft, painted white and blue. If that's the case, they would have no use for them."

They stood and shook themselves, and then J.J. began packing her survival kit. Jess crawled up the sand embankment to the cave opening for a look around. There was no one in sight, no noise of vehicles, aircraft, or men. He motioned for her to stay in the cave while he looked around outside.

With the twilight from the morning sunrise, Jess could see across the ravine to the OV10 Bronco wreckage. Using his binoculars again, he searched every ravine, washout, hill and valley he could see. The spray planes were not in his line of sight, because they were on the other side of the hill.

"J.J., come on out," Jess said. "The sun will be completely up in a few minutes. We'd better make our way over to the aircraft as soon as possible. You feeling up to a hike?"

She shoved their two survival kits out to him. He pulled them to the side and assisted her out of the cave. They strapped on the kits.

"Sure, cowboy!" she said with somewhat of a western accent. "Lead the way. And, please go slow and easy, my ribs cause me to gasp for breath." She paused, watching him, "Why are you limping?"

"Must have sprained it when I hit the ground in the parachute. It's a lot better than it was yesterday."

"You should not be walking on it, Jess. Your boot looks awfully tight," she said. "Quit being so *macho!*"

"Later, nursey. We've got to saddle our horses first," Jess said with his best Irish accent. He was not getting any better with it either.

Earlier in the night before, during all of the confusion with the paratroopers and General Rashid, Eric and his wife were forced to hide, leaving Hastings to the mercy of the troops. Hastings had pleaded for them to leave him behind.

General Rashid now had two wounded men to attend, and he was not pleased. He was mostly aggravated about the escape of Jess Hanes. But even so, he had captured Bushta and Samain, really not knowing who they were, except they were Moroccans at the scene of the wrecked aircraft. They seemed to be of some stature in the government by the way they spoke different languages, and were not intimidated by his military rank.

The only person the general did not know about was Aliba, who had been shot. Bushta had found him and buried him on the hill before the soldiers arrived. Samain and Bushta were trying to get to the aircraft in the valley when they were captured.

CHAPTER TWENTY-NINE

General Rashid marched his troops with Samain and Bushta toward the little town of Ksar Morhel, ten kilometers to the southwest of the wreckage. Two soldiers with Samain and Bushta were carrying Charlie and Hastings on stretchers to a small medical clinic in town used by miners from the mountains. The general's troops had taken over the small town and had transportation waiting for his men there.

He did not call for a helicopter to take the wounded to a hospital in Mecheria, Algeria, 300 kilometers away. Keeping the wounded with him was the only way he could guarantee Samain and Bushta would not try to escape.

Colonel Alvarez could use them now for ransom with the Moroccan government in exchange for drugs, firearms, money or political prisoners in Casablanca. It did not matter whether they were dead or alive; they would be profitable to him in his plans. General Rashid needed the prisoners for exchange, hopefully for gold, which he expected to be awarded by Colonel Alvarez.

The general had not found Eric, Gina, J.J. and Jess. The remains of the helicopter crew and passengers were left in and around the wreckage, unburied. His men scavenged the dead. The general knew he had two important Moroccan government men and did not want to waste further time hunting for others that may have escaped. The general also knew the barren mountains and desert would soon take care of the bodies.

He had no interest in the two small Thrush aircraft, because they were not military aircraft and he had no pilots. At least that was what he was informed by his men. But, his biggest financial loss was not finding Jess Hanes after having him in his grasps. The reward of the million in gold francs had vanished.

That loss infuriated the general, causing him to become impatient and short tempered with his men. The needle wounds from the cactus the general had fallen into poisoned his body, and it was affecting his mind. The wounds had been inflamed by one of the soldiers falling on him and the others trying to drag him from the cactus bush. The general and Hastings had the same reactions from the cactus needles.

The soldiers did not appear to be hardened troops, just a rag-tagged unit the general had thrown together. They were from bribed and threatened groups of *Amazigh*, 'free men', the *Tuareg* of the Sahara, and the *Kabyle* men of Algeria. Dissension among his men had always been a problem because of poor equipment, food and pay.

He almost had a mutiny on his hands when he informed them of parachute training the week before. Then those who refused to jump at night were put in a tribal political prison waiting execution.

General Rashid now found his men tired of marching. They wanted to rest from the morning heat. He persuaded them to continue following his orders with threats of violence to their families.

This rebelliousness was at its peak during a rest period only five kilometers from Ksar Morhel. The general and his men found shelter from the wind and sun under a low cliff overhang. Their prisoners were left in the sun.

Finally, he quieted them down enough that all could hear him speak. General Rashid told them of large amounts of arms, food and money that would be in their hands in a few days. He needed their cooperation in order to make the exchange.

During this ordeal, Bushta and Samain were trying to take care of Charlie and Hastings. Charlie was very close to death, and there were no medical supplies available for his burns. Hastings' cactus-needle poisoning still kept him immobile. They knew it would not be long before both of these men would be dead if they did not get medical attention.

Hastings was an essential part of the puzzle in trapping Colonel Alvarez as a terrorist, murderer and drug dealer. The information he had would put the colonel away for a long time in a Moroccan prison, and the terrorists knew it.

Samain and Bushta could not help Charlie or Hastings, and were hopelessly sitting next to them, watching them die slowly.

These men had never been in such a desperate situation. If the clinic had the needed medicine, maybe Hastings could be saved. But Charlie would not live much longer; he was too badly burned. He needed to be taken to a burn center, but none was close enough to save him.

The stretcher-bearers were off arguing with other Arab soldiers and not guarding Samain and Bushta. These two friends were squatted between Charlie's and Hastings' stretchers, whispering to each other, trying to decide if they should stay with the two wounded men or escape up to the mines. No promises were made for medical attention of the two wounded men lying beside them. If they should sneak away, it may anger the Arabs enough to kill the wounded.

But the wounded needed medical attention now, not a week later. Plus, there were no guarantees that help or safety would be at the mines.

Bushta had his back to the noisy soldiers. They could not hear him whispering to Samain, "You are more familiar with these zinc and copper mines than I am. I inspected them two years ago for drugs, but you have been up there since then. Did you leave with a good relationship?"

Samain shrugged and frowned, "Who knows what the attitude is toward government law enforcement out here? We had no arguments. They did not refuse my erratic searching, and I found nothing out of the ordinary during the inspections for drugs and contraband."

"But what if you showed up unexpectedly looking like you do? Would they recognize you? I would not know you," Bushta snickered. "You are in a dirty pilot's flight suit. You are bruised and cut, with dried blood all over you. And, your body odor!" He held his nose.

"Your sense of humor is back!" Samain said with a half smile.

They were interrupted by loud moans as Charlie tried to turn over on the stretcher. The two nearest Arabs turned to see where the moaning came from, then returned conversation with the others.

Bushta and Samain held him from turning. There was no place on his body to touch that was not burnt flesh. His clothes had already soaked the blood dry, and liquid from the open flesh matted the canvas stretcher. They continued to shade his face from the sun.

"Samain . . . Bushta . . . ," Charlie moaned. "They will kill us anyway. Let me die. Don't stay here. Get away. Now!" His words came as an urgent whisper, "God will take care of me. I'm sorry for getting you in this mess!"

Samain leaned down close to Charlie's missing ear and whispered, "You're not at fault for this mess! No one has and no one will blame you for any of this situation. We will not leave you as long as you are alive. If you die, we promise to come back and take you home to the United States."

Suddenly, a gunshot fired within a foot of Samain's right ear, caused him to fall back across Hastings on the stretcher. He was deafened by the concussion of the muzzle blast. The general's shadow partially covered Charlie as Bushta jumped to his feet.

Immediately, a 9mm automatic pistol was pressed between Bushta's eyes. "You next?" The general asked in Arabic. His hands were shaking, and his eyes were wide like he was transfixed

Bushta squatted between the stretchers again. Samain, holding his hands over his ears, sat next to Hastings on the other stretcher. The noise of the gun had left Samain badly shaken, and it had wakened Hastings from his coma. He began to mutter and jabber incoherently.

The soldiers were hushed and backed away from the four men on the ground. They began jabbering to each other and began throwing their hands in the air. Fright could be seen on their faces.

Charlie had been shot in the forehead, almost point blank.

"Dump body in ravine. Vultures will take care of the rest," the general said, with no expression on his face. Waving the pistol at the soldiers, he stumbled toward them. They backed away from his advances, making a wide space for him.

He looked drugged and glassy-eyed, becoming thick-tongued when he spoke. He could not control his left arm. He began to shake all over with convulsions. Turning away from them, he gasped and fell dead. His pistol fired twice before he hit the ground. The general lay motionless, face down in the dirt. No one made a move toward him.

The soldiers began talking among themselves, breaking up into small groups. One of the younger ones wearing an officer's jacket approached Samain, pointing at the general. He was asking if the general was dead.

Samain stepped over Charlie's dead body, leaned over and checked the general's neck for a pulse. He straightened up and nodded his head, yes; the general was dead.

The answer started a disorderly stampede of soldiers. The troops began disappearing into the distant barren ravines and outcropping of rock formations to the southeast toward Algeria. All but six ran away.

The six soldiers who remained tied Samain and Bushta's hands in front of their bodies. They forced one of Charlie's wooden stretcher poles between their bent arms and their backs, putting them shoulder to shoulder on one pole. Two of the soldiers picked up Hastings in his stretcher and headed up the hill toward the mines. Samain and Bushta were being shoved foreword, following the stretcher-bearers.

Samain wondered why most of the soldiers ran away, and only six stayed behind? One of those who remained was the young one who had asked Samain to check the general. He could not have been over seventeen or eighteen years of age.

Samain also wondered why he and Bushta were tied now, and not before? More unanswered questions!

CHAPTER THIRTY

Jess and J.J. finally reached the remains of the Bronco aircraft. They remembered that a sealed container was stored on the wall of the cargo compartment. Not knowing what it contained, they were going to check it out. It could have first aid supplies in it, or it could be empty.

Having satisfied themselves no one was around; they searched through the wreckage uncovering the container. Inside, they were surprised to fine two M16 rifles and four full magazines of ammo for each, all in good shape. Now they had long-range protection.

They discussed the possibility of taking both crop-duster aircraft to find the others. They talked about how good they felt for not getting any sleep, and how they both were in good spirits.

They had started down the hill toward the ravine, when Jess noticed a large number of soldiers in the valley west of them, between them and the mines. J.J. saw them at the same time. Three gunshots caused the two to drop to their knees behind a crop of cactus. Most of the soldiers dropped their weapons and took off running like a covey of quail.

"Who was shooting at the soldiers?" J.J. asked.

They all disappeared from sight, running south into the ravines and outcroppings of sandstone. Just a small group was left behind.

Hiding under cactus, Jess and J.J. crawled to the edge of a ridge where they could watch with their binoculars. They could see one man laying face down on the ground. He had on an officer's uniform. Two men were on stretchers, and two other men squatted between them, with six armed soldiers surrounding them.

"Can you read lips?" Jess asked.

"No, can you?" J.J. replied.

"If I'm looking straight at someone, I can understand most of the conversation if it's English. But, I'm not good at all with a foreign language."

"That is Samain and Bushta being tied together!" she said. "See what they are doing?"

The soldiers had rolled a body from one of the stretchers into the ravine next to the trail, and then tore off a stretcher pole. For some reason they left the officer on the ground alone, as if he had the plague. Samain and Bushta's arms were tied in front of them, and the stretcher pole was forced through the curve of their arms behind their backs.

"Yeah! It's them!" Jess exclaimed. "That's got to hurt! It has to put a strain on the muscles with that pole."

Two soldiers roughly grabbed the other stretcher and headed up the dusty road toward the mines, bouncing the unconscious man. J.J. and Jess could not recognize who it was.

Samain and Bushta, in step with each other, followed them on the rocky, graveled road. Whenever one of them tripped, they both fell. No one helped them to their feet, but they were prodded with rifle barrels until they stood up again.

Jess was looking to see if the soldiers carried anything like portable 60" Stinger or Redeye rocket missiles. No one carried heavy containers, like a portable missile launcher, or a Light Artillery Weapons System (LAWS) rocket.

"We'd better watch them until they get inside the buildings," Jess said. "Then we can figure how to help them get away."

Suddenly, Jess was startled by the presence of someone kneeling next to him on the ground. He tried to bring his pistol up, when a big hand enveloped both his gun and hand. His hand was pressed to the ground and another huge hand grabbed him by the neck, turning him around. The sun was behind the guy, and Jess could not see for the glare, but he was someone big.

"Hello Jess! Take it easy! How's my long-lost buddy's broken nose?"

"Eric, you scared me to death!" Jess said, out of breath. "I thought for sure I was a goner."

Eric released his grip. Then Jess saw that Gina was on the other side of him with her binoculars. J.J. was startled too, and had started to get up until she realized who they were.

"You two turn up at the most unlikely places," J.J. said. "We heard the shots and headed this way. Happy to see you both are fine."

They scooted under the cactus, peering over the ridge and continued watching the soldiers. They began making plans for getting closer to the mine. All the men went inside an adobe building near the mine entrance. The four observers slowly backed away from the ridge, out of sight.

Down the backside of the foothill, the four inspected the two aircraft and made plans on how and when to use them. They needed a diversion, a plan for getting the soldiers away from Samain, Bushta and the man on the stretcher.

Eric and Gina told Jess and J.J. that Hastings was on the stretcher and was bloated from cactus needle infection. They had talked to Samain before the paratroopers separated them. It did not look like the soldiers had used first aid on any of their hostages.

During the planning, Jess asked if anyone had seen Aliba, "The last I saw Aliba was when he stood up and hollered at me last night. He hit the ground before I heard rifle shots. Where is he?"

"When he was shot," Eric said softly. "He fell into the ravine on the east side of the hill. Samain found him last night and buried him. The grave is marked, and we'll put it on our map so we can come back for him later."

Jess dropped his head, shaking it. He looked at J.J. with tears in his eyes. Folding his arms, he walked away from them and around to the other side of the aircraft.

Quietly to himself, Jess said, "Lord, Aliba was loyal and good friend. He wasn't just doing his job, he protected me like an older brother."

Jess blew his nose and leaned across the tail of the aircraft, "I have never known anyone who was such a stickler about being a bodyguard. He was always close when I needed something. He took care of it, or got someone else who could." He moved around the tail of the aircraft and stood next to J.J., "He did become a close friend these past few months. I'll certainly miss him." He choked up again, and could not go on.

J.J. cleared her throat, "Aliba and I . . ." She hesitated. "We did not get along very well. It seemed we were constantly in competition over you, Jess. When the missile hit the hospital in Casablanca, and when we completed our training together in the mountains, it was only then we finally began working around our differences. I will miss him, too. He was a good bodyguard."

Eric and Gina just nodded as they listened to the conversation.

J.J. went to one of the aircraft and brought back a sectional flight map. They marked the positions of the two wrecks, Aliba's grave, and the body across the ravine from the mines.

"I think you are right!" she said, pointing to the map. "That has to be Hastings on that stretcher, which leaves Charlie in this ravine."

"The last I saw Charlie was when the paratroopers dropped in," Jess said. "I was giving him water when they almost landed on top of us. He was burned really bad from the helicopter explosion, and I don't think he would have made it to a hospital."

They all looked angrily at each other over what they were thinking.

"Did they shoot Charlie and dump him?" Eric asked with gritted teeth. "Or, did he die from his burns? Either way, he didn't have a chance. They didn't have to dump him that way. Hell, he's been our closest friend for years. He was best man at our wedding. What am I going to do without his support? Damn it all to hell!"

Jess shrugged his shoulders, not knowing what to say, "Two friends dead, because of drugs and greed."

It was quiet for a few minutes before Jess spoke again, "I really don't know who was on the stretcher, but I have an idea the officer on the ground was shot. We'll find out once we're rid of those other soldiers." He stuck out his hand to Eric, "I'm sorry for the loss of your friend. I feel responsible for everyone's misfortune out here, and I can't change it."

Eric shook his head, "No, Jess! No! You happened to be at the wrong place at the wrong time in Casablanca. This misfortune is not of your creation. He was a Christian young man, morally strong. Why him?"

"This is impossible!" J.J. said, and began to cry. "There seems to be no end to this 'kill or be killed.'" She lost control of her emotions and sobbed.

Gina put her arms around J.J., and they cried together. Eric and Jess had tears in their eyes, too, but they looked away in the direction of the mines.

"Therein lies our problem," Jess said pointing at the mine. "Our God in Heaven will take care of this mess, in Jesus name we pray."

"We need reinforcements," Eric said. "Our radios still work. J.J., you've talked with the AWAC's. Wake them up! Tell them we never received the air cover they promised yesterday, and we haven't seen anything today. We will need air cover to keep other outsiders from bothering us again. With our two planes, we can attract attention with low fly-bys and drop whatever we can on those six soldiers."

J.J. began to make notes as to what she needed to tell the AWACS people.

Eric coughed, "No rockets or heavy firepower! Bushta, Samain and Hastings are too close to the soldiers."

Gina's crying stopped, and she began to laugh, clapping her hands, "Let me fly! I can do it! I'm the best Swedish crop-duster around! Join me, J.J.?"

Jess nodded his approval to Eric and J.J. "Fine with me!"

"Okay, hotshot!" Eric said. "What do us boys do for fun?"

"Big man, you and me are going to get our friends out of the mines, alive!" Jess said. "And, in one piece! By God's grace, even Hastings!"

They pooled their suggestions again on final plans for the attack. Jess was elected their leader, mainly because he talked so much, and no one else wanted the job.

"First, we'll wait until just before sunset and come at them out of the sun," Jess said. "If you ladies will circle to the north of that peak where the mine's entrance is, and then come in from the west, fast and low, you'll catch them off guard."

They all nodded in agreement.

"They shouldn't hear these turbo engines on take-off, even if the wind is in their direction," Jess said. "The five-bladed propellers will help keep the noise down. Hopefully, three or four passes will be enough of a distraction for Eric and I to locate Samain and Bushta."

J.J. put her hand over her mouth.

"What is wrong?" Gina asked.

"Nothing really, just got an idea. Those parachutes are still on the hill, right?"

"Yes!" Gina replied.

"We can make a basket of rocks and dirt for dropping on those soldiers," J.J. said. "Like a smoke screen, but this would be a dust and dirt screen. What do you think, Jess? That way I will not have to use the guns or missiles loaded on the Vigilante."

Jess and Eric looked at each other with frowns, shaking their head. The two woman joined arms together, with their other hands on their hips, staring at the men.

The men smiled and finally agreed to make an attempt, hoping it would not cost the lives of Samain, Bushta and Hastings.

"Great!" Jess said. "The Vigilante's firepower can be used on bigger targets when the time comes. Go get a couple of parachutes and put them together. I don't have a better idea, do you Eric?"

"Nope, let's go," he said.

Jess stayed with the aircraft and made sure they were ready to fly. Next, they had to figure out a way to rig a parachute for dropping rocks.

Jess stood there with his hands on his hips, thinking, *They can't let it drag underneath the plane, but it has to be tied under the fuselage some way. Opening the two small access panels below the aft cockpit and taping the shroud lines to the roll bar should do the job. Then cut the lines to drop the load, which means cutting them all at one time. But there won't be enough time for that on one pass.*

He rubbed his nose and scratched the back of his neck. He dug into his flight suit vest pocket for a small note pad. He was surprised it was not soaked like everything else.

Let me see . . . What if I tied it up like a hammock and just cut one end? Knot the individual ends of all the shroud lines and separate them into two groups. Then, knot the individual group of lines together and stretch the parachute between the roll bar behind the back seat and front seat roll bar.

Jess sketched it out with a stubby pencil. *Each knotted group would have one single piece of extra line tied to the roll bar. Cutting one of the single lines tied to the roll bar would release the load out of the parachute.*

"Sure, that might work," Jess said to himself.

When the others returned, he showed them his drawing. They made other adjustments with the rigging and studied their plans again. Finally, they felt confident everything was ready.

"Okay, Gina," Jess said. "Are you ladies ready to fly?"

"We are as ready as we will ever be," she said.

"I agree," Eric said, "but make sure there's enough fuel for you both to make it back to Ksar Es Souk's airfield for refueling," he said, pointing to the map again.

"Right!" Jess said. "Good point, we don't want you ladies stranded again."

"I will contact the authorities in Casablanca about Samain and Bushta," Gina said. "It may help move reinforcements faster."

"We have no more than thirty minutes to get this together, so we'd better get to it," Eric said. "Jess and I have a short, steep hike ahead of us before you ladies get in the air. And, one more thing! Don't forget, you have those emergency signal flares if a missile is launched at you. Fire it out the cockpit access panel. You only need one hand to do it. If it is a heat-seeking missile, hopefully the flare will attract it."

"The panel is locked open now for the parachute shroud lines, so we should not have to worry about it," Gina said. "We should be able to put them in our jump suit pockets."

They shook hands, hugged, and saluted each other.

"Let's get with it then!" Jess said.

CHAPTER THIRTY-ONE

The mines in the hills above the town of Ksar Morhel had been abandoned only a short time. Electricity was still available from generators, and there was fresh water in large storage tanks, but no food.

When the Arab terrorist soldiers settled down from trudging up the road from the valley below, they untied Bushta and Samain. The young officer kept a sharp eye on the three hostages, because they would bring about a big exchange for gold from Colonel Alvarez. Because he was in charge, his poor family would benefit from the gold reward.

They were all resting inside the office building next to the mine entrance. Samain had found a first aid kit in a sink cabinet and attended to Hastings' cactus needle wounds. The swelling had gone down enough for him to breathe easier and open his eyes. He was still not able to sit up straight or stand.

Bushta sat at one of the office's dusty, well-worn desks looking out a large double window to the north. He had moved to that side of the room to get out of the direct sunlight and heat. It was cooler in the mud brick building than being out in the sun.

With a pencil from the desk, he began drawing lines and circles, and scribbled Arabic, in no special way. One of the soldiers, who stood next to him watching, broke out in laughter. Pointing at Bushta's doodles, he continued to laugh and walked away. He motioned to the others, with his finger in a circle next to his temple, indicating 'this man is crazy'.

Bushta snickered to himself, "You laugh now, but I will laugh later."

Something white moving down in the valley outside the

window caught Bushta's peripheral vision. He glanced up to barely see the Thrush aircraft disappearing behind the hills to the west. He had not heard the engines and neither did the others.

Who was flying the aircraft? Were Jess and J.J. still alive? What about Eric and Gina? He purposely dropped his pencil, and stretched back in his chair until it tipped over. The sudden crash of Bushta's chair caused everyone to look toward him as the blue Vigilante aircraft sped below them to the south. Samain had seen it and looked at Hastings, winked, and stood up.

"Did you fall asleep over there?" Samain said in Arabic. He used a dialect familiar to both of them, but not the soldiers. Clapping his hands, stomping the floor and laughing as loudly as he could, he went over to Bushta and lifted him up. Still laughing, he spoke in English for Hastings to understand, "I saw a Vigilante aircraft to the south of us. They are up to something. We should get out of here!"

"Yes," Bushta nodded and smiled. "I saw a white spray plane to the north, down in the valley. That is why I fell backward in the chair, to draw attention to me." He threw up his hands and began to laugh.

By now, the whole group of soldiers was laughing, except for the young Arab officer. He walked over and told them to shut up in Arabic, pointing his gun at Hastings. They pretended not to understand. The young soldier understood some English, but the laughter drowned out Bushta and Samain's conversation.

Suddenly, Samain swung a high right punch to the young officer's ear. He did not see the fist coming and the blow knocked him into two other soldiers sitting on the floor. The others did not see what had happened and started laughing at the officer falling over the seated soldiers.

Bushta and Samain picked up the stretcher Hastings was on and ran out of the office door toward a stack of old railroad ties near the mine entrance. They had no plan where to run for cover.

One of the aircraft swooped down over the road toward the office, dropping something that hit the door. On that side of the building, the adobe walls caved in. A dust cloud billowed skyward, completely covering the building with the soldiers still inside.

Sounds of shouting, coughing and guns firing came from inside the remaining walls of the collapsed office building. Three of the men ran out into the open and fell to their knees, coughing and rubbing their eyes. The young officer stumbled out and fell off the porch into a copper slag pile. He tried to stand up, but kept sliding down toward the hopper opening. He disappeared inside the machine's opening, which was not operating.

In front of the collapsed building, frightened soldiers stood in the road. Samain and Bushta crouched behind the stack of railroad ties. Hastings had risen up from his stretcher to watch.

"Samain, is there dynamite in this shed behind us?" Bushta asked as he crashed through its door. Falling between wooden crates, he broke his arm. He got up and dragged one of the crates outside, dropping it next to Samain. It broke open, and sticks of dynamite rolled out with the sawdust packing. Samain quickly moved next to the box, and his face turned white as a bed sheet.

"You could have killed us dropping that box!" Samain said. "Old dynamite can be real touchy. I could have pulled this box out for you. Right now, this dynamite can wait! Your arm does not look good!"

Samain lifted Bushta's arm and laid it against Bushta's chest; unbuttoned his shirt, and then pulled it out from under the broken arm, and pulled it over the wrist. Using it for a sling, Samain buttoned the shirt up under the wrist. Bushta gritted his teeth while Samain moved the broken arm, but he would not cry or yell from the pain.

"Sit still and I will tie your arm against your body, before you damage it," Samain said.

While Samain put a splint on Bushta, Hastings had propped himself against the wooden pile of railroad ties. He leaned over and grabbed three sticks of dynamite, sliding them inside his shirt.

"This dynamite feels wet. If they are wet with water, can they still be used?" Hastings asked.

"Hastings, do not move!" yelled Samain, staring at him. He picked up a stick of dynamite and examined it. It had been sweating, so he placed it back in the broken crate. He moved over to Hastings and carefully unbuttoned the shirt to get a view of the dynamite sticks, "That is nitroglycerin you feel, not water! Let me remove those sticks before we are all blown up."

Slowly, the sticks were removed and placed back in the sawdust. The sticky sawdust was also soaked with the wet nitroglycerin. Samain pointed at Hastings' shirt, which was also soaked.

"I have never been in this situation before with nitro," Samain said. "If we do not wrinkle your shirt, it may not explode. Let me take it off of you."

"No, take your knife and cut that section off," Bushta suggested.

Samain's sharp knife easily removed the front bottom of Hastings shirt. He tossed that part of the shirt away from them. It floated to the ground on the other side of the pile of wood ties. Then, he slowly wiped the wet nitroglycerin from Hastings' stomach with his handkerchief, and laid it in the box of dynamite.

One of the recovered soldiers walked around the pile with his rifle pointed at Bushta. He had seen the cloth float to the ground after hearing them talking, but he had not seen the dynamite until Bushta reached for a stick.

His eyes got wide as he stepped back. Suddenly a bullet hit his chest with a thud, and his boot crunched the wet piece of Hastings' shirt. His foot was blown out from under him, throwing him against the soldier behind him. They both hit the ground. The second soldier got up and ran down the road, heading toward a taxing blue Thrush aircraft coming up the road at him. He jumped into the ditch and kept running toward the valley below.

Samain stood up and waved when he heard the aircraft approaching. He did not see another soldier in the ruins, who had his rifle aimed at him. The soldier jerked back and then fell out the destroyed window opening he had been standing in. Then Samain heard a rifle shot echoing behind them in the hills, and turned to see Eric running down toward them from above the mine entrance.

Jess came up on the road from climbing the hill and walked out behind the blue Vigilante aircraft as J.J. had taxied passed him. He turned his back as the dirt and gravel from the propeller's backwash pelted him. Gina, in the other aircraft, swept overhead in a slow turn, watching their movements, and then glided down toward the valley. She added power to gained altitude and began circling above the mine area.

Higher above her were two military aircraft making a wide circle. Jess could not recognize what type they were, or who they belonged to.

"Let's get Bushta and Hastings in the aircraft," Samain said, motioning to Jess and Eric. "We will wait for the next ride."

J.J. climbed down and cut the remainder of the parachute from the plane and pitched it down the hill. She gave Jess thumbs up as they hurried to Samain.

"Are you all right, Bushta?" Jess asked pointing to his arm.

"I heal fast. Just a broken arm," he grabbed Jess around the neck with his good arm. "Jess, it is good seeing you again. You look worse than Samain! You injured?"

"No!" Jess said. "Nothing wrong with me! A good home cooked meal, your biscuits and a bath would fix me up real good!"

They laughed, happy they were leaving. They helped Hastings up the side of the aircraft and tried to get him in the back seat. His legs were still bloated from the cactus needle poisoning, and he could not bend his knees to get into the cockpit. Even if they could lift him in, he would not be able to sit in the seat, because his hips were too swollen. He would have to wait for the cargo aircraft.

"Let me stay for the flight with Hastings," J.J. said. "I'm the only nurse here, and I can take better care of him than any of you. Someone else fly this plane with Bushta as passenger."

"Jess, you fly! Eric will go with Gina," Samain said.

Jess shook his head, "Ain't no way, Samain! You and Bushta

get out of here. Eric and Gina will be right behind you. J.J. and I can take care of things until someone picks us up. You have more government clout to get us out of here than anyone else."

"Who is in charge of this team?" he yelled at Jess. His face was getting red.

"I don't care who is running this outfit," Jess said as sternly as he could. "The terrorists know that you and Bushta are out here, so take off. They have no need for me anymore, so get going. We'll be alright!"

Samain put his hands on his hips and started to say something. Jess pointed to the plane again, with his hand on his automatic pistol, smiling. Samain knew there was no way Jess would draw his weapon, and he also knew Jess could not be talked into leaving, not on this trip, anyway.

Samain and Bushta shook Jess' hand and gave him a kiss on both cheeks, as was their custom. But, this time it meant more than a formal gesture. They got in the aircraft, buckled in, and closed the canopy. J.J., Eric and Jess picked up the tail and moved the aircraft around so it would be headed down the dirt road. They took off, leaving a cloud of dust behind them.

No sooner had they banked away, than Gina made her landing. The others circled, waiting for her. She jammed the left brake and rudder pedal down to the floor locking the wheel brake. At the same time she increased the throttle, swiveled her plane around, heading its nose downhill. She then decreased the throttle to idle, keeping the engine running.

Eric grabbed J.J., lifted her off the ground with a big hug, and kissed her. She moaned because of her damaged ribs. After he put her down, she stood there, a little bit startled. Eric turned and grabbed Jess, lifting him off the ground too.

"Jess, you're a great guy, but hasty. Don't ever pull your gun and point it at Samain. He's my friend, too, you know!" He smiled and winked.

Jess could barely speak while being held so tightly! "Okay!"

Eric put him down and ruffled his hair. "Take care of yourself,

Jess. We may not be there when you get back. Again, sorry for the broken nose."

"Thanks for helping out, Eric. Tell Gina that I'm sorry we didn't get to visit."

Eric climbed into the aircraft with Gina and buckled in. The two were soon in the air, joining the other aircraft. They flew low back over the mine for a final pass, waved their wings and disappeared into the sunset.

J.J. and Jess went over to Hastings on the stretcher. His eyes were closed, and tears were dripping from his cheeks. They carried him into a shack next to the collapsed office, which protected them from the cold night.

They ate rations left behind by the others, and J.J. nursed the infected holes in Hastings' body with medicine from the first aid kit. She needed water to wash his face and to give him aspirin. Jess searched for a container and found a clay bowl and an empty jug, but no water in the shack.

Hastings grunted, motioning for Jess to come to him.

"What do you need, old friend?" Jess asked, kneeling next to him and J.J.

"Jess, there's still running water in the building that was knocked down," he said, and then pointed at J.J. "You'll have to tell me how you did that."

She nodded she would.

Jess stood up and stretched, "Great, I'll find water to cool you down. It's going to be dark in a few minutes, so I'll be back shortly. I don't like fumbling around in these old buildings without a flashlight. I won't use one, just in case someone comes snooping around." He headed for the building.

"There may be some blankets or rugs in those storage rooms to cover up with," J.J. hollered after Jess. She continued checking the festered needle punctures in Hastings' arms and back.

Jess paused, put his hands on his hips shaking his head, and looked out across the desert from the height of the mine. The big yellow moon was up already, shining beautifully across the desert. Some stars were out, too.

It sure is an unusual twilight, he thought. *The sun is set behind the mountains, causing those rays of white streaks to reach eastward through the white, gold and blue sky. The streaks reach out toward the moon, as if to say 'It's your turn.' Only God can make that happen, and in a few minutes, that scene will all change again.*

It was silent, except for the crunching of Jess' boots on the gravel road.

Boy, he thought, *I feel like the world has been lifted off my shoulders.* He was looking forward to the next day, when someone would pick them up. *Then I'll be heading home.*

Thoughts of sweet home! *Home again! Lord Jesus, home to Marie Ann!*

CHAPTER THIRTY-TWO

Hastings' moaning woke Jess before sunrise. Jess started to rise up, but J.J. was pressed against his back with her arm around his waist. The cold mountain air had moved them together in the night. He lifted her arm and scooted out from under a dusty rug they were using for cover.

Again, Hastings moaned before Jess could get to him. Kneeling beside Hastings' stretcher, Jess felt his forehead. He was burning up and sweating.

"J.J.! I need your assistance over here."

She rolled out from under the ragged rug and crawled over to them, banging her knee against two M16 rifles on the floor.

"Damn it, that hurt!"

"Careful, you might get messy crawling on this dirt floor," Jess kidded.

She dismissed his comment, "I am sorry. I must have dropped off to sleep." She motioned for the bowl of water, and Jess almost spilled it on Hastings in the dark. Again, she began washing his arms, legs and face to cool him down.

"Is there anything I can do, J.J.?"

"I need clean drinking water," she said. "He is dehydrated and may chill, so bring me that blanket and tarp. I may have to get on the stretcher with him to keep him warm. You will have to get things for me, if I need them."

Jess pulled his last water container from his flight suit pocket and zipped it closed. Her hand was hard to find in the dark room, and he hit her shoulder with the container.

"Sorry! Lost my grip on the water container and nearly dropped it."

J.J. reached out and grasped the bottle firmly. "No wonder. It is coated with that slick hydraulic fluid. Your pockets must be soaked through with it."

"When we get more light, I'll have to empty my pockets and wipe everything off," Jess said. "It's probably not doing my skin any good."

Hastings was getting depressed, "I don't think I'll ever get back to normal with all this swelling. It's what I deserve anyway; especially after all the grief I've caused everyone. I'll be in a body bag before I leave here."

"Hold on there!" Jess said, "Cancel that thought! You'll recover nicely, now that J.J. is taking care of you. She's the best nurse in Morocco. I know from personal experience, because she took care of me when I was in the hospital at Casablanca."

"I heard you were there," Hastings said. "Colonel Alvarez forced me into taking part in the attempt to assassinate you by threatening my children stateside. I should have died in the desert. That would have prevented all these problems." He moaned turning on his side, facing them. "Forgive me for the pain I've brought you two. My association with that terrorist has caused all this pain and death, after I refused to comply with his demands. In fact, that was the same day at the airport, when he forced Charlie and me onto his plane." He began coughing again.

J.J. held his head up and pushed a small wooden beam under it. He lay still, licking his chapped lips. She moistened a cloth and dabbed his lips.

"Do you want some water?" J.J. asked.

"Please."

"Take these three aspirin," she said. "They will help reduce your fever and swelling."

"Not on an empty stomach. They will give me heartburn."

J.J. took a cracker ration from her survival kit, opened it, and fed them to him. Then she helped him with the aspirin. After taking them and satisfying his thirst, he took a deep breath and slowly exhaled.

The sun was coming up, giving better light in the shack. The swelling in Hastings' face had gone down considerably during the night. He could close his hands enough to hold the water container and drink by himself.

"Where's Charlie?" Hastings asked. "I don't remember seeing him after we crashed. What happened, anyway?"

They gave him all the details, bringing him up to date about their situation. While they talked, they ate more of their food rations, and J.J. gave him more aspirin.

Every hour, jets would fly low through the valley and vanish toward the Sahara Desert. Their noise echoed against the hills.

Hastings felt better as he talked, continuing to give them information on his dealings with Colonel Alvarez. J.J. was taking notes on a writing pad from her kit. This was his confession time, and he had a captive audience. Finally, he became tired and went to sleep.

J.J. and Jess walked outside to watch the morning sunrise over the desert. It was a quiet morning, except for noise from an animal near the damaged office. It sounded like it was in pain.

J.J. turned to Jess and frowned, "Something is hurt!"

"Let's find out what it is. There could have been a dog or something in the office when it collapsed yesterday." Jess went back inside and picked up one of the M16's, then headed toward the noise with J.J. at his side.

The sound was coming from a copper slag pit behind the buildings. Jess could not see anything from where they stood on the road.

"What is it, Jess?"

"Beats me! Sounds like a trapped animal of some kind," Jess said. "Stay here and listen for Hastings. I'll go around to the backside. If I can't help it, I'll shoot it."

"Let me look at it first, Jess. I may be able to help it."

"I'll check it out."

The office was built on a stacked reddish rock foundation, protruding over the cliff. Jess held onto the rocks, making his way down the cliff to the bottom of the foundation and behind the building. Part of the porch above had collapsed, and it dangled along side of the foundation. The greenish and gray copper slag spread all the way down to the ravine below, from years of dumping.

Jess could see an Arab soldier buried up to his armpits in the slag, halfway down the slide. When the soldier tried to move in the slag, it reacted to his movements like quicksand, causing him to sink deeper.

Jess motioned with his hands and yelled for the soldier to be still. He began searching for anything to toss to the man to keep him from sinking. He found a coil of rusty fence wire hanging from a spike driven into a wooden beam at one corner of the collapsed porch. He wrapped one end of the wire around the beam, and tossed the coil out towards the man.

The soldier grabbed the thin wire with both hands and tried to pull himself out. That just caused him to sink deeper. Jess motioned for him to put the wire around his back and under his arms. He slowly looped the wire behind him, twisting the remainder of it together.

There was no way Jess could pull him up. The wire was too small to grip, but it was strong and heavy enough to keep the soldier from sinking or sliding further into the slag.

Jess motioned to him again that he was going to get help and would return. At first, the soldier did not understand all the sign language that Jess was sending down to him. Then he nodded his head and smiled and waved.

Hastily climbing up the hill next to the front of the office building, Jess ran back. The sun and his excitement made him pant heavily. He was getting overheated.

"J.J.," he yelled as he went up the steps of the front porch and sat down on the middle step.

"What?" she called from inside the shack.

"There's a man in the slag down the side of the hill," he yelled, trying to catch his breath. "I need your help to get him!"

"Come in here first," she yelled back.

Jess slowly got up and went inside the shack. The brightness of the sun had temporarily blinded him; he did not see the rifle butt coming.

His head exploded and he reeled. Dropping to his knees onto the dusty floor, he clasped his face. Everything was a blur to Jess as he peered out between his fingers, trying to focus his eyes.

"My nose, it's broke again," Jess yelled, covering it with his arms for protection.

Then someone hit him in the back of the head. This time he went face down, sucking dust from the floor.

Get up Jess and fight back, he said to himself. But he could not; someone was sitting on his back.

"Jess, just sit still," J.J. said, pressing him back down with her weight. "A young Arab soldier just hit you with his rifle. He was in here when I got back."

The young soldier mumbled something in Arabic. J.J. just grunted and pointed to the survival kit next to Hastings' stretcher. He picked it up and went back to the open door of the shack.

"He told me to shut my infidel mouth," she sneered.

The soldier shouted something at her again and kicked the door facing with his boot. His rifle was pointed at them.

Jess was feeling weak from the loss of blood, and was thinking, *Why does everyone have to hit my nose?* "Let me up!" Jess whispered.

J.J. moved off his back and gave him a dirty cloth to wipe his face. Sitting cross-legged, Indian style, Jess held the cloth to his nose, staring at the young officer. He had opened the emergency kit and poured its contents on the floor in the doorway. *What was he looking for?* Jess thought.

The sunlight silhouetted the soldier in the doorway. He was very young and slender, about sixteen or seventeen, but he was wearing an officer's jacket.

I wonder who he stole that from? Jess was thinking. *He's too young to be involved with all this violence.*

The young soldier shielded his eyes from the sun when he

looked down the road toward the valley, like he was waiting for someone. He continued pointing his rifle at Jess and J.J.

Jess gained his strength back, and began to think of a plan. *If the sun blinded me when I came in, it should do the same to him. The rifle needs to be taken away from him, but I can't move fast enough at this distance to take it away. He could spray bullets all over the room, killing the three of us.*

Jess just realized Hastings had not moved at all, but was not willing to move closer to him. He had a bad cut above his eye where the blood had already clotted. The young Arab had knocked him unconscious, and almost did the same to Jess.

Jess nudged J.J. and nodded at Hastings. She said something in Arabic to the young soldier, pointing at Hastings. He stepped inside and leveled the rifle at her. He stood next to Jess, and Jess could see the rifle had its safety 'on'. Jess was convinced he could grab the rifle, pull it down, and then be able to roll the young soldier over and get on top of him.

"J.J.!" Jess yelled, grabbing the middle of the rifle stock. With all the force Jess had, he yanked the rifle and boy over him and rolled. Jess' weight, plus the hardness of the rifle dropping on the boy's chest, caused him to gasp for air. But he would not let go of the rifle until Jess had pressed it against his throat. He released it, and Jess tossed the rifle to J.J.

The soldier suddenly drew a knife from his belt and slashed at Jess.

Warm blood continued running across Jess' mouth into his beard from his nose. He was able to deflect the blade, but the boy still hit Jess in the nose with its handle. For some reason, Jess was not blinded with tears this time, just numbed. He wrapped both his hands around the young soldier's fist, which held the knife.

Jess screamed in his ear, startling the boy, "This is the end for you, young man!"

Jess jammed the knife half way up the blade into a slit on the wood floor, and their hands slid down its sharp blade. The soldier jerked away, snapping the blade off between the boards in the floor.

Jess grabbed him by the nape of the neck, lifting him off the floor. Then with his other hand, Jess grabbed the seat of the soldier's pants and tossed him through the open door onto his back, outside on the porch. His bleeding hand splattered blood all the way. He bounced and rolled off the porch, lying still in the dusty road.

Jess snatched up what was left of the first aid kit on the floor and ran out to him, leaving J.J. to take care of Hastings. The young boy was still dazed as Jess sat him in between his legs on the ground and locked them around him. The fingers on his left hand were cut and bleeding badly. Jess took the roll of gauze and loosened it. Then he opened a can of disinfectant salve. With his red bandana handkerchief, he wiped the blood away from the wound as best he could and emptied the tube of salve into the cuts.

Pressing the salve into the deep wounds helped stop the flow of blood. Jess then made a thick roll with part of the gauze and pressed it against the cuts on the young boys fingers. He put his hand under the cut hand, curling the cut fingers around the gauze roll, making the boys small hand into a fist. Holding it closed, Jess then wrapped the gauze around the fist to hold the fingers in that position.

Jess released his leg grip, but the young boy continued to lean against him, making no attempt to move. Jess pushed away from him and sat him up straight. The young soldier's body odor was as bad as Jess'.

At least Jess could still smell through his damaged nose. It had stopped bleeding, but the blood stench was bothering him in the heat. He got up and stood the young soldier to his feet. They both were still groggy.

"Nice job, Dr. Jess!" J.J. said from the shack door. "I have been watching you. You are full of surprises, mister." She walked out to them, and examined the wrapped fist.

Jess held onto the upper arm of the young soldier making sure he did not get away. Terror came to his face when he realized who had a hold of him.

"Tell him I will not hurt him again, if he will not hurt us," Jess said to J.J..

She told him, but he never stopped looking at Jess.

"What's wrong now?" Jess asked.

Slowly the boy pointed at Jess' blood-soaked beard and began to smile.

"What you see is what you get!" Jess told him and J.J. translated.

"He wanted to know if he did that to you, and I told him, yes."

"He must be pleased with himself," Jess replied.

"Yes, he has never shed the blood of an infidel before, and it pleased him," she said.

Jess did not return his smile. In some way, this boy was going to show some respect, even if Jess had to pull his pants down and spank his butt. Jess was getting very upset.

"Yeah, I know! He was just protecting himself," Jess said angrily, glaring at the boy. "That's his God-given right. But twice he hit me in the nose. He could be a dead young boy if I had not restrained myself earlier."

"But, he would have considered that as Allah's will, his life for the life of an infidel in mortal combat," she said. "His glory is to kill all infidels."

"He doesn't know I'm not a Moslem. Right? Ask him!" Jess demanded.

J.J. looked at him with a surprising smile and asked the young boy if Jess was a Moslem. He just shrugged his shoulders, and told her Jess was too white to be a Moslem. She translated.

"Tell him that Moslem people are not all dark skinned like him and his soldier brothers."

"This is a very interesting conversation, Jess," she said. "I do not think you have a chance to convert him to Christianity."

"I know, but that's not my motive. I'm sure it would be a full-scale war to even try introducing him to Jesus Christ. Anyway, ask him if his hand hurts, and if he knows who bandaged it for him."

J.J. asked the boy. He had forgotten about his hand for there was no pain to draw his attention. He held up his fist, looked at it, and sniffed it, wrinkling his nose as if it did not smell good. He looked at Jess, then at his fist again and back to J.J.

She motioned for them to sit on a stack of wooden railroad ties. J.J. asked him again and he told her that Allah knew. She shook her head and pointed to Jess, calling him by name.

"Monsieur Hanes," she said.

Jess had released his grip on the boy's thin arm and reached out to shake the young boys unhurt right hand, "La bes! Hello! What is your name?"

He would not react or shake Jess' hand. Jess suspected the young soldier would show weakness if he responded. He just sat there for a few minutes, pondering his situation, stood up and walked away from them.

Suddenly he stopped. Then they all heard that sound again. The soldier in the copper slag pile began hollering again.

Jess told J.J. what had happened as they ran, following the young boy. He started down the hill next to the building, and J.J. yelled at him to be careful. The boy came up short when he saw the man down the slope in the slag.

He began yelling at the man, and he replied. Then the man pointed at Jess, and the young boy screamed back at him. The boy shook his head and held up his bandaged hand, then pointed at Jess.

J.J. walked up next to the boy and put her arm around his shoulder, pulling him close. She told the man what had happened, and he told her how he got into the slag.

"That man is the boy's father," she said. "He was knocked off the back porch up there when we dropped the rocks on this building. They told each other what you had done for them, and this youngster cannot understand."

Jess started back up the hill again, "I'll find some rope to help pull him out. I'll check on Hastings while I'm at it. Be right back."

J.J. explained to them where Jess had gone, and that he would return.

Now let me see, Jess thought to himself. *Maybe the shed behind that stack of railroad ties will have supplies in it. The stink from these dead bodies are about to make me vomit. Pew, what a mess!*

He noticed a broken case of something in front of the shed? "Dynamite!" Jess hesitated to move closer. *Don't move too fast, Jess, this could be a booby trap of some kind.* He could not see any trip-wires or stings attached. *Just leave it alone for now and see what's in the shed.*

Jess carefully stepped inside the shack. Stacks of dynamite cases lined the back wall of the shed. There were rolls of fuses in boxes under the window and digging tools leaning against the other wall. *But, where is the rope we need?* He turned to go out and saw rope hanging behind the broken door that was halfway shut.

Now, what else will I need? Block and tackle? There were two hooked over the rim of a barrel of railroad spikes. "If this keeps up, I'll need a wheelbarrow to carry all this stuff."

With his hands and arms full of things, Jess walked passed the dynamite, noticing it was wet. *Dangerous stuff to mess with,* he was thinking, *but we might need some later.* He laid everything on the porch and went inside to check on Hastings.

"Hi, Jess!" he said when Jess entered. "What's happening out there? I feel like I had a freight train hit me in the head. Why's all this gauze on my head?"

"One of the young soldier 'boys' . . . hit you with 'our' rifle butt," Jess said.

"I didn't see anybody and don't remember anything," he said.

"He got me too," Jess said. "Broke my nose again with the rifle and his fist. Got us both!"

"You're covered with blood! You all right?" Hastings asked. "Where's J.J.?"

"She's out there. We'll be back directly. We've got to rescue somebody right now, explain it later. Need anything?"

He shook his head.

"Be back," Jess said, and hurried out with his load of gear.

CHAPTER THIRTY-THREE

All five of them, Hastings, J.J., the young Arab boy-soldier, his father and Jess sat in the afternoon shade of the mine entrance. J.J. had translated the whole story to them about why they were there. The two Arabs had become very interested, and soon began to smile talking to her.

Jess found a large metal bucket and filled it with water. The young man pointed at him, wanting to know what he was going to cook. Jess noticed and told J.J. to tell him he was going to heat the water for them to wash themselves with. It did not take long to heat the water with the small fire they had built.

Pulling on his beard, Jess had knocked some of the dried blood and dirt out of it. With a tin cup, he poured hot water into a large clay bowl and started washing his beard with water and no soap.

Jess held his breath thinking to himself, *This stench is enough to gag a maggot.* It reminded him that the four dead men needed to be buried. They had been lying in the sun for two days.

"When I get finished here, will they help me bury these soldiers?" Jess asked J.J.

She spoke to them, and they immediately got up. Jess dried his beard on his sleeves. The young boy was told by his father to look in the shed for a shovel. J.J. told them Jess already had the tools from the shed.

With two shovels and a pick, Jess started down the road. The father halted him and shook his head, pointing at the tools.

"What's his problem, J.J.?" asked Jess.

Hastings cleared his throat. "They want to burn the bodies. If bodies are not burned, they fear disease will come."

"I didn't know you knew their language," Jess said.

"Neither did I," J.J. said.

"I can understand some dialects of Arabic," Hastings said. "These two are like English in the south, both in America and Australia. Sometimes it's slurred, mouthed words, not very distinct Arabic."

"Okay, ask them where's the best place," Jess said. "I can help."

J.J. asked them, and they said they would take care of it all. They pulled a cart out of the mine tunnel and took the bodies down to the valley below. The two disappeared around a distant bend in the road, never to be seen again by the other three.

"I never did get their names, J.J., did you?" Jess asked.

She shrugged her shoulders, "I do not believe it will be important for us to know. They might even refuse to tell us. Anyway, they would not say where they were from, other than . . . ," spreading her arms toward the immense desert, "The Sahara."

#

The mountain shadows began to reach across the valley below the mines and extended eastward toward the desert. Hot wind increased as a sand storm on the eastern horizon was building in the desert, heading their way. It would not be a cold night nipping at them, but one with high temperatures and winds. The Arabs called those storms *Haboobs*, and the Mediterranean countries called their windstorms a *Sirocco*.

The storm reminded Jess of dust and sand storms in West Texas, but these in the Sahara were worse. They could last a couple of months, with no letup. He remembered the last one he was in, it lasted three days back in 1962 near Kenitra. During those three days, they could not breathe properly because of the heat and the sand in the air. In a matter of a few hours, the sand would cover a man and camel lying on the ground. It could be a killer storm.

The three hoped to hear from Force One before the storm hit. J.J. was using her radio, talking to someone in French, and gave Hastings and Jess thumbs up. She had already made contact.

Samain had a problem securing a cargo plane or helicopter to pick them up, but he would call again the next morning.

Hastings was much better, and slowly helped them move everything they needed inside the mine entrance to get out of the approaching storm. J.J. would stop every so often and hold her ribs; she was still suffering from the explosion. Jess favored his bad ankle, but was walking better. His nose would ache when breathing hard, but he could tolerate that.

The mine's entrance opened into a gigantic man-made cave, large enough for massive trucks to drive in and turn around inside. Approximately 200 feet inside the entrance, there were three smaller tunnels, each with an opening of only ten feet. Railroad timbers, treated with creosote, were used for shoring the walls.

On top of an old rusty truck frame were warped sheets of half-inch plywood. In the dynamite shed, Hastings found nails and hammers for building a windbreak along one wall of the mine. His body was still swollen, which slowed his movements, but he was deliberate with his tasks.

The walls inside spread wide and curved back away from the mine opening, making a natural windbreak from the east. If the wind would shift to the north or northeast, they would have a blast of hot wind coming in.

They slanted two sheets of plywood from the ground up to three feet, and then nailed scrap two-by-fours to them for bracing. The sandstone floor was easy to pound the wood stakes into for vertical supports. With two more sheets, they enclosed the space using the mine wall as one side.

J.J. made masks from burlap sacks found in the shed, to cover their nose and mouth. She brought in a five-gallon container of fresh water, and used its weight to hold down the tarp covering their supplies. With the limited survival kit rations, they could hold out for a few more days. Plus, the water supply was plentiful.

Jess thought to himself, *Once the storm clears, if for some reason we have another delay getting out of here, I'll take J.J. and go down the hill to town. Maybe we can find additional food there.*

The sunlight had disappeared into the thick blowing sand like someone had turned the switch off. The sand, heat and wind developed into a severe storm for the night.

The darkness was so thick with sand in the air; they could not see the shed, shack or other buildings outside, even though they were only forty feet away. Everything that was not tied down or securely nailed was flying passed the mine entrance, making screaming noises. The wind was becoming such a deafening roar across the mine opening; Jess could not hear J.J. and Hastings without shouting. They shrugged their shoulders at each other, then hunkered down under the plywood sheets and against the mine's cool wall for its protection.

Jess could see through a crack between the plywood, and every so often, the sand in the air would part like a drapery, leaving an opening. The sand and gravel was hitting the adobe walls of the buildings, stripping them. On the east walls of the buildings, holes began to appear from pounding rocks and gravel punching through. The sand began making it harder to breath, and Hastings was beginning to hyperventilate.

J.J. motioned for Hastings to lay down facing the wall. She covered him with one of the ragged rugs she had found and gave him a small closed container of water to sip.

If the wind would shift toward the entrance of the mine, it would be like someone shooting an automatic shotgun at them. Jess did not know if any of the three tunnels opened to the other side of the mountain. If one did, he figured they would have hurricane force winds through their section of the mine.

Jess yelled in J.J.'s ear that he was going to search the far left tunnel. He was hopeful that they could get further into one of the tunnels, where the sand and wind would not bother them. J.J. shook her head, no, and wrinkled up her forehead with her disapproval. Pretending he did not understand, he gave her thumbs up, grabbed another plastic container of water, and zippered it into his flight suit pants pocket.

He leaned against the wall, feeling his way toward the tunnel's entrance to his left. The flashlight was no help in the thick cloud of sand that was settling in the large mine opening.

He flashed the light down the first tunnel, thinking, *This is much better! It's clear back in here and not bad at all, except for stinking of stale air.*

The walls were cold and damp to his touch, "Is this condensation on the walls or is it moisture seeping in? I can't really tell," he said to himself.

Fifty feet into the tunnel, he banged his head on something hanging from an overhead beam.

"Hey! Hey! How lucky can you be, Jess?" he said aloud. "It's a kerosene lantern, and there's a miners carbide lamp, too. Wonder if they have any fuel in them."

He shook the lantern, and heard no sloshing of liquid. It was empty. Disappointed, he hung it back on the nail. The carbide lamp had some calcium carbide in it. He remembered all that was needed was moisture on the carbide, so he spat on it. Then he stirred it to activate the gas, acetylene, to burn for fuel.

After stirring the mixture, he screwed the top back on, which housed the reflector. In front of its concave reflector was a striker mounted next to a gas tube outlet. He flicked the striker like a cigarette lighter, and it just twirled. No flint.

"Doggone! Just when I thought we had something worthwhile. I don't have a cigarette lighter or matches to light the carbide gas," he said disgusted. "Come on, Jess, think!"

J.J. did not smoke, but Hastings did. Plus, the survival kit had either matches or a striker for starting fires. After searching the wall with his flashlight, he knew there was no flint stone in the mine, just sandstone or copper matrix. He wondered if the copper had any silver mixed with it, remembering copper nuggets did in the area along the upper peninsula of Michigan.

Returning to the exit into the larger outer mine, it was dark, and the wind had not ceased its angry howling. Their hastily built protection was still intact, so he crawled back under with his two companions. They were both lying with their faces to the wall, and they were not only covered with ragged rugs, but mounds of sand.

Finding the fire starter in the kit for the carbide lamps, he crawled over to J.J.. Jess bumped her on the arm, but no reaction. Shaking her shoulder did not arouse her, either. He reached under her neck to feel for a pulse, and found that her heart was still beating. Pushing his way further underneath and using the flashlight, he found her head covered in sand. He lifted her head and placed it on his leg. When he shown the light in her mouth, he saw that it was still moist. The handkerchief that was over her nose and mouth had covered with sand, almost cutting off her air intake. The situation was as bad as the cave they had been trapped in earlier.

Pulling the rugs from over her, he slid her from under the makeshift protection. Jess picked her up and with the mini-light in his mouth, he leaned against the wall and scooted toward the tunnel.

Further inside the tunnel, he sat J.J. on a wooden beam and against a wall timber. "Now, what did I do with that water container?" he whispered. "Too many pockets in his flight suit."

Taking her handkerchief, he soaked it good with fresh water, rinsed the sand off and wiped her face. Her breathing was becoming better, and she tried to open her eyes. They were stuck together with sand and her tears.

"It's all right now, J.J., don't try to breathe through your nose. It's clogged with sand. Breathe through your mouth."

"Hmm . . . where are we?" she asked.

"In one of the tunnels, out of the wind and sand. Let me wash your face with water again, and then you can wipe it off with this handkerchief. Your eyes and nose are full of sand, be careful," Jess said. "Blowing your nose will help. Are you all right, until I come back?"

She nodded, "Yes, please leave me some water." Jess stood up and banged his head on the beam again. He grunted and moaned, "I bet I lifted the roof off this tunnel. I'm out of here! Be right back!" Rubbing his head, he turned to leave. "I'll bring Hastings in here, too."

Realizing he had not lit the miners' lamp, Jess turned around, "Sorry, I forgot to get the carbide lamp for you. Here, hold this light for me, so I can get the lamp started."

The striker from the survival kit worked great, and he left J.J. smiling at him, "Please do not be long. Remember Jess, I am uneasy in caves and tunnels, you know."

"Okay."

Hastings was doing better than J.J. had done with the sand. Jess shook him, and he immediately raised his head, and coughed. "Hi, Jess! What's happening?" he hollered.

"Do you feel strong enough to help me move this plywood to the entrance of the left tunnel?" Jess yelled over the roar of the storm. "We may be able to block the sand and wind with the plywood over the entrance, just enough to keep it from blowing in so bad. J.J. is in there now."

Hastings nodded his head and crawled out. Jess pointed to the two survival kits for him to carry and picked up the large clay water container. They left them with J.J. and went back for the plywood.

It took both of them to manhandle and slide on edge, two four-by-eight feet, three-quarter inch plywood sheets, to the tunnel entrance where J.J. was waiting. It did not take as long as Jess thought to get the sheets braced in place. It not only helped keep the sand out, but it also reduced the noise of the storm's roar.

He reached out, grabbed Hastings hand and shook it, "We make a pretty good team."

"The pay ain't much, but we do a dandy job, don't we?" Hastings replied.

They walked back to J.J., laughing and joking with each other. She was standing, shaking her head and running her fingers through her hair.

"Watch out Jess, we have another sand storm in here," Hastings joked. He was feeling better.

"Hey, you two! Have a seat and I will give you the menu," she said. "Dried prunes or peaches. One, Meal-Ready-to-Eat, (MRE), is left for each of us. You two can flip a coin for those, and I will take what is left."

She and Jess sat down next to each other on a wooden beam.

"You sound much better! How you doing?" he asked.

"Great, except for a headache and sore ribs."

"That's a nice lamp you have there, J.J., buy it on the blue-light special?" Hastings laughed, trying to bend his legs to sit on an empty upside down tar bucket.

"Green light, what . . .?" she said, confused.

"You know, like the blue-light specials they have back stateside in those mall stores," he said.

"No, I do not think so," she said as she suddenly turned her head, shining the lamp further into the tunnel. Weird noises from deep in the tunnel shafts sounded like something from outer space.

"There must be wind moving in the tunnel somewhere," Jess reassured her. "I don't think there's any problem, J.J."

"Let's eat!" she said, trying to stay calm. Closed-in spaces always got to her, especially when she could not see outside.

They felt better after eating their ration of food and drinking enough water to finish filling their stomachs. It was definitely cooler in the tunnel, and they did not have problems breathing. The additional plywood sheets they had toted in were nice to lay on, off the damp floor. They finally had a restful night of sleep, after becoming accustomed to the stale air.

#

Back on the airline heading for Texas, Jess finally took a break from telling his story and paused just long enough for Marshall Madi to say something.

"Jess, would you like more iced tea?" she asked as she stretched her arms out in front of her. She unbuckled her seat belt and stood bracing her knees against the seat next to him. "I should visit the ladies' room. Do you want me to get you anything on the way back?"

"No thanks, I'm fine."

She gave him a little wave, "Be back."

Jess stood up, stretched, and then sat next to the window. The land they were flying over was green and the farmers' fields made uneven patterns across the ground. They were not far from Austin. He was glad the whole thing was finally behind him. Maybe he would be able to rest easier at night, in his own bed, with Marie Ann.

Now that was a pleasant thought, Jess. Together again! Not for sexual desires, but to have her in my arms, close, quiet and nestled comfortably together . . . safely at home! He smiled to himself.

Madi returned with some peanuts, cashew nuts, and two sodas. She smiled and handed Jess the tray. After buckling in again, she turned and pulled her seat tray out.

"I know you didn't really want anything, but I'm sure you're dry from talking so much," she said smiling, giving him a wink.

"You know something, Madi?"

"No, not much," she replied with her broad grin.

"You're a flirt!"

"Why, Jess! You finally noticed," she said patting his hand.

Jess ate a handful of nuts and washed them down with the soda. Closing his eyes a moment, he opened them and leaned toward her. "Are you ready for the ending of this Texas tale? We're not far from home!"

"Carry on, young man."

Where I had left off was in the copper mine tunnel, waiting for the sand storm to stop, thinking to himself.

"We had spent the night in the tunnel, and woke up the following morning with sunlight reflecting through the cracks of the plywood sheets, which we had used to board up the tunnel entrance."

CHAPTER THIRTY-FOUR

Walking out of the mine the next morning, they noticed right away that the sandstorm had changed directions, blowing to the south and had lost most of its strength. The air had cleared enough for J.J., Hastings and Jess to see the valley below through the light dust. Sand had made drifts through the valley and had built up against the outcropping of sandstone. The ruts in the road were level with sand, which stretched across to the small shed where the dynamite was. The broken dynamite case in front of the shed was completely covered with the light brown sand.

J.J. was in radio contact with Samain, and found that he was still unable to make arrangements for an aircraft to pick them up. He wanted them to leave the copper mine and go down in the valley were Charlie had been shot. They were to wait there until a supply parachute was dropped at twelve noon. He asked them to find Charlie's body and wait one more night before being evacuated. The airdrop would include a body bag, camp equipment, medical supplies for Hastings and food. A C-123 cargo plane would pick them up the following morning.

They had stored the rifles and ammo in the dynamite shed. After retrieving them, Jess gave J.J. and Hastings each three dry sticks of dynamite. Jess put three in each of his flight suit leg pockets. Then, they headed for the valley below to find Charlie.

With M16 rifles slung over their shoulders and the survival kits on their backs, they looked like lost survivors who had walked out of the desert. Unkept, dirty and smelly, they were on the move again. The only thing out of place was the ragged carpet Hastings and Jess were carrying between them for Charlie's body.

It did not take long for Jess to realize his pants leg pockets were not the place for sticks of dynamite. They swung around his leg as he walked and bumped against whatever got in the way. He moved them to the almost empty survival kit on his back.

There was not much conversation as they walked down the road. They kept a sharp eye, scanning the area around them and further down the road, at the bottom, the road split. To the south, it entered a town a few miles away, and to the north they would soon find Charlie. Jess still felt like they were being watched.

"Samain said Charlie's body was rolled into the ravine somewhere near that flat area over there," J.J. said.

"Isn't that about where we saw them from the hill?" Jess asked.

She hurried ahead of them to look, and disappeared from their sight as she went into the ravine. Hastings was slow, but walking much better than before. He and Jess stood at the edge of the ravine, but could not see her.

"Where did she go now?" Jess asked. "See her?"

"No! I'll go down if you want to stay up here."

"Good, but do you feel like climbing back up? Are your legs strong enough?"

"This exercise will help loosen my joints. I'll be okay," Hastings said.

Jess nodded, "I'll walk north along this ridge. If you find her, one of you call me on the radio."

Hastings slid on his butt all the way to the bottom and headed slowly south around a bend in the ravine.

Jess could see the buildings of the mine, high on the mountainside to his left. To his right, across the ravine, another mountain rose to the location of their wrecked aircraft. It would be awhile before anyone could get to the wreckage and remove those bodies. For now, they needed to find Charlie.

What a mess the terrorists left behind! Lord Jesus, help us! Jess prayed.

"Jess, I'm up the ravine to the north," J.J. said on the radio. Her voice was shaky, "I found Charlie . . . at least what is left of him."

Hastings said he was on his way, so Jess jogged along the ridge of the sandstone ravine. There she was.

"I'm right above you, J.J.! Coming down," Jess said on the radio.

The sandstone slopes has sharp rocks, and a guy could be cut to pieces before getting to the bottom of this ravine, Jess thought. At the bottom, he stood up and examined his flight suit. Sure enough, he had cut the seat of his pants and also the calf of his legs.

"Dumb, dumb!" He said to himself.

J.J. had her back to Charlie's body, and had watched Jess' graceful decent from the ridge above.

He walked passed J.J. and over to Charlie.

Jess could see why J.J. was so sober. Most of his body was covered with sand from the storm, but enough was uncovered to see the damage done to him. His head, hands and feet had been severed, and were laying several inches from the body. Some terrorist butcher tried to make sure Charlie's infidel spirit would not roam the earth. Jess wondered if Charlie had been ready to meet God. Some day they would know.

Jess and Hastings rolled up Charlie's remains in the old rug they had brought down from the mine, and carried him to the top of the ravine.

The airdrop was late, so they sat in the dusty sun, not talking. Jess stood up, taking out a smoke flare to mark their location.

"You hear a plane?" Hastings asked.

"Not yet," he replied.

J.J. was quiet, with dried tear streaks down her dusty cheeks. She was staring at the rug that was wrapped around Charlie's body. They were not friends, but they had worked for the same anti-terrorist team.

"How well did you know Charlie, J.J.?" Jess asked.

"Not at all. He did not know that we were working for the same end result, using you," she said. "I only knew him when I saw him."

Hastings sat cross-legged next to the body, and gripped one of the ropes tied around it. He had not been listening to their conversation. It was the first time in the whole ordeal that he had stopped long enough to reflect on what had happened.

Jess had been watching him closely, and thought about the years in the past they had known each other. He really did not like Hastings for what he had been a part of, but felt sorry for him. They had been friends years ago, not close, but they often partied together.

Jess was thinking, *Will Hastings be punished for the crimes he shared while associated with the terrorists? There will always be a day of reckoning for him, as well as for the rest of us. It may not be in this lifetime, but be assured, we all will stand before God Almighty in the life to come and be accountable for our past deeds.*

"You knew Charlie for a long time, didn't you?" Jess asked, looking at Hastings.

He sat on the ground, leaning on his knees with his elbows, and would not look at either J.J. or Jess. A moan came from deep in his throat, and he covered his face with his hands as he sobbed.

J.J. looked at Jess and stood up, "I will walk to those distant ruins, and stay in sight."

"Fine, just keep your radio on."

Jess' shadow covered Hastings and Charlie when he moved closer. He put his hand on Hastings' shoulder.

"We better move Charlie down to the road where the aircraft had been parked. That area is the best strip for the landing, and we'd better be ready. Okay?"

"Sure, Jess. Whatever you think!" he said quietly.

"You going to be alright?" Jess asked.

"Physically, I'll get better. But, this thing about Charlie . . . why did God let him die such a horrible death? Did God take care of us in the desert just to let Charlie get burned and be tormented with all that pain, and then let him get shot by that greedy Arab? I don't understand this at all! Especially after Charlie spoke so highly of how God had been taking care of him." Hastings stood with his arms stretched toward the hot sun, sobbing.

Jess did not have any words of wisdom or comfort for him at

that time. Charlie was dead. Aliba was dead. And the other men who were in the helicopter were dead.

"How many of us will be in the same condition before this situation is over?" Jess whispered to himself. "If it weren't for the grace of God . . ."

Their load became heavier for them, carrying Charlie's remains to the clearing east of the ruins. Jess could see J.J. from there. Up the mountainside to the south, he could also see the remains of their OV10 Bronco and the Huey helicopter. There were at least two-dozen green parachutes dotting the same area of the mountain, giving a definite contrast in color to the landscape. They were still caught in the brush and cactus, flapping in the light breeze. Jess was surprised they were still there after the storm.

"We should bury this dynamite before getting on an aircraft, don't you think?" Jess asked Hastings.

Hastings did not answer; he just gave Jess a blank look. Then he removed the three sticks from his pocket and laid them on the ground against his foot. He sat next to Charlie again.

"Tell me something, Jess. How come you are always so cool, calm and collected about everything? You don't really seem to get excited about anything, do you?" he asked, not giving Jess time to reply. "Except when Eric popped you in the nose. Wish I had a cigarette. I haven't had one for two weeks . . . or is it three."

"I don't think I'm so cool, calm and collected," Jess said. "Not by any means! I have deep problems I fight every day. But, I try to remember to pray about them and then leave them with the Lord." He drank from his plastic water bottle, and then continued, "There may be times I don't outwardly show my fear, shock or sorrow, but it's there. I've tried to always look on the bright side of an issue and not be so hasty in making a judgment. Sometimes, that doesn't always work for me either!" Jess shielded his eyes from the sun. "You know I've made some stupid mistakes, like getting my nose busted by Eric. You surely can remember what my life was, years ago?"

Hastings' face suddenly changed and he began to laugh, "Yeah, you're right! After Eric hit you, you were a bloody mess. We thought you were for real. Yeah, a real hotshot pilot! I didn't know I was being set up, until Samain told me in the helicopter. Then I realized you had played a great acting part, even though you were bleeding a lot. Your beard kept me from recognizing you. That was a great show!"

"But that wasn't part of my show!" Jess said. "Eric threw that in for free, and boy did he ever."

They laughed again as the sun got hotter. Both of them were soaked with sweat and needed shade to get out of the sun's rays. Jess slid his survival kit off his back and searched through it for the light canvas lean-to. It would provide a small amount of shade for them.

"Give me a hand?" Jess asked.

They stretched the small canvas between two outcroppings of sandstone and placed large rocks on the top edges to keep the wind from blowing it away. Hastings pulled the rug that held Charlie's body into the shade, and pushed it back against some brush.

He leaned back against the rug with his arms around his bent knees. The swelling in his legs had disappeared completely. With his chin on his knees, he watched J.J. in the distance.

"We should drink some more water before we get dehydrated any further," Hastings suggested.

Jess nodded, "You're right." He drank a few mouthfuls of hot water, and thought, *This would taste better with instant coffee mixed in it.*

After collecting the dynamite from Hastings and J.J., Jess laid it gently on the ground next to a hole under a rock, where the sun would not shine on it. Some animal had dug a good-sized burrow large enough for holding nine sticks of dynamite. Carefully covering them with dirt and gravel, he placed a large rock on top and continued filling in the hole. Now they would not have to worry about those unstable sticks anymore.

Jess wondered, *Would animals eat into the cover of the dynamite sticks? Hope not. Don't know what it would do to them.*

The shade they had erected reduced the heat of the sun, and it felt pleasant and cooler leaning against the cool side of a boulder. The canvas did not cover much of an area, so they sat close together under it. Their body heat did not help the situation. To give them more room, they needed J.J.'s lean-to canvas to attach to this one.

"Hastings . . .I mean Larry. We may never see each other again, once we get back to Casablanca," Jess said.

"That's probably right! If they don't shoot me, I'll be in prison for the rest of my life," Hastings said. He continued telling Jess about his relationship with Charlie, before and after Colonel Alvarez kidnapped them.

"I'm sure Samain and Eric will speak on your behalf," Jess said. "If Charlie were here, I'm sure he would share how you two helped each other in the desert."

He patted the rug, nodding, "Made it out all right, didn't we, Charlie? I'll make sure you get home," he said, leaving his hand on the rug.

"May I get personal with you?" Jess asked. "If you feel I'm out of place, just tell me and I'll shut up." He moved around in front of Hastings and sat down. His face grew somber. "Larry, we knew each other fairly well years ago, and we did some partying around together."

"Didn't we though! We weren't so bad, back then. Not like the mess I'm in now, anyway."

Jess sat cross-legged and ran his fingers through the dirt on the ground between them. *Lord, you know what is on my heart,* he prayed silently. *Don't let me mess this up.*

"I had a big change in my life since those good old days. A big change for the better," Jess said. "It was such a change in a short period of time that Samain and Bushta were shocked. They know about it."

"What?" Hastings said with a smile, "Don't tell me you got religion?"

"If that is what you want to call it, yes!" Jess said wiping the sweat off his neck. "I got religion, born again, saved. My sins were washed away by Jesus Christ's blood that was shed for me at Calvary's cross," Jess blurted out.

Yes, that is what it is all about in a nutshell, he thought to himself. Jess surprised himself for such a sudden response, because he did not want Larry to think he was preaching at him. He wanted to help Larry as much as he could, and this was the only way. It was Jess' responsibility at that moment in time to speak from his heart.

Hastings sat quietly, waiting for Jess to finish what he had to say.

"I had such a change in my life that those things we used to do are the furthest things from my mind. I have no desire for that way of life anymore. Sometimes, I can't put into words what I mean." Jess paused and stretched out his legs to get the circulation back in them. He rubbed them because they tingled from going to sleep.

"It didn't happen in church back home, but in a friend's home here in Morocco," Jess said. "There wasn't a brilliant flash of light from heaven, just a conviction in my heart that I needed help, and Jesus was the only One who could help. My friends had introduced me to God's Son, Jesus Christ, who has made huge changes in my life." Jess hesitated a moment to let Hastings think about what he had said, then continued, "And . . . Jesus still does every day, because I've not reach perfection, yet! That won't happen until I'm in heaven with Him. Larry, He can help you, too!"

"I'm listening," Hastings said, looking up at Jess.

"Am I making you uncomfortable?"

Hastings shook his head, no.

Jess felt awkward, because it had been a long time since he had shared his heart in this way. He clasped his hands together, putting his elbows on his knees and rested his chin on his hands, facing Hastings eye-to-eye.

"Do you remember a time in your life when someone shared Jesus Christ with you?" he asked. "By that I mean, have you ever asked Jesus to come into your life, save you and forgive you of your sins?"

Hastings looked at Jess for a long time with no expression or reply. Then, leaning to the side, he rose to his feet and walked away from Jess. Hastings turned and replied, "I think Charlie did that in the desert with me, when he was remembering scripture verses to keep us going." He turned and walked up the road.

"Lord, he's in Your hands," Jess whispered.

Jess turned around and saw J.J. waving at them. He stood up and shielded his eyes from the sun. She was pointing to the west, towards the far mountains. Hastings waved back to her. Sure enough, a high-winged, single-engine aircraft was heading their way.

Jess changed channels on his radio and listened to her conversation with the pilots. She began running toward Jess and Hastings on the dusty, rocky road. She fell, got up, and continued on her way. Out of breath, she ran past Hastings and up to Jess, throwing her arms around his neck. She was sobbing so hard with emotions, that Jess could not understand what she said. But the big smile was enough to explain her happiness.

The small aircraft flew over them at a very low altitude to check out their approach, and then circled. A supply bundle was dropped by parachute, and it hit the road right in front of Hastings. He slowly strolled over to it as J.J. started folding up the parachute. Evidently, Samain had not yet been able to make arrangements for their pickup.

They pulled the package over to the shaded area. J.J. made a larger shaded area with the white parachute, and held it down with large rocks from the ditch along the roadside. The small aircraft passed over dipping it wings, and headed west.

Hastings and Jess transferred Charlie to a body bag they had taken from the dropped supply bundle. They then separated the food, water and other goods into three piles. Jess and J.J. filled their survival kits and a backpack for Hastings. J.J. found a short note from Samain, telling them he would see them the next day, if the weather was good.

Their spirits were heightened, and the conversations continued about the future, and what could eventually happen to Hastings. They felt certain his prison term would not be lengthy, and that he would be able to return to his family in the United States.

Then they were quiet for a while, resting in the shade during the hottest part of the afternoon.

The ruins were visible from where Jess lay on his side with his head propped up in his hand. He wondered if J.J. had seen anything interesting while she had been walking around in the ruins. They were adobe ruins, but with square cut rocks and an arch like the kind Romans would use.

"Did you find anything worthwhile in those ruins?" he asked. "Are they Roman or Berber?"

"No, I did not notice anything, because my mind was not on archaeological discoveries," she said in a disinterested way. "I have no idea who built them, nor do I know why they are no longer used."

She certainly was not in the mood for treasure hunting conversation. She was thinking about getting out of there. Their tensions were less since the aircraft dropped the supplies.

"If you two don't mind, I'm going to nose around those ruins for awhile. Maybe I can find our hidden fortune. If I do, we will split it three ways," laughing, Jess did not wait for a reply.

Taking his well-supplied survival kit, M16 and two water containers, Jess leisurely strolled toward the ruins. With the sky clear, and no hat, the sun beat down on his head and shoulders, something fierce. Jess soaked his dirty red bandana with water, and tied it around his forehead so that it covered the top of his head. He supposed he was trying to steam his brains, but the damp cloth did seem cool flopping in the breeze against his head. At least it kept the direct sun from feeling so bad. He pulled up his jump suit collar to protect his neck from the burning sun's rays and unzipped the front down to the waist, letting in a little breeze to blow some of the stink off.

The barren land did not look like it would ever produce a living plant, even if water were available; even so, the experts say it was very possible with the right amount of moisture to grow almost anything. The dust from the road was so fine; it just hung in the air when Jess stepped in it. The parched land was void of any life above ground, only the three of them. Jess reflected that maybe that should be telling them something.

The road divided at the ruins, going south past the copper mines to the left and then continued on west ahead of him. He climbed up to the rock foundation entrance of the first ruins and stepped inside the archway. It did have the influence of the Romans in the archway, but the foundation was sandstone. The ruins were not more than a hundred years old. Some dried weeds had grown on the inside dirt floor, but they had died there.

Jess stepped down onto the ground inside, knelt down and picked up a handful of sand. It was a very fine grain, and most of it blew away when he poured it into his other hand.

Then a heavy item fell in his palm. Looking closer, he saw that it was a silver coin about the size of a dime, with Arabic inscription and a date of 1862. It definitely had more silver than the U.S. minted clad dimes. It was much heavier. "Found my wage for today," he said, and put it in his vest pocket, zipping it closed. "Didn't find that with a metal detector, but wish I had mine to hunt with here! Never know what's lost or intentionally buried."

He ran his fingers through the sand a few more times and found nothing. *Lucky find*, he told himself. *Not really! It was there on purpose for me to pick up. But, why?*

While he fingered the coin and rubbed it under his thumb, Jess still had a funny feeling that he was being watched, not just by J.J. and Hastings. He put the coin in his flight suit vest pocket and zipped it shut. Turning around to look down the road and up to the mines, he searched those areas with binoculars. *Nothing! Lord, I don't like this uncomfortable feeling. I'm resting in You for our safety*, he thought quietly to himself. Looking back to where the shelter was, he could see they were using their binoculars watching him, and then they would glance at the mines. They were probably curious about what he had seen up there.

"I need to found some shade," Jess said out loud. He did not like standing in the open; anyway, especially when he felt like someone was watching him. There was a good place down behind one wall, where it was thick enough to stop most high-powered rifles. He wondered if there were poisonous snakes or scorpions in the ruins.

It would have been nice to have a good riflescope on this M16, he thought and leaned the rifle against the wall. *But, open sights are better than none.*

From Jess' viewpoint, he could clearly see the mines to the south. Hastings and J.J. were still under the shade of the white parachute with Charlie's body, to the east. He could not see anyone up the mountain behind him to the north; but then, he could not see to the west because of the ruins' high wall.

There was no one to be seen anywhere toward the mines, or down the dusty road toward Ksar Morhel. *What about the east road that goes past our shelter and the crashed aircraft? Over there, somewhere is Aliba's grave and the cave where J.J. and I had hid. The only things moving with any life are the parachutes left by the paratroopers, flapping in the breeze.*

Nothing at the two crash sites was moving. Jess was thinking, *If the 50 caliber machine guns on the helicopter were still in working order? It might not be a bad idea to check them out. We don't want to leave weapons there for wreck-scavengers, especially if they still operate. No one had looked for personal things belonging to the dead flight crew, either. And no one had buried the dead. Jackals probably roam around these parts at night, even thought we haven't seen any. Hope Samain will take care of the dead.*

Jess spoke into the radio, "How's every little thing over there, baby sister?"

Silence, then Jess saw her move and pick up the transceiver.

"Partner, I'm plum tuckered out!" she replied, in somewhat of a Texas accent.

"Would you and Larry feel like a short hike?"

Silence again. Jess saw her bend over, probably to wake up Hastings. He sat up, and she handed the radio to him.

"What's happening, Jess?" He asked.

"Do you feel like walking over to your crash site?"

"Sure, but why?"

"Have J.J. check out the weapons on board. They may still be good. If they are, we'd better secure them!"

"Sounds good to us. What about the crew's remains?"

"Better let Samain handle that area. If you find anyone, make a mental note of the location so he can find them. But the heavy firepower from the helicopter should be in our possession. Also, keep a sharp eye around you at all times. I still feel like someone is watching us. I guess I'm getting paranoid."

"Right! We're on our way."

"I'll be out of your line-of-sight for awhile. Curiosity has got the better of me. I'm going back up to where we spent the night. Keep in contact!"

"Yes, sir!" J.J. said.

Jess saw her wave at him.

Talking to himself again, Jess said, "Well, we have at least eight hours of sunlight to burn. Better use it. Check out the area before crawling out of here first, Jess. Never hurts to double check."

He searched with his binoculars.

"Looks good!" Slinging the M16 on his shoulder, Jess checked his .45 automatic and the two containers of water. If he needed more water, he could refill at the mines. After washing down a chocolate bar, he was ready to head up there.

His mind wondered again, *All I need now is a helmet, a dozen well equipped U.S. 101st Airborne Screaming Eagle soldiers for backup, and to complete my field equipment requirements, I would need . . .* Smiling to himself, *Dream on, Jess!*

He stepped out on the dusty road and headed south toward the town of Ksar Morhel. Every so often, he would suddenly change to the opposite side of the road to check the water run-offs where they cut into the sandstone making ruts and ravines. Plus, it is harder to hit a moving target. Then he decided to take a short detour up to the mines. There was something unusually strong drawing him back up to the mines.

The Lord works in mysterious ways, Jess thought.

Jess had not noticed any movement of nomads or caravans while they had been stuck at the mines. It was possible that the little town in the valley was abandoned, since the mines were closed.

But I want to check it out anyway, he thought to himself. *Just for the fun of it, just because it is there. There might have been something of historical value left behind. I'll never know unless I check it out.*

If anyone were up there, they would not see Jess approaching the mines from the north side. It was the same approach he and Eric had taken the day before. The climbing was punishing to his legs, bruised ankle and boots. He had to stop often to drink some water and catch his breath.

Even though the rocks and gravel were sandstone, they were sharp as razor blades. His gloves would not last long under these conditions. They were made for pilot's gripping aircraft controls and knobs, not for rough ground conditions.

Thinking again that he had not flushed a living creature from its hiding place during his climb, he remembered the desert rat with her little ones in the cave. The only vegetation around was small clumps of dried grass along the sides of the ravines. There was no surface water for large animals, only the watering troughs close to the hand-dug wells near the desert. The mine had the only well water he had seen, and he was not making fast progress climbing up to it.

Finally reaching the mine entrance, Jess sat in the shadows for a few minutes to drink and relax. The area looked like a war zone, after the past few days of the storm tearing things down and the aerial bombing by Gina and J.J.

The mine property could be privately owned, he thought. *But not likely. The Moroccan government probably owns it.* There were no signs posted as to ownership, so Jess hoped he was not trespassing. *It would be a shame to get shot for that, especially, after all I've been through.*

Most of his visits to Morocco were on the west side of the mountains. Jess' knowledge of the eastern part of Morocco's early history was zero, so he did not know what to expect or what to search for around the mines relating to relics or antique items.

"Relics should not be plentiful, and pirates treasures shouldn't be hidden this far from the coast," he mumbled to himself. "But, bedouins or modern day terrorists could use abandon mines for storage of contraband."

There was not a sound from anywhere, just the quietness of the desert and mountains. During the few minutes of relaxation, a small whiff of cool air from the mine twirled dust into a funnel, twisting and dancing around, passed by Jess. The little dust devil grew in size, jumping around like it had a mind of its own. It continued on its way until it hit the dynamite shed.

Jess' mind flashed to the wet dynamite sticks that Bushta and Samain had found. Half-expecting the nitroglycerin to explode when the little twister hit the dynamite sticks, he threw up his arms in front of his face and rolled over with his back towards the shed for protection.

Nothing happened!

"Thank you, Lord!" Jess said, setting up.

As he thought about it, he was surprised that dynamite had not been locked in better storage, especially in such a large quantity. Perhaps that was an indication of frequent visits by someone? Jess did not know about Bushta breaking the door down.

After filling his water containers, he went to the dynamite shed. Inside, everything seemed to be as they left it. No paperwork lying around, no journal books, no records for inventory. There had to be at least fifty cases of dynamite stacked against one wall.

Why so much, he wondered?

The remains of the damaged offices were empty of papers, magazines and files, or any other form of written material. No information he could use around there.

Returning to the shed, he found a five-pound tin of calcium carbide. "I can use this to fill the carbide lamp in the tunnel. Better do that while I'm thinking about it," Jess whispered to himself. "I want to check out the interior of that mine shaft, just because it's there."

Jess entered the large entrance of the mine, and felt the coolness of its interior. Decision time, which of the three tunnels to enter first?

That reminded Jess of what they would say back home. "I was thinking, and nothing happened!" He laughed at himself and snickered when it echoed in the mine.

Entering the left mine shaft where the three of them had stayed overnight, the hair on the back of his neck suddenly stood up! Goose bumps popped out on his arms, and he felt a chill. It was not cold, because his flight suit sleeves were rolled up and he was covered with perspiration. Jess had the feeling of someone close . . . or the feeling that he was about to be pounced on. Someone must have heard him talking to himself.

Dropping to his knees with the rifle at ready, he released the safety and leaned flat against the wall to make himself a smaller target. A black cloud of bats flew over him toward the mouth of the tunnel.

Something had disturbed them, because it was the wrong time of day for them to be leaving the dark depths of the mine. Their wings beat the air, and their squeals subsided once they entered the larger mine cavern. They flapped around squealing frantically, and finally attached themselves to the ceiling of the large room. The floor became a slimy mess of their droppings caused by their fear and excitement. The stench, along with the heat from outside, forced Jess further into the tunnel.

The noise from the bats quieted down. He could not hear anything from inside the tunnel, so he continued until he found the carbide lamp hanging on the overhead wooden beam. The old calcium carbide in the lamp had hardened and would not dump out. Pouring water over the carbide made it like a paste, and he could scrap it out with his finger.

The newer carbide from the five-pound container made a brighter flame for the lamp. Jess made sure no carbide was spilt in the water on the floor. Mixing it with water produced acetylene, which was the burnable gas for the lamp. If the carbide was in the water on the floor, could it be a hazard? Well, he didn't know and was not going to drop any to find out.

Jess put the five-gallon container of carbide on the plywood sheet they had carried in earlier, where it would be safe, away from the water on the floor. He planned to take it to the shed when he went out.

The lamp was designed to wear on a head strap, belt buckle, or carried by hand. He used the ragged head strap that was on it and placed it over his bandana around his forehead. The flame from the acetylene gas created a bright light and reflected with a broad coverage. The strap still had some life, and it adjusted to a tight fit.

Jess needed to find something to mark the tunnel wall for his return trip. There were no spray paint cans in this part of the world. He slung the M16 rifle over his shoulder again. Using his combat knife to mark every tenth vertical wooden beam in the tunnel, he notched the edge towards the exit.

Continuing on, all Jess could hear was the echoing of his boots on the floor and their sloshing water from the condensation collected in small pools on the mine floor. He rolled the flight suit long sleeves up to his armpits and began to feel air across the dampness of his sweaty bare arms. *There must be another opening somewhere in the mine*, he thought.

After about thirty minutes of gradual downgrade walking, the tunnel leveled and the light breeze on his face become stronger. But, he still could not see any light up ahead, and the tunnel was narrowing. The walls were slimy with some type of growth like moss, saturated with moisture, and the air stunk of mold.

Jess stopped to drink from his water bottle, squatted and listened for any sound. Nothing. The tunnel's ceiling was so low he had to bend over to walk.

He was not going much further stooping over; his back would not take it. All Jess could hear now was the steady increase of the wind whistling across the tunnel's surface. It would have been easier lying on a cart mounted on the rails, but he did not remember seeing one back at the entrance.

Jess' compass still worked after an hour or more walking in the tunnel. He was surprised there was so little natural ferrous mineralization, or iron content, in the mine. None seem to be present to interfere with the compass. His course at that point was 265 degrees in a westerly direction.

After another thirty minutes or so of stooped walking, he stopped for another drink and squatted against a wooden beam. *Why did I have the thought of blowing a whistle? I guess it was the little boy in me. Just wanted to hear it echo.*

"Could it cause a cave in? Why take the chance?" Jess spoke softly so it would not echo, then dismissed the thought.

He took another swallow of water to wash down the remainder of the candy bar he had opened earlier. That would hold him until he returned to J.J. and Hastings.

Jess was wondering how they were getting along with the guns from the helicopter. He squatted, and sat on the heels of his boots, and squeezed his thighs and calf muscles, then relaxed them. Rising up again, he stretched as best he could in the low tunnel, figuring he would go just a little further and then head back.

#

While J.J. and Hastings were searching for weapons from the crashed helicopter, they were not aware of the camel and mule caravan passing above them on the road. Along the top of the ravine and up the side of the hill, the dust stirred by the animals' hooves and men walking made bad visibility in the direction of the wrecked aircraft.

Only the braying of the mules alerted them, causing the two to kneel in the helicopter's burned wreckage. All they could see was the cloud of dust and hear the animals' discontented braying. The westward movement of the caravan passed the shelter and ruins without stopping. They disappeared in their own dust cloud.

The two scroungers carried a pair of black-soot covered .50 caliber machine guns between them on their shoulders from the crashed helicopter. In step, they marched back to the shaded shelter where Charlie's remains were in the body bag. J.J.'s ribs hurt when she bent over to lay the guns down.

"Can I be of assistance, J.J.?" asked Hastings.

"No, thank you." She put her hands along her rib cage and took a deep breath, "I will take some more aspirin with you in a few minutes to keep the pain and swelling down. Are you hurting in your joints?"

"Nope! Under the circumstances, I'm feeling pretty good."

"From the way you looked yesterday, I did not think you could carry on like this," J.J. said. "But, your swelling has subsided considerably, and your color is good. Without medication, your recovery is a miracle."

Miracle, Hastings thought to himself, *Is it possible?*

They sat under the white parachute's shade and shared a water container and each took a couple of aspirin. The extra physical work produced a great deal of sweat in the arid heat and dust. They both were soaking wet through their clothing. The wind across their wet clothes helped to cool them off.

"We were very fortunate that caravan stirred up that dust storm, hiding everything on this side of the road," Hastings commented.

J.J. nodded and yawned.

"You're not afraid of manual labor, are you?" Hastings said, making idle talk.

"No, and I am not afraid of relaxing when it is finished," she replied with a smile, not noticing him staring at her. She pulled her long hair back behind her head with her hands together, lifting it so air could flow across her hot neck. She glanced at Hastings and he looked away.

J.J. turned and knelt next to the supply box and began opening the rations of food for their meal. She knew Jess would be returning soon, and they all needed to eat.

Hastings stood up and turned his back to her. He turned

around to say something, but her back was to him as she busied herself with the rations. He walked away.

The silence was broken only by the noise J.J. was making and the stones Hastings was kicking down the road.

#

Back in the tunnel, the constant stooping was getting to Jess. He felt like he was on a wild goose chase anyway.

Then he noticed something lying on the floor to the right of the rails, like a bench. It was long and about two feet wide, waist high and was covered with a heavy canvas.

Interesting! Someone has stored supplies back here. What could it be? He thought smiling to himself, already feeling the thrill of discovery, even though he had no idea what he had discovered.

He tried to untie one of many ropes of the netting, which held the canvas in place, but it was too tight. At the far end, he found the canvas draped loose and pulled it back enough to see stacks of waxed bundles, about the size of a loaf of bread. When he pressed one with his thumb, whatever it was, was packed hard.

"Why is it stored back here where it's so damp and cold?" Jess asked himself quietly.

He was chilled from the dampness of the tunnel and from his wet flight suit where he had been sweating in it. The wind blowing through the tunnel did not help as he continued to snoop around the pile.

Samain and Bushta would know more about this, or even J.J. with all her Interpol experience. "It looks like drugs to me!" he whispered.

Jess was thinking of breaking open one of the bundles to see what it was. Then he thought maybe he should leave the stuff alone, because his curiosity was peaked and it might get him into trouble again.

"I know! I'll put a bundle in my survival kit, if it will fit. Good idea, Jess!"

He unslung the M16 rifle, laid it on top of the canvas and unstraped the survival kit. Sure enough, one bundle did fit. After zippering the kit closed, strapping it on his back again, slinging the rifle over his shoulder, he was ready to go.

Checking his time, he could go westbound at least thirty more minutes. "Wait, put the canvas back in place." He slung the canvas back in place, "Okay! Let's go!"

He had to get on his hands and knees to go further. The kit on his back banged and scrapped the top of the tunnel. Ahead of him was a piece of equipment leaning against the wall, partially blocking the tunnel.

Sure enough, it was an old flatbed on small rail wheels. The wheels should turn unless they were rusted in place.

He pulled the flatbed away from the wall. "Yea, the top two wheels turn, and one on the bottom turns. I bet that fourth one will turn with some persuasion."

Jess used the handle of the combat knife to beat the rust loose. His pounding and the squeaky noise of the rusty wheels echoed through the tunnel.

"If you grunt harder Jess, it might break loose!" he muttered to himself. "Use both hands and push against the bottom of the bed with your feet."

Well, self did just as self suggested and the wheel broke free and turned, Jess though to himself.

"Now keep moving! It's time to put this flatbed to work on the rails."

Pulling on the edge of the wooden bed just broke a board loose and did not move the flatbed at all. Jess fell against the opposite wall.

"Well, what's holding it in place? Check it out!"

Sure enough, it was chained, and rail spikes held the chain to the wall. How was he going to pry them out of the wall or break the chain loose from the bed? He looked behind it to see where it was attached to the bed.

"This is taking too long," he said to himself. "Damn it! I don't have time to mess around with this! Excuse me, Lord, I'm getting impatient!"

He could see that where the chain came down over the one axle and laid on it, they were rusted together. Then it was attached to the other end where it lay across that axle and back to the wall.

"Okay! Just pry the rusty chain off the axle, and its weight should pull it off the other axle."

It rattled and banged against the water soaked wooden bed, knocking a hole in one of the planks. Jess kicked the chain loose. It hit the tunnel floor with a thud as the flatbed fell away from the wall and banged against the track rails.

"Well, I couldn't have put it on there any straighter, even if I had tried! Now will it move?" He gave it a shove, "Sure enough!"

He cleared the tunnel ceiling lying on the bed of the cart. It looked good to continue on through the tunnel.

"You could run into trouble, if anything hanging down from this low ceiling snags you," he told himself. "Just be careful, Jess!"

Pushing with the toes of his boots against the wooden rail ties easily moved him on the rails. *To be so rusty, it moves along all right. It squeaked some, but that's not so bad.* In fact, he forgot the noise and gained speed through the tunnel. The flatbed turned out to be the best thing around!

After pushing for twenty minutes, his compass heading began to change, indicating the tracks were coming around to the south and beginning to climb. Jess knew the easy coasting would not last long!

Then he realized there were light reflections on the walls ahead of him. Before getting any closer, he stopped the noisy vehicle and listened. Nothing! As he cautiously moved on the tracks toward the light, the tunnel began to widen and the ceiling heighten as the tracks began a slight downgrade.

"Stop and listen again," Jess whispered. "Nothing!"

He stood upright slow and easy, trying not to make any noise. The bats must have clung to the ceiling and made their home;

their mess was all over the floor. The slimy stench of many years accumulating turned his stomach.

The tunnel opened into a natural cavern of icicle-like calcium carbonate stalactites formed by water dripping through cracks hanging from the ceiling, and stalagmite mound deposits rising from the floors. They did not have much color, not like the caverns from back home.

Jess walked toward the light. The cavern floor looked like a salvage yard of metal left by the miners. The air had become warmer and the breeze picked up. Jess checked for trip wires and booby traps ahead of him in the rubble.

Old pieces of metal beams, rusty gears, cables, pipe and electrical wires covered the floor and were propped against the walls. An old electrical generator and gasoline motor looked ancient, but Jess thought they probably did not run anymore. The cavern humidity was lower than in the tunnel.

The cavern became a larger, man-made room, with a huge caged entrance to the outside where the light was blinding. The opening was covered with heavy meshed flatiron strips, reinforced vertically with I-beams fastened into the ceiling and buried into the floor.

Looking at the huge room with its giant caged door, Jess thought to himself, *Dynamite would be the only key to open this exit. This must have been the west mine entrance at one time, which is marked on the maps.*

Jess' compass went wild near the iron gate, so he put it back in his pocket.

To the south, Jess could see out across the desert for miles at his altitude. He was up 5,000 feet or so above the desert floor. It was still hazy in the distance from the sandstorm the day before.

Focusing his binoculars, he spotted a caravan of six camels and three mules in the valley below. They were slowly moving west, about six miles from the opening of the mine where he stood.

A vehicle of some kind had left a high cloud of dust traveling further west toward Beni Tajit. On a clear day looking to the southeast of that point, Jess should have been able to see aircraft at the Algerian airports of Bechar/Leger or at Bechar/Ouakda. But not this day!

A sheer cliff dropped off on the other side of the iron barrier down at least a thousand feet to another slope. Then it abruptly dropped off to the foothills of the mountain to where a road from the west ended.

"I'll bet the digging stopped here, and the tunnel was dug from the east," Jess said, mumbling to himself. "They just left all this equipment and machinery here to rust away. Where did they mine for copper in this tunnel? Nothing resembles raw copper in the walls or ceiling? I don't remember seeing any tunnels leading off of this one. Maybe the other two tunnels have the copper ore? The search through those other tunnels will have to wait for another day!"

Overall, Jess had only been gone two hours. He used the portable transceiver and started calling J.J. and Hastings to find out how they were doing, although he was not sure if they would hear him from this side of the mountain.

"Hello, little sister! Do you have a copy on this homesick old Texan?"

He turned up the volume. Just noise. No reply.

"Okay world! Anyone speak English out there, please reply."

"You have no patience at all, Tex!" Came a male voice. "Little sister is waiting supper for you! When can they expect you home?"

Jess frowned. Was that Hastings' voice? "Who am I talking to?"

"This is Main Force, Samain."

"Well, I'll be dog-gone," Jess said. "Where the heck are you, old friend of mine?"

"Main Force base. You are sending me a strong signal. So, do not send a long transmission. Supper is waiting! Signing off!"

Jess pushed the talk switch twice to let him know he understood the message. He turned off the radio and returned it to his survival kit.

On the rails again, Jess kicked hard and fast with the toes of his boots to get the momentum downhill on the flatbed. He picked up good speed heading eastbound through the tunnel. There did not seem to be any reason to stop going back.

It did not take long to arrive at the east entrance of the mine. Jess lifted the flatbed from the tracks and headed down the dusty road for the sheltered area. With the binoculars, he could see J.J. and Hastings waving at him. He waved back and took a shortcut down the side of the mountain.

After they ate, Jess spent the rest of the afternoon sharing his mining tour with his two companions. The three agreed the bundle he picked up in the tunnel was drugs, and they should wait for Samain to open it.

They talked for a while until the mountain's shadows moved over them. The coolness of the night made them drowsy, so they said their goodnights, checked their bedrolls for bugs and scorpions, and stretched out to sleep. The heavens were certainly clear and the stars seemed exceptionally bright, especially after the sandstorm earlier.

The sand in the atmosphere to the east had cleared. The evening star was brighter than the previous nights, and Jess just laid there staring at it, waiting for sleep. He prayed for Marie Ann to rest peacefully at home. She would be watching the moon tonight, too.

J.J. and Larry were both breathing deeply, and the stargazing finally put Jess to sleep.

#

Morning came early as they prepared for an aircraft to pick them up. Breakfast was over, and everything was packed before the sun rose above the eastern mountains. It was a clear blue sky with no sand and a good day for flying.

It did not take long for them to load, once the cargo door of the C-123 aircraft lowered. Charlie's body was secured in netting on a pallet, along with the machine guns from the helicopter.

The three companions moved forward to rows of web seats facing each other in the cargo bay, and buckled in. Samain came out of a radio room and buckled in next to J.J. She hugged him and held onto his arm while they became airborne. They all were extremely exhausted from all that had happened.

At cruising altitude, the engines' throttles were readjusted to synchronize them, and the outside noise decreased. Samain took J.J.'s face between his hands and kissed her lightly.

"I am most happy to have you three alive and well," he said.

Samain and Jess looked at each other, unbuckled at the same time, meeting in the center of the cargo bay. Jess thought his lungs would burst before Samain let go of him. Holding each other at arms length, they had tears blurring their vision.

"God bless you, Samain!" Jess said.

"He has, and He is!" he replied, and they hugged again.

Bushta came down from the cockpit area to join them. Samain turned to Hastings and shook his hand. He unbuckled and grabbed Samain around the neck with both arms, and then Bushta also. Hastings was in uncontrollable tears as their arms encircled him. J.J. joined their group, and they all held on to each other.

Finally, Hastings controlled his voice enough to say, "Thank you all for not leaving me in the desert and not making me stay behind back there. I know my activities and business have not been lawful in your country or anywhere else, for that matter. I couldn't find my way out of that mess I was in. Forgive me? Indirectly, I'm responsible for many deaths, and I'm ready for whatever consequences come."

They all embraced each other again.

One of the aircraft crew members brought coffee and French pastry. They buckled into the web seats again, because wind turbulence began to bounce the aircraft around. The food and drink hit the spot while they related their information to Samain. They were finally heading safely back to Casablanca, unwinding, laughing, crying and clapping their hands.

Jess showed Samain the bundle found in the mine tunnel. His

eyes got enormous and he yelled something in Arabic at the top of his lungs. J.J. began to clap her hands and sing with Samain. Whatever the bundle was, it made a hit!

He took his knife and punched a hole in the bundle of white powder, which came out on the blade. Jess knew then it was drugs. What type it was did not really matter. Samain sampled the white powder with a wet finger and gave them another big smile, nodding his head in approval. They had found where drug dealers had hidden one of their shipments.

"I reckon you'd like to know where I found that," Jess said. "Well, give me a map, and I would be happy to show you."

Samain laid out a map on the floor in front of Jess, and he marked the two mines with a note: 'Far left tunnel, halfway to the west end, under canvas on the right side of the tunnel.'

"From your description, this will be our largest find to date," he said, and went forward to the cockpit area.

This news topped off their happy mood!

Hastings elbowed Jess, offering his handshake, "Thank you for helping me, too, Jess. You really didn't have to." He settled back into the webbing of the seat. "Sometime you'll have to tell me how you got involved at the airport when the assassination took place."

"It would be a long story!" Jess said. "I may write a book about it sometime and send you a copy. We should try to keep in touch after this ordeal anyway, no matter the outcome of your trial."

He closed his eyes and leaned back into the web seat. Listening to the throb of the turbo engines was putting him to sleep. Hastings elbowed Jess again.

"I'm ready to take you up on that offer you made me back there at the mines," he said. "How can I get Jesus in my life? Charlie told me about the power of prayer while we were in the desert. I definitely need a change for the better."

CHAPTER THIRTY-FIVE

Jess felt a hand on his shoulder as he sensed the aircraft beginning a turn.

"Jess, I need to talk to you up front," Samain said.

"Sure!" Jess said, excusing himself with Hastings and unbuckling from the web seat. He turned back to Hastings, and said, "We can finish that discussion later. Be back."

From the expression on Samain's face, something had upset him. The aircraft was slowing down, and the landing gears were being lowered. The landing lights reflected on thin clouds as the aircraft descended through them. Jess knew they had not been in the air long enough to be making an approach landing to Casablanca. He could not see the city lights of Casablanca out the cargo bay porthole window.

When they got into the cockpit cabin, Samain motioned for Jess to sit in a crew's seat and buckle in. Samain sat next to the radio operator. They were talking in French to someone on the radio. He swiveled his seat around to Jess and locked it in place. From a paper, he began to read the message, "Urgent! Return to Force Headquarters! Immediately!"

Jess looked at him blankly, "What's happening?"

"I am not sure what this message is about. It is from our king in Rabat," Samain said. "We will learn more once we are at headquarters. I am sorry for the delay arriving in Casablanca."

"Sure, but for how long?"

"I do not really know. When we land, I will go to our headquarters and then return to the plane. It should not take long. I wanted you to know about the delay first. If it is necessary, I will tell the others . . . only, after I return!"

Once the aircraft taxied and parked, the engines were shut down. Samain motioned for everyone to stay in the aircraft, and he left.

Bushta went over to Jess, "Why have we landed here?"

"Samain got a message for us to land. He said he would tell us all about it when he returns. He apologized for our delay getting to Casablanca."

Bushta shrugged and asked if anyone wanted coffee or something else to drink. No one wanted anything, so he poured himself a cup, then walked over to a porthole and looked out. Everyone else stretched out on the web seats and closed their eyes, including Jess.

Shortly, Jess was awaken by the pilot and Bushta talking. He rolled on his side, facing them. Their voices had lowered, and reading lips that spoke in Arabic still did not work for him.

He slowly stood and walked to the exit doorway. It was dark and quiet outside, not even an airport beacon tracing the sky. The brightness of the stars in the west silhouetted the mountains.

"I have your gear and emergency kit," Bushta told Jess. "A truck is coming for you."

"I'm staying here?" Jess asked, stunned by Bushta's statement. He put his hands on his hips, "What now?"

"I do not know anymore than that. Be safe, and we will see you soon," Bushta said with a handshake and hug.

"I should say goodbye to the others."

"Let them rest, I will explain to them. Your transportation is here." He said pointing outside.

Jess shook his hand again and left the aircraft. Its engines started as soon as he was out of the way, and it was taxing before Jess was underground inside the headquarters.

Samain met him at the elevator, and the guard handed him the picture ID badge that he had previously. Samain's expression had changed to a smile, but he did not speak until they were in the commanding officer's office.

They had a satellite monitor set up for communications. The Commander pressed a button inside his desk drawer, and a large screen TV lowered from the ceiling at the back of his office. King Itssani was on the monitor. A Moroccan airman moved a video camera on a tripod in front of Jess, and at the bottom left corner of the TV screen, Jess could see himself. The airman left the office.

The king, commander and Samain spoke shortly in Arabic. Then Samain nodded to Jess, "King Itssani wishes to speak to you again, Mr. Hanes."

The king was standing next to his desk, which had a picture of his family on it, three young children and his wife. He wore a light colored beige European business suit with a bright red tie. His smile was real, but his face also carried a serious expression.

"Yes, Your Highness. I am pleased to see you again," Jess said, with a bow.

"Thank you, Mr. Hanes. I am most happy you are in good health, and you have returned to us again. I will not talk long, but I must impose again."

"Yes, Your Highness?"

"Colonel Alvarez has escaped from the Algerian prison and is somewhere in Morocco. I feel he is searching for you. From reports I have received, it is evident he was the person responsible for the death of my older brother, and the death of the others returning from Algeria. My agents tell me you found drugs in a mine not far from where you crashed. Is this correct?"

"That is correct, Your Highness," Jess said. He knew what was coming, and he did not want to hear anymore. He wanted to go home.

After clearing his throat, the king proceeded, "Will you please resume assisting my agents? The information I have substantiates the cache of drugs belong to Alvarez. It is conceivable he is there now."

Jess was silent for a moment. He looked at Samain, and then nodded to the King. "Yes, Your Highness. Although I'm anxious to get home, I will continue to help."

"Thank you again."

Samain said, "We will promptly see to it, Your Highness."

The King nodded to Samain, and the screen retracted into the ceiling. The video camera and other equipment were removed, and the commander left the two men alone in his office.

"That was short and sweet!" Jess said. "Straight and to the point!"

They shook hands.

"You know, you did not have to agree to this again," Samain said.

"Yes, I did! And you know I have to help finish the job. It would be too much to expect Colonel Alvarez to stay in prison with all his millions in gold on the outside. Probably in Swiss banks! That would be wishful thinking, don't you think?" Jess put his hands on his hips, "I wonder who he bought off with his gold?"

"You are right. But we had planned to take him from Algeria tomorrow. He must have bribed someone in the prison." Samain led Jess from the room. "We must leave as soon as we have cleaned up. You do not have to wear that beard anymore, unless you like it."

"I may shave it off. Haven't made up my mind. Could we get something to eat after I clean up? I'm awful hungry and thirsty."

"Yes! The aircraft will be ready by then. You do not have problems flying at night, do you?" Samain asked.

Jess slapped him on the shoulder, "Are you kidding? Not as long as you're my wing man!"

"We will have two helicopters of Moroccan soldiers and the Vigilante," Samain said. "You and I will fly it to the mine and land on the road to the entrance. The men will secure the road in the valley and above the mine. We will search all three mine tunnels. There may be more than the one cache of drugs."

"You're probably right," Jess said. "Hopefully we will beat Alvarez to his stash of dope."

They entered a private stateroom for officers. "You will have privacy here," Samain told him. "Lock the door and do not let anyone enter, other than me! I will bring food to you. Okay?"

"Understood! I need a change of clothes and shaving gear."

"You will find everything in the bathroom, and there is a variety of flight suits in the closet. Underwear is located in the bottom drawer with socks. All sizes. Help yourself."

Samain excused himself, locking the door behind him.

The room was nicer than most expensive hotels back stateside; at least it was fully furnished, and there was satellite TV and radio.

Jess had showered, shaved and dressed when a knock at the door woke him from a restful nap. Using the peephole in the metal door, he could not see anyone on the other side.

He thought, *Someone must have been playing a game.*

A feeling came over him to move against the wall, away from the door. The door may not be bulletproof, and the walls may not stop anything either.

For several minutes, he stood against the wall without moving.

Bang! Bang! Bang!

This time the knock was harder and more rapid. Jess took the chance and looked. It was Samain with a tray of hot food. He let him in, and then locked the door behind him.

"Are these walls and doors bulletproof?" Jess asked.

"Yes! Why do you ask?"

"Someone knocked a few minutes before you banged on the door, and I was slow getting to the door. No one was there!"

"That is unusual, but I would not worry about it," Samain said. He sat the tray down and uncovered two plates filled with beef and vegetables.

Jess' mouth watered, "Looks like beef stew with a loaf of French bread."

With a big smile, Samain said, "We eat well tonight!"

"I'll bet it tastes as good as it looks. Thanks, Samain."

"Thank our Lord for us, Jess."

He prayed asking the Lord to bless their food and the events to come. They did eat well.

Afterward, they reviewed the route to the copper mine while walking to the hangar. Jess thought flying at night through the mountains at low altitude would be great. Also, the moon would still be full, which was in their favor.

Samain kidded Jess about his smooth shaved face. The guard had to look at him twice to make sure Jess fit his photo ID card. He handed them both an M16 rifle, ammunition bandoleers, two canteens of water, two backpacks of food rations and supplies, and ammunition for their side arms.

A Hummer drove them to the aircraft, an Ayres Vigilante (V-1-A). Jess reviewed its capabilities from the aircraft's flight manual. It was a modified spray plane, specifically designed for two missions: surveillance and close ground support. It was an unsophisticated aircraft, easy to operate, easy to maintain in a field environment and inexpensive to fly with a tremendous load-carrying capability. The Moroccan agents depended on its proven ability against drug running. The small aircraft's surveillance and weapon systems were the state-of-the-art field-replaceable units with high reliability.

Jess thought it sounded like an advertisement from the manufacturer. It could be right out of the owner's manual. It had two 50 cal. gun pods and two 2.75 rocket pods mounted under each wing, with two AIM-9 Sidewinder missiles on the wing tips. The little aircraft was loaded for bear for this trip.

Both Jess and Samain were fitted with slim-style airfoil parachutes. Seated in the small aircraft, they were ready to leave, Samain in the front seat and Jess in the back.

Jess was happy for the hours he spent with J.J. flying the Vigilante, *because now we are ready to use it to fight to the death if necessary.* He lifted mental eyebrows at himself for that thought, *It could happen. Was that mighty brave talk, or foolish thinking?*

Samain turned on the red master power switch and all the green and red-lighted instrumentation lit up. It was not long before they were in the air and well on their way, skimming through the dark valleys. Two armed Huey helicopters trailed behind with Moroccan troops on board.

They had the electronic countermeasure systems running, just in case another missile would be fired at them. Radar surveillance from the NATO AWACS aircraft had been contacted. Information received confirmed there were no aircraft near the mine.

Their aircraft responded for Samain like it was an A10 Thunderbolt II, the ole Warthog. He landed on the incline of the road to the mine, taxied to the entrance, and spun it around in front of the dynamite shack. One of the helicopters had landed behind them, off-loaded soldiers wearing desert tan uniforms, and left to join the other one at the bottom of the road in the valley.

With men in the valley below and at the mine, all that was left to do was load the drugs into the helicopters and get out. Three of the men took the flatbed on the rails and hurried into the left tunnel to retrieve the stack of drug bundles. Samain and Jess, both took a pair of soldiers into the center and right tunnels of the mine. One of the two soldiers with Jess was a young officer, and the other had no rank on his uniform.

Jess picked the center tunnel, for reasons unknown to him at the time. It just felt like the right choice because it looked like the first of the three to be dug, but more out of curiosity than anything else.

They had brought the latest industrial miners hard hats with the halogen lamps mounted on them. The halogen lamps were brighter and covered a broader arc than the old style carbide acetylene lamp found earlier in the other tunnel. The beam reached further into the mine tunnel, almost like using an automobile headlight on high beam. With three lamps turned on together, it flooded the mine with light.

They had not walked far before the tunnel came to a dead-end, except for a shaft opening above them. It was thirty feet to the ceiling of the shaft. Cables were hanging from a pulley mechanism mounted on steel beams across the shaft above. Another tunnel opened into the shaft from the left twelve feet above them, toward the first tunnel where the other soldiers had entered to get the bundles of drugs.

Jess could not remember seeing openings in the left tunnel, except in the cavern at the very end where it was caged closed.

That piqued his curiosity all the more, and now he was determined to climb the old cables to get to the tunnel above. There was another tunnel at the same level as the one to the left, to the right, but it did not interest him.

The officer spoke to Jess in French and motioned with his hands he would climb first. After swinging into the tunnel above, he held the cable stable for the rest of them to climb.

They had no problem getting into the tunnel, but sat down for a few minutes to catch their breath. Jess needed it more than the others; his arm muscles were not as strong as the younger men.

While resting, he scribbled a sketch of the tunnel they were in, comparing it to a sketch of the tunnel the drugs were in. The two soldiers watched him and realized his question about their tunnel, especially when Jess put a question mark at their location with an arrow toward the end of it. They discussed the possibility of where it went and shrugged. Jess smiled and shrugged too, but motioned for them to follow him again and stuck the paper in his pocket.

They had no sooner stood to their feet, than a roar in the tunnel below came up through the shaft. An explosion had erupted, and dust bellowed up through the shaft into their tunnel. They fell to the floor from the tremendous quaking of the explosion, covering their heads from the falling rocks. They put handkerchiefs over their faces to keep from choking on dust. They were covered with rocks and dust, which made Jess thankful for the hard hats.

There was an immediate rush of air through the tunnel in the direction they wanted to go, clearing the dust, which had swirled around them. Their lights still worked, and nobody was badly hurt. They were only bruised from the falling rocks.

"Are you Okay?" Jess asked them.

They understood, "Okay!" Nodding their heads. "Okay!" They repeated.

He muttered a, "Thank you, Lord!"

They stood again, brushing the rocks and dust off. Jess smiled at them and pointed toward the end of the tunnel—or at least where he thought it should be. They quietly talked to each other. He tried the transceiver radio as they walked cautiously down the tunnel, but no answer.

Jess wondered if someone had found the dynamite in the shack and had accidentally set it off. But for now, they needed to find out where the airflow was from, and where the tunnel wandered. Hopefully, Samain and the others were not hurt. Jess' tunnel did not seem to be blocked by the explosion.

Then they began to hear voices ahead of them, and as they moved further through the tunnel, the voices got louder. Jess stopped and listened, but his companions smiled and motioned to continue as they began to shout to the others. The others finally answered as Jess and his crew approached a hole in the tunnel floor. Light was coming up through it, and Jess knew that below them was the cave he had been in a few days before. They climbed down to the soldiers, and a lot of hugs were exchanged.

Jess asked if anyone could speak English, but no one could. He tried understanding French and some Arabic, while they tried to understand him scribbling on paper.

The officer with Jess pointed their route to the others, and where Jess had marked the stack of drug bundles. They nodded that the bundles were still there, but the explosion had collapsed their tunnel further back toward the entrance. As yet, they had not removed any of the bundles.

Jess motioned for the officer to follow him into the room where the caged entrance opened to the west. He was hunting for a container with gasoline or diesel fuel. Pointing to the old filler cap on a generator, he pantomimed pouring gasoline into the tank. The officer knew exactly what Jess wanted and relayed the message to the others. It did not take long to find containers of both gasoline and diesel fuel.

Jess gestured for everyone to take their undershirts off and tie them together. The officer read Jess' mind and found a pile of rope. After they tied everything together, they followed him to the stack of drug bundles. He indicated that he wanted them to soak the rope and undershirts in an open bucket where he had mixed the gasoline and diesel fuel.

The soldiers stretched out the soaked rope and undershirts up into the tunnel from which Jess and his crew had come. They uncovered the drug bundles, spreading them out on the tunnel floor, across from wall to wall. The bundles were split open. The officer and Jess poured five-gallon buckets of fuel into the drug bundles, between them and over them. The dry, powdered drugs soaked up the fuel fast, so they poured more on the bundles. Then they cut the canvas in strips and soaked them with fuel, and placed them on top of the bundles. Jess pushed the last soaked undershirt into an opening of one saturated drug bundle. The remainder of the fuel was poured over the whole stack.

He nodded to the officer, and they all headed for the upper tunnel. The gasoline fumes were terrible, burning their eyes and nose. Jess grabbed the officer's arm and signaled with his finger to wait, he would be back. Going to the caged entrance, he tried the transceiver again. No reply from Samain, but the NATO AWACS aircraft operators answered. Jess told them what they were doing, and he would contact them once they got out.

Back with the others in the upper tunnel, Jess asked the officer if all his men were accounted for. He understood and nodded, yes.

Jess gave him his lighter, offering him the opportunity to light the soaked rope. The other soldiers clapped their hands and whispered their approval, reacting to the burning of the drugs in a most positive way. They quietly laughed and jabbered among themselves as the flame raced down the rope and disappeared below.

A flash of flame from the explosion passed the tunnel opening into the cave below them and blew into the caged room. The pressure, flame, smoke and dust exited out the west entrance. The smoke was forced up the hole into the tunnel where the men were, but they were already hustling back to the center shaft and tunnel.

They made their way outside the center tunnel into the large mine entrance to the east and found a mountain slide. It had covered the first tunnel's main opening and caved in the roof of the dynamite shack. Jess was surprised it had not exploded. The Vigilante was covered with dust from the rockslide, but it did not look damaged. The third tunnel's main entrance had collapsed where Samain had entered.

Jess climbed over the rocks and timbers to the closest point of the third tunnel entrance, which was covered. Using the transceiver radio again, he called for Samain.

"Samain, can you hear me?"

He heard the usual static with the squelch off, but no answer. By that time, the officer and a few of his men were at Jess' side.

"Samain, this is Jess. Can you hear me?"

He only heard his own voice echo in the big mine entrance. They strained to hear a reply. Jess waited long enough and transmitted again.

"Samain, answer me buddy. Can you hear me?"

Then a weak reply was heard, and everyone hollered. The officer got his men under control, hushing them down.

"Are you injured?" Jess asked.

"No! My men are all dead. My body has taken a beating, again. I have a headlamp, but I am running out of air."

"Stay where you are. We'll get you out."

Smoke began to fill the mine entrance, burning their eyes. It was coming from the center tunnel where they had come out. The drug stash continued to burn back inside the mine, and its smoke got thicker.

Then gunfire erupted from the valley. Jess and the others moved into the ruins for protection. He did not think the opposition could see them, because the Moroccan soldiers at the bottom of the road were in intense fighting with someone farther down the valley, to the south.

Two problems faced Jess. One was Samain trapped in the tunnel with little air to breathe, and the other was the fighting in the valley. Which was priority? If they were to help Samain, how were they to get him out? And if they supported the troops down the road, they would be exposing themselves in the open to gunfire.

The helicopters were still on the ground because their crews had to stay under cover from the gunfire.

Jess and the soldiers at the mine entrance had rifles, but that was the limit of their protection. Plus, it was after midnight, and the moon was high above them.

From Jess' position, even with his binoculars, he could not see around the foothills as to whom the Moroccan soldiers were shooting at. Mortar and heavy-rifle fire sounded like Vietnam again.

CHAPTER THIRTY-SIX

Samain passed out due to the lack of oxygen in the collapsed mine tunnel. He had been unconscious for only a few short minutes, when he finally began to stir.

After several minutes of frustrating effort, he managed to take his miner's headlamp from the hard hat. He hung the lamp around his neck. If the hard hat was knocked off again, Jess and the others could still be able to see the light around his neck. He put the hat back on.

Leaning back against one of the many huge rocks that now had blocked the mine entrance, he took a slow, painful breath of whatever air was left for him. He was still dizzy from the concussion of the explosion and lack of air. Despite his desire to remain awake, he slowly fell into a deep sleep. Darkness slowly closed in over him as his headlamp began to dim.

#

Outside the closed mine tunnel, Jess told the young officer he was going back into the tunnel from which they had come and try to find a way to get to Samain. The tunnels had to be connected together somewhere. The officer tried to discourage him, but Jess was determined to go.

He took a rifle and three extra ammo magazines, and ran into the center mine tunnel, and then turned on the headlamp.

Most of the smoke had cleared because the wind had changed; it came from the desert, not from the other side of the mountain. The wind had forced the smoke of the burning drugs back inside the tunnel.

The west tunnel opening probably looked like a smokestack, Jess though.

The center tunnel shaft at the other end was clear, so Jess climbed rusty chains up to the next level cross-tunnel. Instead of going the direction as before into the tunnel to the left, he took the tunnel to the right and moved at a fast jog through the mine.

Hopefully, there's a shaft down to the tunnel Samain is in, and his tunnel is parallel with the center one.

Sure enough, there it was, a small shaft going down. He paused just long enough to take a swallow of water, and then slid down the only thing available: a rotten rope. The rope broke before he had gone a few feet. The drop was a good ten feet further to the bottom. He landed on his back, knocking the wind out of him.

Squeaky noises and stench filled the cavity he lay in. Catching his breath, he sat up and felt things crawl up his back. Little beady eyes glowed in the dark from his light. Rats! They were all over the floor! He had fallen into a nest of them, and they were wasting no time pondering their unexpected bounty. They were chewing at his pants legs and boots. He jumped up and down to keep them off.

Now I have to figure a way to get out of this rat's nest.

The bottom of the shaft was eight feet below the entrance to the right tunnel opening where Samain was located. He was surprised that he had no broken bones from the fall.

Jess tied both ends of the broken rope around the middle of the rifle, doubling the rope's strength. After removing the ammo, he tossed the rifle up into the tunnel and pulled on the rope, hoping it would catch on something. On the second try, it wedged under the top of a trolley rail.

The rats were gnawing the rope and following him up, and he had to keep stopping and knocking them off. Their squeaky noise and stench was getting to him.

He finally pulled himself up into the tunnel. The rats tried to follow, but fell off when he shook the rope. Pulling it up, he laid it in a heap, figuring to use it again.

Jess leaned out into the shaft to look up. He had not fallen as far as he thought, but far enough. Loading the rifle again, he headed into the tunnel to find Samain.

The further he went, the harder it became to breathe.

It did not take long to find Samain. Samain's headlamp was still bright enough for Jess to see his location. The other men were crushed under the fallen rocks.

Moving rocks off of Samain, Jess checked him for bleeding and broken bones. He could not get him awake. Samain's breathing was slow and shallow as he labored to get air. His nose and mouth were full of dust.

Jess took the water bottle and washed Samain's face, then soaked his red bandana and wiped out Samain's mouth. He wanted to keep the water from going down Samain's throat and choking him, so Jess propped him up. The inside of his clogged, crusty nose was hard to clean out with the edge of the twisted bandana. He moved behind Samain and gave him a Heimlich thrust with his clasped fist just below the rib cage, above his belly button.

A chunk of mud flew out, sticking to his pants leg. Samain gasped for air, throwing his arms about. Jess released the pressure, and Samain slumped against him, breathing easier and more deeply.

"Samain! Hey old, friend, it's Jess!" he whispered in Samain's ear.

"Yes . . ." he said weakly.

"I'm going to lean you back against these rocks."

Jess moved from behind him, easily resting him on the rocks. Washing his face again with fresh water caused Samain's eyes to open. He set his headlamp on a rock so it would illuminate them. A slow smile came across Samain's face as he recognized Jess.

"Can you blow your nose? It would help you breathe better, my friend," Jess said, handing him the bandana. "It's full of dirt."

Samain shook the dirt off his head and blew his nose. Jess handed him the water bottle. He washed his mouth out and took a long drink. Catching his breath again, he laughed.

"I did not think I would ever see you again in this life!"

"Again, our Lord answered prayer, and is still taking care of us both," Jess said, holding Samain's shoulder. "He's not finished with either of us. Not yet!"

"Help me up. We must get out of here," he demanded.

Air began to stir. They both took in deep breaths.

"Hold on a minute," Jess said. "We're getting air from someplace. Take time to eat this chocolate nut bar and drink some more water. You need the energy."

Samain finished the little snack and relaxed a few minutes. His facial features seemed to be back to normal, and Jess helped him to his feet. A quick inventory revealed no broken bones.

"Thank the Lord!" Jess exclaimed. "Let's go!"

As they made their way back to the main mine opening, Jess explained what had happened outside, and what they had done. Samain was glad the drugs had been destroyed.

The rifle fire was still hot and heavy down in the valley when they reached the opening of the mine.

"I left that officer and his men in the ruins of this building," Jess said. "But, they aren't here now!"

"They may be in the valley. There!" Samain pointed at another group of soldiers right below them in the valley. The rifle fire exposed their position. They were being pinned down by rifle fire from the ravine where Charlie's body was found.

Jess and Samain began firing at the people in the ravine, giving some support to the men below. The night glowed of red flame coming from the automatic rifles. Every so often, someone used a magazine with tracer bullets that could be seen ricocheting in all directions off of the rocks and boulders.

Suddenly, Jess saw a dim moon shadow move across him from behind.

Samain yelled, "Colonel Alvarez!"

Jess turned to see a huge arm grab him around the neck. His feet came off the ground, and he dangled like a rag doll. Jess' face was buried into this giant's armpit. His head was being crushed, and he thought his eyes would pop out.

The colonel was shouting harshly at Samain in Arabic, and swinging Jess around by the head. Samain could not shoot for fear of hitting Jess. He thought for sure Jess was going to die.

Jess forced his hand between the colonel's fat stomach and his body to reach for his own .45 automatic in its shoulder holster. Gripping it tightly, he pulled on it, but it would not slide out because he was being held so tightly.

Still holding onto Jess' head, the colonel began swinging him like a merry-go-round. That was exactly what Jess needed. His body swung out, separating from the colonel's body and giving Jess better access to his gun.

Jess fired one shot with the gun still in the holster, hitting the colonel in the knee. He crumbled to the ground with Jess under him. The colonel released him and grabbed Jess by the throat with one big hand. Jess brought the barrel of his .45 autos up between the colonel's eyes.

The colonel knew it was a large-caliber gun, pressing hard between his eyes, and he knew that sudden death was coming unless he released Jess' throat.

Samain yelled, "No, Jess! Do not kill him! He has information we need!"

Grinding his teeth and groaning, the colonel was like an old turtle that would not let go. Jess pressed the barrel against the ridge of the colonel's nose as his eyes crossed looking at it.

The colonel slowly released Jess' throat and rolled off of him. Jess rolled with him, sitting astride the huge shape of a man and insured the barrel stayed pressed against his nose.

There is no other way to rid the world of such terror, Jess thought. *Just kill him.*

He earnestly wanted to squeeze the trigger and put an end to the sorry hulk of a creature! For all the terror, murder and ruined lives the colonel had caused throughout the world, Jess wanted to kill him right then and there!

Hate welled up inside him, and then subsided. Jess slowly moved away from the colonel keeping his weapon pointed at him.

I'm not a murderer! Jess reminded himself. *Why should I be like him?*

Colonel Alvarez was sweating profusely, eyes glaring, staring up at the automatic. He looked down at his knee and groaned after he tried to move, grabbing the under side of it. He could not use his leg. It was bleeding badly; Jess must have blown off the kneecap.

Jess stood up, holstered his weapon and moved away from the colonel. Samain removed the colonel's gun from its holster and searched him for other weapons. He took the colonel's wallet and other papers found on him. Neither of them attempted to give the colonel first aid.

The colonel was muttering something in Arabic and finally spoke in English, "I find you both together, alive! My millions in gold have been wasted! I will roast you both alive before this is over!"

Jess grit his teeth and shouted, shaking his fist at the colonel, "Over! What do mean over? It's over for you! You're not in any position to make threats like that big boy! There's more than one person who knew you at the Casablanca airport and saw you!"

He pointed again at Samain, and then to himself. "We didn't know who killed the king's brother, not until my bodyguard remembered seeing you leaving the airport. He watched you exit the hole that was blown through the restroom wall and leave in your big black limousine."

The rifle fire had ceased in the valley below. All at once, noise in the mine tunnels could be heard. The mine was making unusual moans again, like a volcano would do before it blew its top. The ground trembled and shook.

They looked up to see an avalanche above them in the moonlight. The ground beneath them vibrated violently.

Samain yelled and grabbed Jess by the arm, and they ran toward the Vigilante. The colonel had managed to get up on one leg. Stumbling, dragging his bad leg, he entered the mine opening as the landslide covered him and sealed it. He was caught under it.

Samain kicked away rocks that had been placed in front of the wheels to keep the aircraft from moving down the hill, and pointed for Jess to get in the pilot's seat. The roar from the avalanche was deafening, keeping them from hearing each other's shouting.

Jess switched on the main power, and turned on the fuel pump, then the ignition switch. The propeller rotated twice, and the engine jumped to life. Samain yelled for Jess to go as he got one leg inside the cockpit.

By the time Jess lifted the aircraft from the dirt road and slowly banked away from the mountain, Samain had just buckled into the seat.

Jess looked back while tightening his shoulder harness with his left hand. He gave Samain thumbs up, and he returned the gesture. With the aircraft still climbing, Jess pulled his shoulder straps tighter, then abruptly pulled the nose up higher, and sharply banked over toward the mine. In an upside down dive, they could see a tremendous explosion erupted from the entrance of the mine, where the dynamite shack had been. The whole side of the mountain at that level crumbled to the valley below. There was no mine entrance to be seen.

Jess rolled out of being upside down and banked away from the billowing dust and smoke, and put on his headset. "Samain, do you know any reason why I shouldn't close the west opening of the mine?"

"Jess, help yourself. That should seal the mine forever!"

The cavern collapsed after he fired all the rockets into the west opening on two passes. There was no way anyone could get in there again, not without major digging. Also, no one would ever get out alive.

Jess did not feel grief over the loss of the colonel.

Our Lord has His ways of taking care of things. Then he issued a deep sigh, *Lord, forgive me for the hate I had felt in my heart toward the colonel, because I did want to kill him.*

They circled back around the mountain from the south, and the soldiers all waved as they passed low over them. Samain talked to someone on the ground that had a radio, and then told Jess to head for the base.

"Jess, our job is finished here and you can finally go home," Samain said with a broad smile.

Jess waved the aircraft's wings, climbed to 8,000 feet and leveled off heading back to the home base at Rissani.

Relaxing back into the seat, Jess said, "Like they say in the old western movies, 'With guns hot and smoking, they headed off into the sunset.' In this case, . . . 'Into the moonset'!"

Samain laughed, "Yes, and another job well done! The good guys can go home now!"

At the same time they both said, "Thank you, Lord Jesus!"

CHAPTER THIRTY-SEVEN

At the Casablanca International Airport, King Itssani and his family, Samain, Bushta, J.J., Eric and Gina were all bidding Jess a safe trip home. The assassin, Colonel Alvarez, was buried in that copper mine and was no longer a threat.

Larry Hastings' review trial would start the next week, and support statements for him had been taken from all of the Force One team. Jess' friends were recovering from their injuries, and they were all getting ready to return to their individual homes.

Before leaving, they met in a private conference room at the airport. The king of Morocco had presented each of them with a special made Moroccan Medal of Valor. He had cleared everyone's debts at home and opened Swiss accounts in their names.

In parting, King Itssani handed each of them a royal sealed envelope and said, "In the future, we will refer to this operation as 'Eye-Witness, Broken Nose'." He winked and laughed going to the door, stopping in front of Jess.

Everyone began to laugh and clap, until the king turned and raised his hand for silence. "Mr. Hanes, a nice surprise awaits you at your home with your wife. Anytime you wish to return to Morocco, you are welcome with open arms. Please contact me in advance so I can furnish transportation and accommodations for you. My family will forever be indebted to you. Thank you, Mr. Jess E. Hanes."

King Itssani saluted and bowed, and Jess returned both gestures. They shook hands, and the king kissed Jess on each cheek, and then made his exit with his family and bodyguards. Jess' friends escorted him to a Royal Air Maroc 747 for his trip home to the United States.

#

Back on the airliner flying the last leg of the trip home, Jess folded his arms and smiled. He sighed, looking at Madi, "The end!"

Madi softly clapped her hands and leaned over, kissing Jess lightly on the check. "Welcome back home, Jess," she said. "It has been a pleasure to know you on these two flights, and I'm sure these will not be our last hours together. We'll be watching many sunsets . . . perhaps not always together, but in Texas."

"Thanks, Madi. Sorry that took so long to tell my story. Thanks, again for listening."

They fastened their seat belts and watched the hill country of Texas pass beneath them as the airliner descended and banked toward the runway at Austin.

Finally, home again! Thank you, Lord. Thank you for taking care of Marie Ann and me, while we've been apart.

CHAPTER THIRTY-EIGHT

It had been a restful trip for Jess from JFK International. The landing was smooth at the newly acquired Bergstrom International, in Austin, which was formerly an U.S. Air Force base. Jess had finished his lengthy adventure story for Madilene before arriving.

Jess and Madi departed through the forward exit and took the maintenance stairs down to the parking ramp from the boarding area. Other U.S. Marshals followed them across the ramp area and into the baggage department. They were ushered into a small room where others were waiting.

Then Jess saw his sweet angel, Marie Ann, standing with their Texas Ranger twin nephews, Charles and Jack Randel. She was a beautiful lady in her early fifties, with short, wavy brunette hair and a well-proportioned five feet six. She wore her favorite navy dress suit with white high heel shoes. Teary-eyed, she had that big wonderful smile Jess had always remembered.

They grabbed each other and held on tight, not saying anything for a long time. The others patiently waited for them to finish their welcome.

Madi broke them up. "Sorry to do this, but we need to move out of here. Where to, guys?" she asked the twins.

They both shook Jess' hand and gave him a hug. "Welcome home, Uncle Jess," Charles said, and Jack replied, "Amen!"

Neither spoke further; they were very stern and businesslike. Madi wrapped her arm around Marie Ann's arm. Charles was on her other arm, both protecting her.

Jack led them out of the small room and into an underground parking lot, where two dark blue cars waited. They used their radios all the way to the cars, checking the planned exits.

Jess was beginning to get very uneasy about all the security. Calm down, *this is not unusual; it's for our best interest. Terrorists could be here in Austin waiting for me. What a rotten thought! Cancel that one! Lord, prevent it from happening!*

Jack, Madi and Jess were in one car, following Charles, Marie Ann and another Ranger in the front car. They stayed on county roads leading south out of town. There was very little conversation.

Jess noticed the Texas Hill Country was greener than when he had left home. It seemed to have had a lot of rain recently.

They continued south and turned west at FM1327 to Interstate 35. Taking the Interstate south to FM967, they headed northwest again, up to State Road 290. Jess thought they were in route to the little town of Dripping Springs, but they left the paved roads. Taking graveled roads, they left a large dust trail behind. Looking out the back window, Jess could see a white helicopter following them high above the dust.

Friend or foe? He wondered. *If someone else was tracking us or following us, these dusty roads would be like waving a red flag at a bull. I hope these Rangers know what they are doing.* He drew a deep breath. He was getting uncomfortable, *Guess I'm getting paranoid again.*

Suddenly, a low flying aircraft swept over them and rose to the west. It was a light tan C-130, just like Colonel Alvarez's aircraft. Jess could not see any markings on it, because it disappeared into the sun. No one paid attention to it, and they did not notice Jess' interest watching it. *Dismiss it, Jess, the colonel's dead!*

Jess sighed deeply and put his mind on the road ahead.

But the white helicopter is still behind us. No foreign aircraft the size of a C-130 could be in this part of the country without being noticed.

Jess lost track of all the turns, except for west. The sun was dropping lower toward the western horizon.

The vehicles crossed a cattle guard onto someone's ranch with an arch above the entrance. It was marked with the brand: *Lazy M.J.* There was a large, recently built, western-style Austin stone ranch house with large, white-fenced corrals next to it.

There were white stables with beautiful horses feeding in the back of the corral. It was built near the west base of a slope rising to a high mesa in the east. Familiar ranch odors made Jess feel right at home.

This is beautiful! Jess thought. It was exactly what he had always dreamed of for himself and Marie Ann.

The countryside was thick with cedar, pecan, oak and cottonwood trees. Weeping willow trees marked the banks on both sides of a creek near the freshly painted red barn. Jess was in love with the beautiful Texas hill country.

Through the trees, he could see two government aircraft; twin engine U-21 Beech Super King Air parked next to a hangar. Jess always had an eye for aircraft. *They must have a lengthy runway for those aircraft. Someone has put out a bunch of money on this place. Wonder who MJ is?*

A nice-looking elderly couple stood at the yard gate to welcome them. They sure had a fantastic home. Men who looked like ranch hands come around the corner of the house from the back yard. Jess missed seeing western clothes like everyone was wearing.

Marie Ann and Jess joined arms when Charles and Jack led them to meet the couple. Madi and the other Marshals followed closely. She was talking on her hand-held transceiver again.

Jack made the introductions, "This is Juan Jordon and his wife, Lolita. They are your ranch foreman and house attendants."

Charles immediately interrupted with a cough, as if he were to make a speech. "Uncle Jess! Aunt Marie Ann! This is your new home, compliments of the king of Morocco. It is yours, lock, stock and barrel. The deeds and titles are in a safety deposit box. Welcome home, folks!"

Juan and Lolita shook their hands as they all walked toward the house. Marie Ann and Jess looked at each other, speechless, not really understanding what was happening. Everyone smiled and clapped their hands as they entered. The tension began to disappear, as they were welcomed into their new home.

"You are under our Witness Security Protection Program from

now on," Madi said. "Your names will stay the same, but your home location and friends are new. Our State Department, the State of Texas and the Moroccan king arranged this. All you have to do is sign official documents, and it will be yours, clear and free from any debts. The Bank of Austin has transferred all of your savings accounts to the local bank in Marble Falls. We also insured their computers erased all evidence of your past. The Moroccan king has opened a Swiss bank account for you."

Jess looked at Marie Ann, kissed her and closed his eyes holding her close. *It has to be a dream! It is too good to be true!*

Standing in the large foyer of their home, they were awed by a staircase that went up on each side of the foyer. It was all typical western furnishings with huge rugs covering hardwood and mosaic tiled floors. Marie Ann and Jess' presence surely make it home.

"This is all too much to take in at one time! Lay this on us a little at a time, please!" Jess cleared his throat with a few tears in his eyes.

"I just want to say this for now," Marie Ann said. "We thank you all! You have gone out of your way to protect us and provide for us. I know it's your job, but thanks anyway. I thank God, also, for our protection getting home. We still need His continued guidance."

She looked up at Jess, he said, "I love you sweet lady."

Someone in the group announced a hearty, "Amen!"

Marie Ann and Jess were in tears when they gave everyone a hug. Jess motioned for all to gather around them. "Please, everybody! Grab someone's hand and let's have a word of prayer. We're going to start this out right and give thanks to Jesus, our Lord."

CHAPTER THIRTY NINE

The sun was setting in the west behind the distant hills. Marie Ann was seated next to Jess on the front porch swing, with his arm around her, slowly swinging. It was a scene of the best he loved in Texas. Quietness of the country, other than the birds and animals, and water rustling in the nearby stream . . . and his Love in his arms, Jess finally had peace.

"Now, you can tell me all about your stay in Morocco," Marie Ann said with a big sigh. "We have all night, tomorrow and weeks to catch up. I'm all ears! Tell me every detail you can remember."

Jess pulled her closer, "Angel of mine, it may take longer than that!"

They put their heads together while watching the sun's rays steak the horizon as it set in the west. A familiar, low-flying C-130 circled far to the west, silhouetted in the twilight.

-THE END-